SUPER BOBA CAFÉ

SUPER BOBA CAFÉ

by **NIDHI CHANANI**

colors by **SARAH DAVIDSON**

Amulet Books • New York

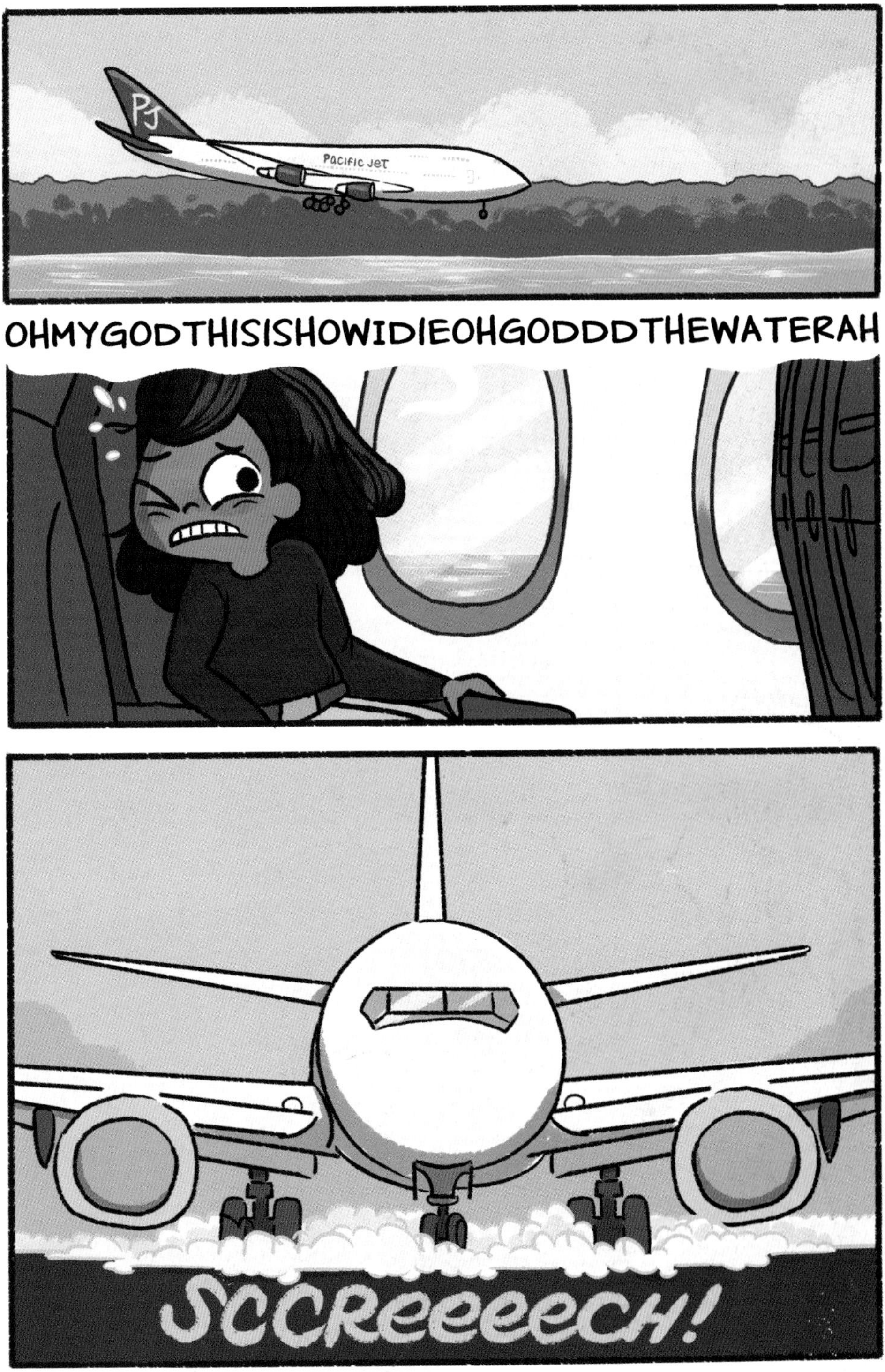
PJ
PACIFIC JET
OHMYGODTHISISHOWIDIEOHGODDDTHEWATERAH
SCCREEEECH!

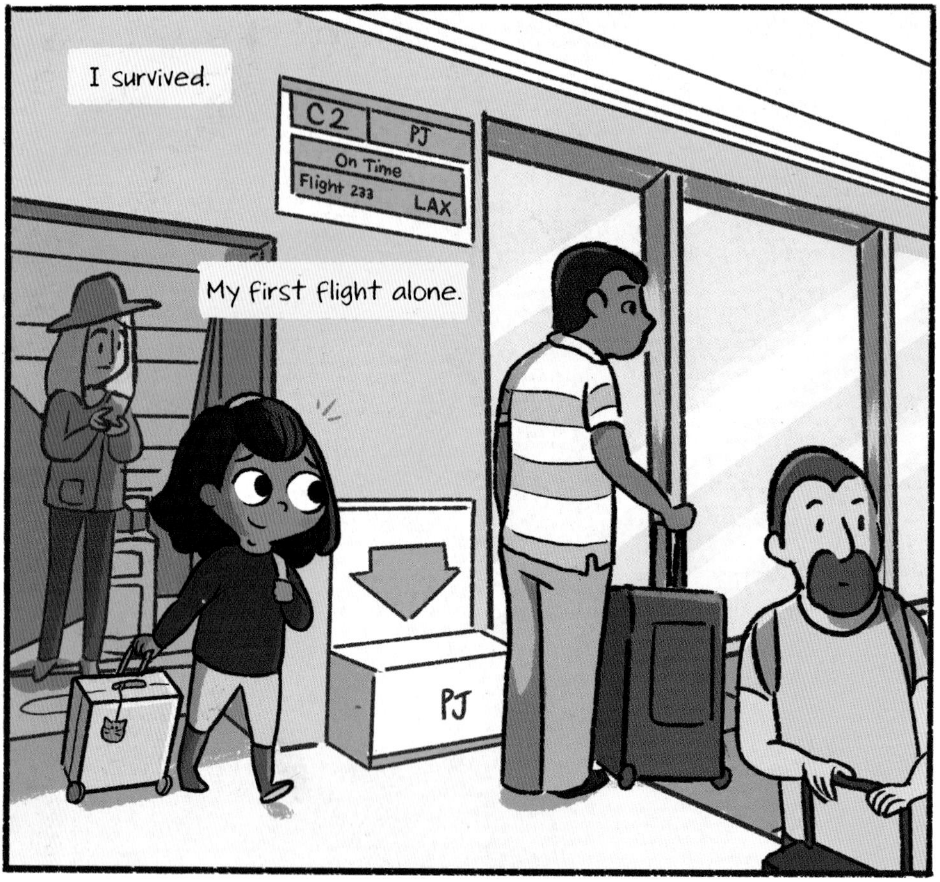
I survived.
C2
PJ
On Time
Flight 233
LAX
My first flight alone.
PJ

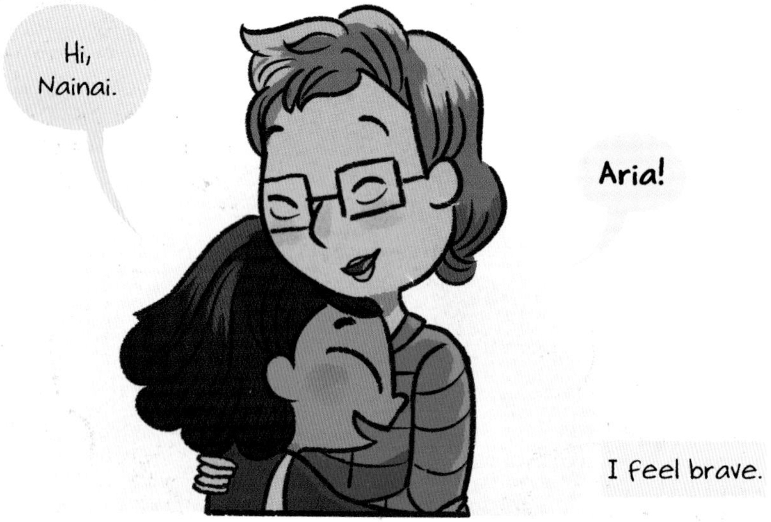
Hi, Nainai.
Aria!
I feel brave.

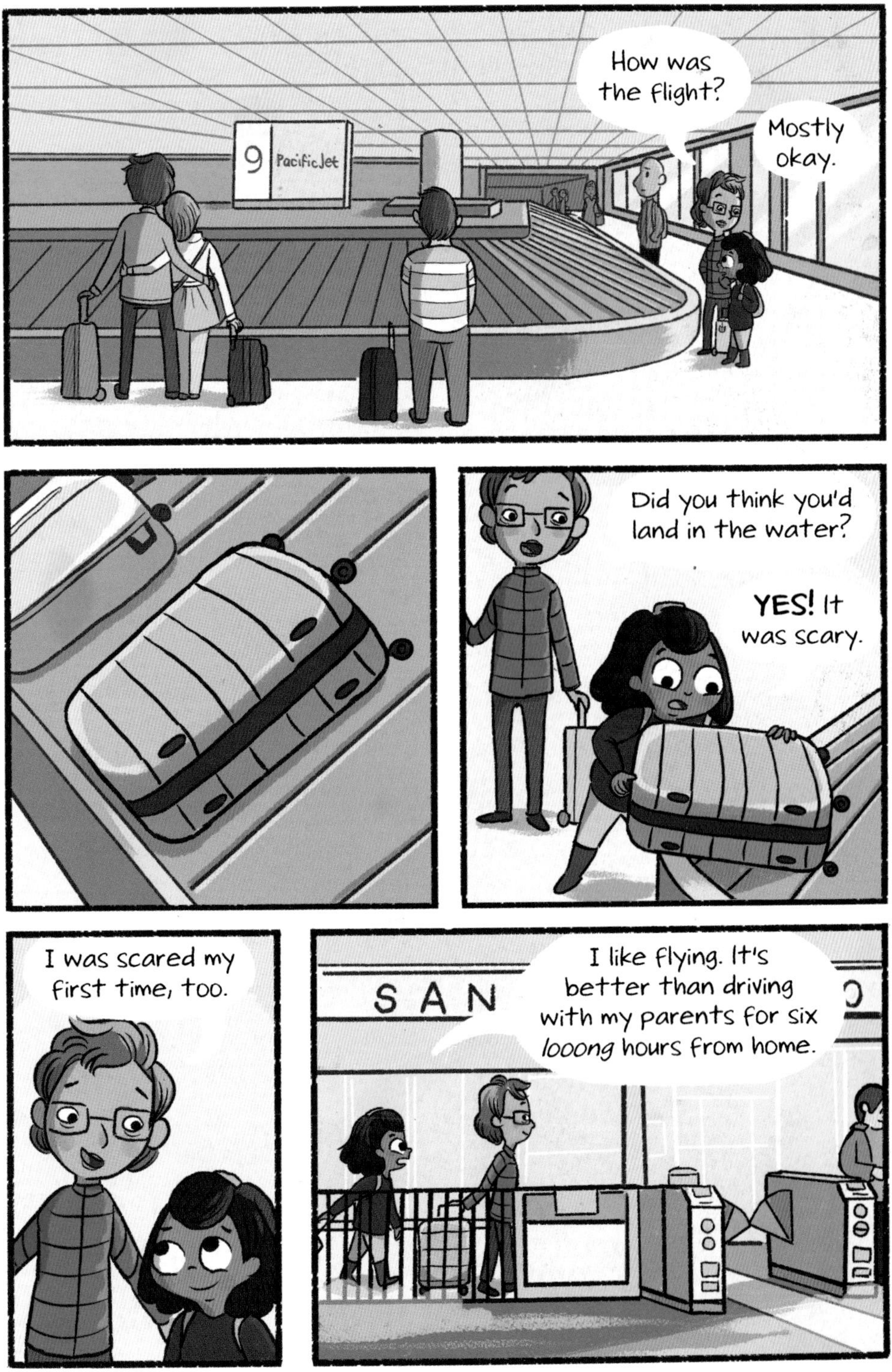
9
PacificJet
How was the flight?
Mostly okay.
Did you think you'd land in the water?
YES! It was scary.
I was scared my first time, too.
I like flying. It's better than driving with my parents for six *looong* hours from home.

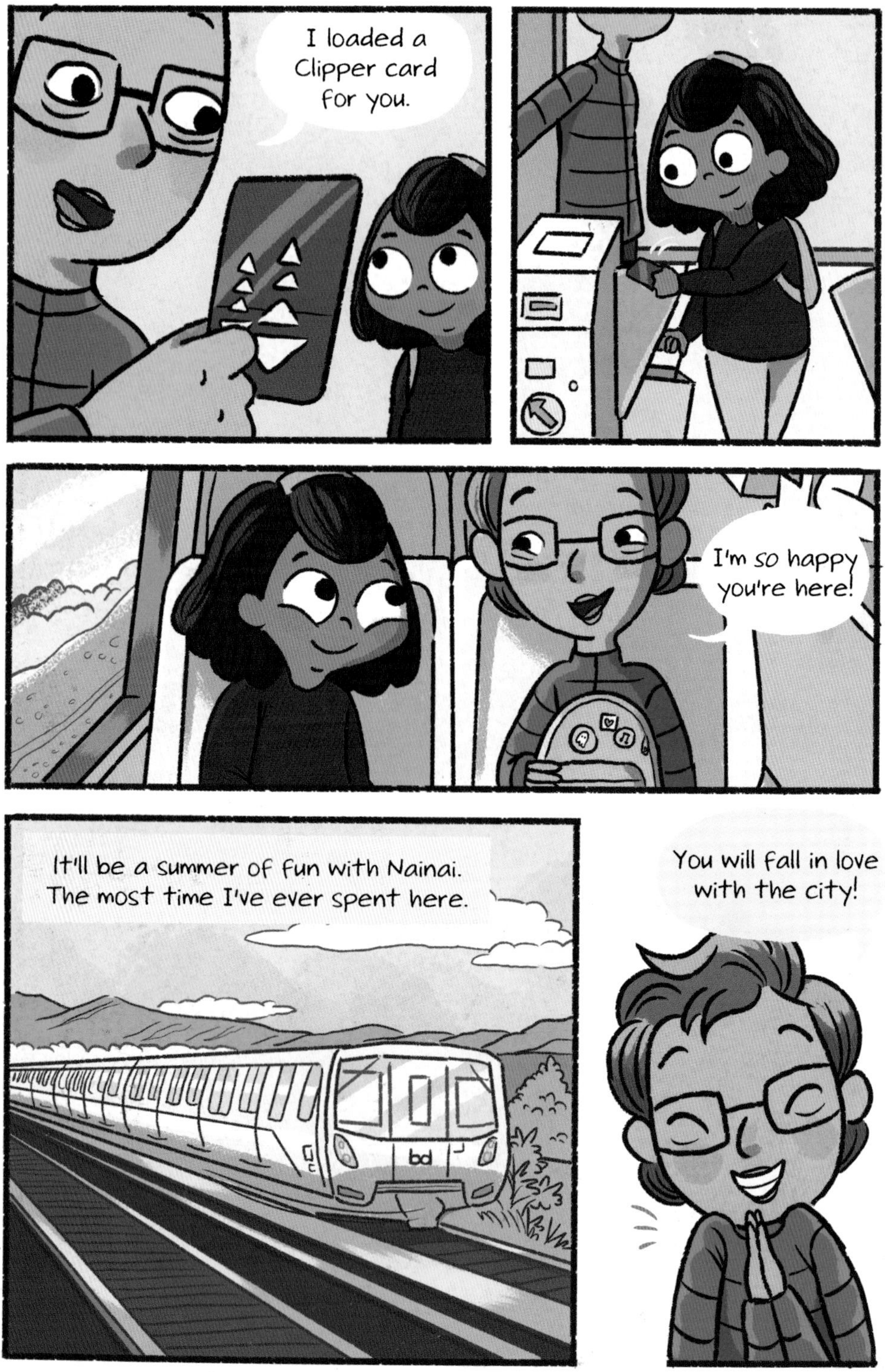
I loaded a Clipper card for you.
I'm so happy you're here!
It'll be a summer of fun with Nainai. The most time I've ever spent here.
You will fall in love with the city!

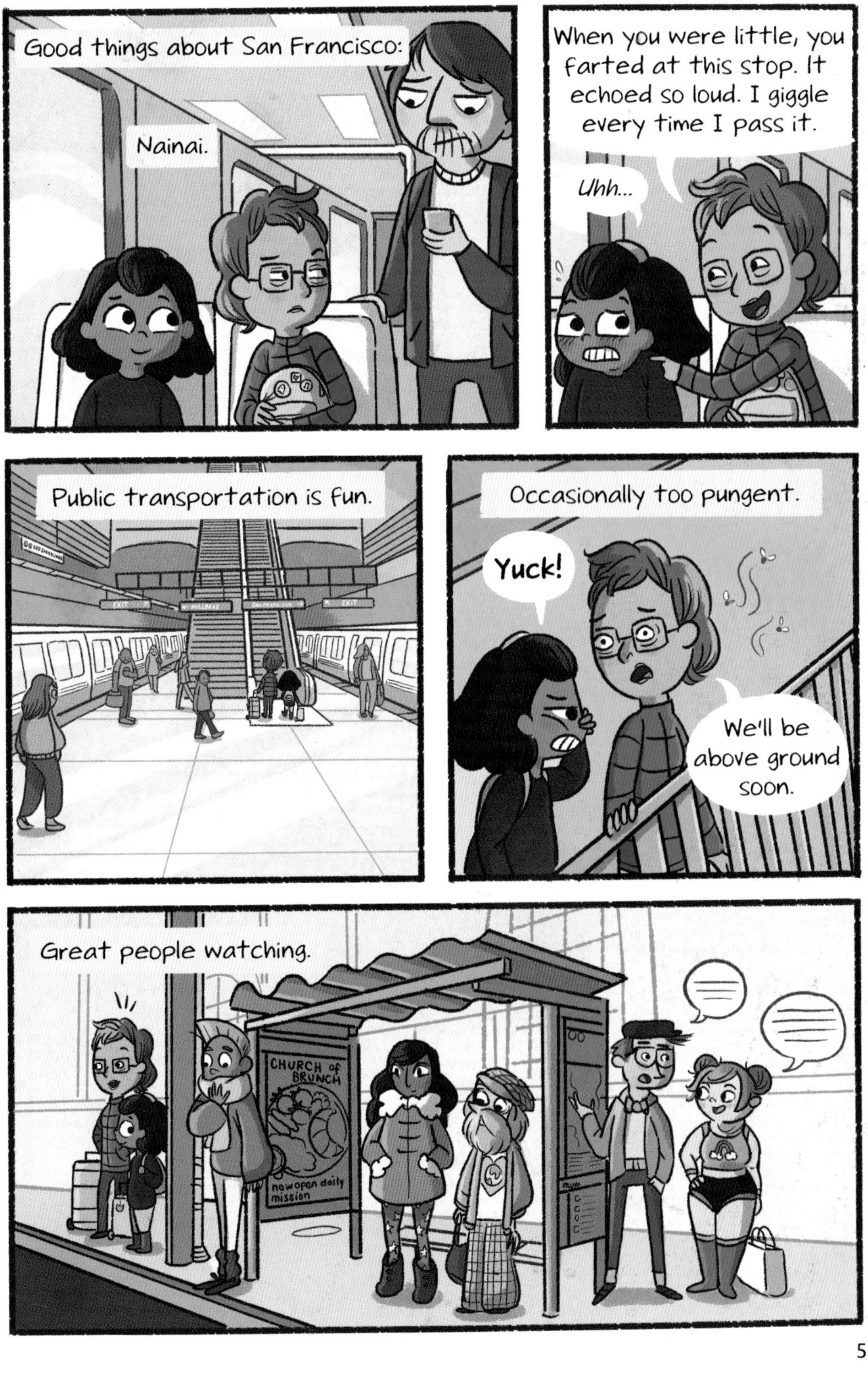
Good things about San Francisco:
Nainai.
When you were little, you farted at this stop. It echoed so loud. I giggle every time I pass it.
Uhh...
Public transportation is fun.
EXIT
MILLBRAE
SAN FRANCISCO
EXIT
Occasionally too pungent.
Yuck!
We'll be above ground soon.
Great people watching.
CHURCH of BRUNCH
now open daily mission

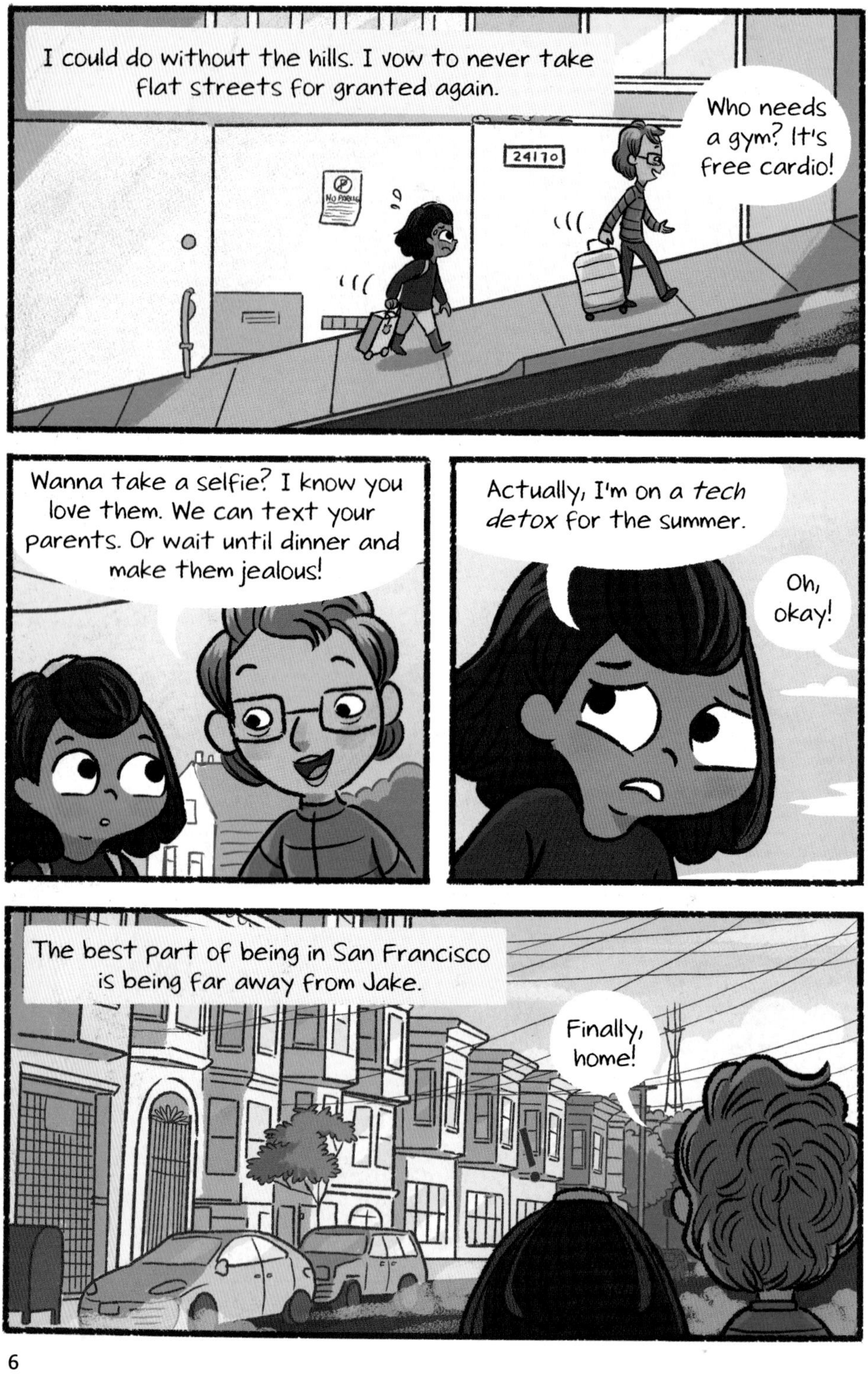
I could do without the hills. I vow to never take flat streets for granted again.
24170
Who needs a gym? It's free cardio!
Wanna take a selfie? I know you love them. We can text your parents. Or wait until dinner and make them jealous!
Actually, I'm on a *tech detox* for the summer.
Oh, okay!
The best part of being in San Francisco is being far away from Jake.
Finally, home!
!

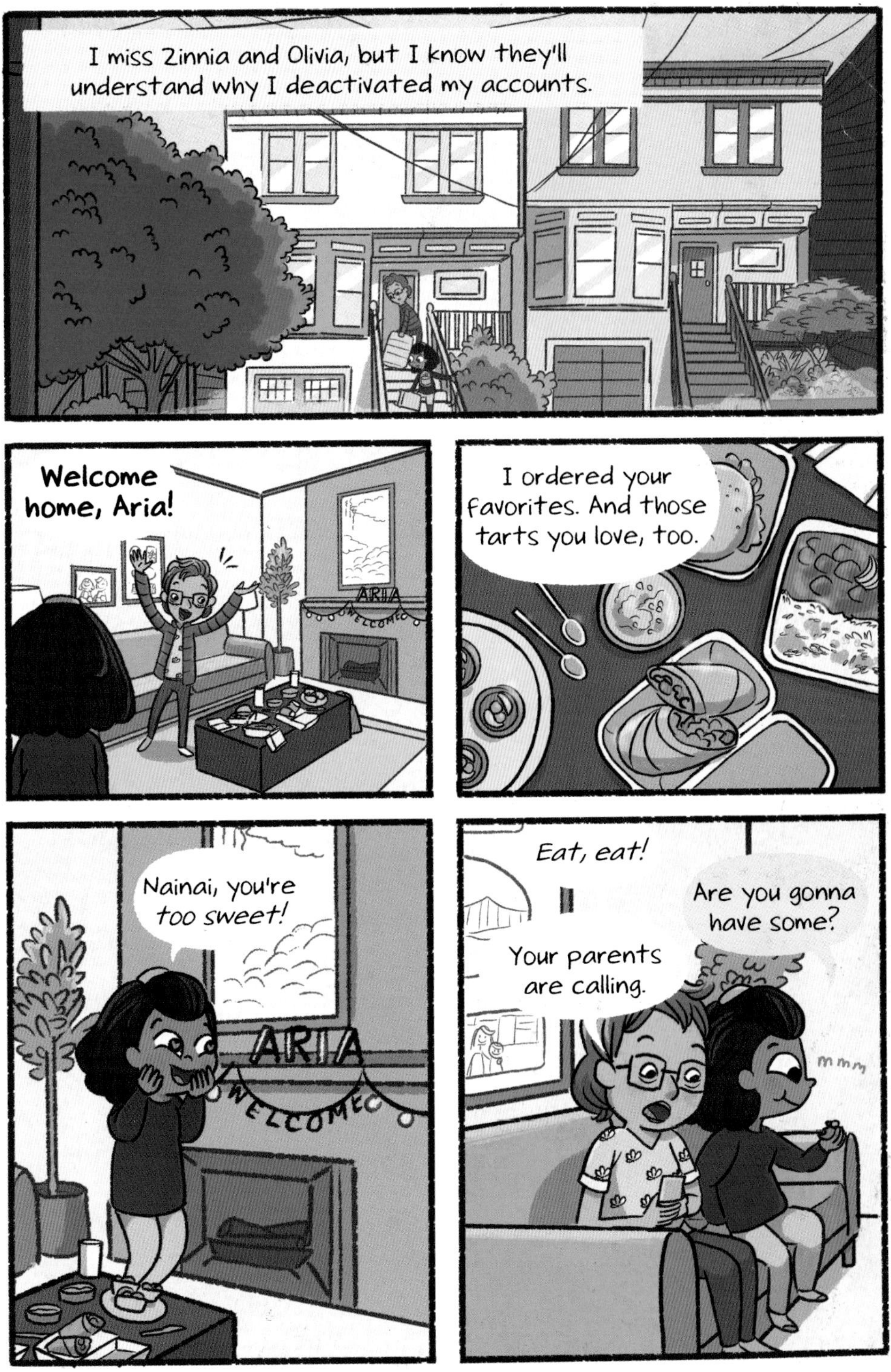

I miss Zinnia and Olivia, but I know they'll understand why I deactivated my accounts.
Welcome home, Aria!
ARIA
WELCOME
I ordered your favorites. And those tarts you love, too.
Nainai, you're too sweet!
ARIA
WELCOME
Eat, eat!
Your parents are calling.
Are you gonna have some?
mmm

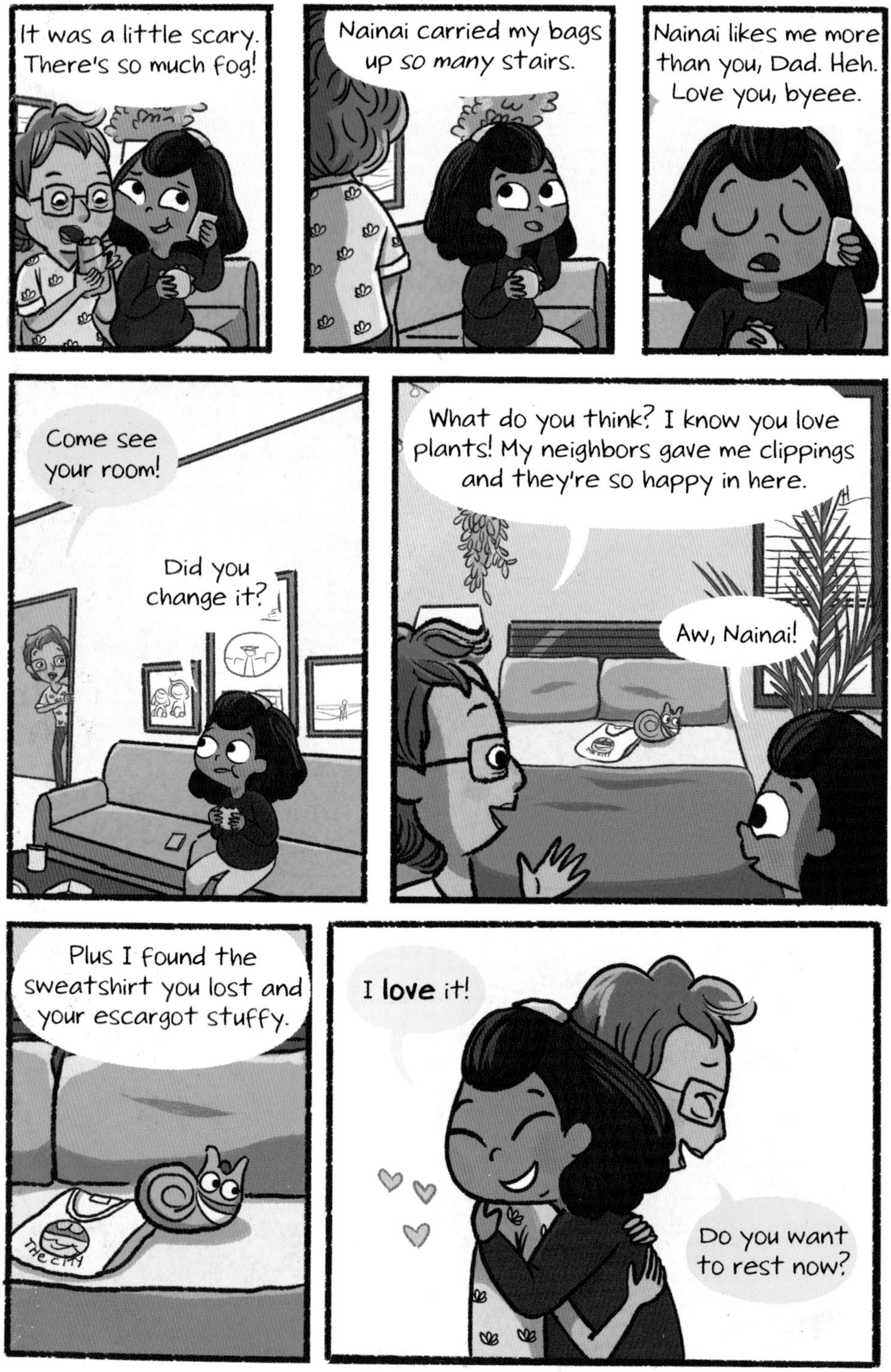
It was a little scary. There's so much fog!
Nainai carried my bags up so many stairs.
Nainai likes me more than you, Dad. Heh. Love you, byeee.
Come see your room!
Did you change it?
What do you think? I know you love plants! My neighbors gave me clippings and they're so happy in here.
Aw, Nainai!
Plus I found the sweatshirt you lost and your escargot stuffy.
I **love** it!
Do you want to rest now?

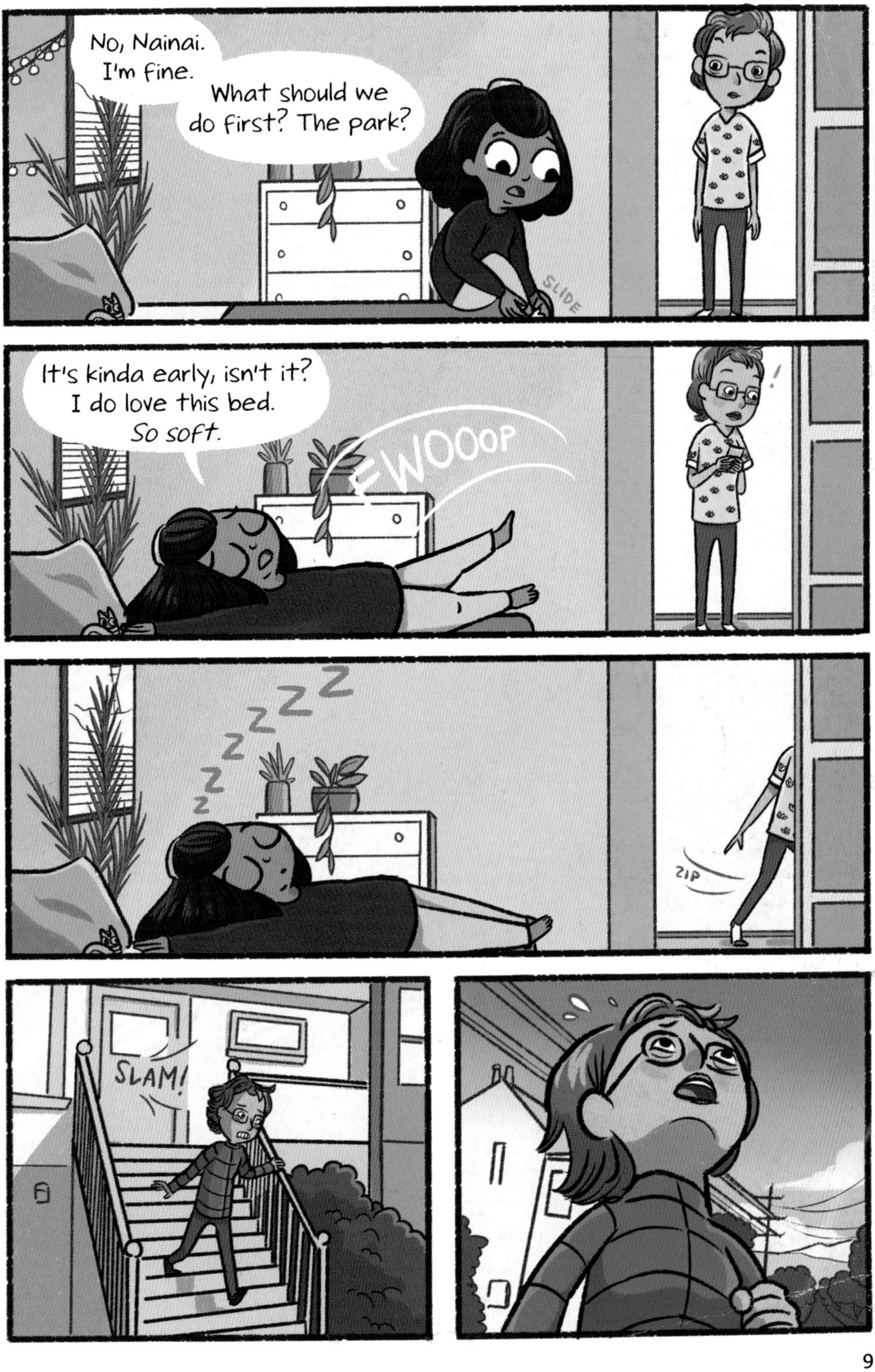
No, Nainai.
I'm fine.
What should we do first? The park?
SLIDE
It's kinda early, isn't it? I do love this bed. So soft.
FWOOOP
!
ZZZZZZ
ZIP
SLAM!

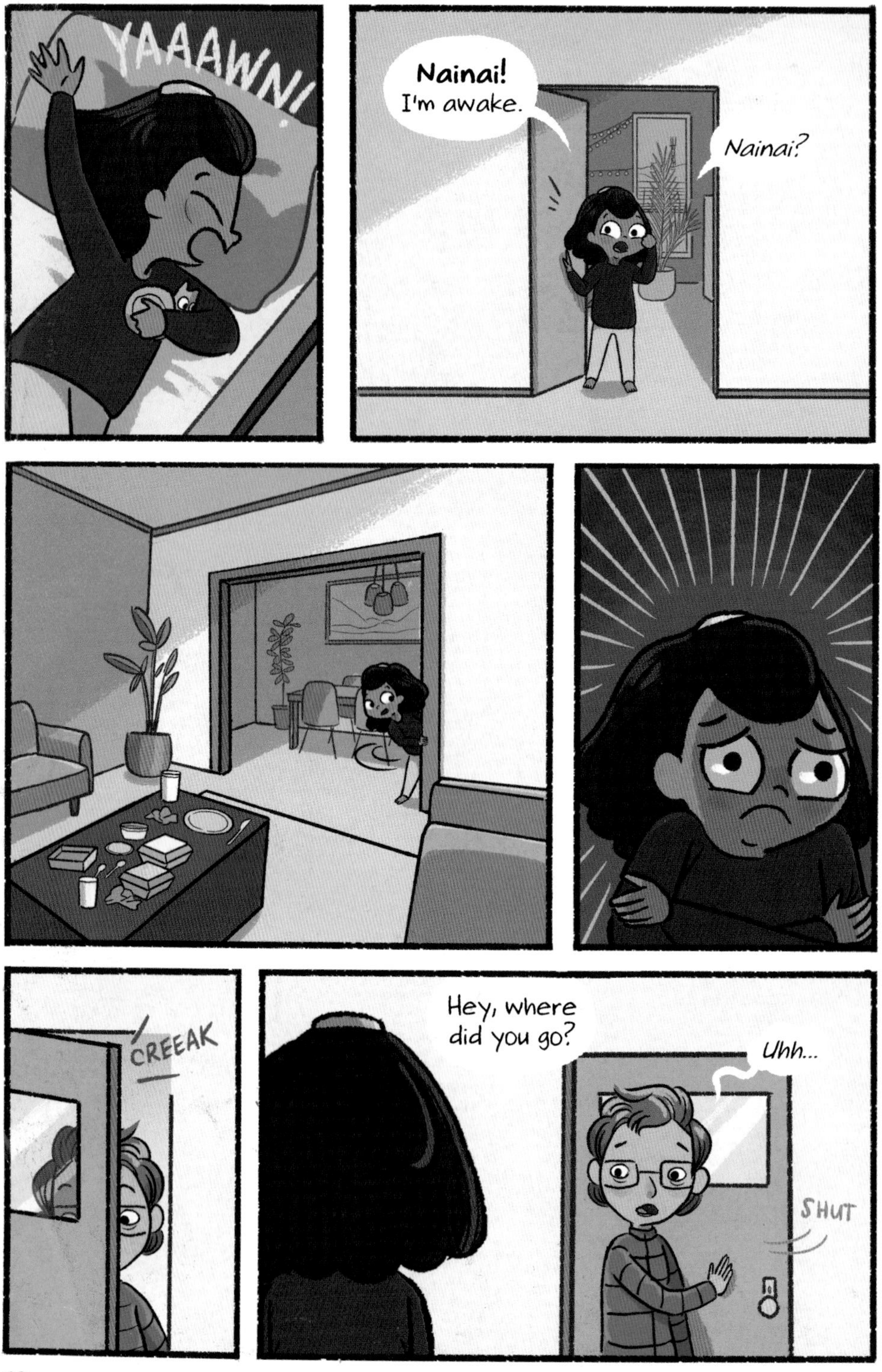
YAAAWN!
Nainai!
I'm awake.
Nainai?
CREEAK
Hey, where did you go?
Uhh...
SHUT

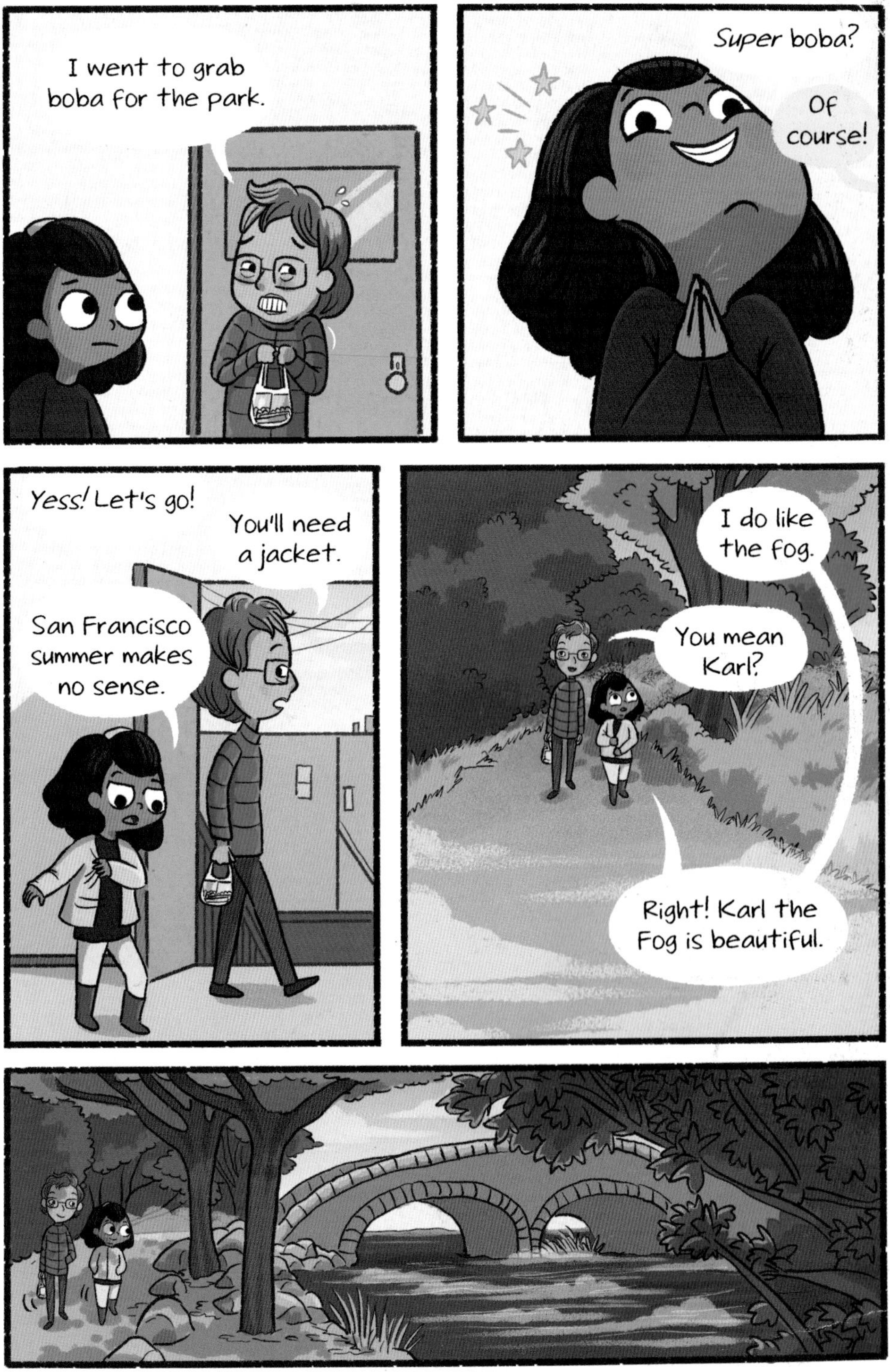
I went to grab boba for the park.
Super boba?
Of course!
Yess! Let's go!
You'll need a jacket.
San Francisco summer makes no sense.
I do like the fog.
You mean Karl?
Right! Karl the Fog is beautiful.

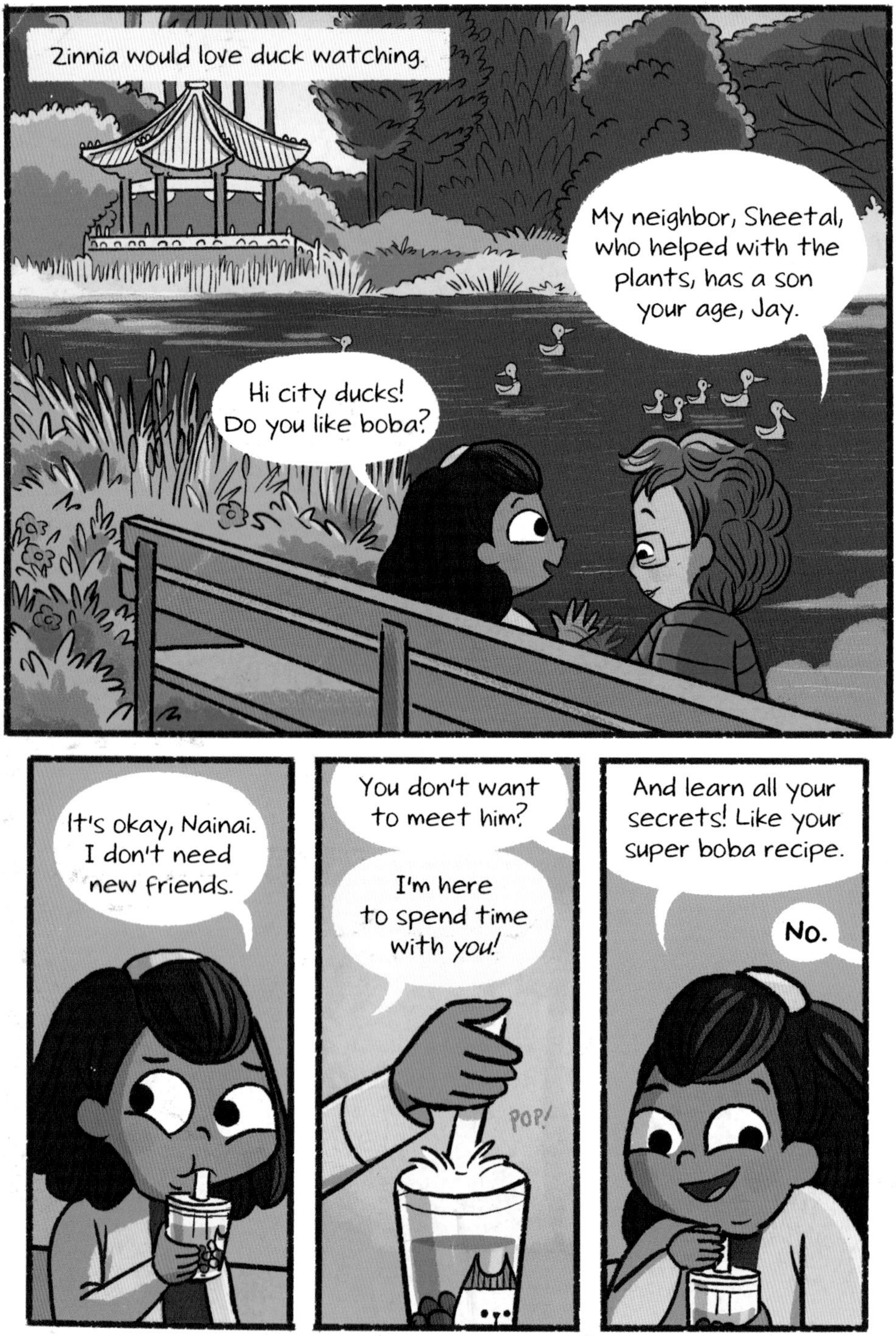
Zinnia would love duck watching.
My neighbor, Sheetal, who helped with the plants, has a son your age, Jay.
Hi city ducks! Do you like boba?
It's okay, Nainai. I don't need new friends.
You don't want to meet him?
I'm here to spend time with you!
POP!
And learn all your secrets! Like your super boba recipe.
No.

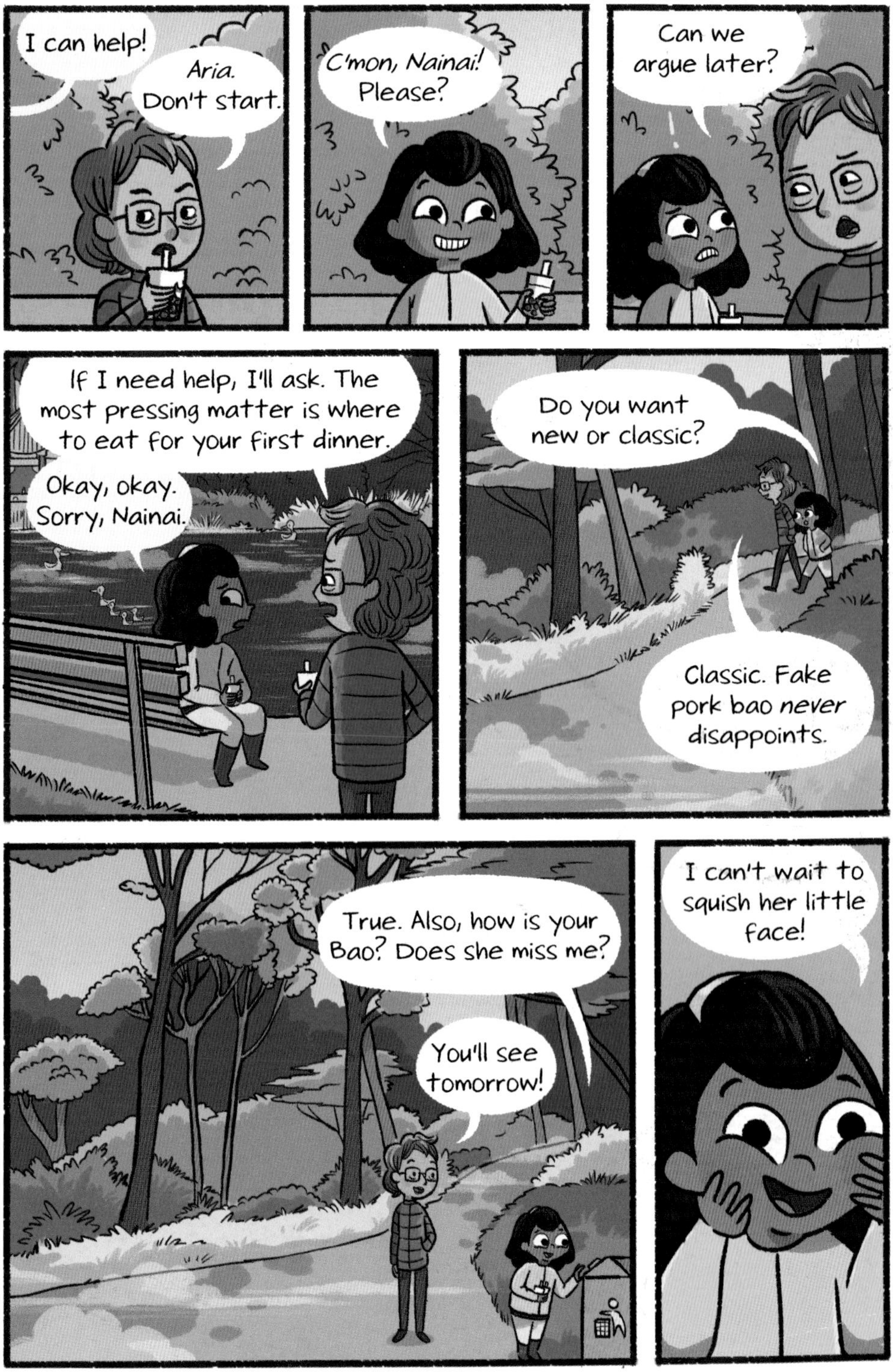
I can help!
Aria. Don't start.
C'mon, Nainai! Please?
Can we argue later?
If I need help, I'll ask. The most pressing matter is where to eat for your first dinner.
Okay, okay. Sorry, Nainai.
Do you want new or classic?
Classic. Fake pork bao *never* disappoints.
True. Also, how is your Bao? Does she miss me?
You'll see tomorrow!
I can't wait to squish her little face!

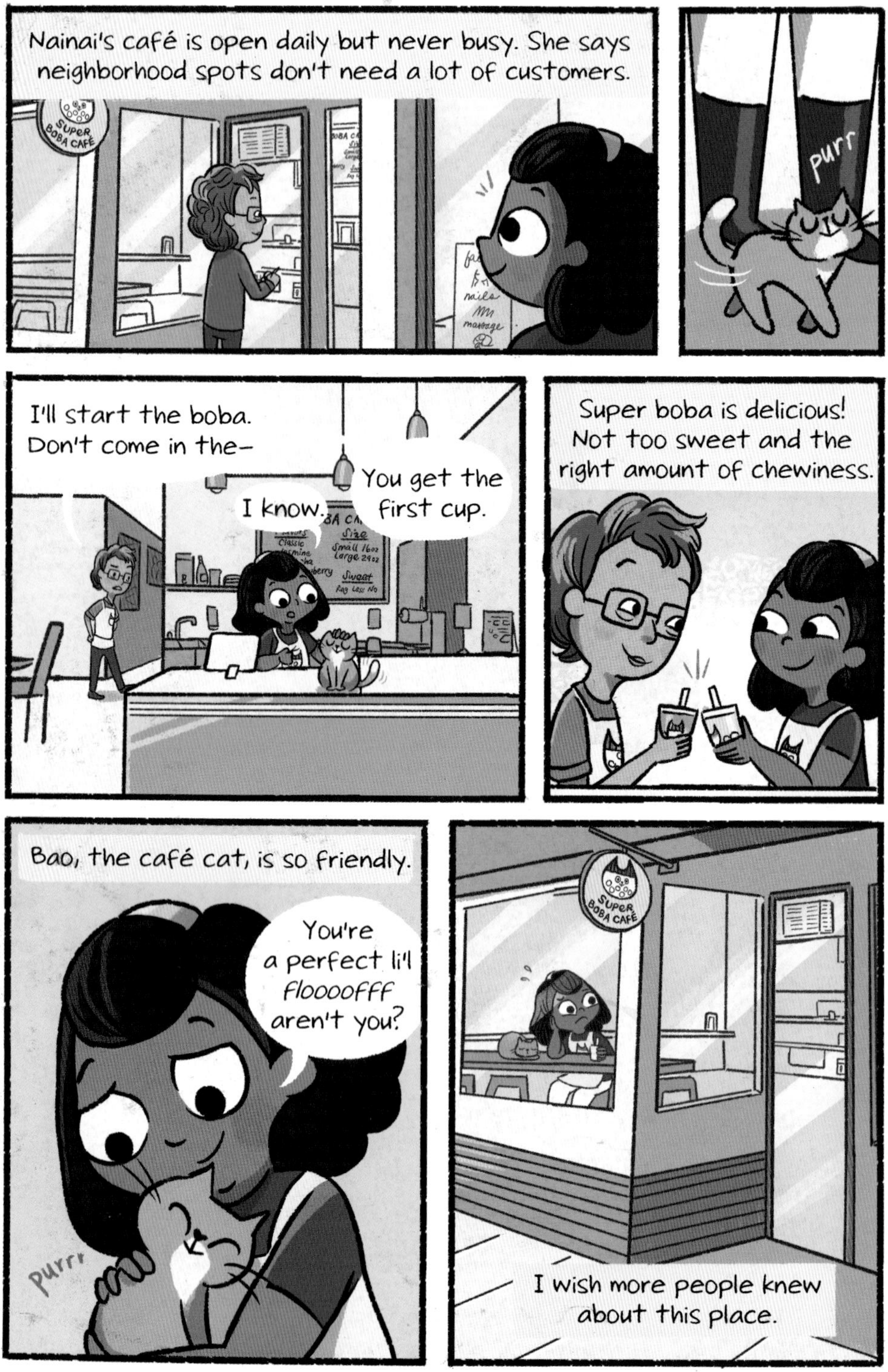

Nainai's café is open daily but never busy. She says neighborhood spots don't need a lot of customers.
SUPER BOBA CAFÉ
nails
massage
purr
I'll start the boba. Don't come in the—
I know.
You get the first cup.
Size
Small 16oz
Large 24oz
Sweet
Super boba is delicious! Not too sweet and the right amount of chewiness.
Bao, the café cat, is so friendly.
You're a perfect li'l flooooFFF aren't you?
purrr
SUPER BOBA CAFÉ
I wish more people knew about this place.

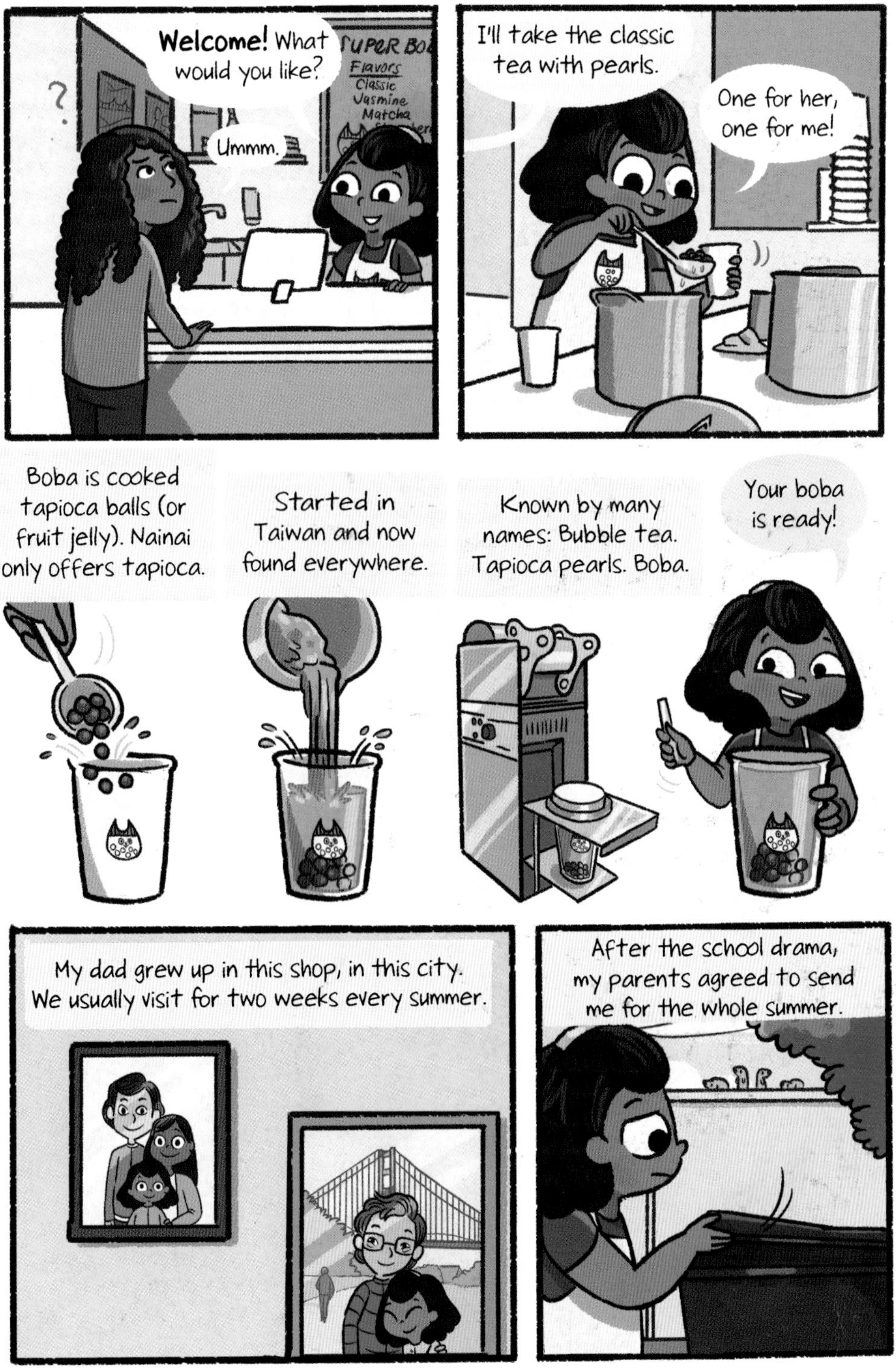

Welcome! What would you like?
Ummm.
Flavors
Classic
Jasmine
Matcha
I'll take the classic tea with pearls.
One for her, one for me!
Boba is cooked tapioca balls (or fruit jelly). Nainai only offers tapioca.
Started in Taiwan and now found everywhere.
Known by many names: Bubble tea. Tapioca pearls. Boba.
Your boba is ready!
My dad grew up in this shop, in this city. We usually visit for two weeks every summer.
After the school drama, my parents agreed to send me for the whole summer.

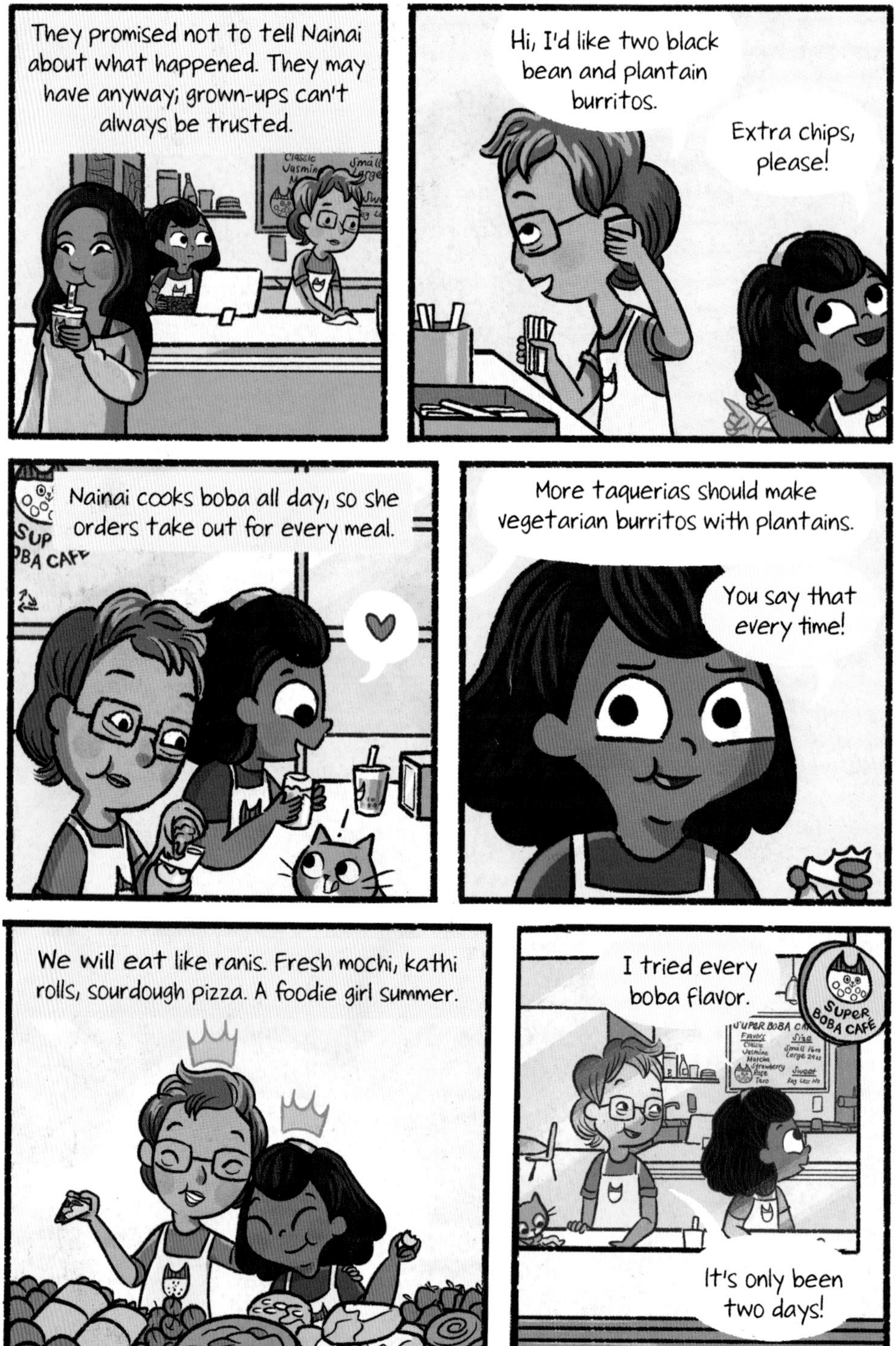
They promised not to tell Nainai about what happened. They may have anyway; grown-ups can't always be trusted.
Hi, I'd like two black bean and plantain burritos.
Extra chips, please!
Nainai cooks boba all day, so she orders take out for every meal.
More taquerias should make vegetarian burritos with plantains.
You say that every time!
We will eat like ranis. Fresh mochi, kathi rolls, sourdough pizza. A foodie girl summer.
I tried every boba flavor.
It's only been two days!
SUPER BOBA CAFE

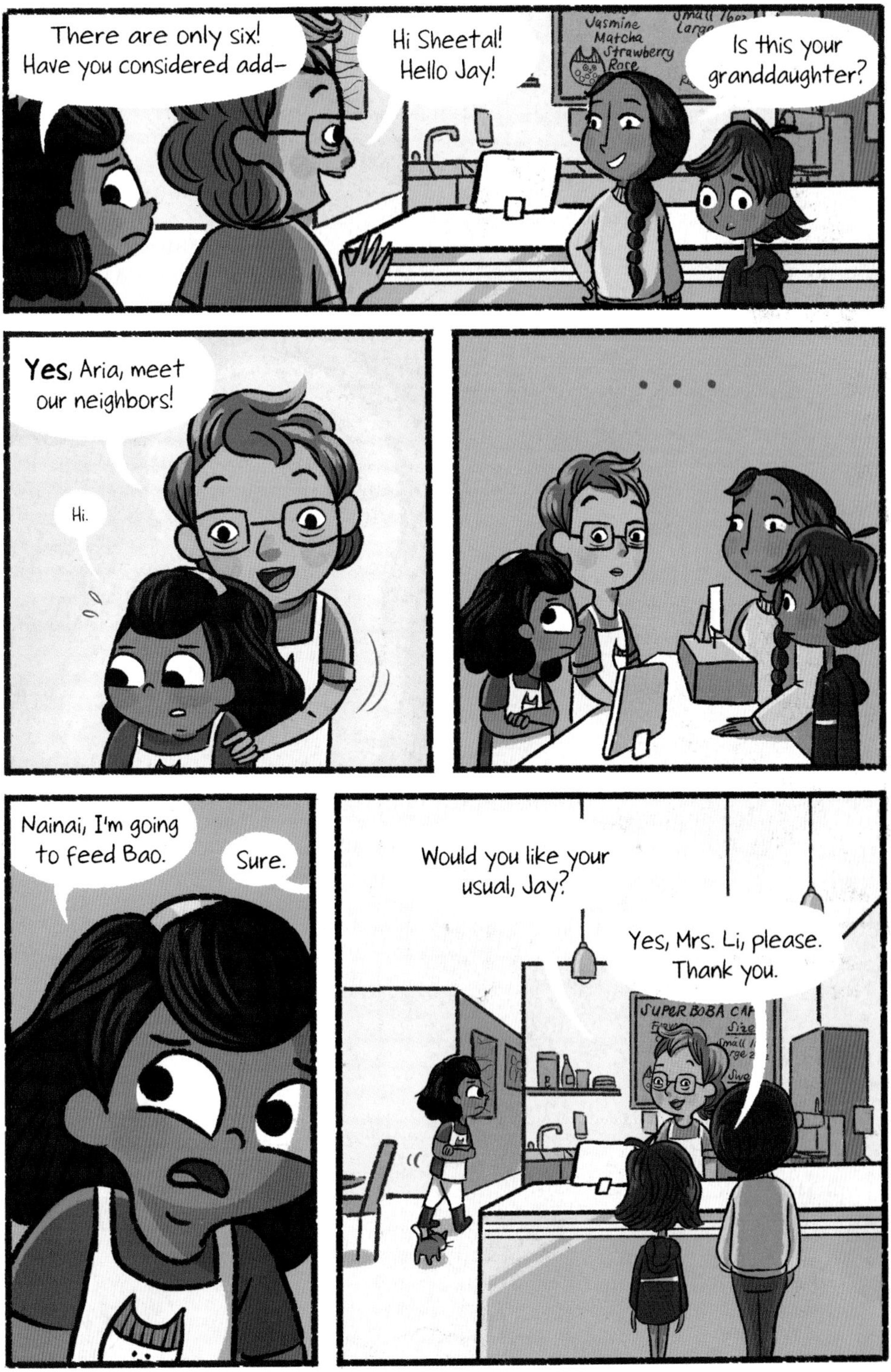
There are only six! Have you considered add-
Hi Sheetal! Hello Jay!
Is this your granddaughter?
Yes, Aria, meet our neighbors!
Hi.
. . .
Nainai, I'm going to feed Bao.
Sure.
Would you like your usual, Jay?
Yes, Mrs. Li, please. Thank you.

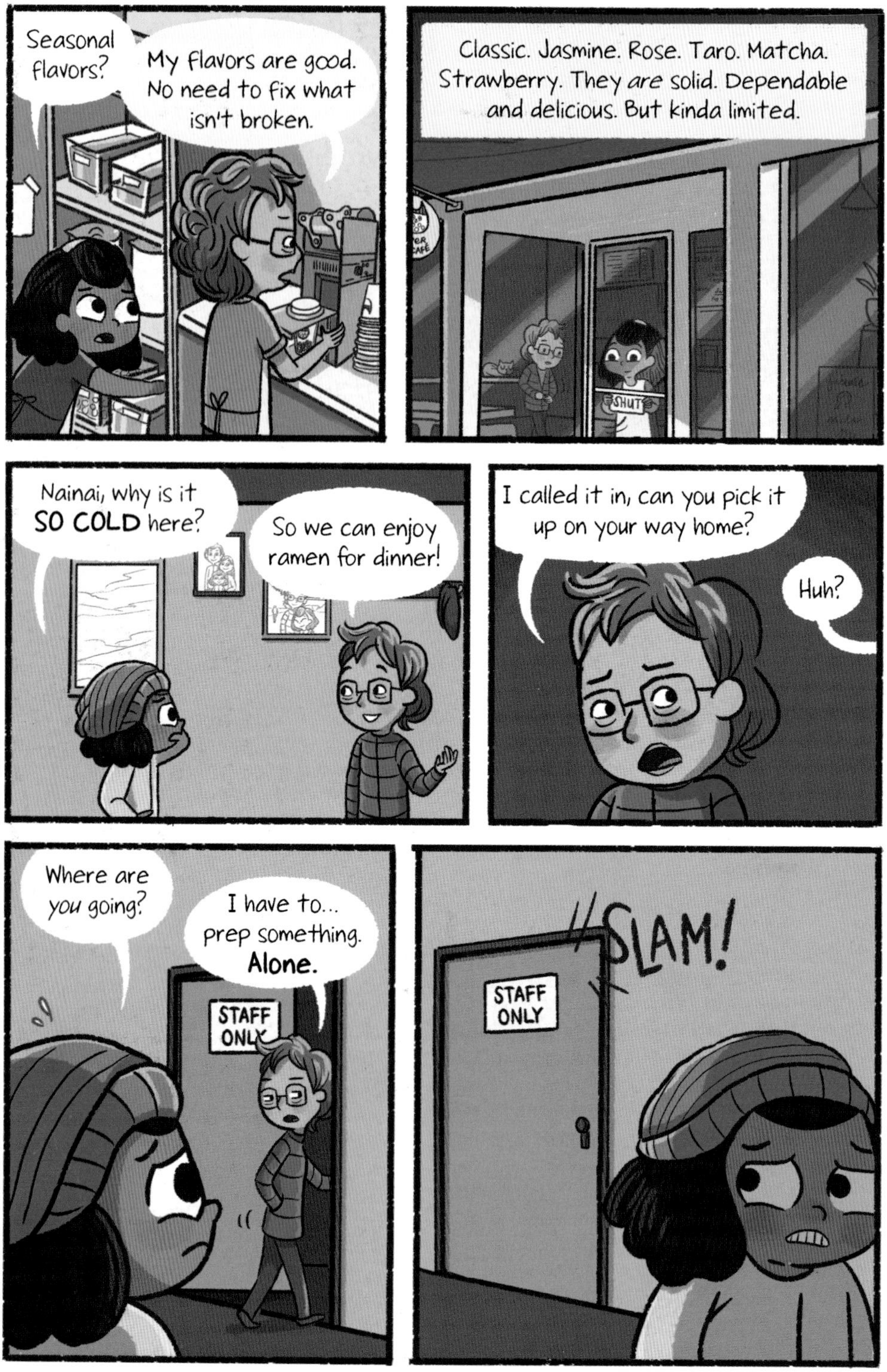
Seasonal flavors?
My flavors are good. No need to fix what isn't broken.
Classic. Jasmine. Rose. Taro. Matcha. Strawberry. They *are* solid. Dependable and delicious. But kinda limited.
SHUT
Nainai, why is it **SO COLD** here?
So we can enjoy ramen for dinner!
I called it in, can you pick it up on your way home?
Huh?
Where are you going?
I have to... prep something. **Alone.**
STAFF ONLY
SLAM!
STAFF ONLY

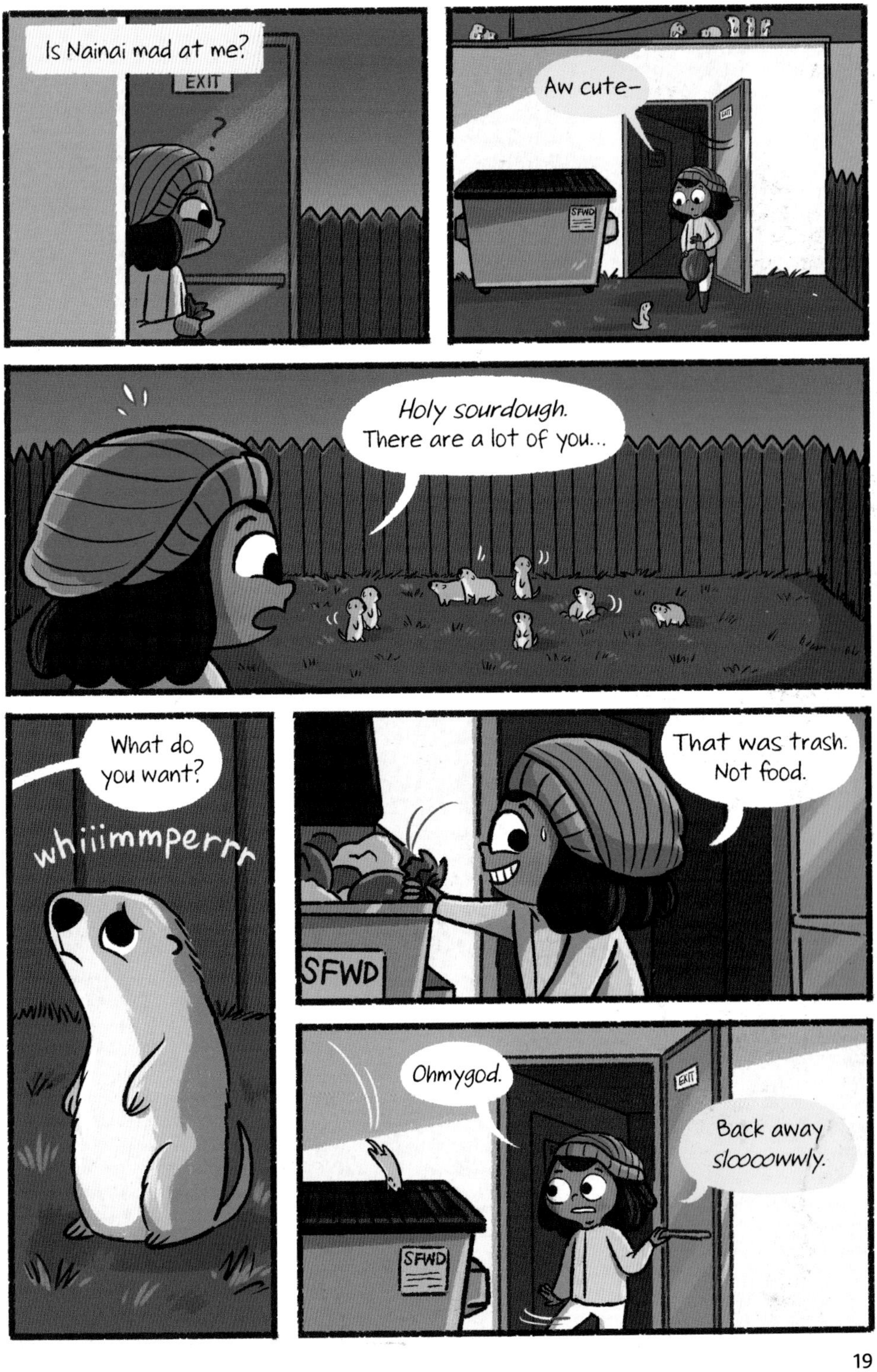
Is Nainai mad at me?
EXIT
?
Aw cute-
SFWD
Holy sourdough. There are a lot of you...
What do you want?
whiiimmperrr
That was trash. Not food.
SFWD
Ohmygod.
Back away slooowwly.
SFWD

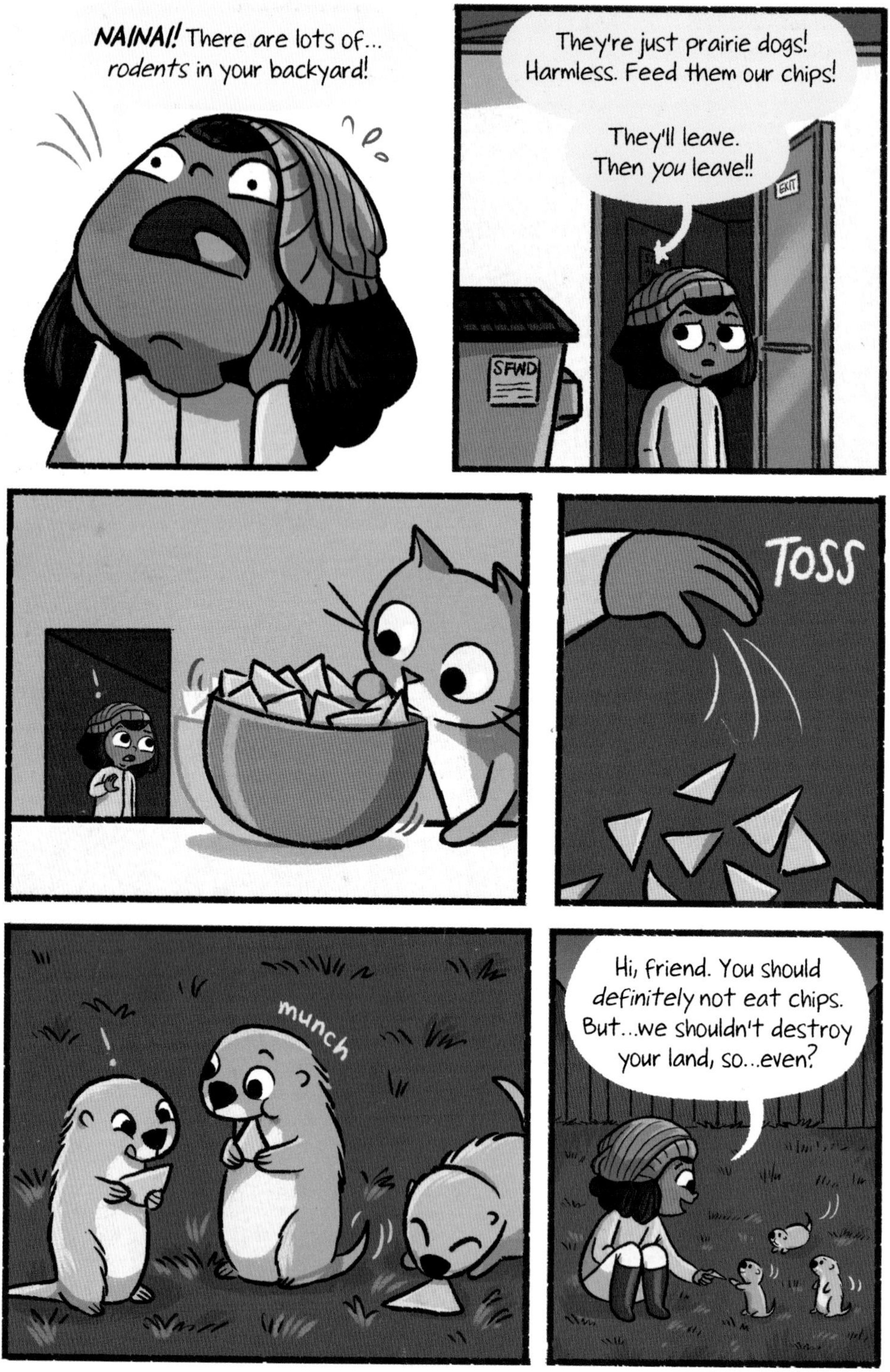
NAINAI! There are lots of... rodents in your backyard!
They're just prairie dogs! Harmless. Feed them our chips!
They'll leave. Then you leave!!
EXIT
SFWD
TOSS
munch
Hi, friend. You should definitely not eat chips. But...we shouldn't destroy your land, so...even?

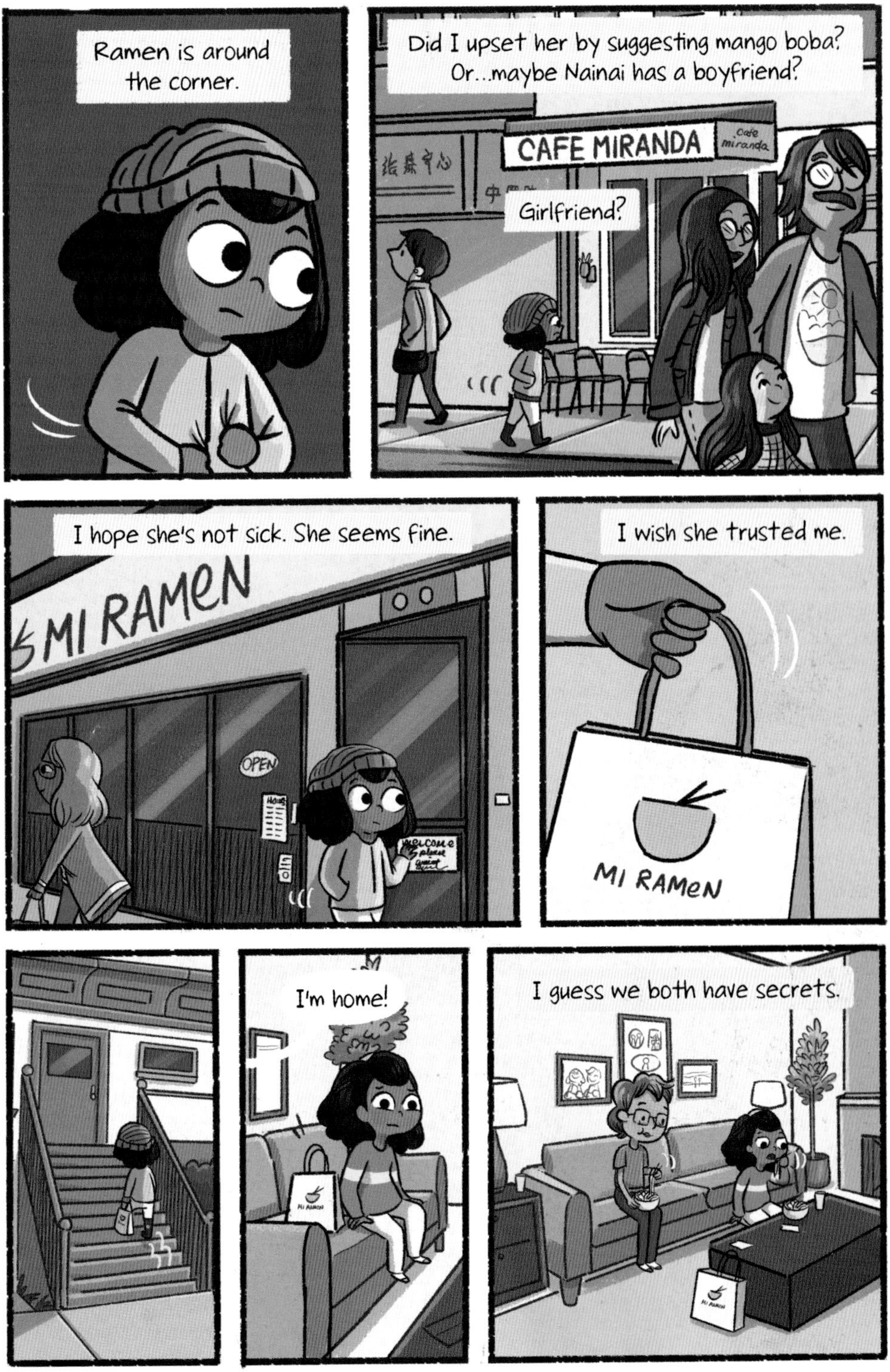
Ramen is around the corner.
Did I upset her by suggesting mango boba? Or...maybe Nainai has a boyfriend?
CAFE MIRANDA
cafe miranda
Girlfriend?
I hope she's not sick. She seems fine.
MI RAMEN
OPEN
I wish she trusted me.
MI RAMEN
I'm home!
I guess we both have secrets.

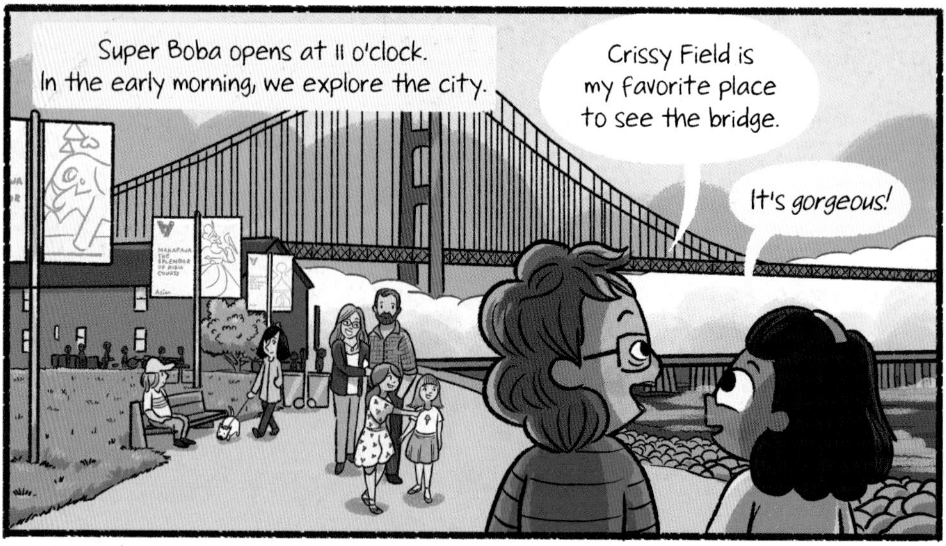
Super Boba opens at 11 o'clock.
In the early morning, we explore the city.
Crissy Field is my favorite place to see the bridge.
It's gorgeous!

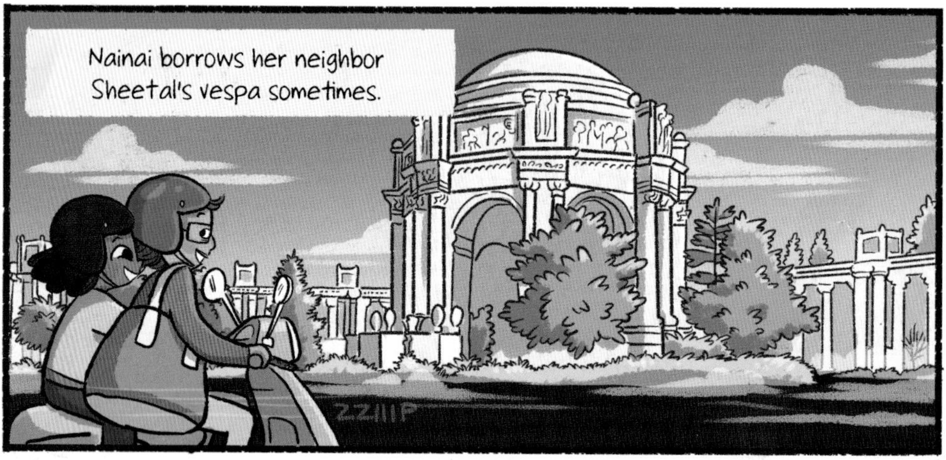
Nainai borrows her neighbor Sheetal's vespa sometimes.

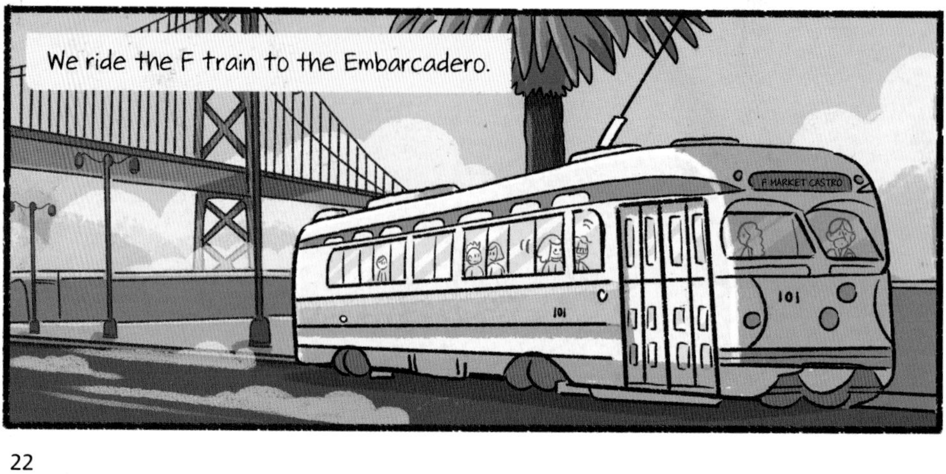
We ride the F train to the Embarcadero.
F MARKET CASTRO
101
101

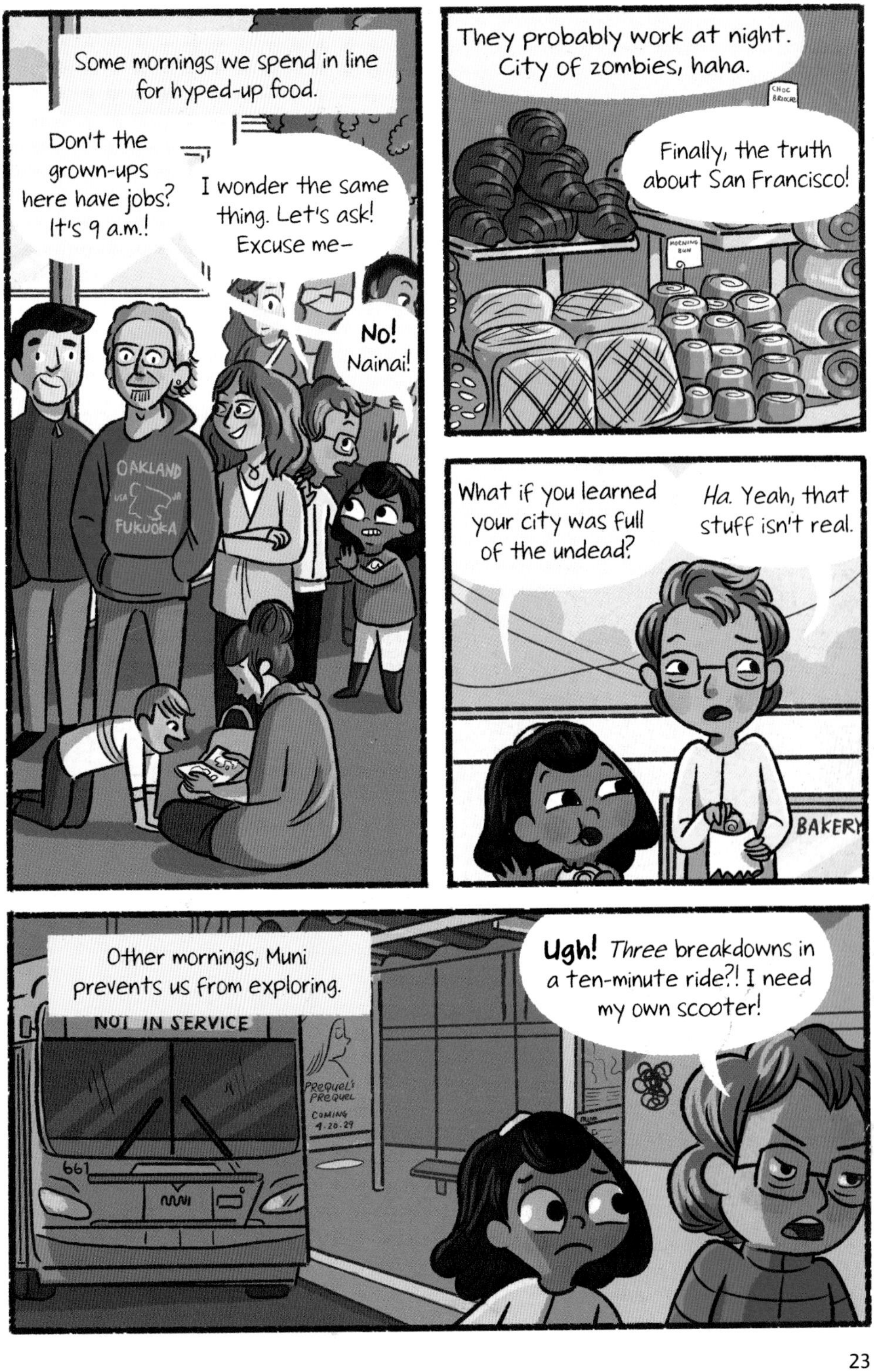
Some mornings we spend in line for hyped-up food.
Don't the grown-ups here have jobs? It's 9 a.m.!
I wonder the same thing. Let's ask! Excuse me–
No! Nainai!
OAKLAND
FUKUOKA
They probably work at night. City of zombies, haha.
CHOC BRIOCHE
Finally, the truth about San Francisco!
MORNING BUN
What if you learned your city was full of the undead?
Ha. Yeah, that stuff isn't real.
BAKERY
Other mornings, Muni prevents us from exploring.
NOT IN SERVICE
PREQUEL'S PREQUEL
COMING 4.20.29
muni
Ugh! *Three* breakdowns in a ten-minute ride?! I need my own scooter!

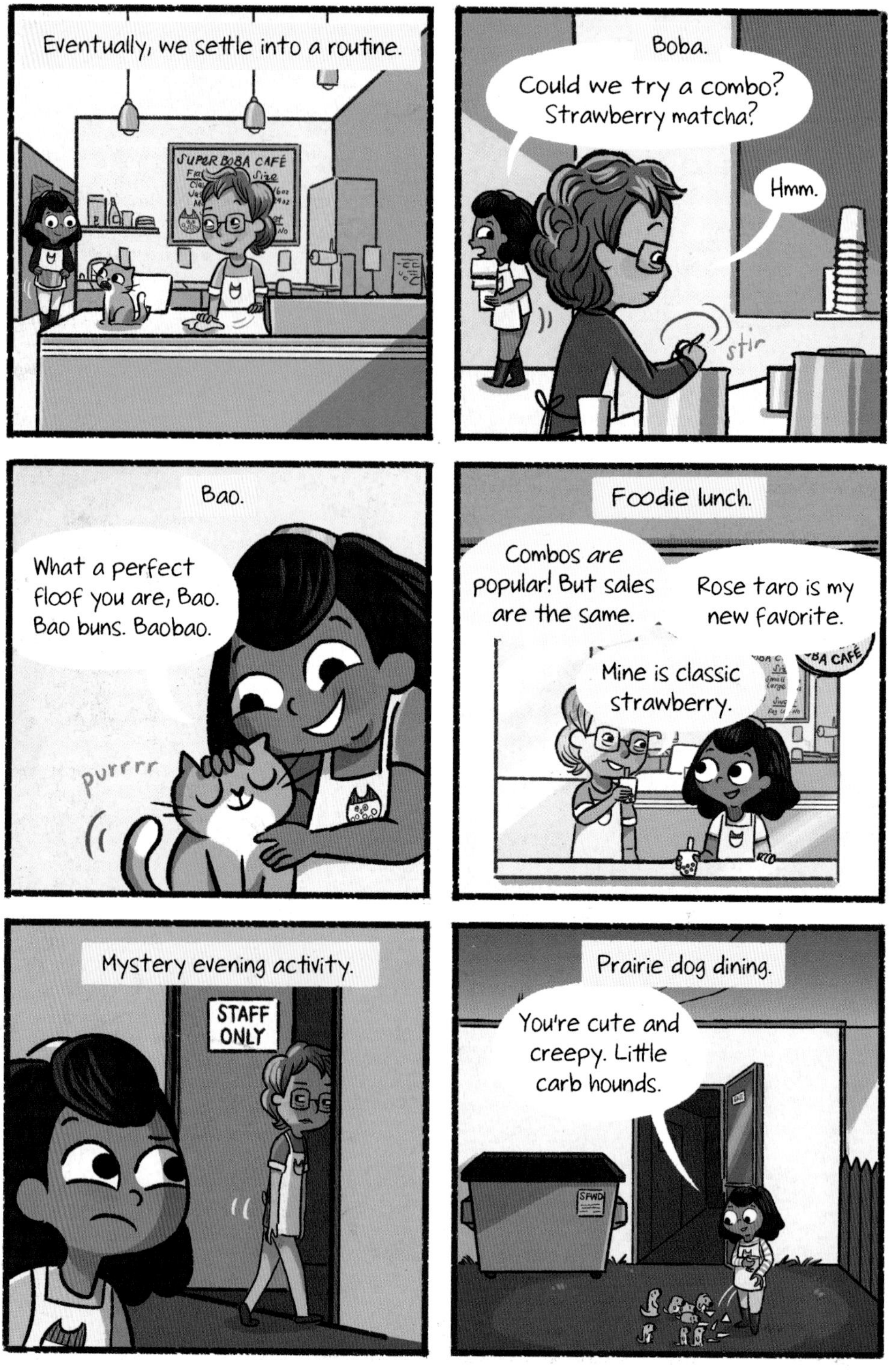
Eventually, we settle into a routine.
SUPER BOBA CAFÉ
Boba.
Could we try a combo? Strawberry matcha?
Hmm.
stir
Bao.
What a perfect floof you are, Bao. Bao buns. Baobao.
purrrr
Foodie lunch.
Combos are popular! But sales are the same.
Rose taro is my new favorite.
Mine is classic strawberry.
Mystery evening activity.
STAFF ONLY
Prairie dog dining.
You're cute and creepy. Little carb hounds.

Day in, day out.

Little changes.

Flavors | Try Combo
Classic | Mix 2 an
Jasmine | Sizes
Matcha | Sm Med
Strawberry
Rose
Ta

Nainai is open to new ideas.

Except in her kitchen, and my theories escalate.

Secret government lab?

STAFF ONLY

Bizarre art?

MWROW

Magic?

Dead bodies?

STAFF ONLY

I need a project.

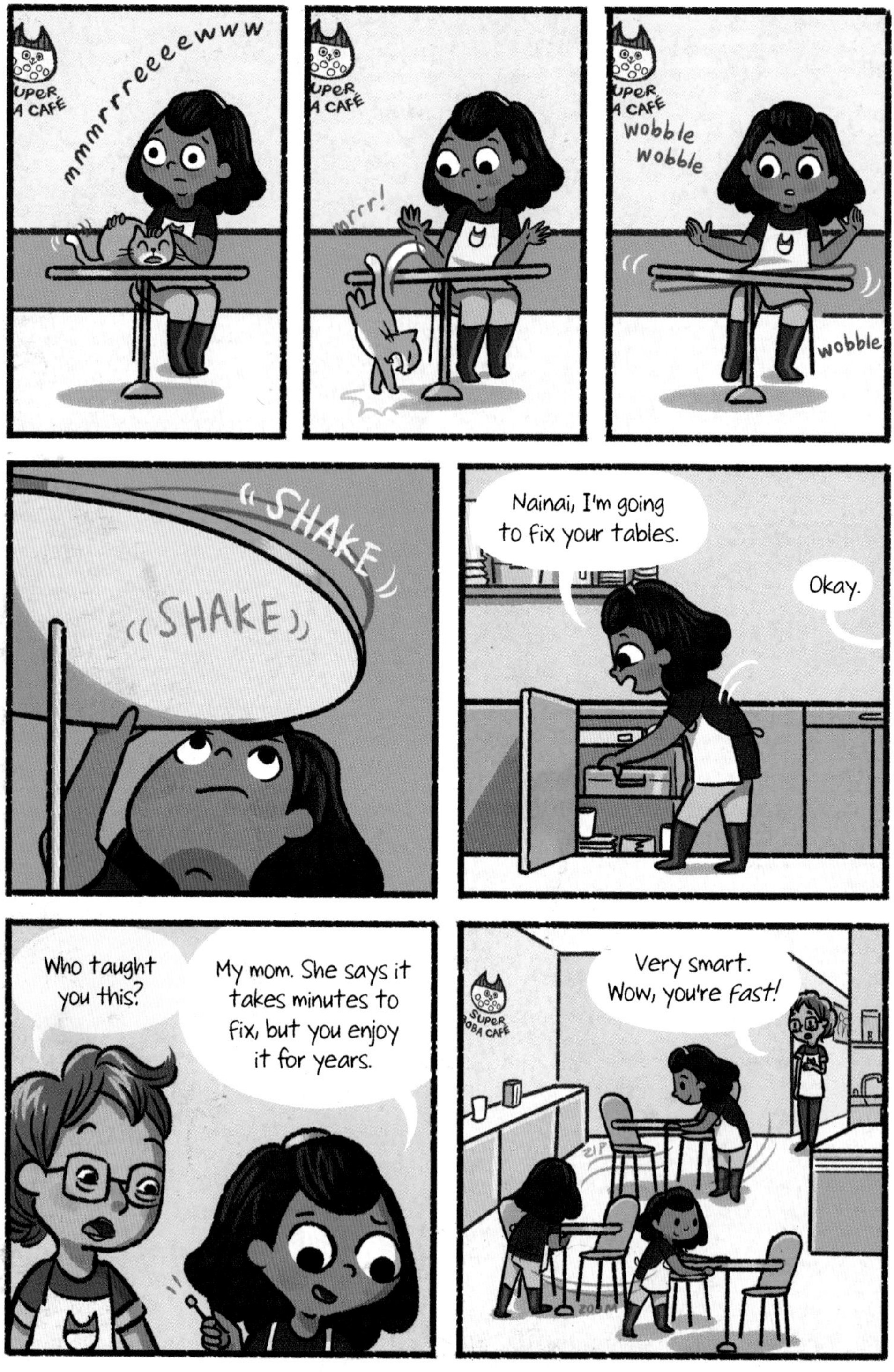
mmmrrreeeewww
mrrr!
wobble
wobble
wobble
SHAKE
SHAKE
Nainai, I'm going to fix your tables.
Okay.
Who taught you this?
My mom. She says it takes minutes to fix, but you enjoy it for years.
Very smart. Wow, you're fast!
ZIP
ZOOM

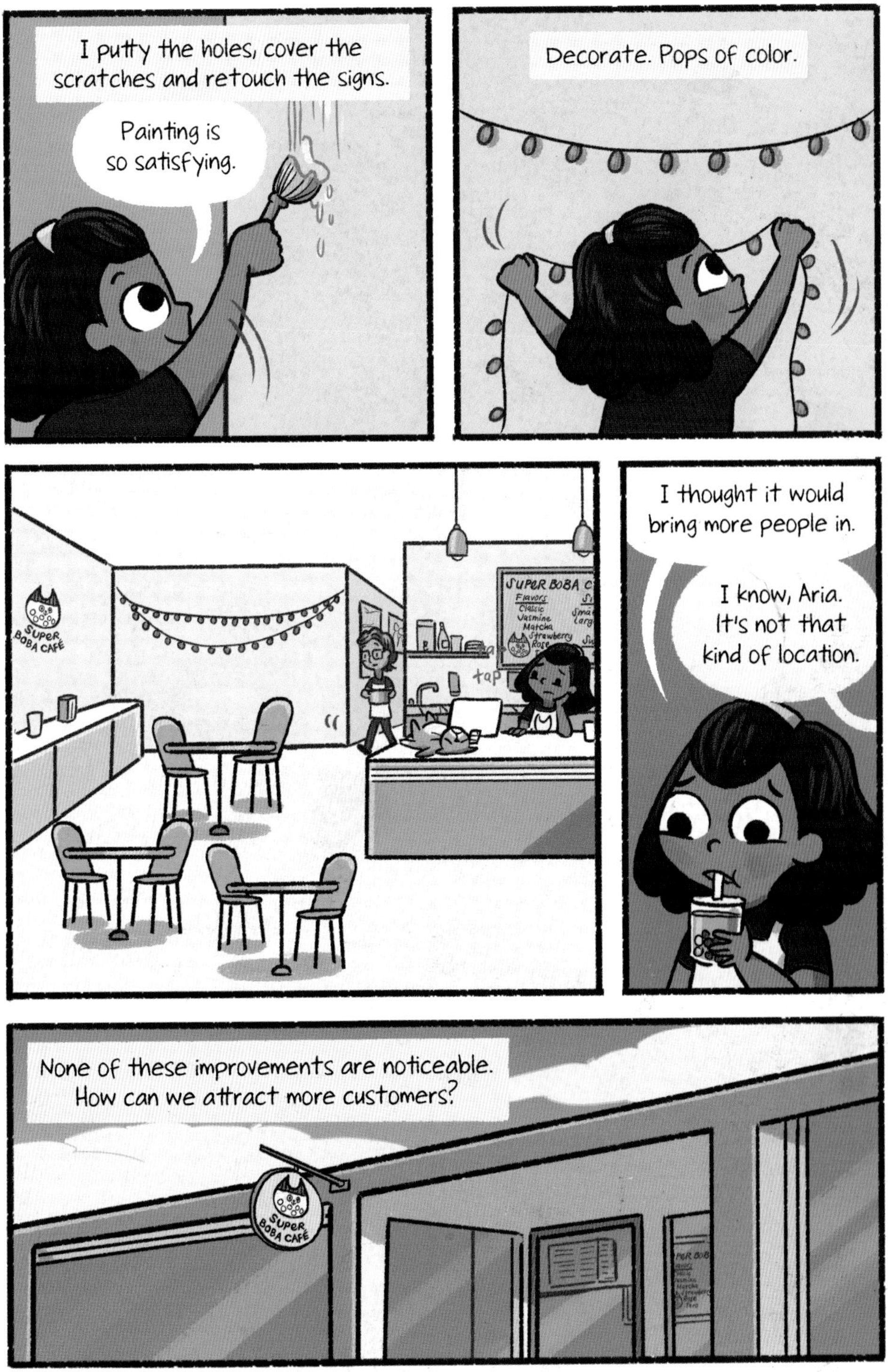
I putty the holes, cover the scratches and retouch the signs.
Painting is so satisfying.
Decorate. Pops of color.
SUPER BOBA CAFÉ
tap
I thought it would bring more people in.
I know, Aria. It's not that kind of location.
None of these improvements are noticeable. How can we attract more customers?
SUPER BOBA CAFÉ

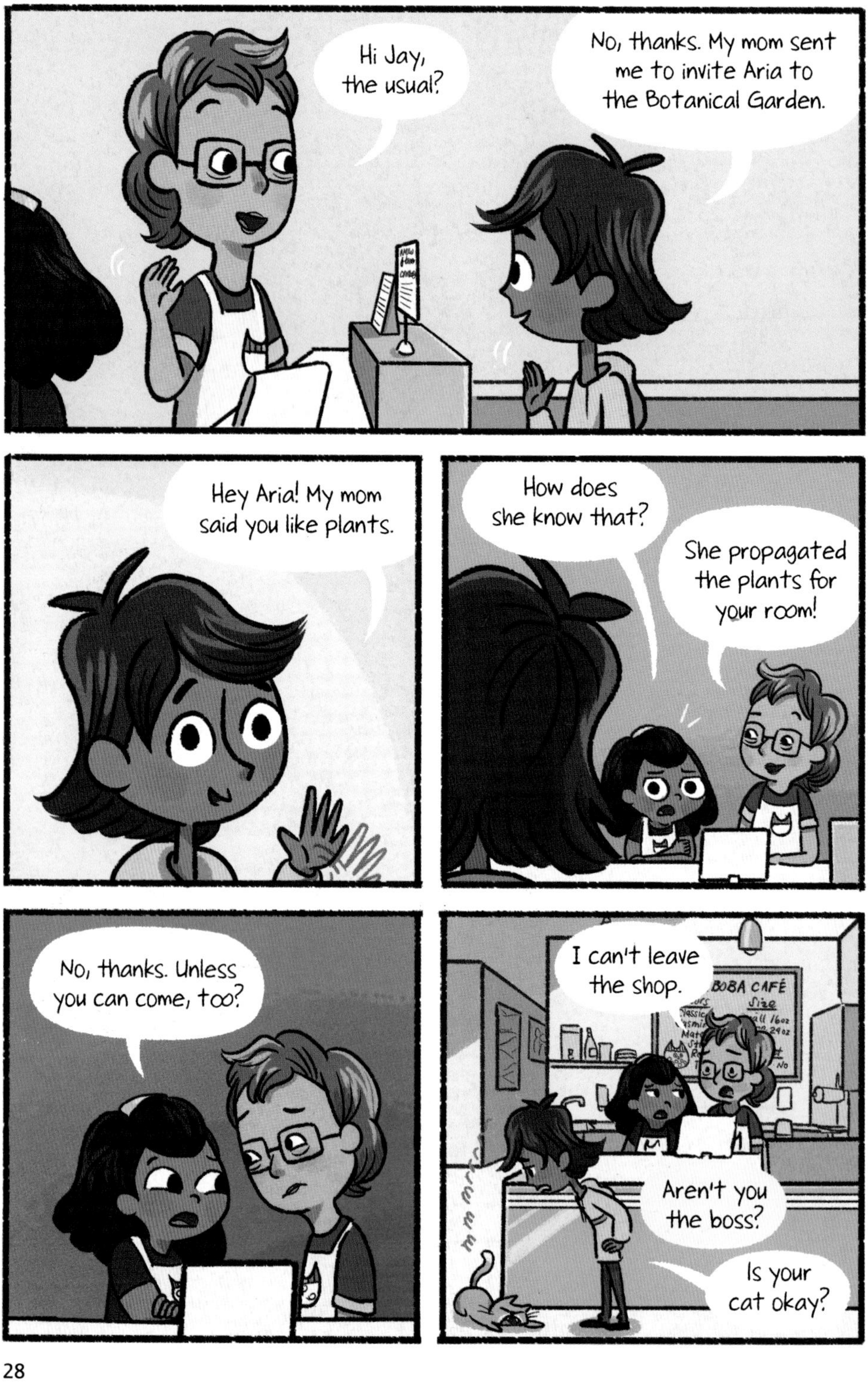
Hi Jay, the usual?
No, thanks. My mom sent me to invite Aria to the Botanical Garden.
Hey Aria! My mom said you like plants.
How does she know that?
She propagated the plants for your room!
No, thanks. Unless you can come, too?
I can't leave the shop.
BOBA CAFÉ
Aren't you the boss?
Is your cat okay?

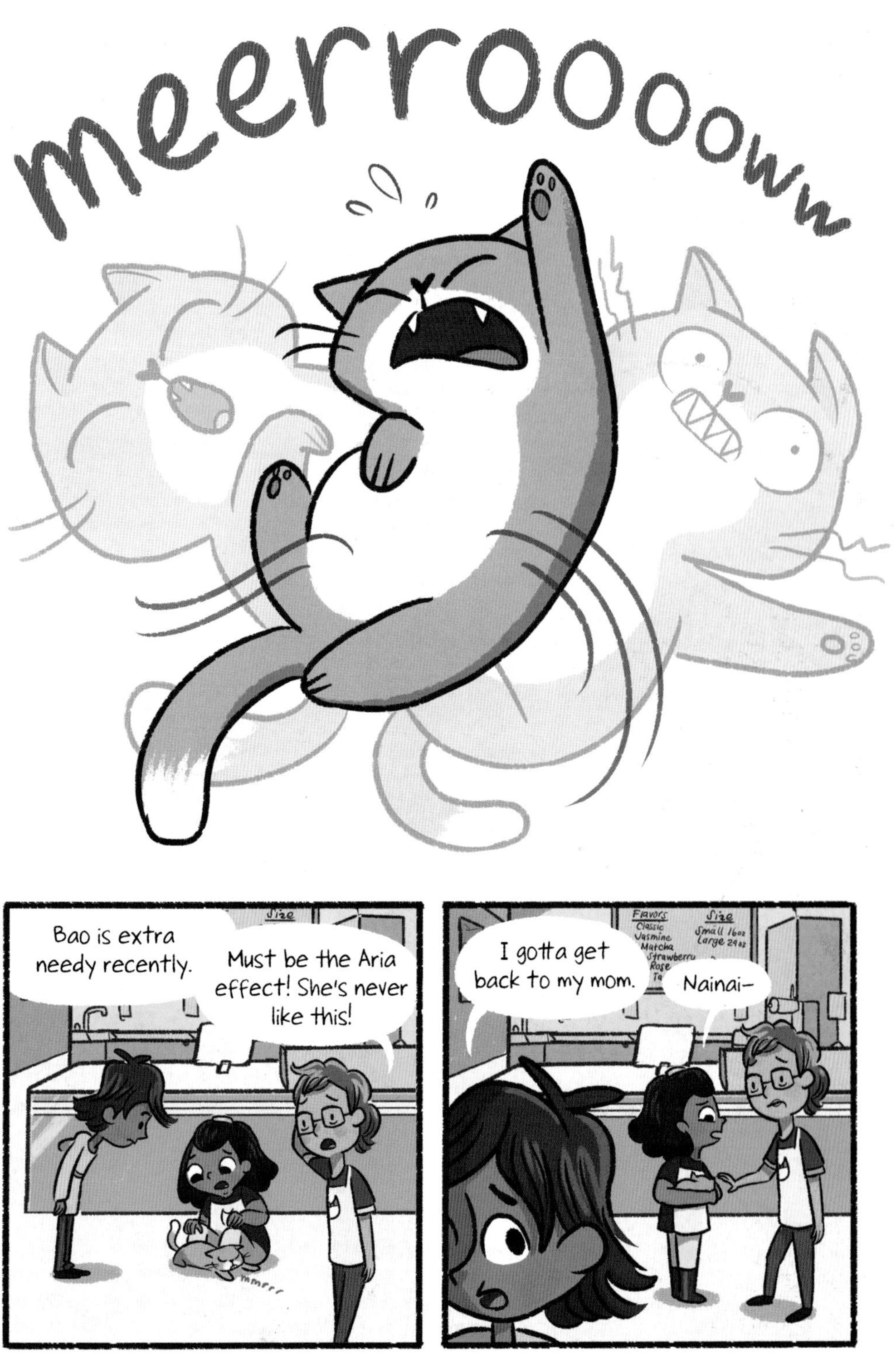
meerroooooww
Bao is extra needy recently.
Must be the Aria effect! She's never like this!
I gotta get back to my mom.
Nainai–

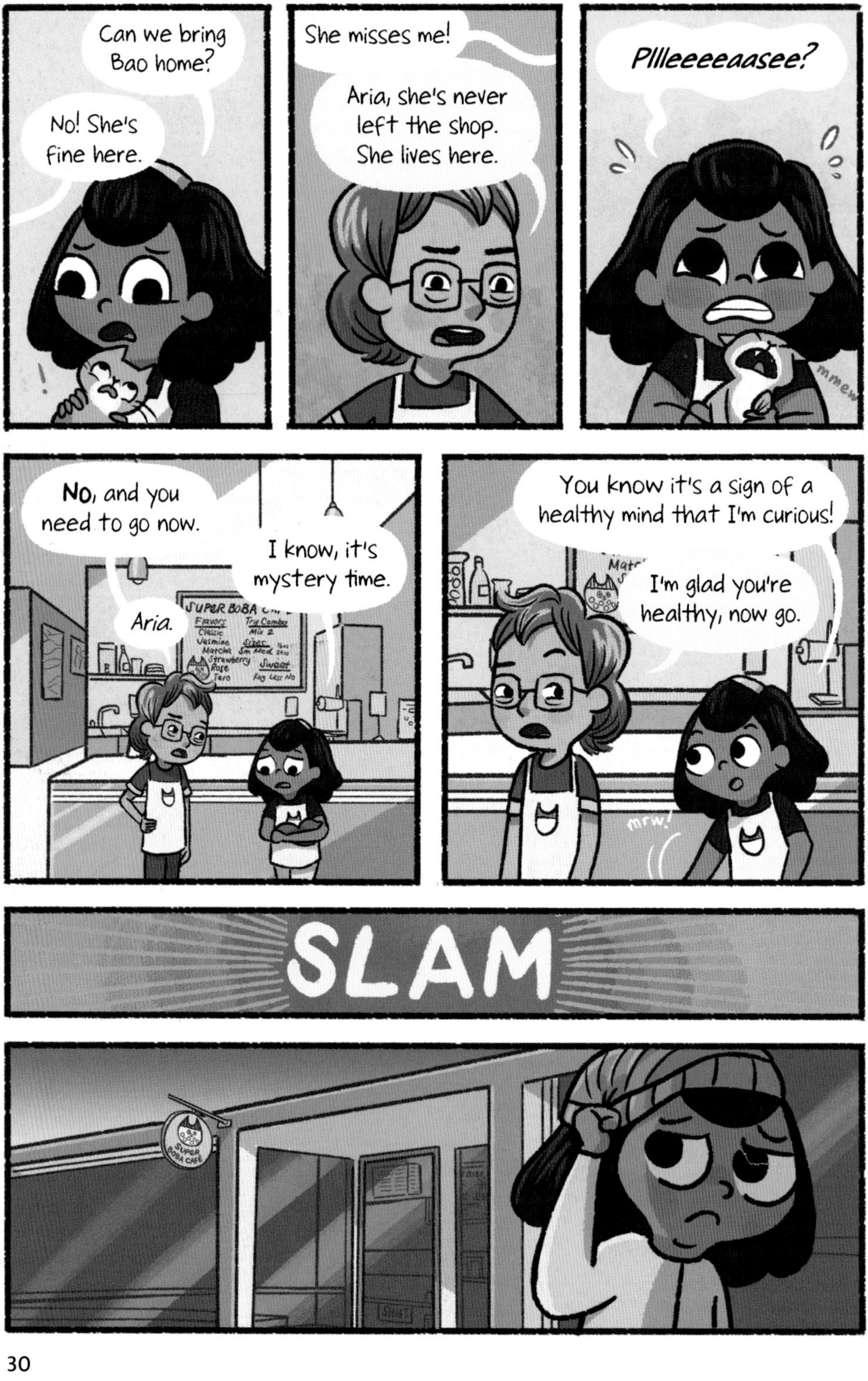
Can we bring Bao home?
No! She's fine here.
She misses me!
Aria, she's never left the shop. She lives here.
Pllleeeeaasee?
mmew
No, and you need to go now.
I know, it's mystery time.
Aria.
SUPER BOBA
Flavors
Classic
Jasmine
Matcha
Strawberry
Rose
Taro
Try Combo
Mix 2
Sizes
Sm Med
Sweet
Reg Less No
You know it's a sign of a healthy mind that I'm curious!
I'm glad you're healthy, now go.
mrw!
SLAM
SUPER BOBA CAFE

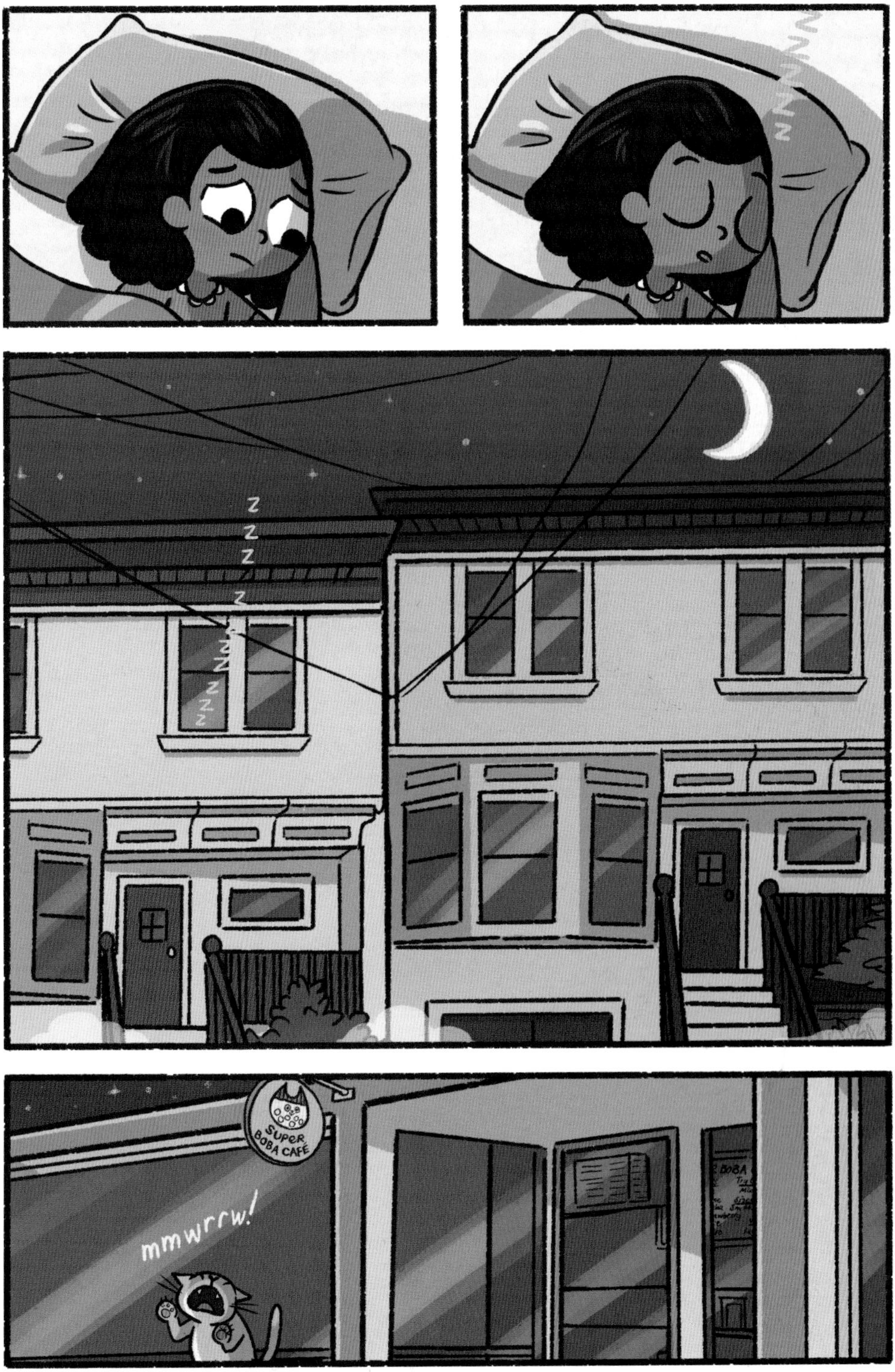
Z Z Z Z Z
Z Z Z Z Z Z Z Z
SUPER BOBA CAFÉ
mmwrrw!

The next morning, a surprise was waiting.

Well, eight surprises.

purr
mew mew
mew
mee
meew
purr
mew
purr
purr

This explains a lot.

Bao!

TURN

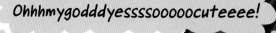

Ohhhmygodddyesssssoooooocuteeee!

This is **it**, Nainai!

What? What's it?

Shake
Shake

There are *too* many cats here now!

mew!

You're the answer!

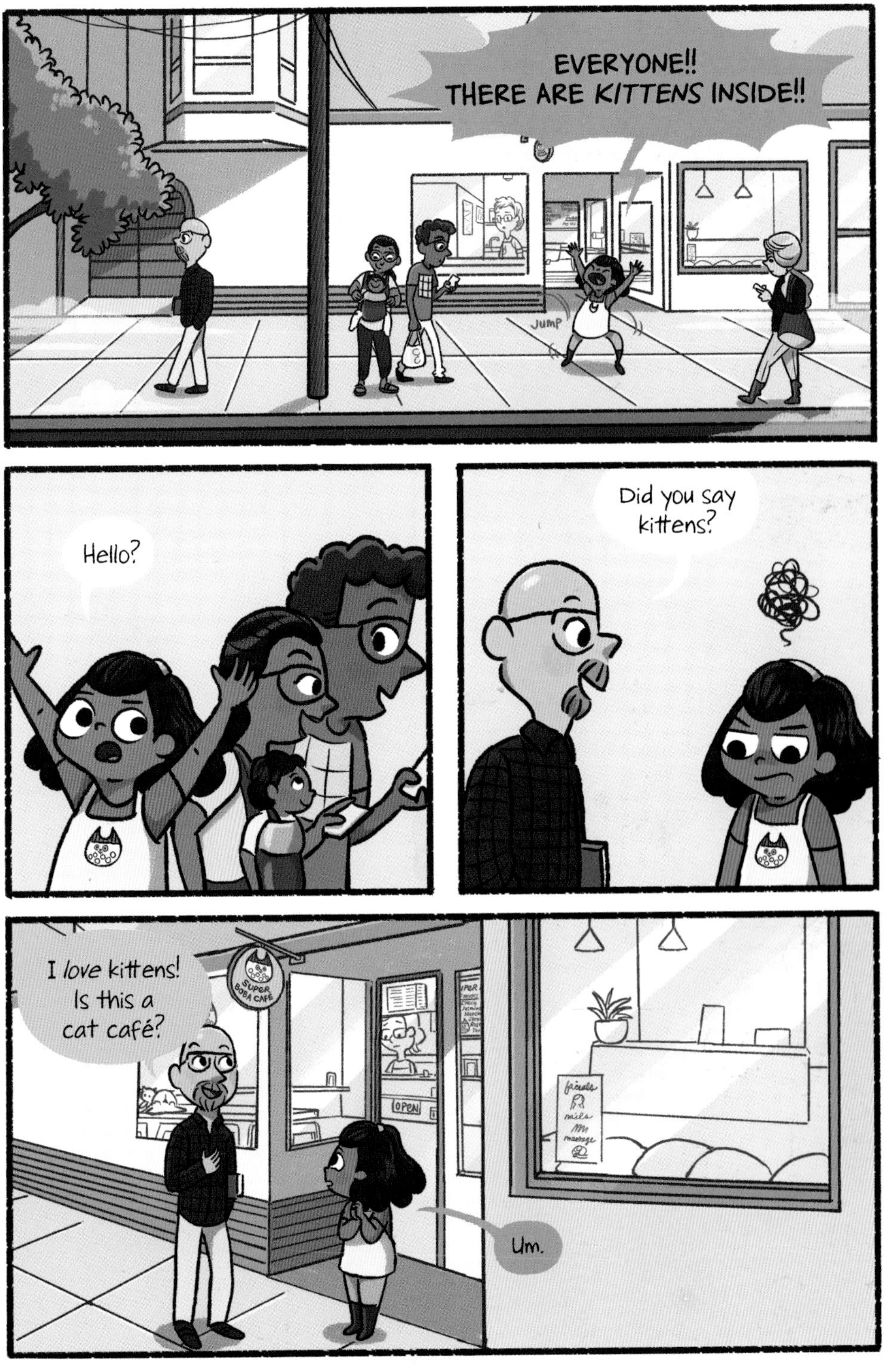
EVERYONE!! THERE ARE KITTENS INSIDE!!
JUMP
Hello?
Did you say kittens?
I love kittens! Is this a cat café?
SUPER BOBA CAFE
OPEN
Um.

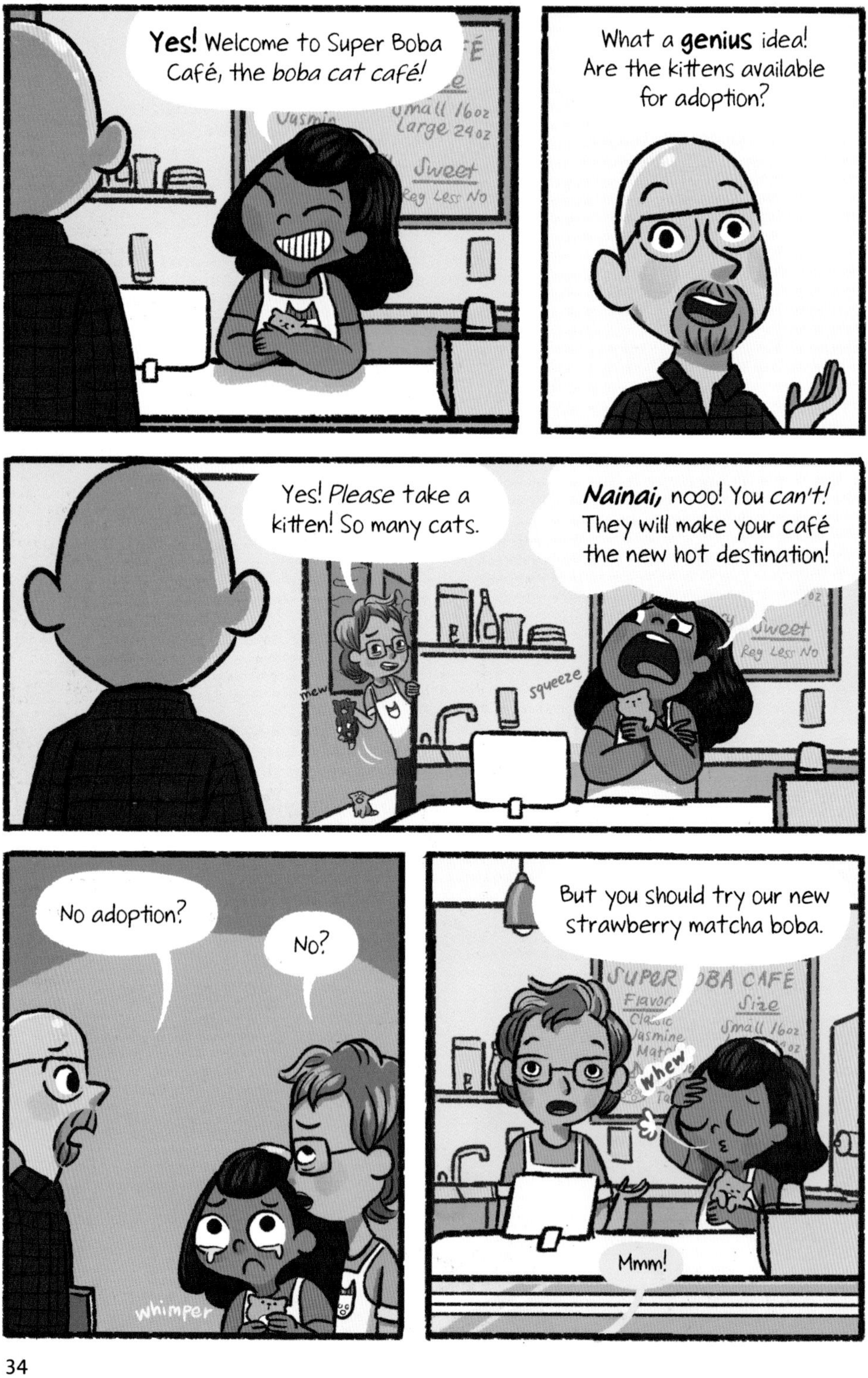
Yes! Welcome to Super Boba Café, the *boba cat café!*
What a **genius** idea! Are the kittens available for adoption?
Yes! *Please* take a kitten! So many cats.
Nainai, nooo! You *can't!* They will make your café the new hot destination!
mew
squeeze
No adoption?
No?
whimper
But you should try our new strawberry matcha boba.
whew
Mmm!

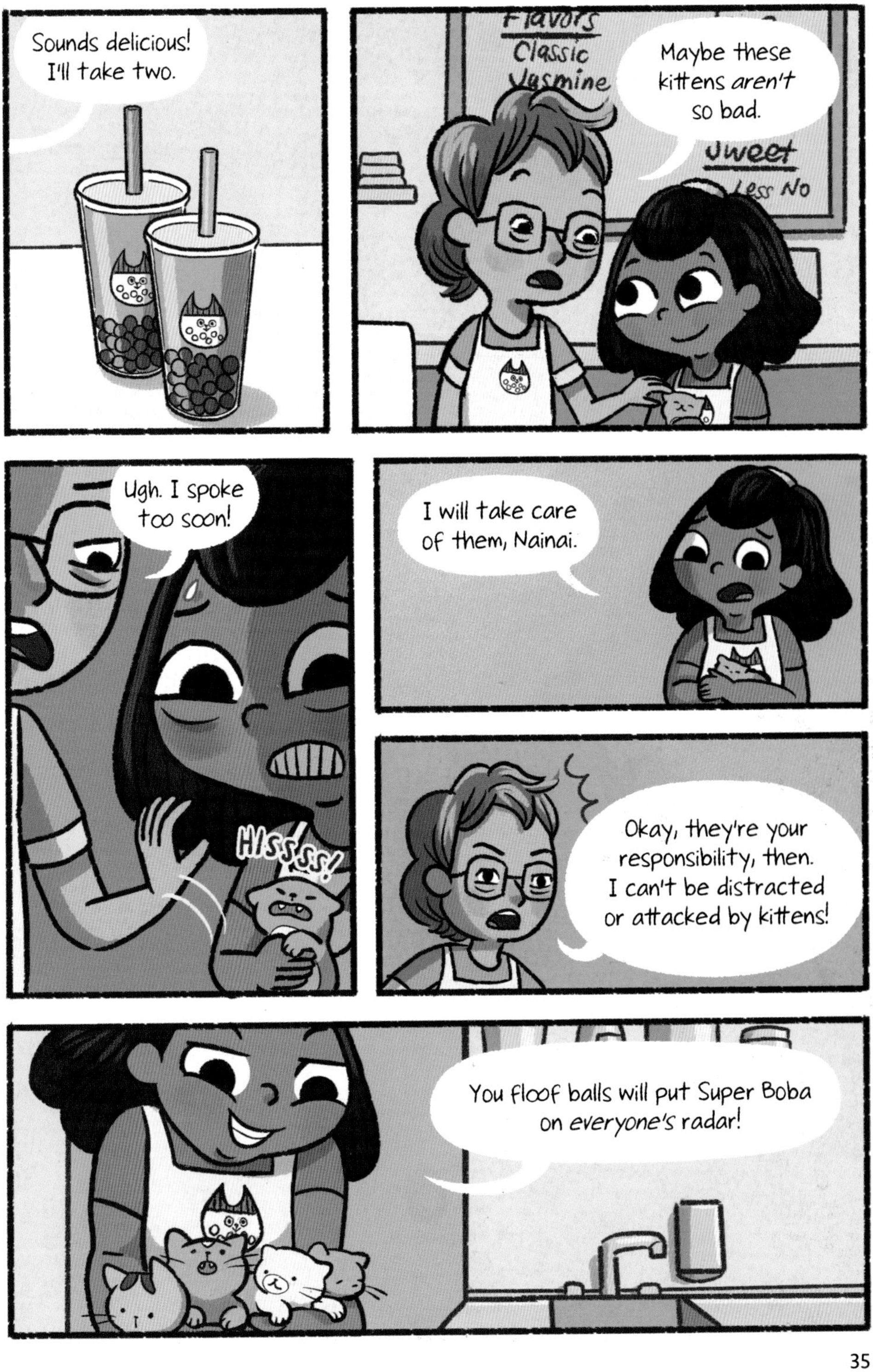
Sounds delicious! I'll take two.
Flavors
Classic
Jasmine
Sweet
Less No
Maybe these kittens *aren't* so bad.
Ugh. I spoke too soon!
HISSSS!
I will take care of them, Nainai.
Okay, they're your responsibility, then. I can't be distracted or attacked by kittens!
You floof balls will put Super Boba on *everyone's* radar!

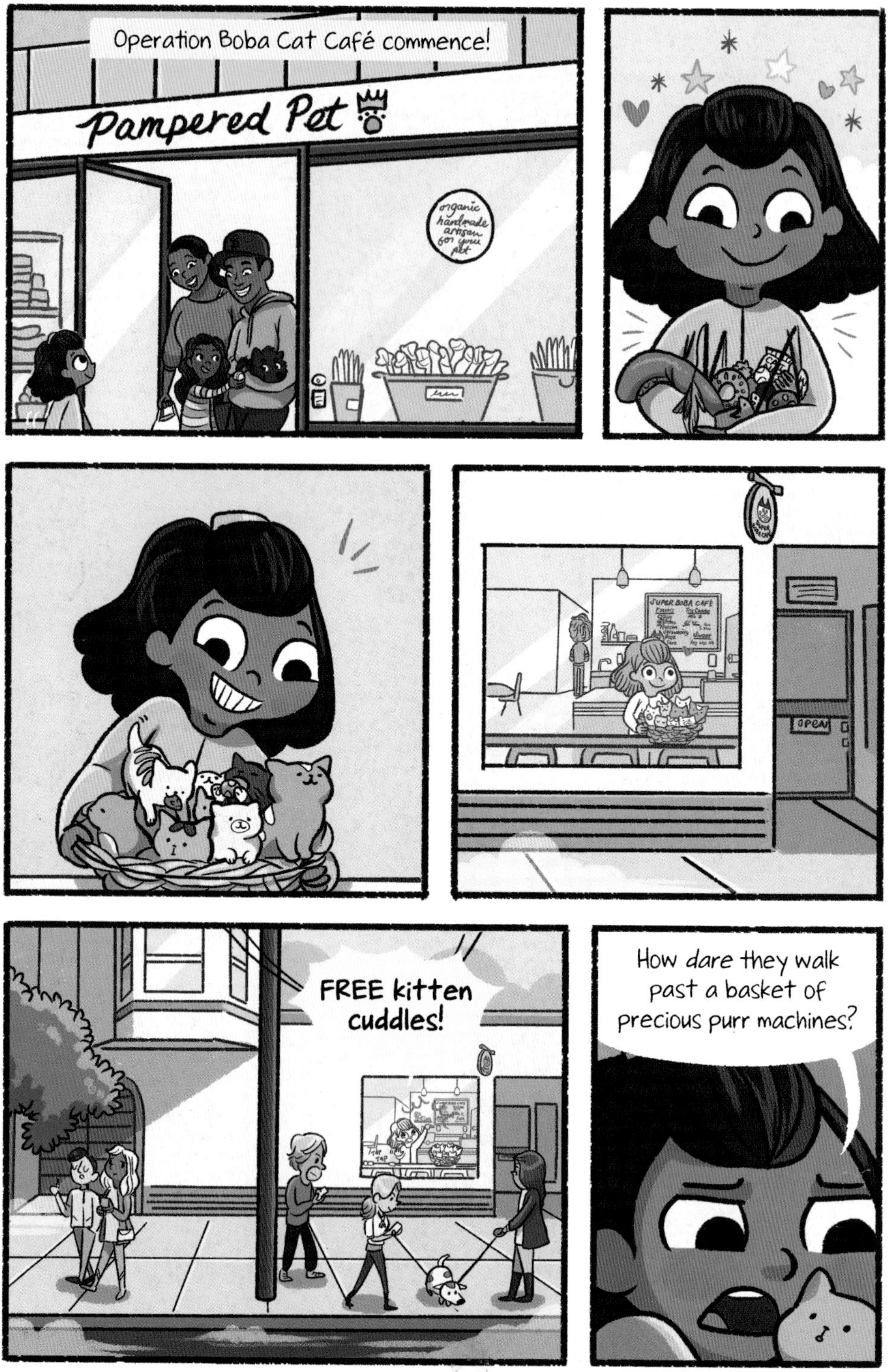
Operation Boba Cat Café commence!
Pampered Pet
organic handmade artisan for your pet
SUPER BOBA CAFE
OPEN
FREE kitten cuddles!
How dare they walk past a basket of precious purr machines?

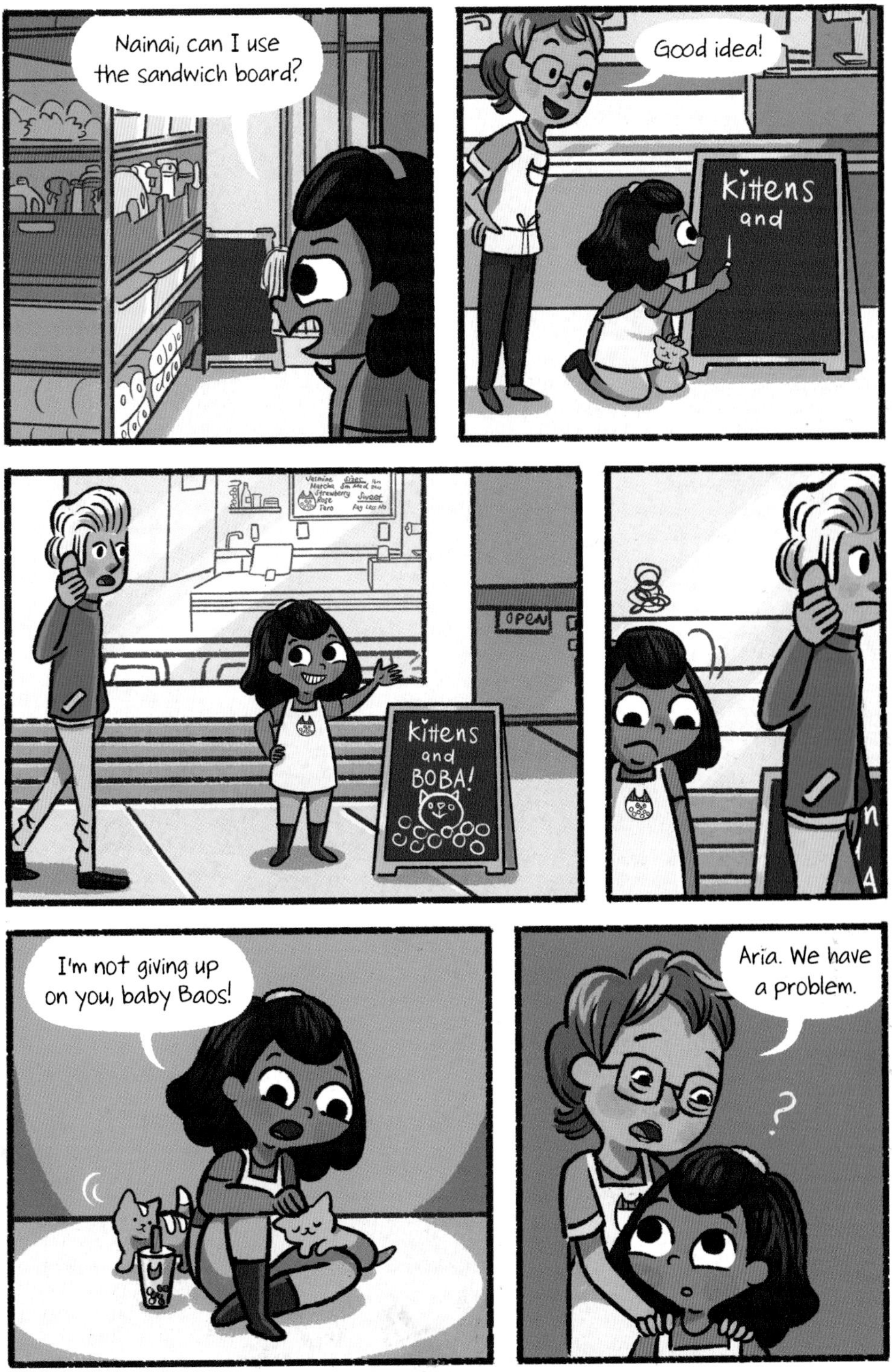
Nainai, can I use the sandwich board?
Good idea!
Kittens and
Kittens and BOBA!
OPEN
I'm not giving up on you, baby Baos!
Aria. We have a problem.
?

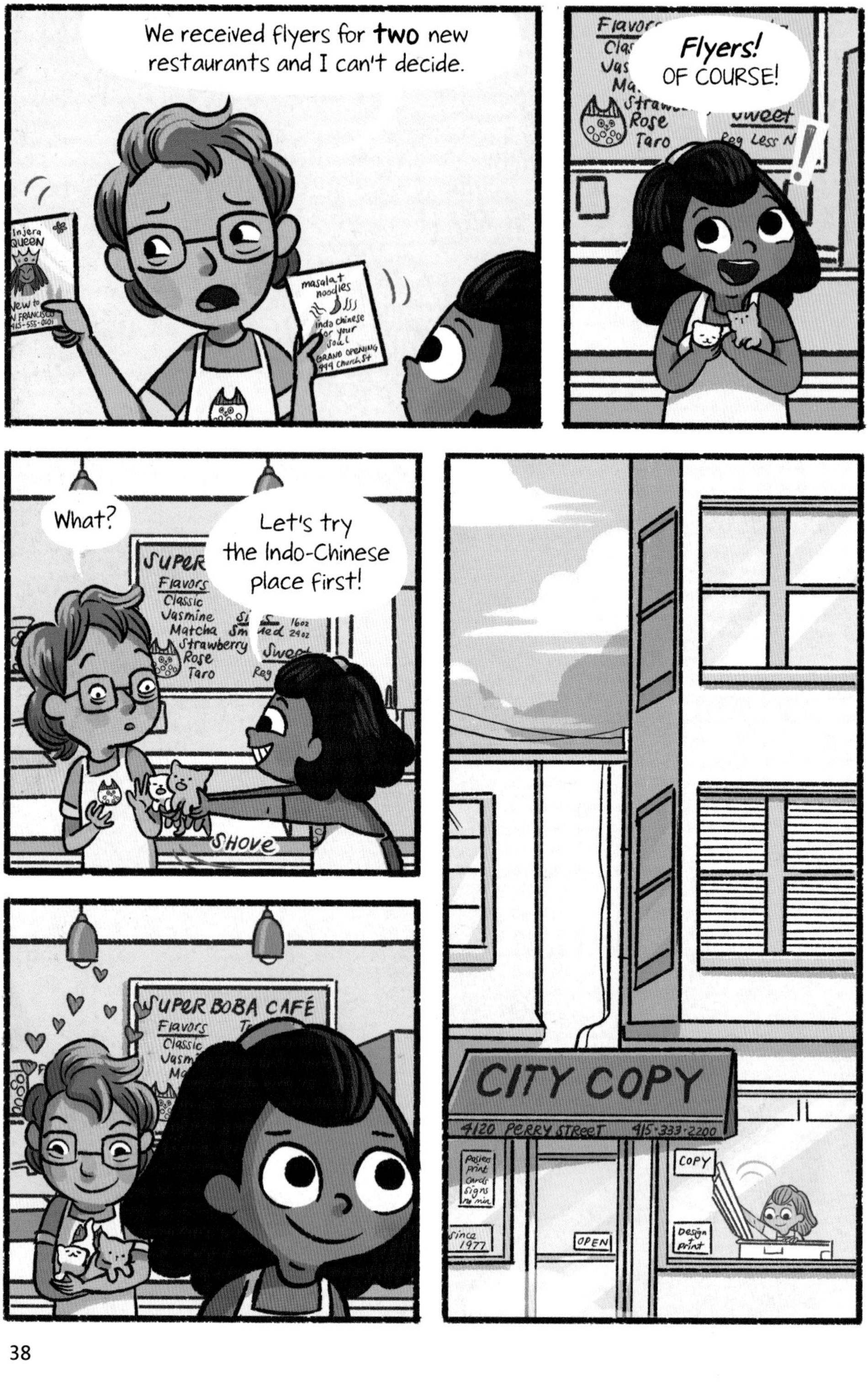
We received flyers for **two** new restaurants and I can't decide.
Injera QUEEN
New to SAN FRANCISCO
415-555-0101
masala+ noodles
Indo chinese for your soul
GRAND OPENING
999 Church St
Flyers! OF COURSE!
What?
Let's try the Indo-Chinese place first!
SHOVE
SUPER BOBA CAFÉ
Flavors
Classic
Jasmine
Matcha
Strawberry
Rose
Taro
CITY COPY
4120 PERRY STREET
415·333·2200
COPY
OPEN
Since 1977
Design + print

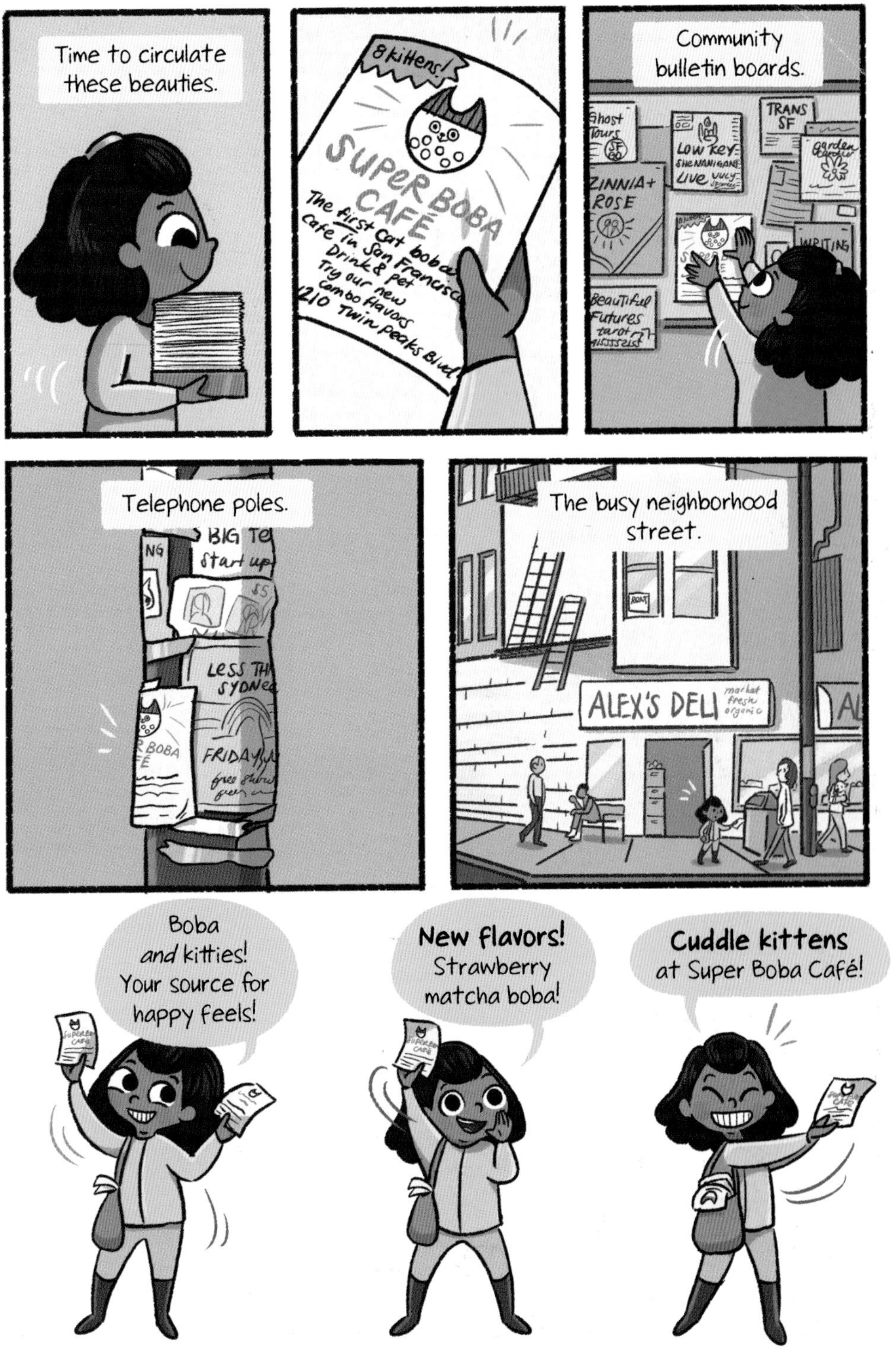
Time to circulate these beauties.
8 kittens!
SUPER BOBA CAFÉ
Community bulletin boards.
Telephone poles.
The busy neighborhood street.
ALEX'S DELI
Boba and kitties! Your source for happy feels!
New flavors! Strawberry matcha boba!
Cuddle kittens at Super Boba Café!

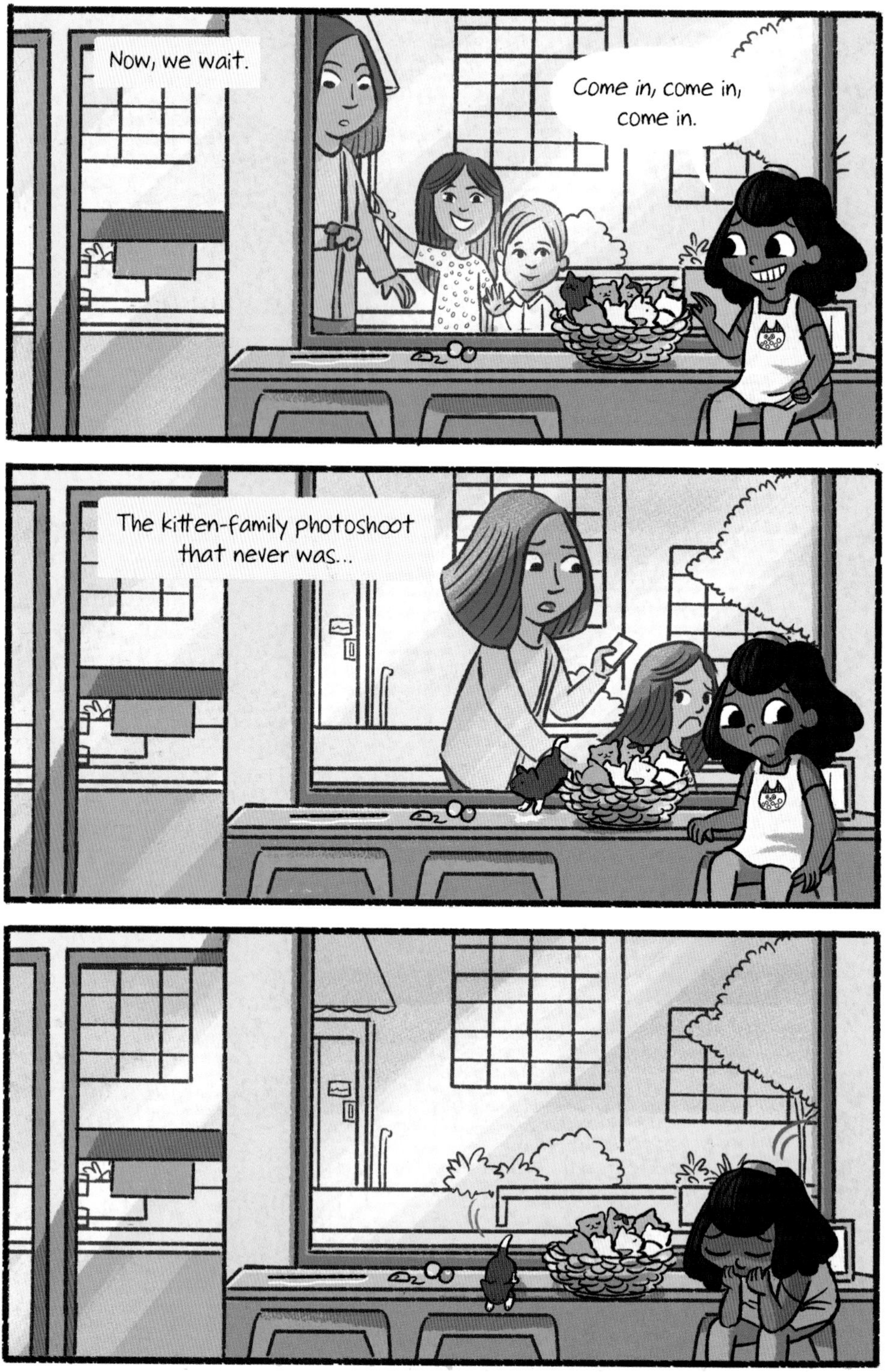
Now, we wait.
Come in, come in, come in.
The kitten-family photoshoot that never was...

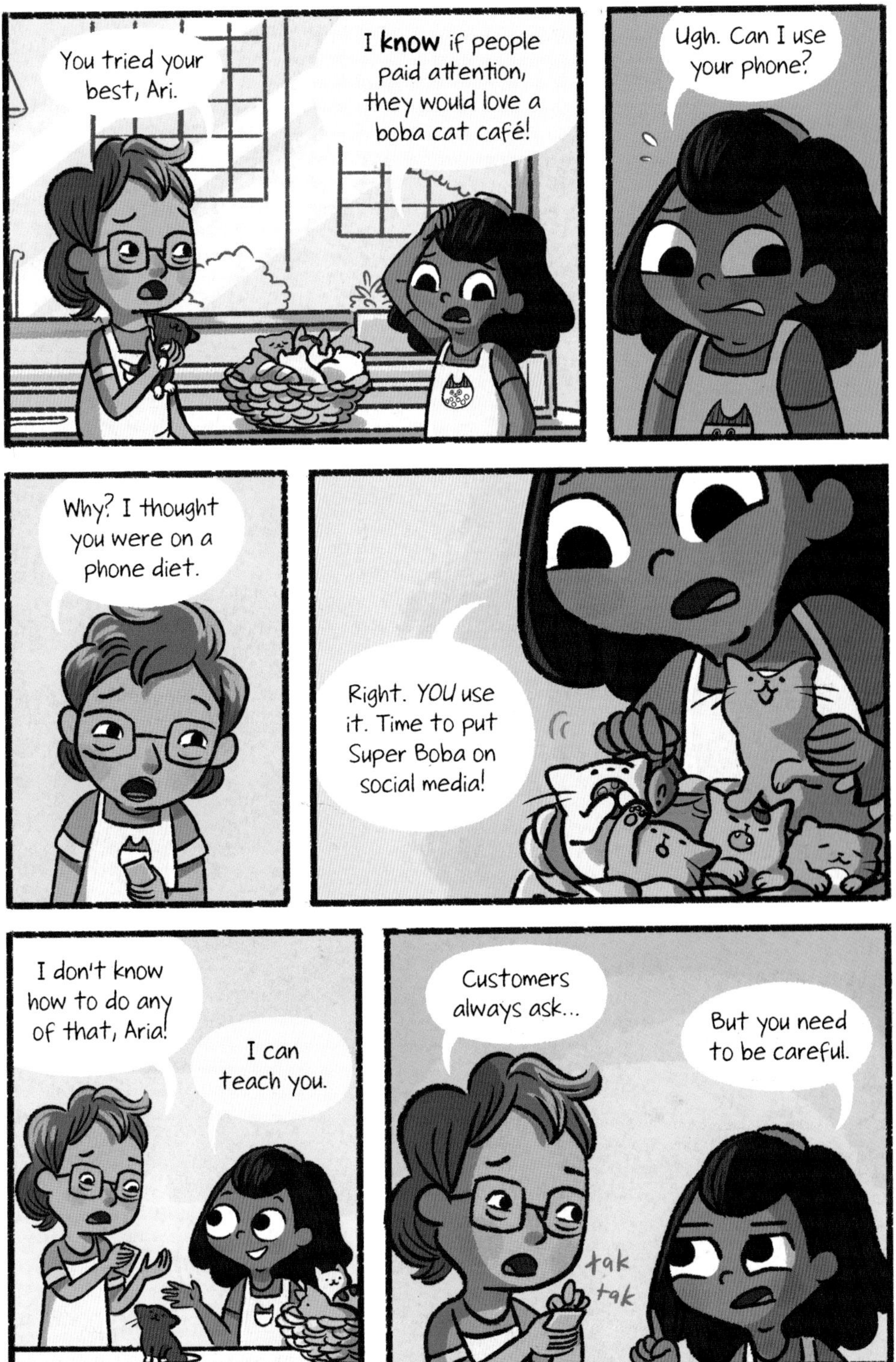

You tried your best, Ari.
I **know** if people paid attention, they would love a boba cat café!
Ugh. Can I use your phone?
Why? I thought you were on a phone diet.
Right. *YOU* use it. Time to put Super Boba on social media!
I don't know how to do any of that, Aria!
I can teach you.
Customers always ask...
tak tak
But you need to be careful.

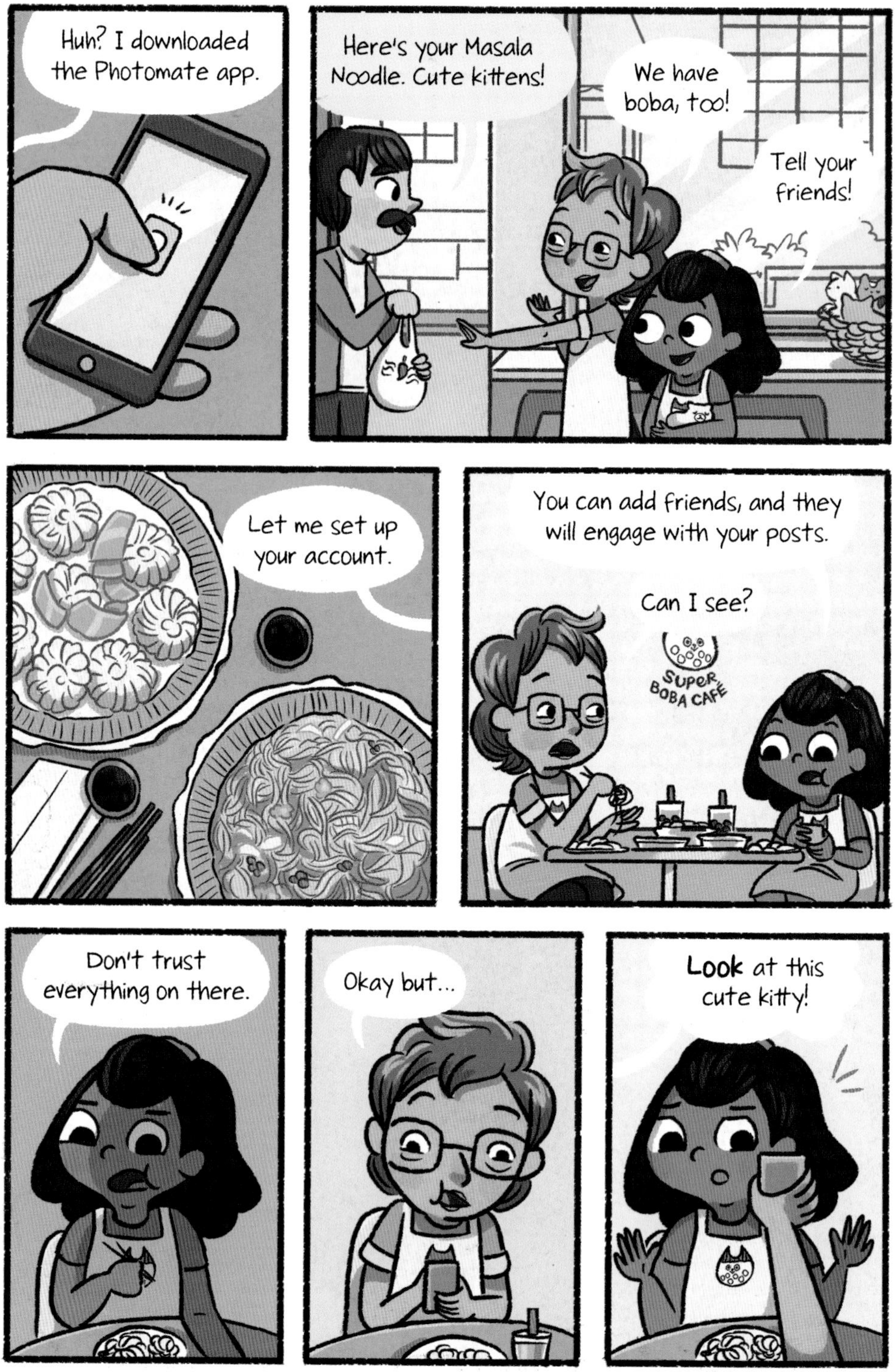
Huh? I downloaded the Photomate app.
Here's your Masala Noodle. Cute kittens!
We have boba, too!
Tell your friends!
Let me set up your account.
You can add friends, and they will engage with your posts.
Can I see?
SUPER BOBA CAFÉ
Don't trust everything on there.
Okay but...
Look at this cute kitty!

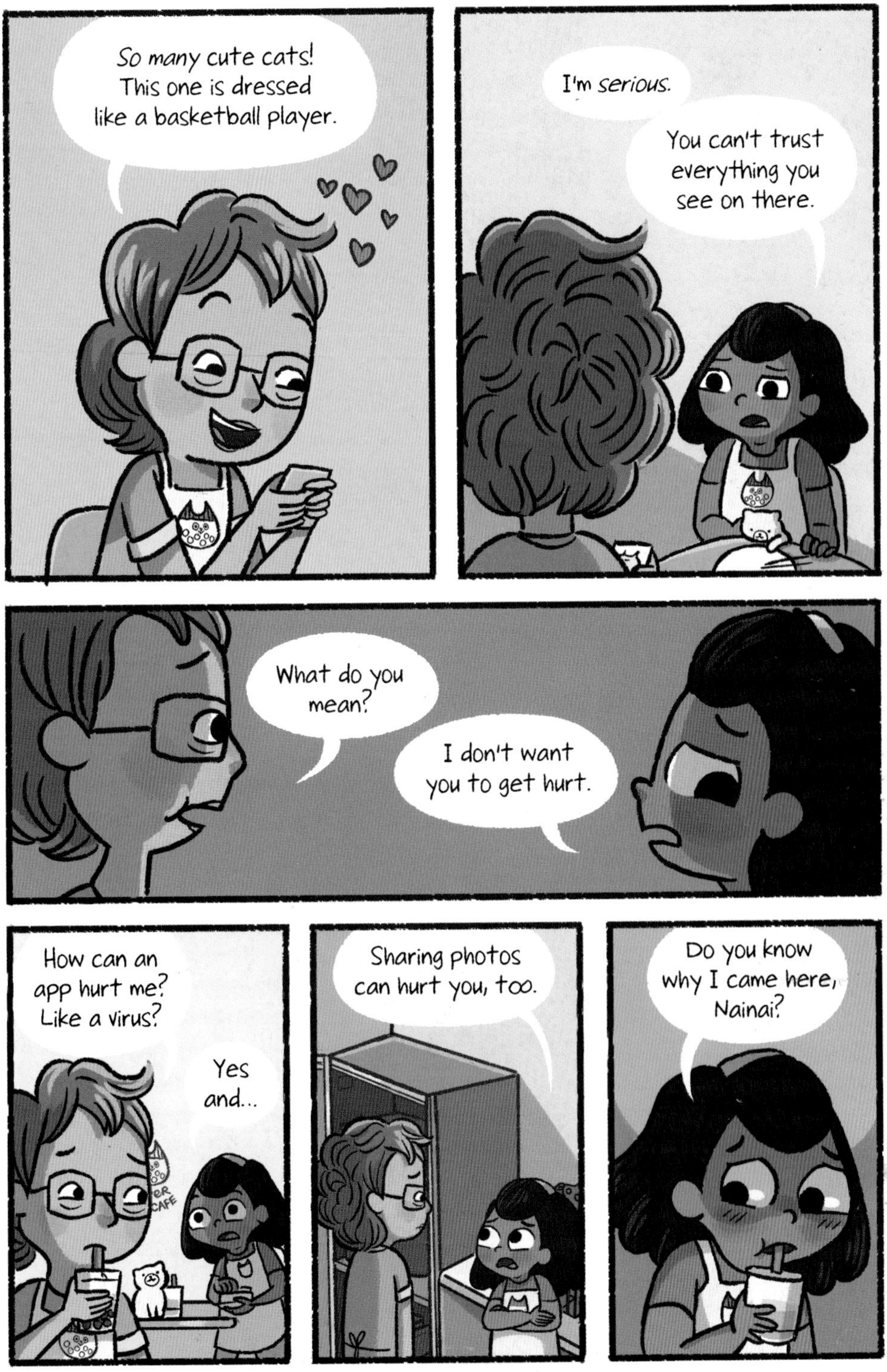
So many cute cats! This one is dressed like a basketball player.
I'm *serious.*
You can't trust everything you see on there.
What do you mean?
I don't want you to get hurt.
How can an app hurt me? Like a virus?
Yes and...
Sharing photos can hurt you, too.
Do you know why I came here, Nainai?

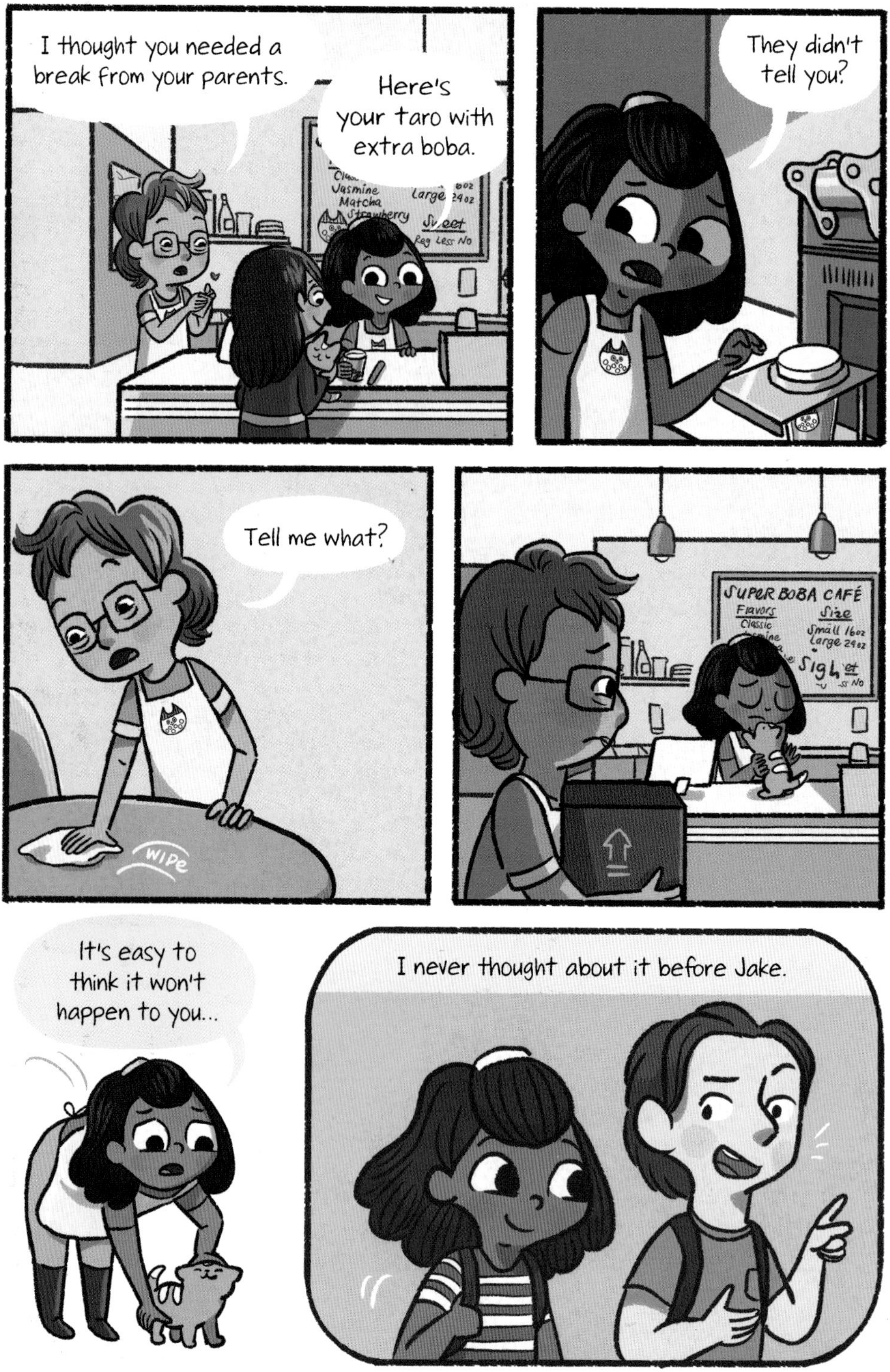
I thought you needed a break from your parents.
Here's your taro with extra boba.
Jasmine
Matcha
Strawberry
Large 24oz
Sweet
Reg Less No
They didn't tell you?
Tell me what?
WIPE
SUPER BOBA CAFÉ
Flavors
Classic
Size
Small 16oz
Large 24oz
Sigh
It's easy to think it won't happen to you...
I never thought about it before Jake.

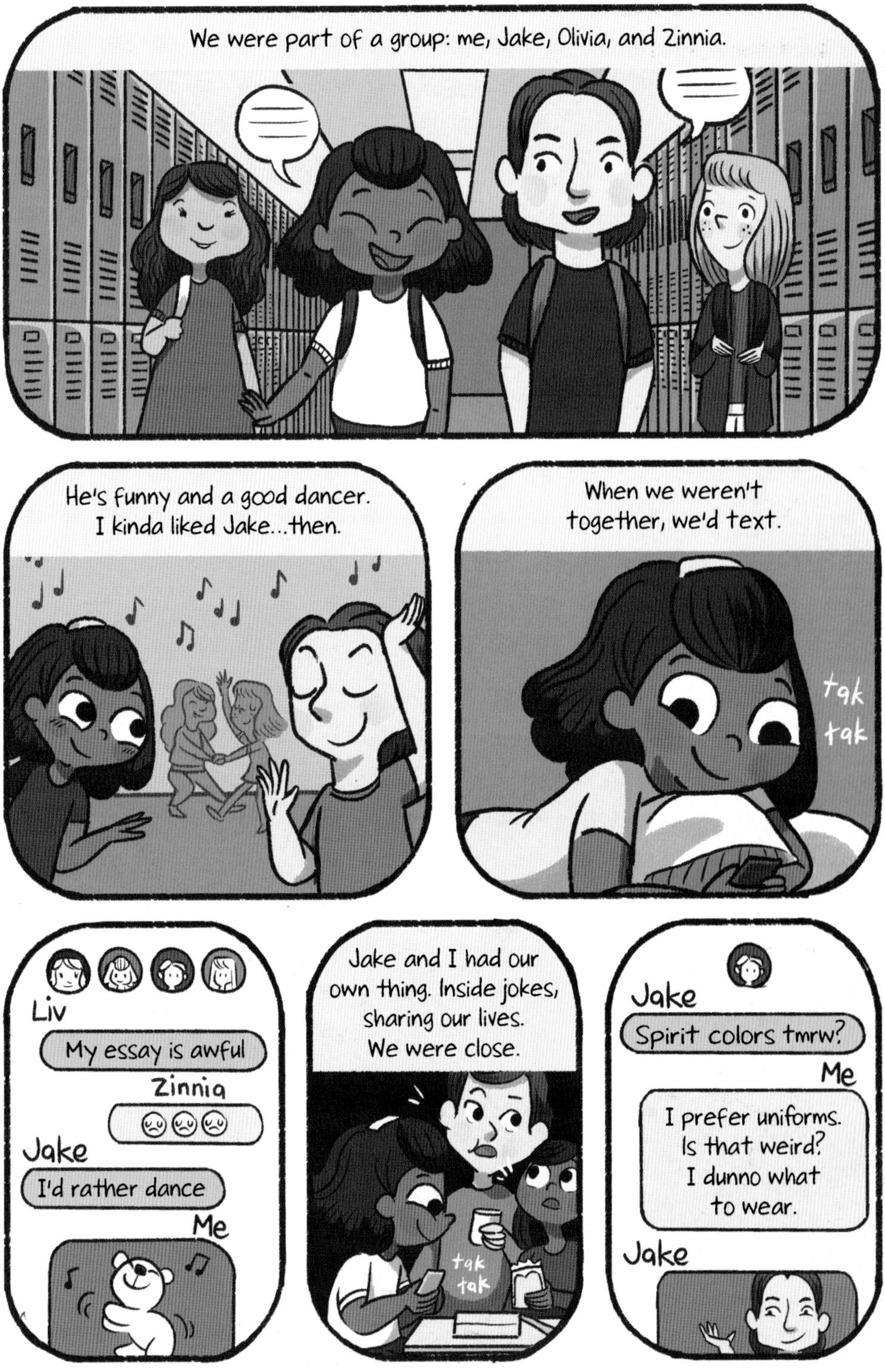

We were part of a group: me, Jake, Olivia, and Zinnia.
He's funny and a good dancer. I kinda liked Jake...then.
When we weren't together, we'd text.
tak
tak
Liv
My essay is awful
Zinnia
Jake
I'd rather dance
Me
Jake and I had our own thing. Inside jokes, sharing our lives. We were close.
tak
tak
Jake
Spirit colors tmrw?
Me
I prefer uniforms. Is that weird? I dunno what to wear.
Jake

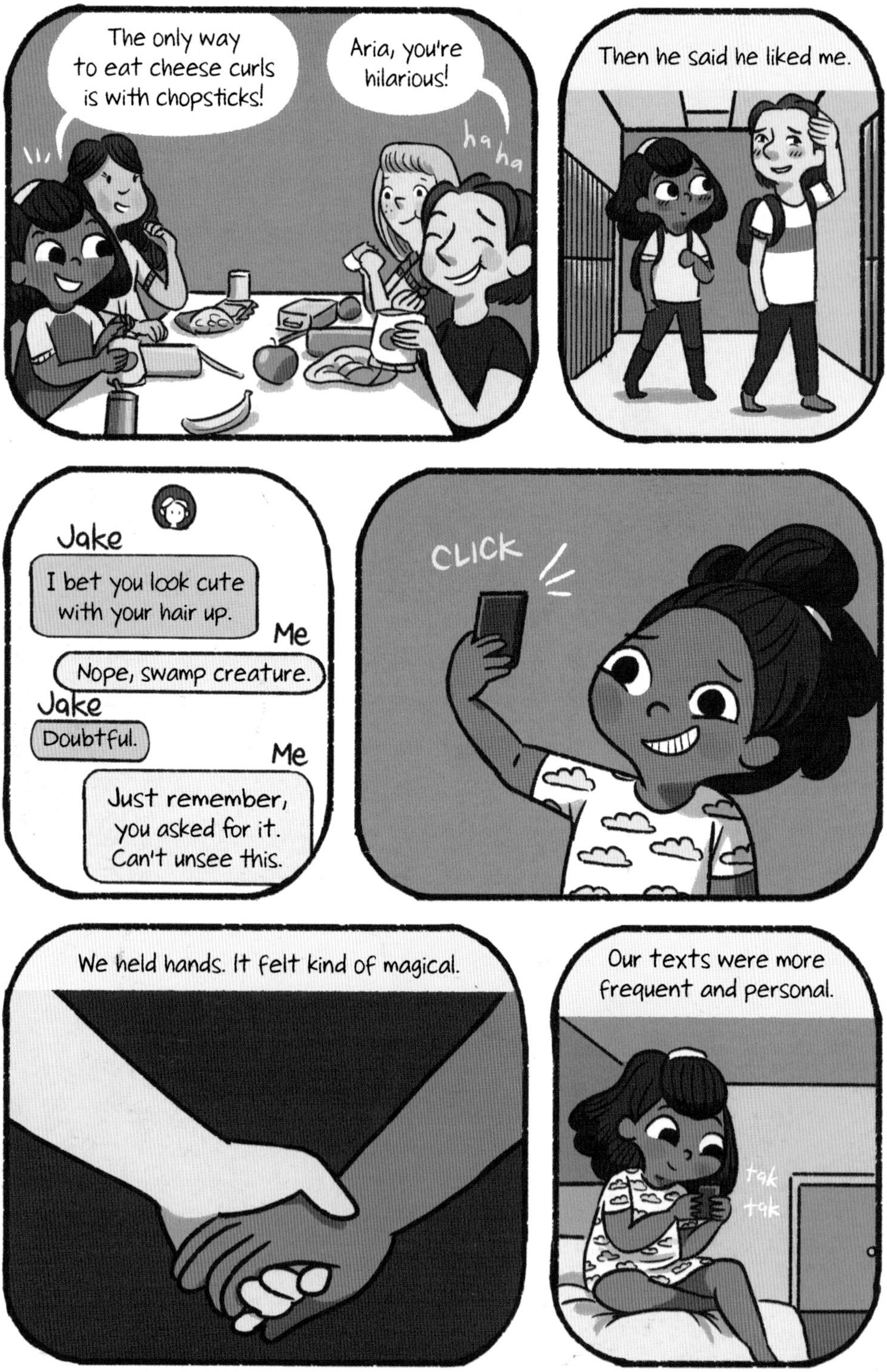
The only way to eat cheese curls is with chopsticks!
Aria, you're hilarious!
ha ha
Then he said he liked me.
Jake
I bet you look cute with your hair up.
Me
Nope, swamp creature.
Jake
Doubtful.
Me
Just remember, you asked for it. Can't unsee this.
CLICK
We held hands. It felt kind of magical.
Our texts were more frequent and personal.
tak tak

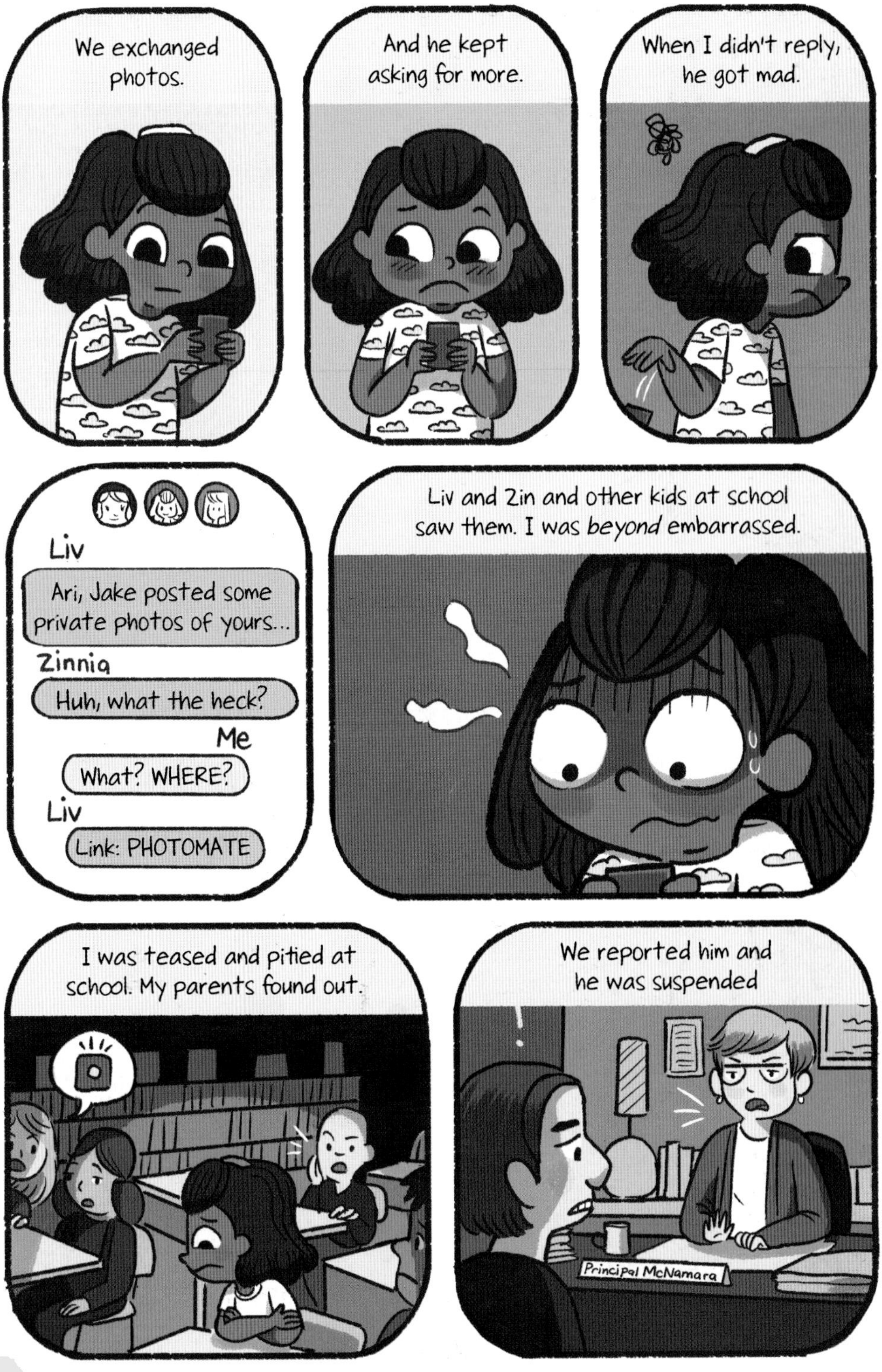
We exchanged photos.
And he kept asking for more.
When I didn't reply, he got mad.
Liv
Ari, Jake posted some private photos of yours...
Zinnia
Huh, what the heck?
Me
What? WHERE?
Liv
Link: PHOTOMATE
Liv and Zin and other kids at school saw them. I was *beyond* embarrassed.
I was teased and pitied at school. My parents found out.
We reported him and he was suspended
Principal McNamara

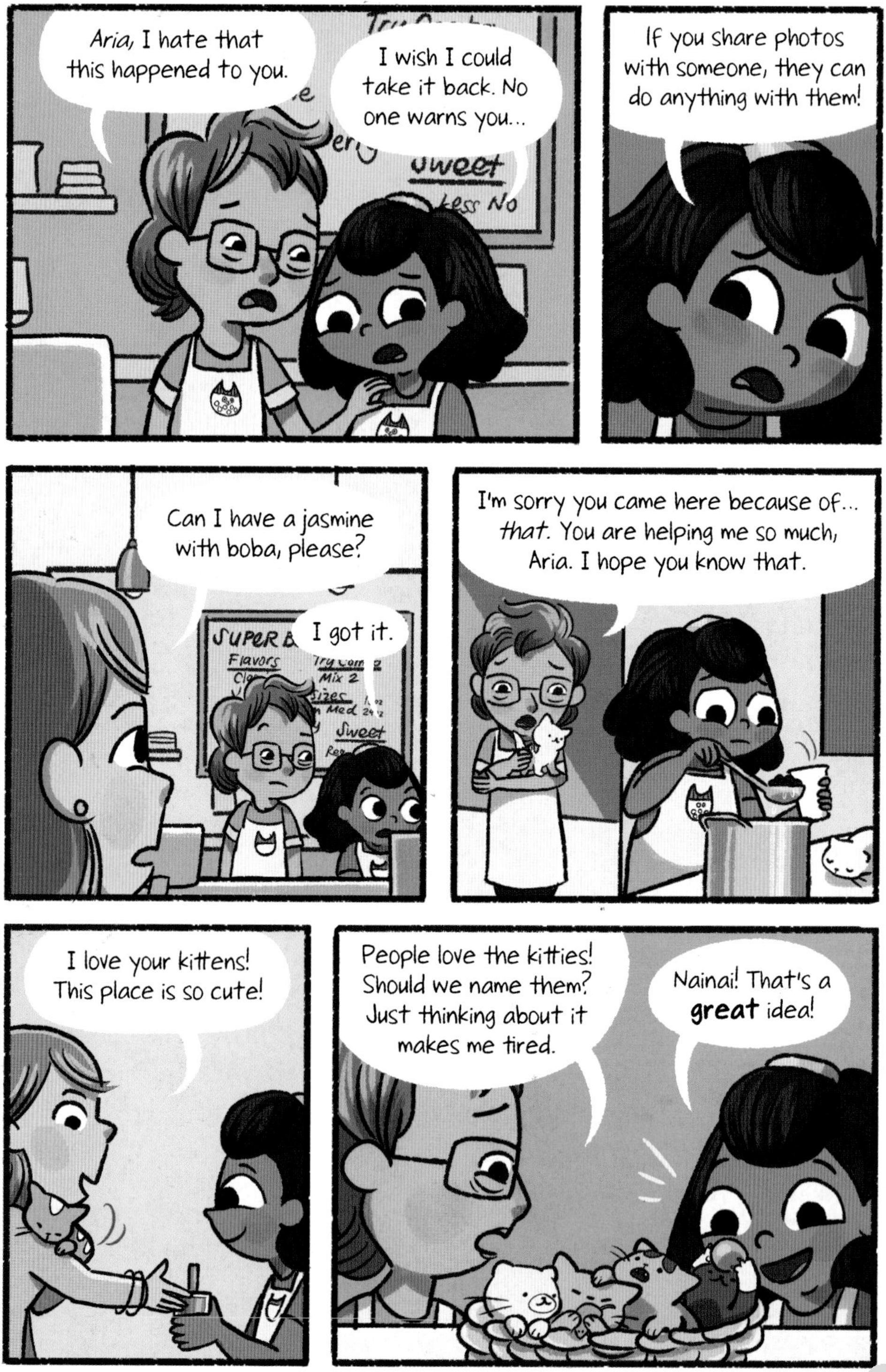
Aria, I hate that this happened to you.
I wish I could take it back. No one warns you...
If you share photos with someone, they can do anything with them!
Can I have a jasmine with boba, please?
I got it.
I'm sorry you came here because of... *that*. You are helping me so much, Aria. I hope you know that.
I love your kittens! This place is so cute!
People love the kitties! Should we name them? Just thinking about it makes me tired.
Nainai! That's a **great** idea!

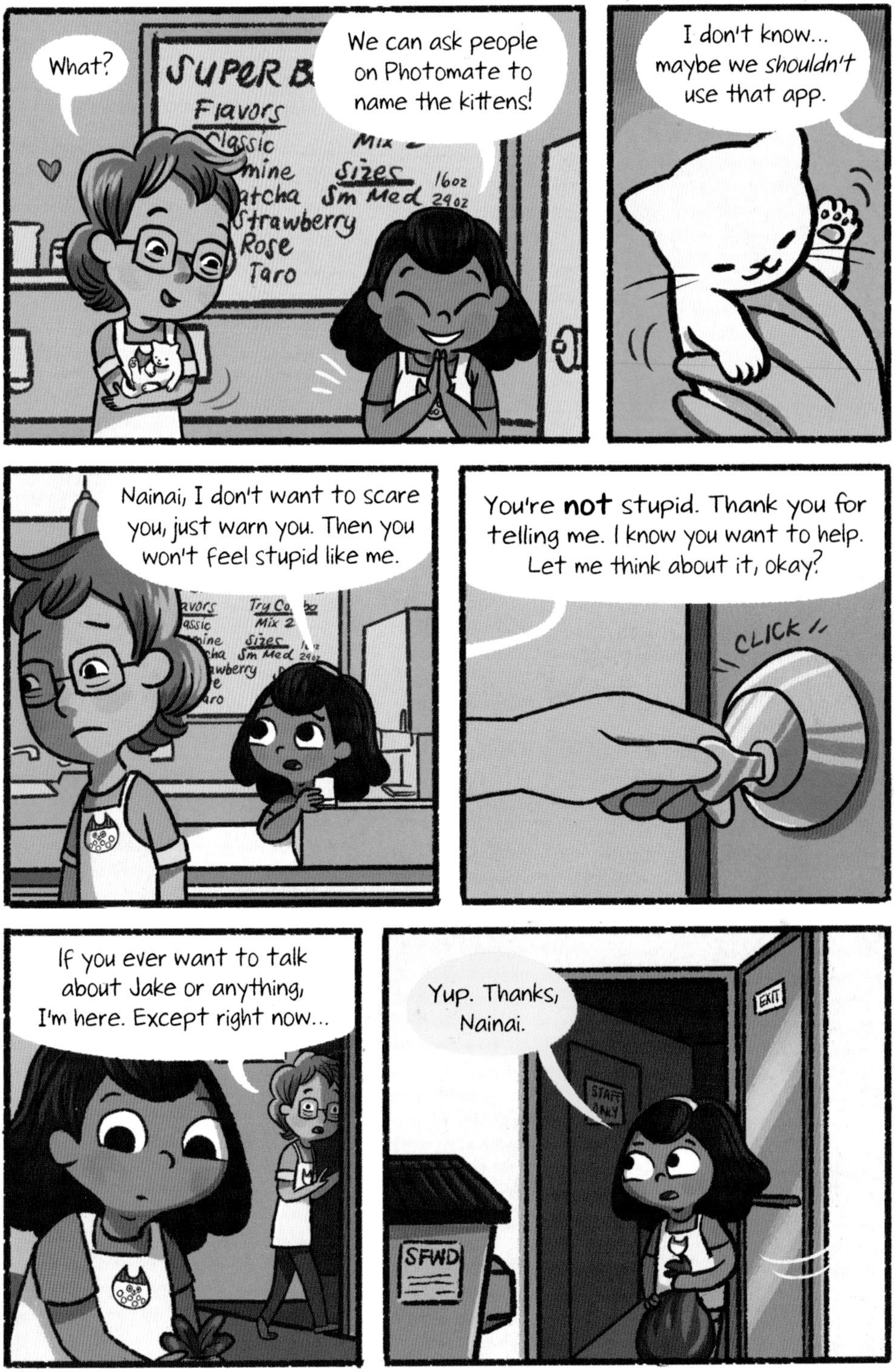
What?
SUPER B
Flavors
Classic
mine
atcha
Strawberry
Rose
Taro
Mix
Sizes
Sm Med
16oz
24oz
We can ask people on Photomate to name the kittens!
I don't know... maybe we *shouldn't* use that app.
Nainai, I don't want to scare you, just warn you. Then you won't feel stupid like me.
You're **not** stupid. Thank you for telling me. I know you want to help. Let me think about it, okay?
CLICK
If you ever want to talk about Jake or anything, I'm here. Except right now...
Yup. Thanks, Nainai.
EXIT
STAFF ONLY
SFWD

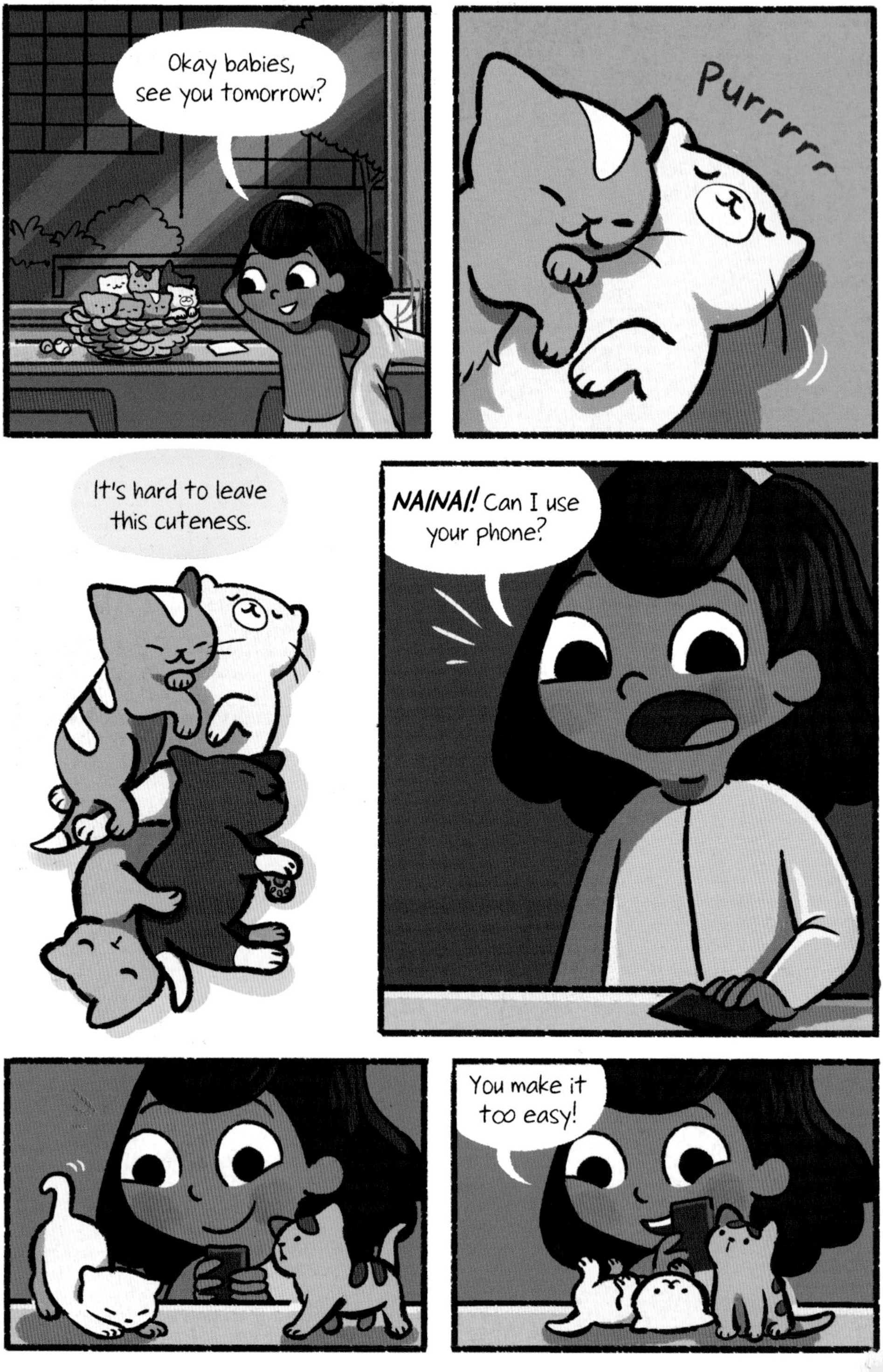
Okay babies, see you tomorrow?
Purrrrr
It's hard to leave this cuteness.
NAINAI! Can I use your phone?
You make it too easy!

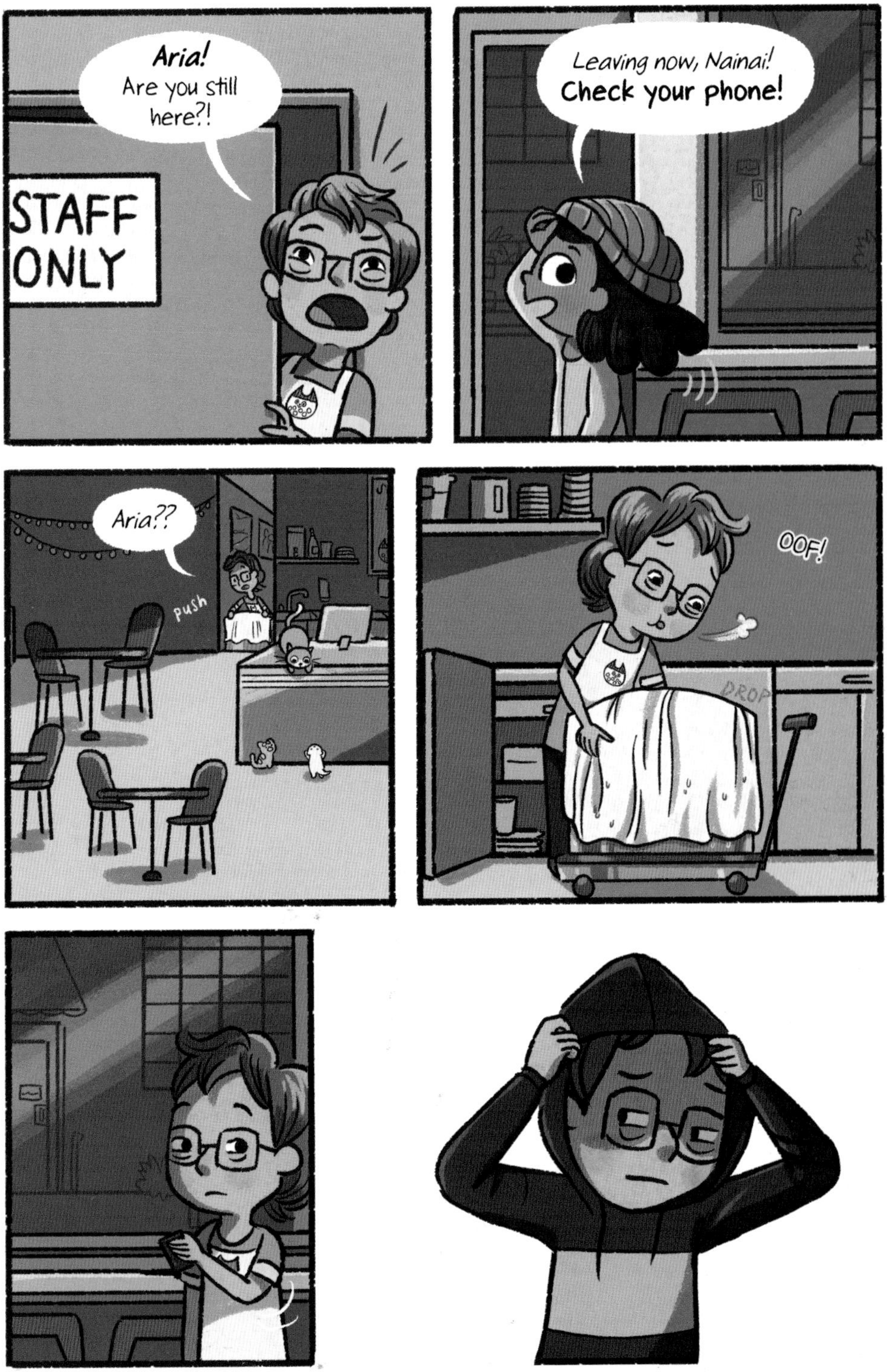
Aria!
Are you still here?!
STAFF ONLY
Leaving now, Nainai!
Check your phone!
Aria??
push
OOF!
DROP

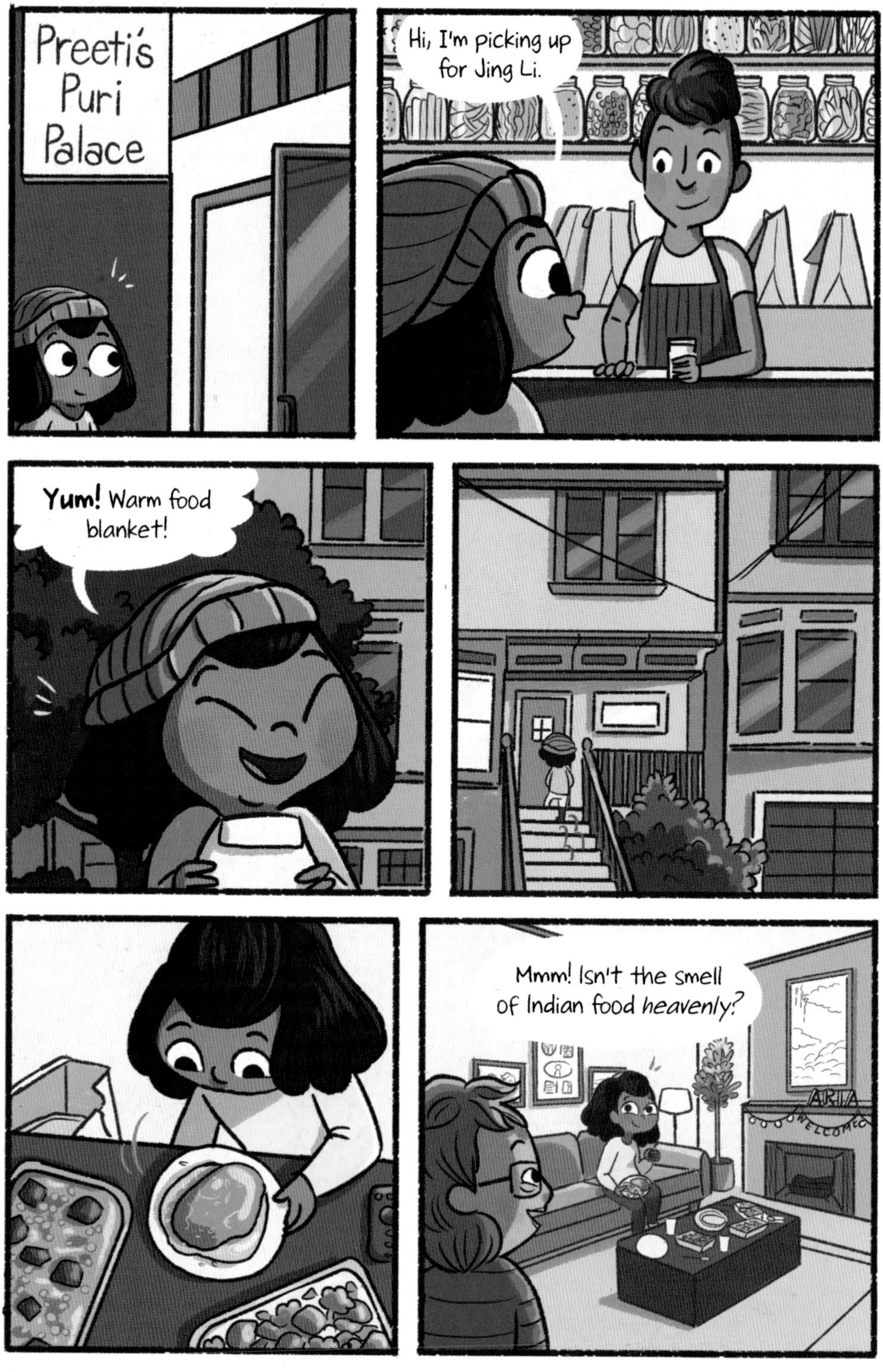
Preeti's Puri Palace
Hi, I'm picking up for Jing Li.
Yum! Warm food blanket!
Mmm! Isn't the smell of Indian food *heavenly?*
ARIA
WELCOME

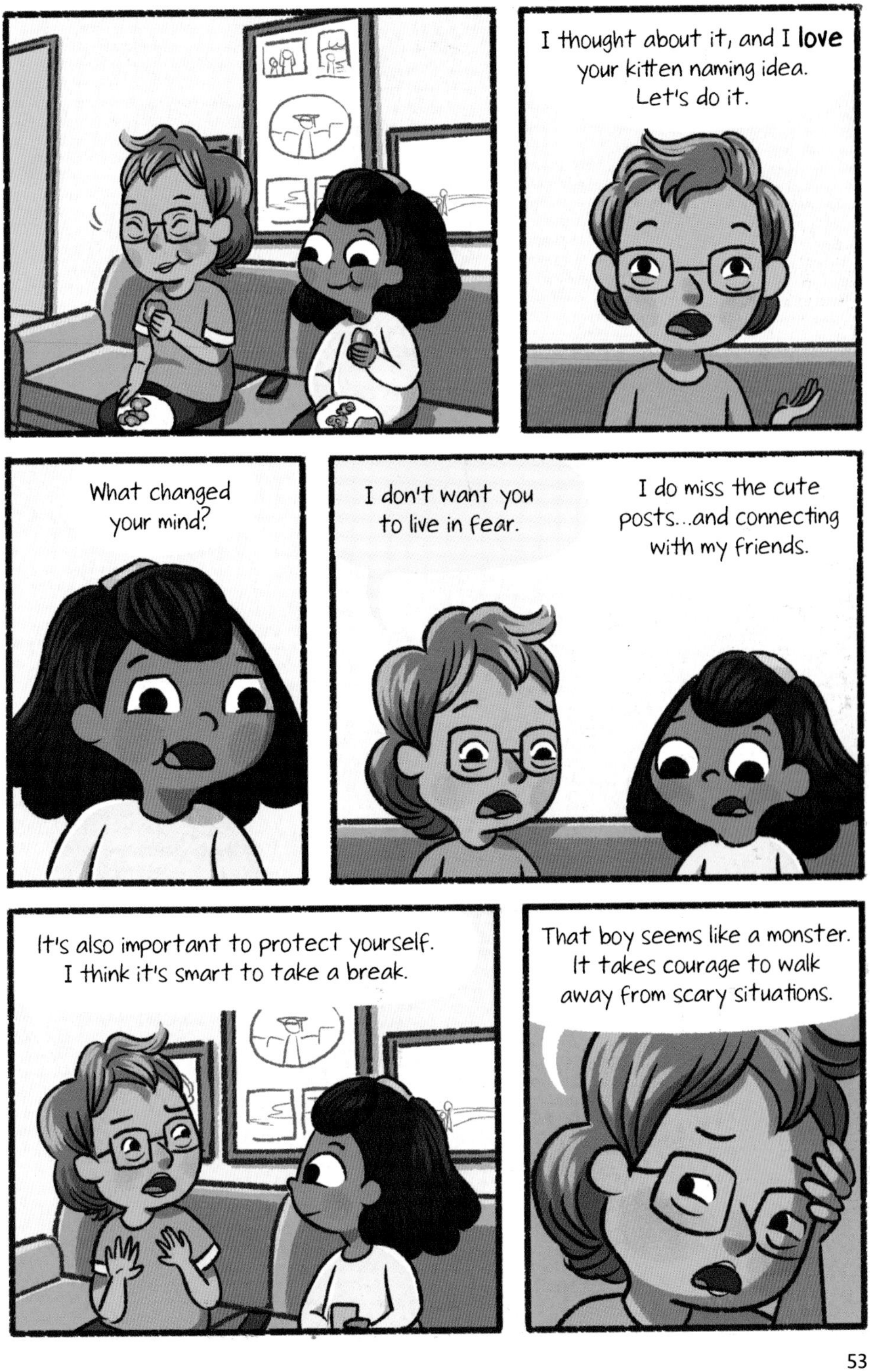
I thought about it, and I **love** your kitten naming idea. Let's do it.
What changed your mind?
I don't want you to live in fear.
I do miss the cute posts...and connecting with my friends.
It's also important to protect yourself. I think it's smart to take a break.
That boy seems like a monster. It takes courage to walk away from scary situations.

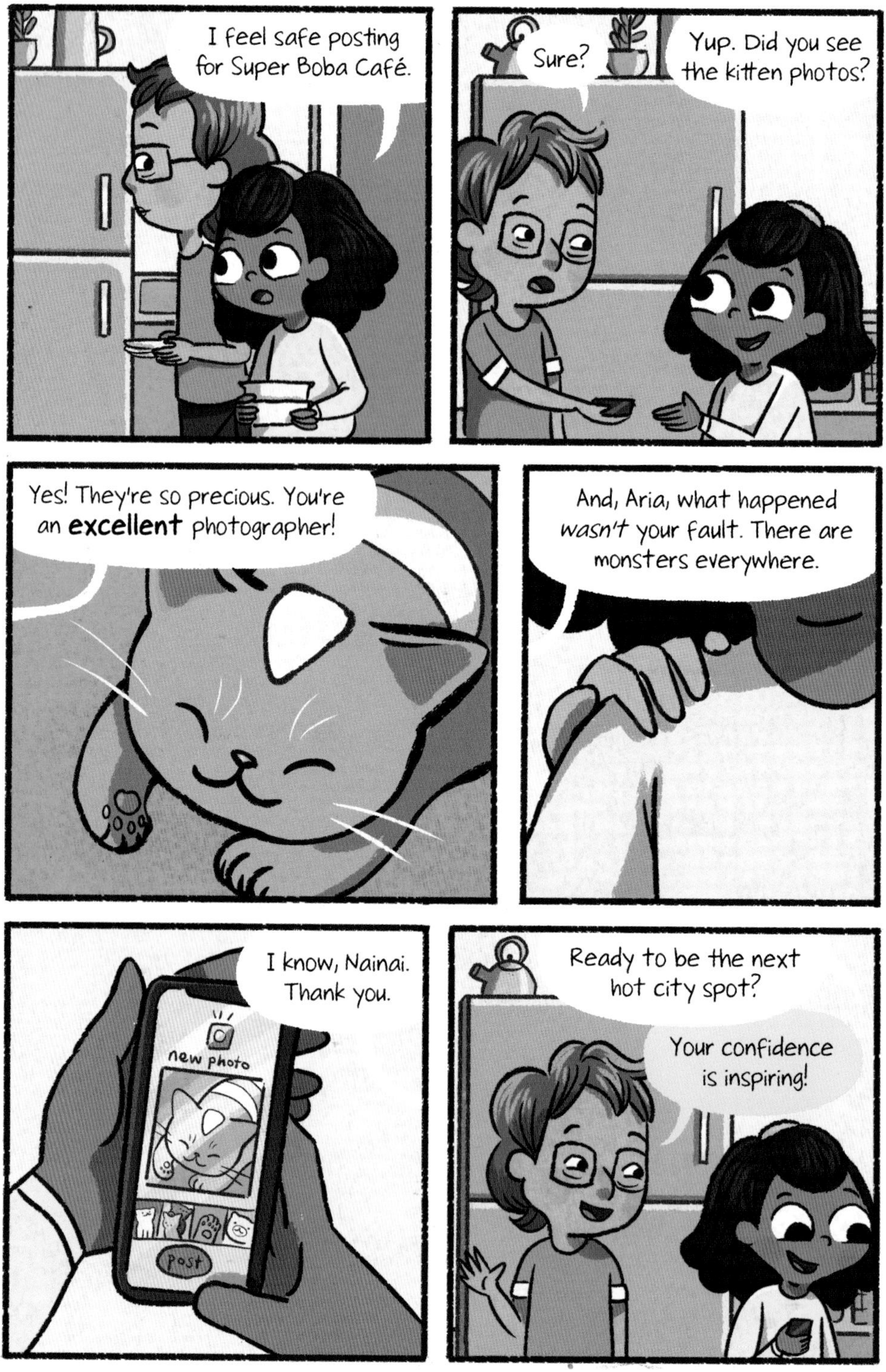
I feel safe posting for Super Boba Café.
Sure?
Yup. Did you see the kitten photos?
Yes! They're so precious. You're an **excellent** photographer!
And, Aria, what happened *wasn't* your fault. There are monsters everywhere.
I know, Nainai. Thank you.
new photo
post
Ready to be the next hot city spot?
Your confidence is inspiring!

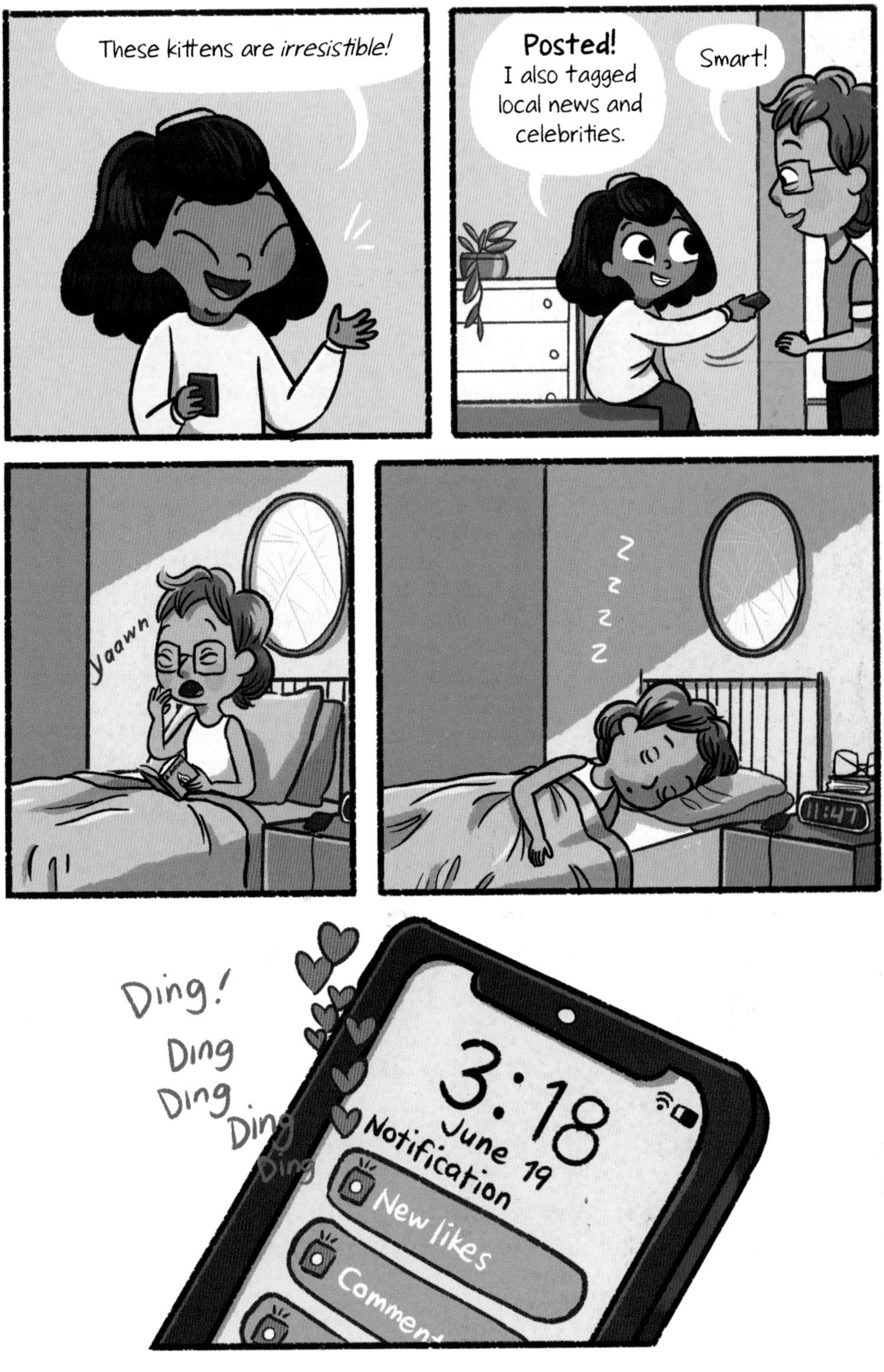
These kittens are *irresistible!*
Posted! I also tagged local news and celebrities.
Smart!
Yaawn
Z
Z
Z
Z
1:47
Ding!
Ding
Ding
Ding
Ding
3:18
June 19
Notification
New likes
Comment

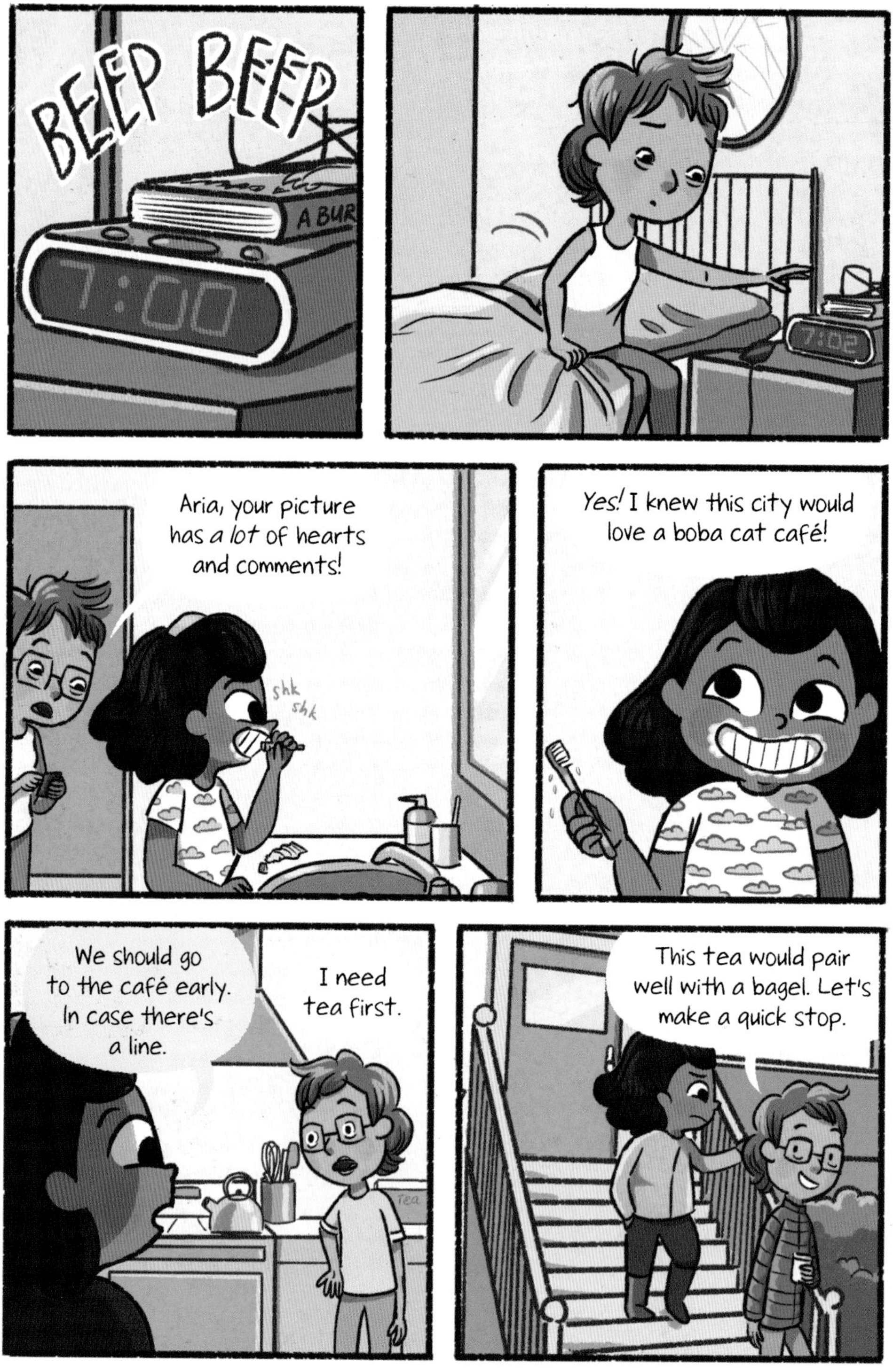
BEEP BEEP
A BUR
7:00
7:02
Aria, your picture has a *lot* of hearts and comments!
shk shk
Yes! I knew this city would love a boba cat café!
We should go to the café early. In case there's a line.
I need tea first.
Tea
This tea would pair well with a bagel. Let's make a quick stop.

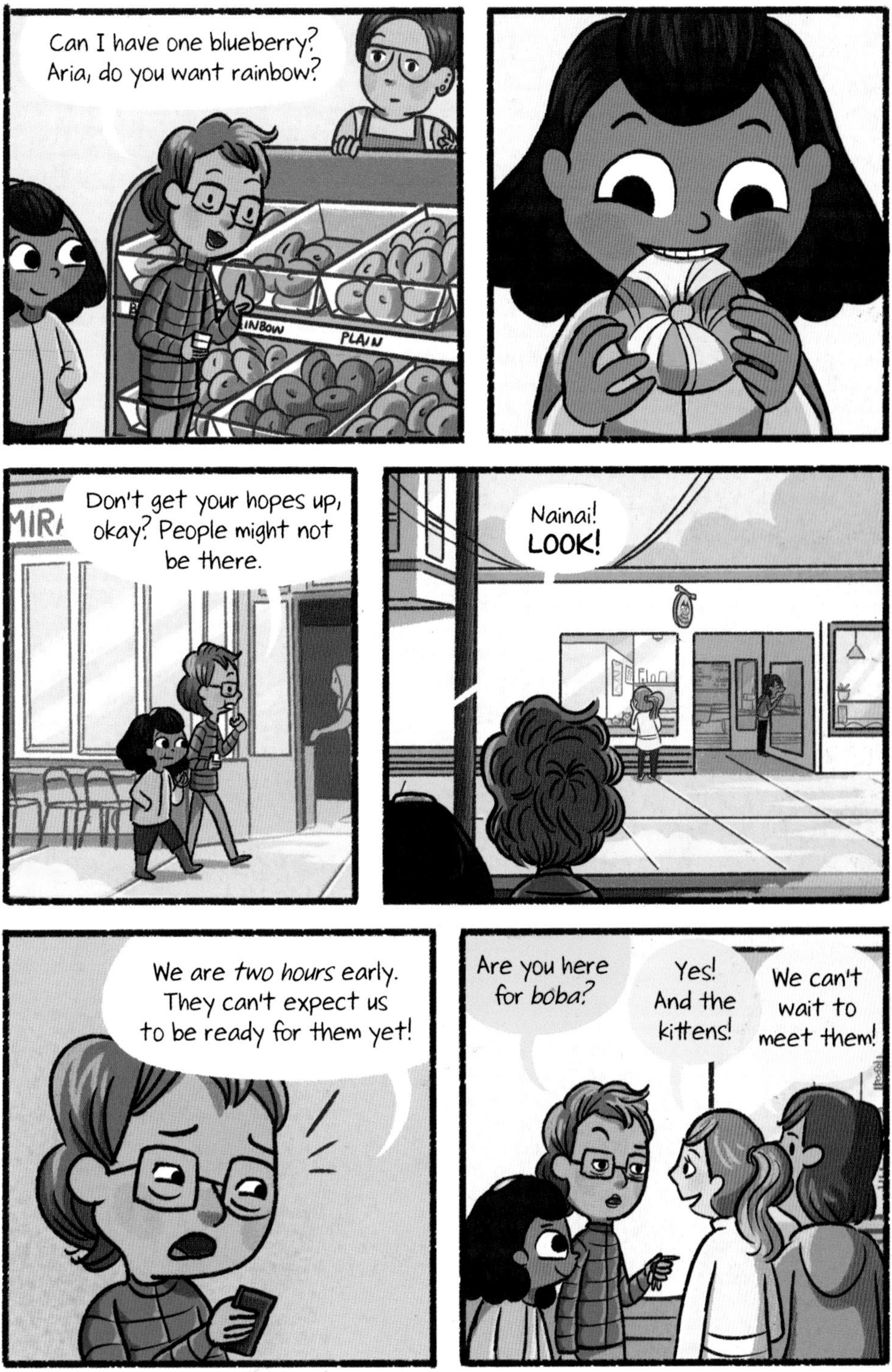
Can I have one blueberry? Aria, do you want rainbow?
INBOW
PLAIN
Don't get your hopes up, okay? People might not be there.
MIRA
Nainai! LOOK!
We are *two hours* early. They can't expect us to be ready for them yet!
Are you here for *boba?*
Yes! And the kittens!
We can't wait to meet them!

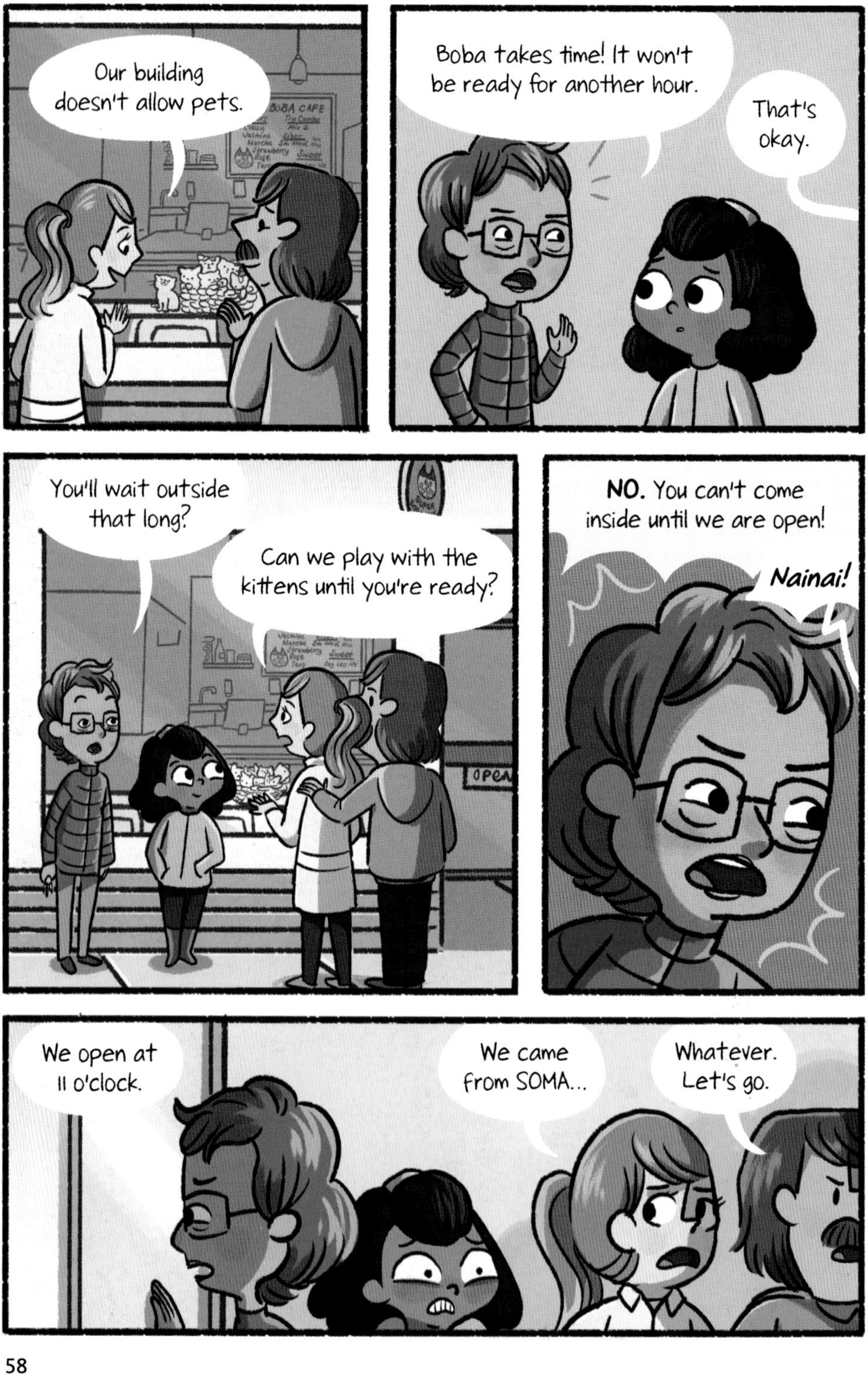
Our building doesn't allow pets.
BOBA CAFE
Boba takes time! It won't be ready for another hour.
That's okay.
You'll wait outside that long?
Can we play with the kittens until you're ready?
OPEN
NO. You can't come inside until we are open!
Nainai!
We open at 11 o'clock.
We came from SOMA...
Whatever. Let's go.

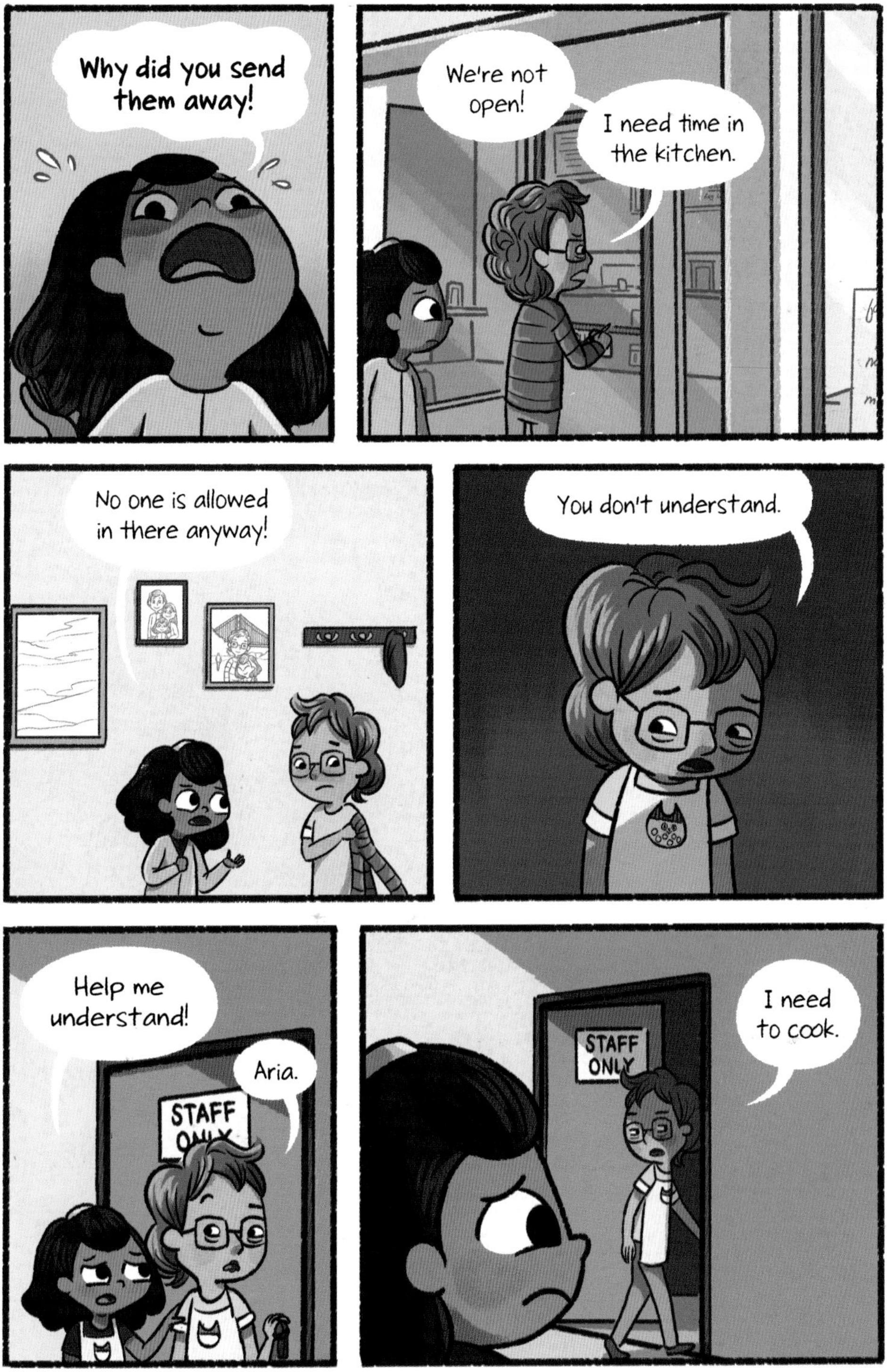
Why did you send them away!
We're not open!
I need time in the kitchen.
No one is allowed in there anyway!
You don't understand.
Help me understand!
Aria.
STAFF ONLY
STAFF ONLY
I need to cook.

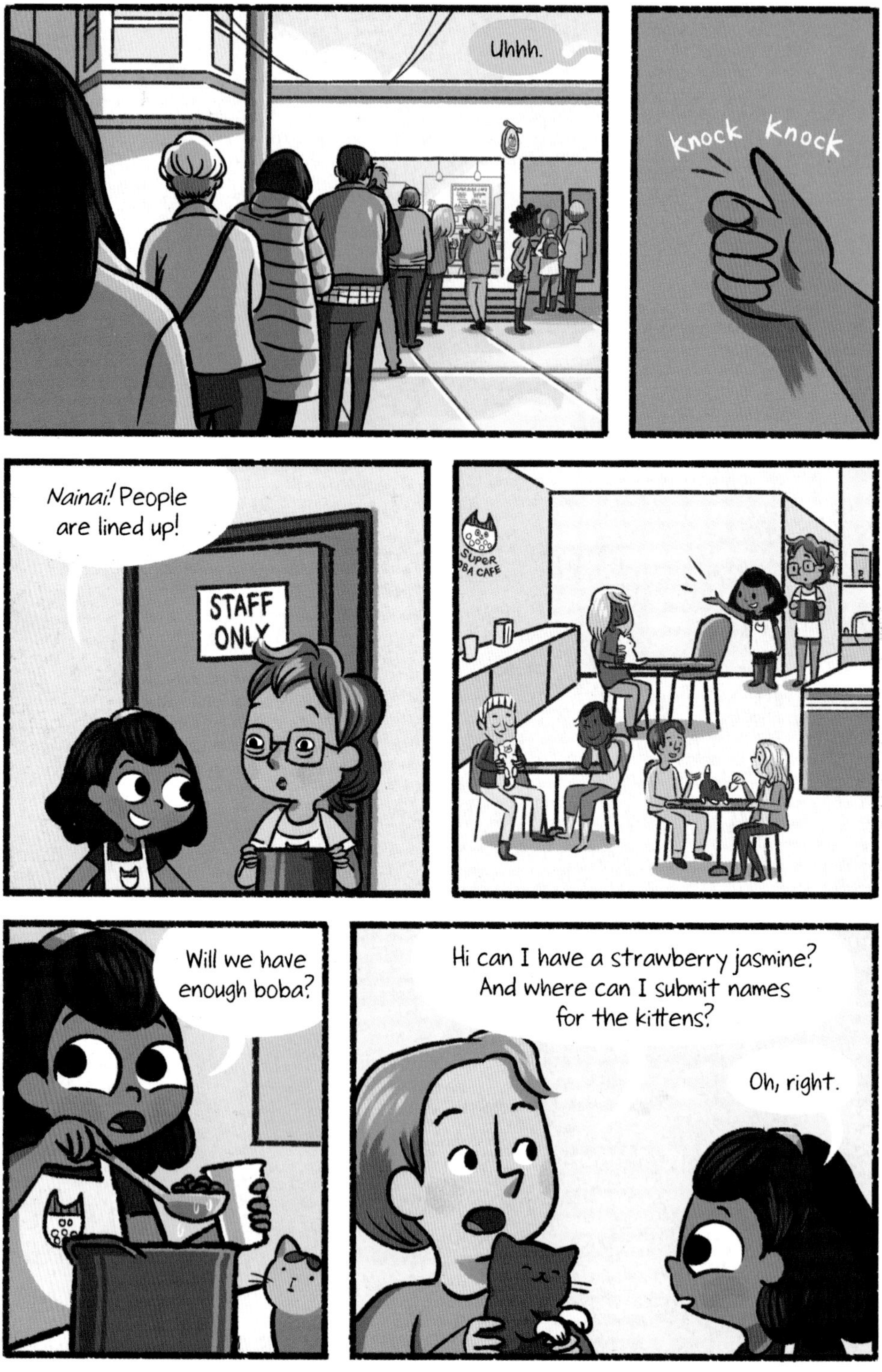
Uhhh.
Knock Knock
Nainai! People are lined up!
STAFF ONLY
SUPER BOBA CAFE
Will we have enough boba?
Hi can I have a strawberry jasmine? And where can I submit names for the kittens?
Oh, right.

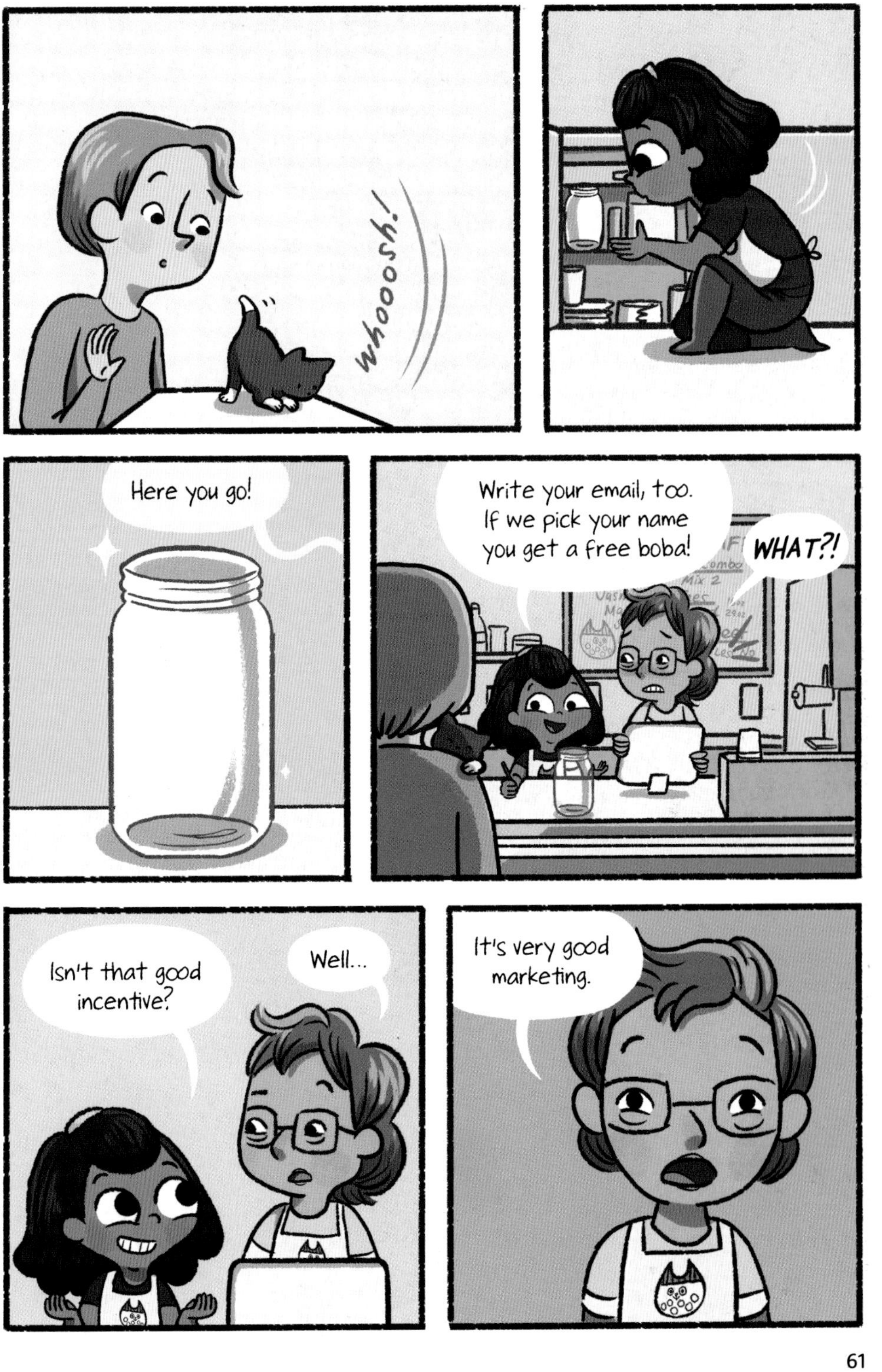
whooosh!
Here you go!
Write your email, too. If we pick your name you get a free boba!
WHAT?!
Isn't that good incentive?
Well...
It's very good marketing.

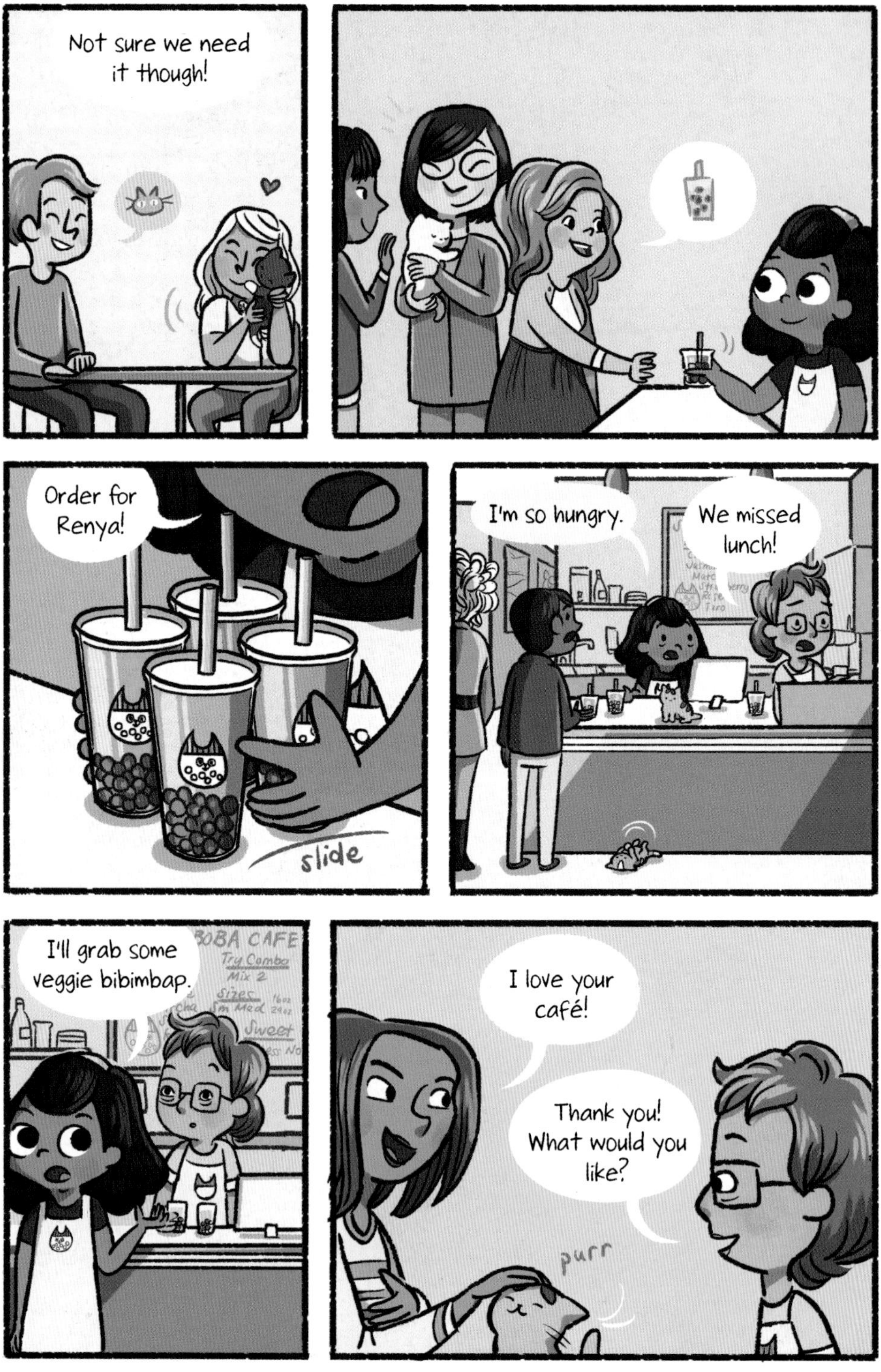
Not sure we need it though!
Order for Renya!
slide
I'm so hungry.
We missed lunch!
I'll grab some veggie bibimbap.
Try Combo
Sizes
Sweet
I love your café!
Thank you! What would you like?
purr

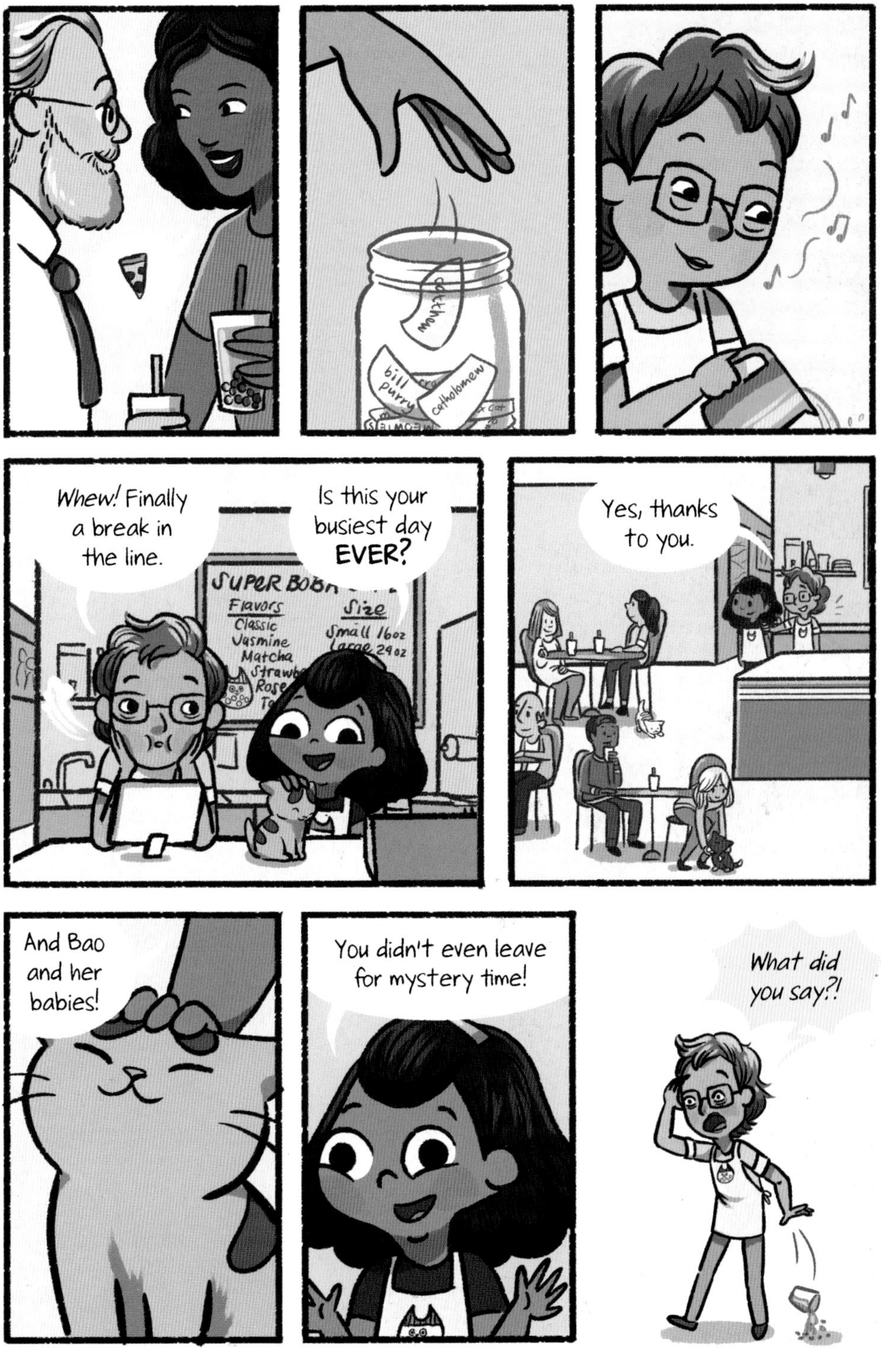
catthew
bill purry
cathalomew
Whew! Finally a break in the line.
Is this your busiest day **EVER?**
Flavors
Classic
Matcha
Size
Small 16oz
Large 24oz
Yes, thanks to you.
And Bao and her babies!
You didn't even leave for mystery time!
What did you say?!

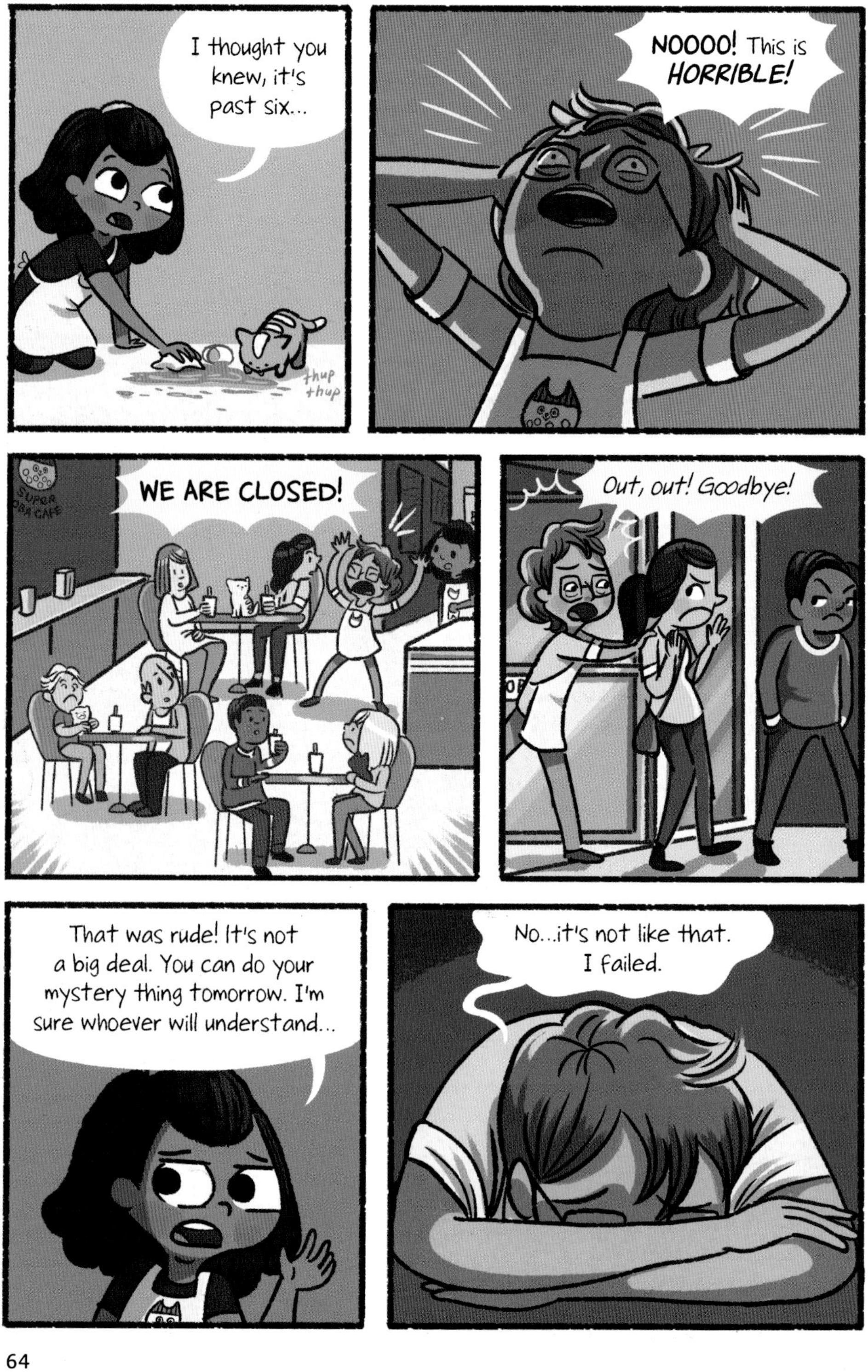
I thought you knew, it's past six...
thup thup
NOOOO! This is HORRIBLE!
SUPER OBA CAFE
WE ARE CLOSED!
Out, out! Goodbye!
That was rude! It's not a big deal. You can do your mystery thing tomorrow. I'm sure whoever will understand...
No...it's not like that. I failed.

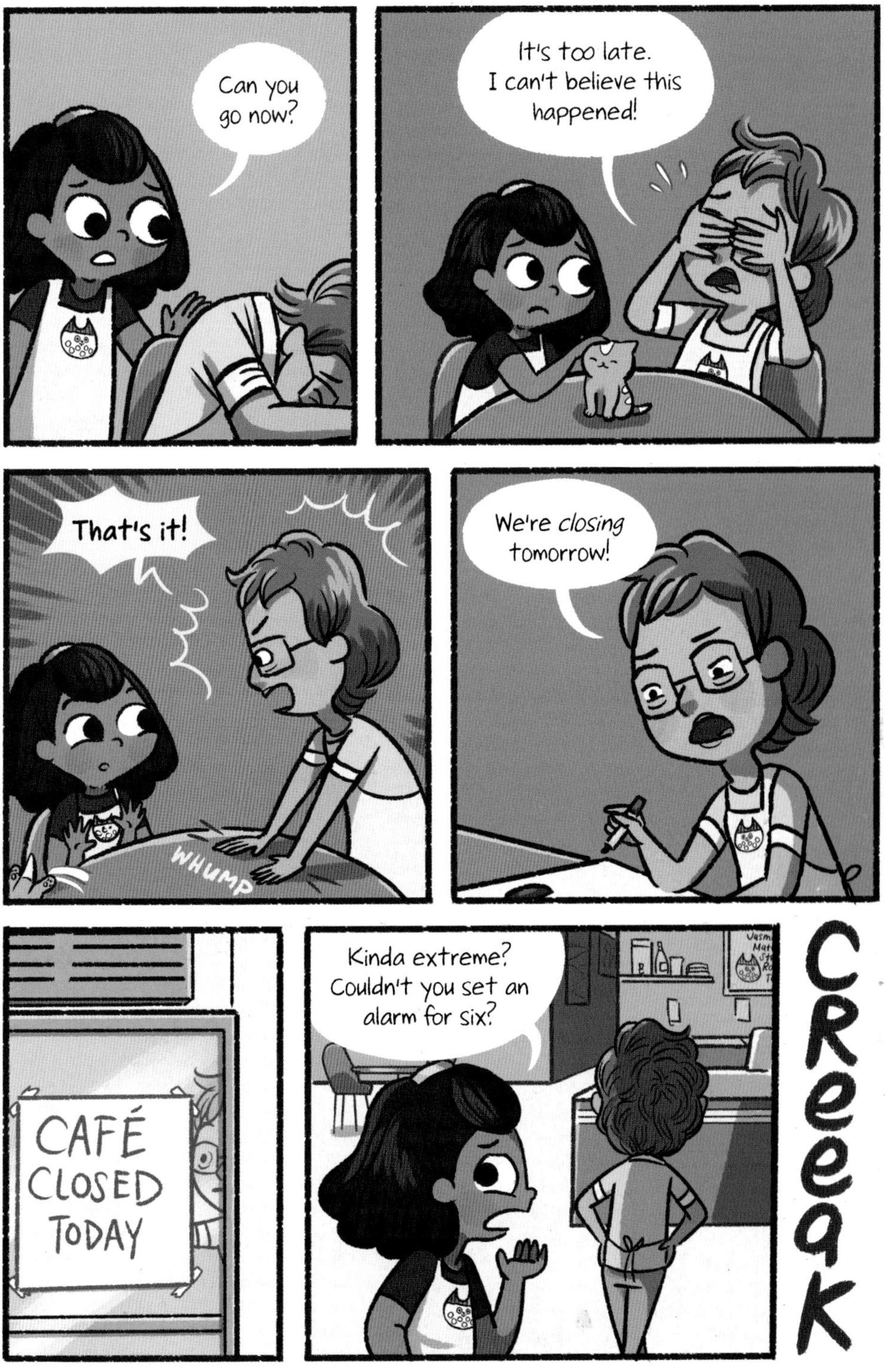
Can you go now?
It's too late. I can't believe this happened!
That's it!
WHUMP
We're *closing* tomorrow!
CAFÉ CLOSED TODAY
Kinda extreme? Couldn't you set an alarm for six?
CREEAK

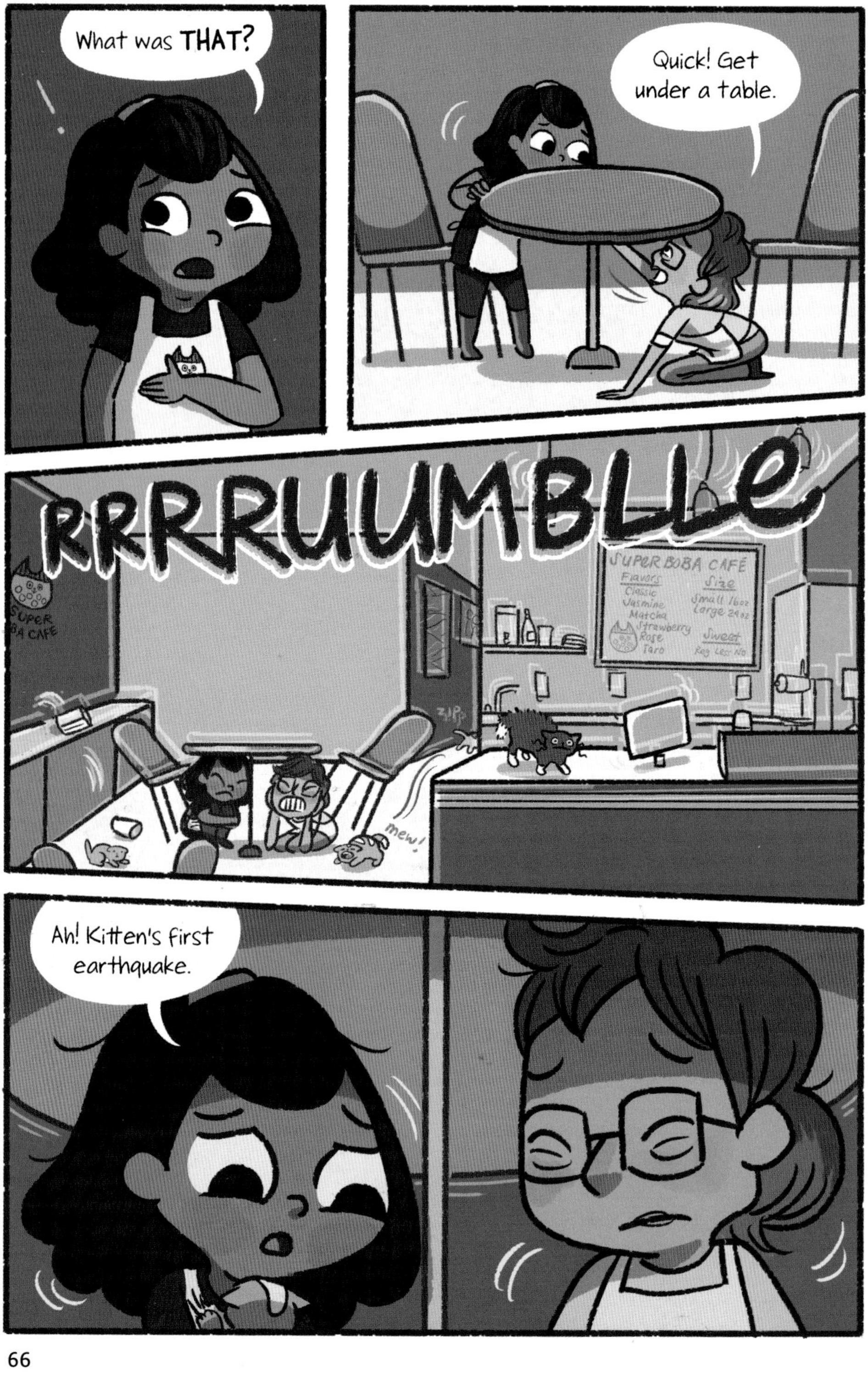
What was THAT?
Quick! Get under a table.
RRRRUUMBLLE
SUPER BOBA CAFÉ
SUPER BOBA CAFÉ
Flavors
Classic
Jasmine
Matcha
Strawberry
Rose
Taro
Size
Small 16oz
Large 24oz
Sweet
Reg Less No
mew!
Ah! Kitten's first earthquake.

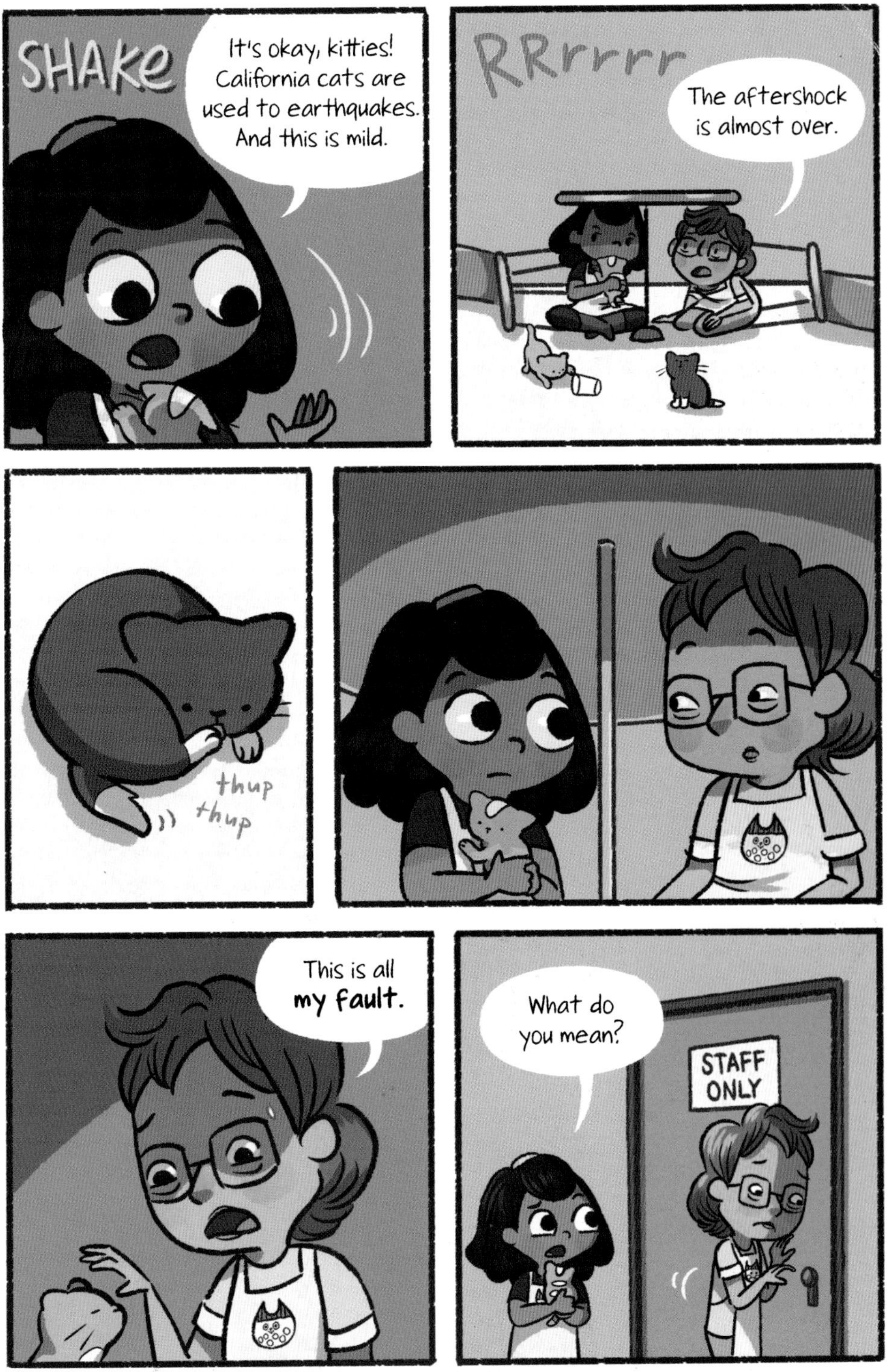
SHAKE
It's okay, kitties! California cats are used to earthquakes. And this is mild.
Rrrrrr
The aftershock is almost over.
thup
thup
This is all **my fault.**
What do you mean?
STAFF ONLY

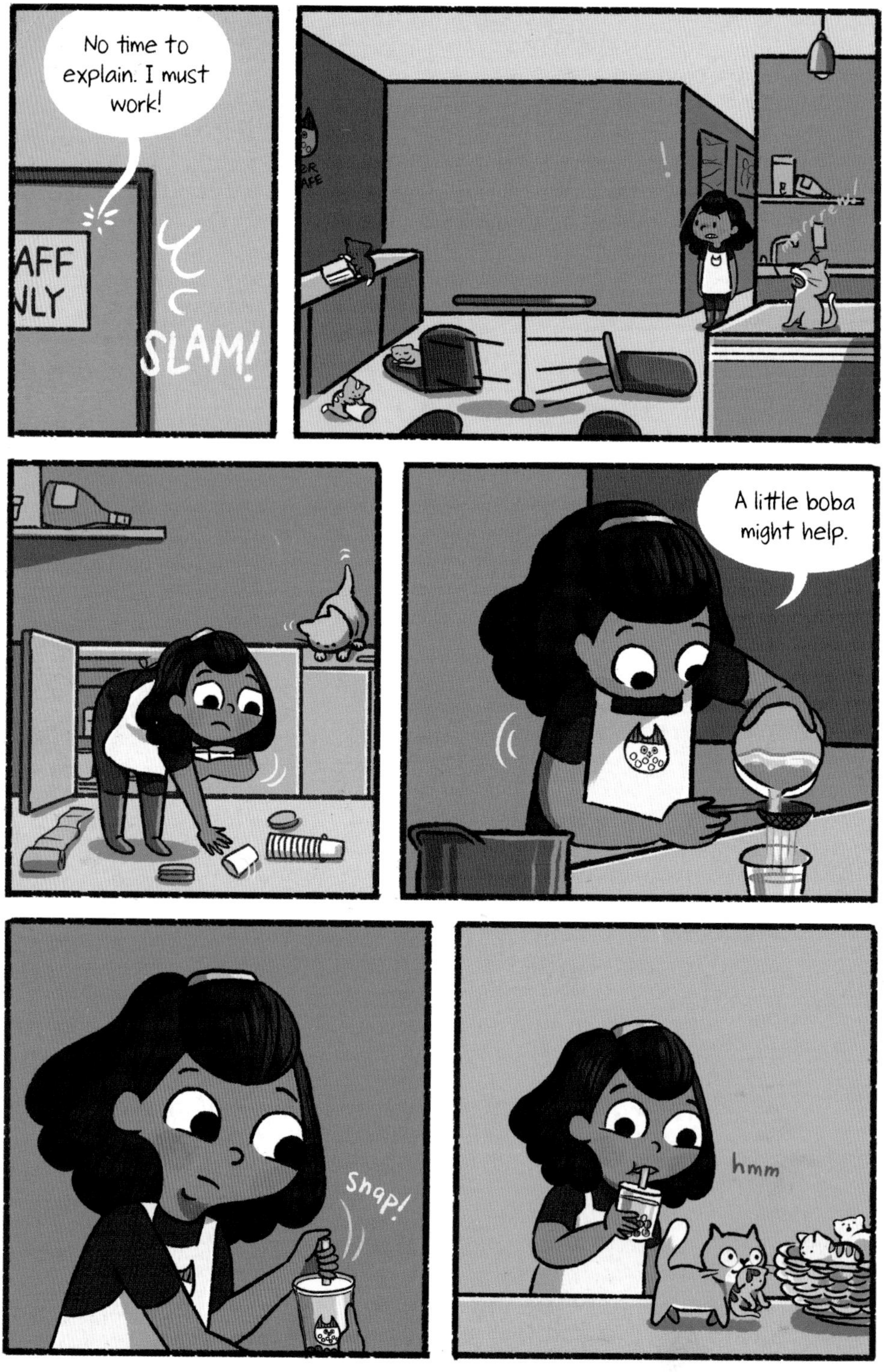
No time to explain. I must work!
AFF
NLY
SLAM!
A little boba might help.
Snap!
hmm

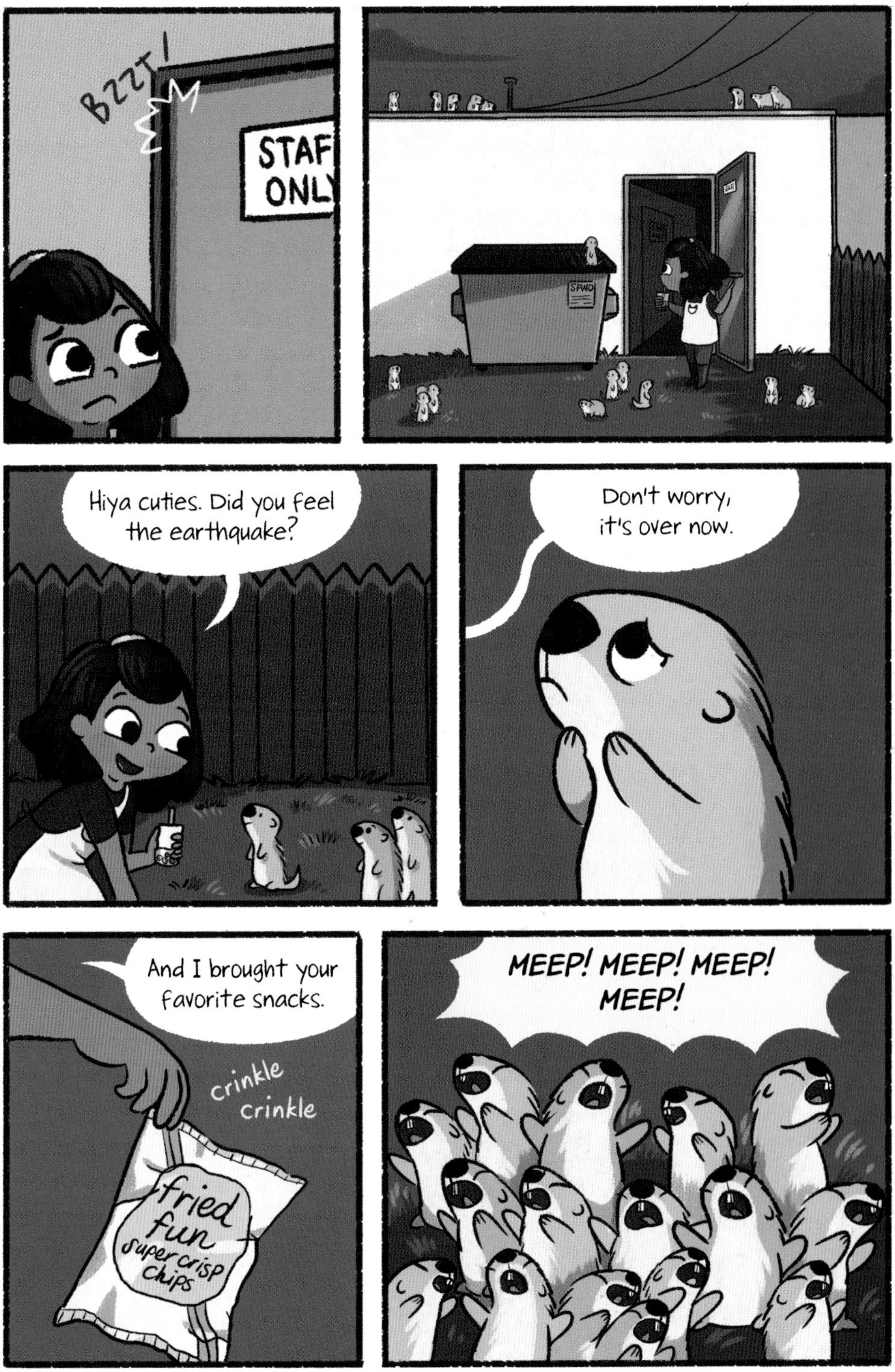
BZZT!
STAF
ONL
Hiya cuties. Did you feel the earthquake?
Don't worry, it's over now.
And I brought your favorite snacks.
crinkle
crinkle
fried fun super crisp chips
MEEP! MEEP! MEEP! MEEP!

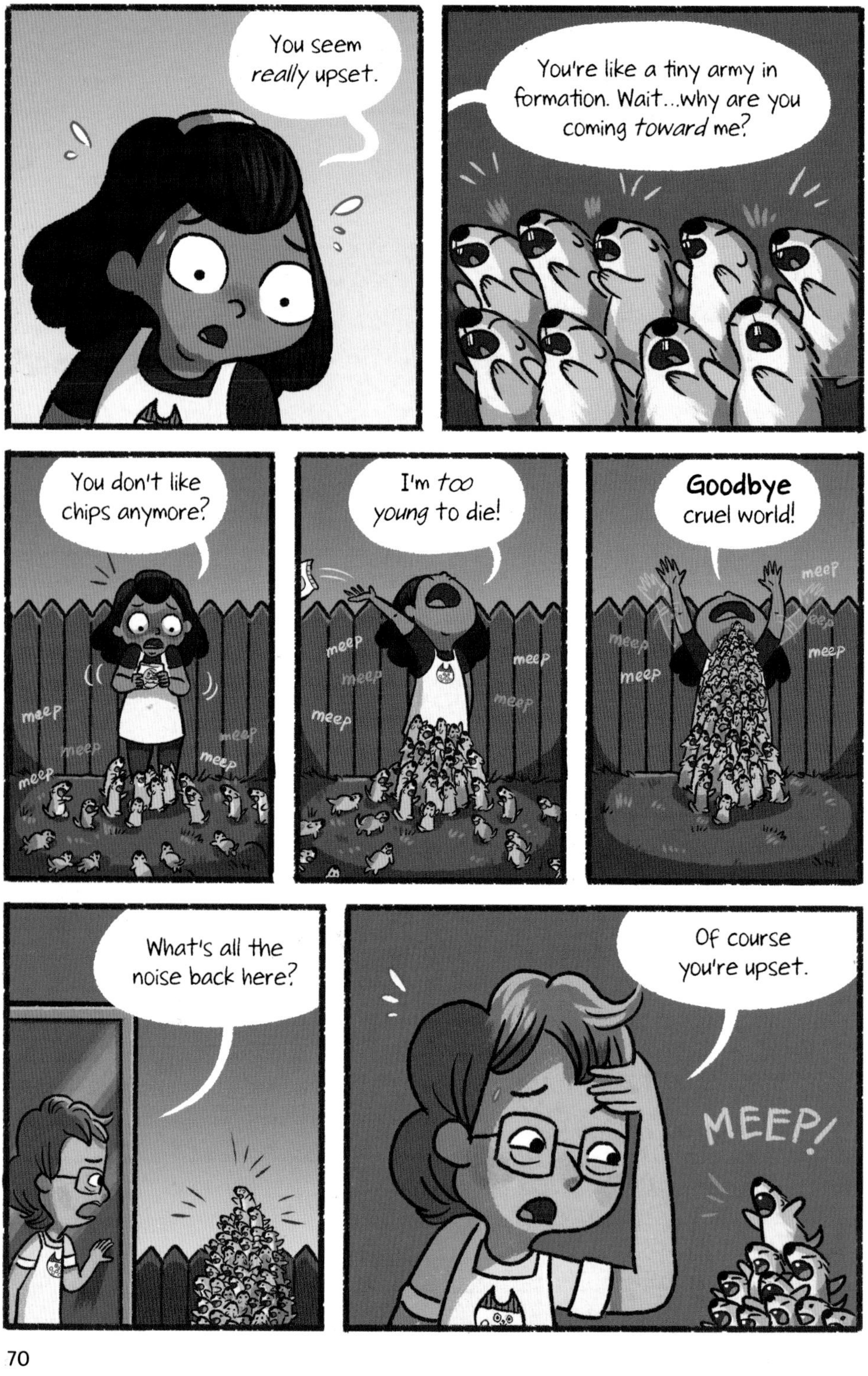
You seem *really* upset.
You're like a tiny army in formation. Wait...why are you coming *toward* me?
You don't like chips anymore?
meep
meep
meep
meep
meep
I'm *too* young to die!
meep
meep
meep
meep
meep
Goodbye cruel world!
meep
meep
meep
meep
What's all the noise back here?
Of course you're upset.
MEEP!

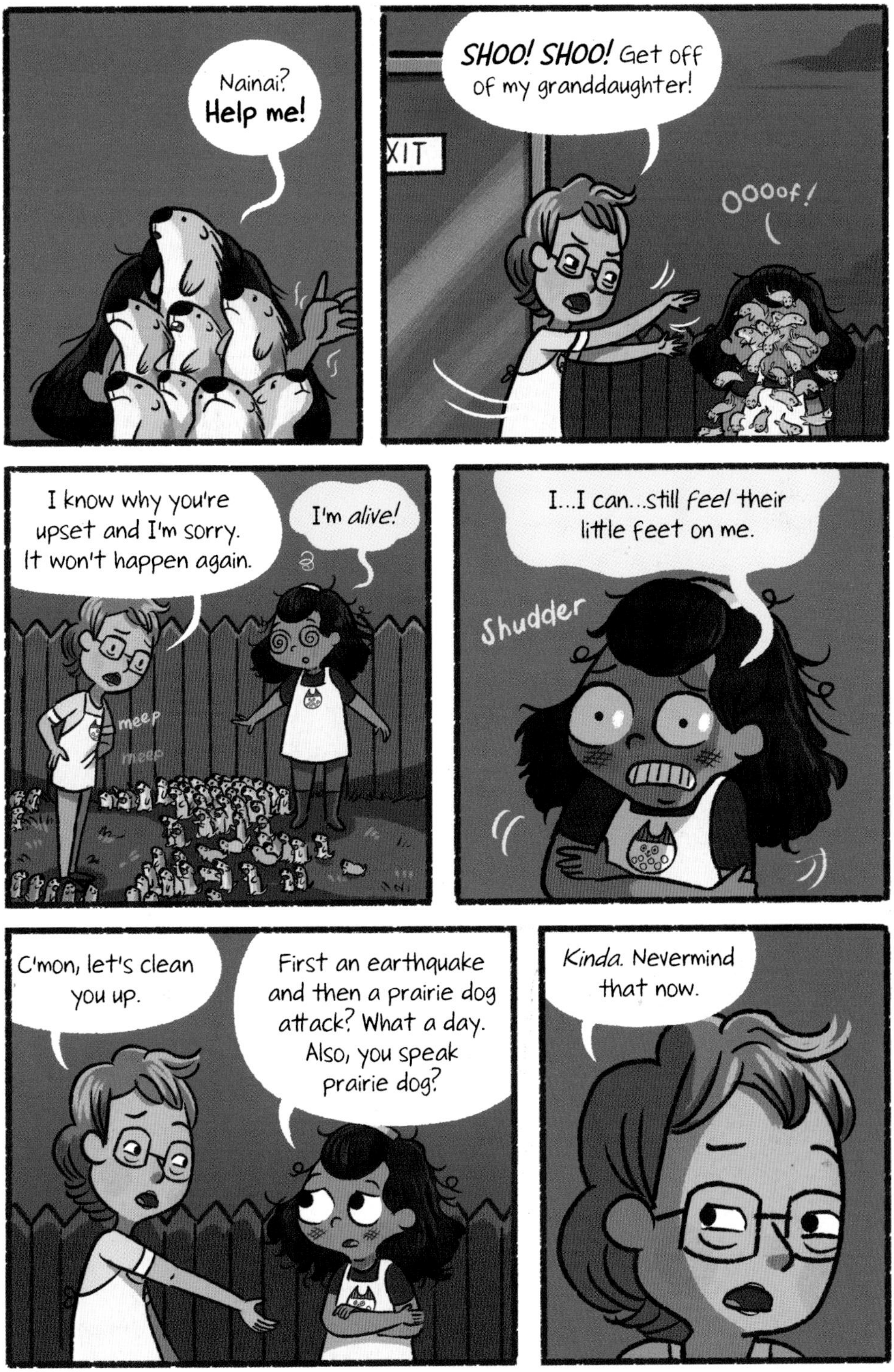
Nainai? Help me!
SHOO! SHOO! Get off of my granddaughter!
XIT
OOOof!
I know why you're upset and I'm sorry. It won't happen again.
I'm alive!
meep
meep
I...I can...still feel their little feet on me.
Shudder
C'mon, let's clean you up.
First an earthquake and then a prairie dog attack? What a day. Also, you speak prairie dog?
Kinda. Nevermind that now.

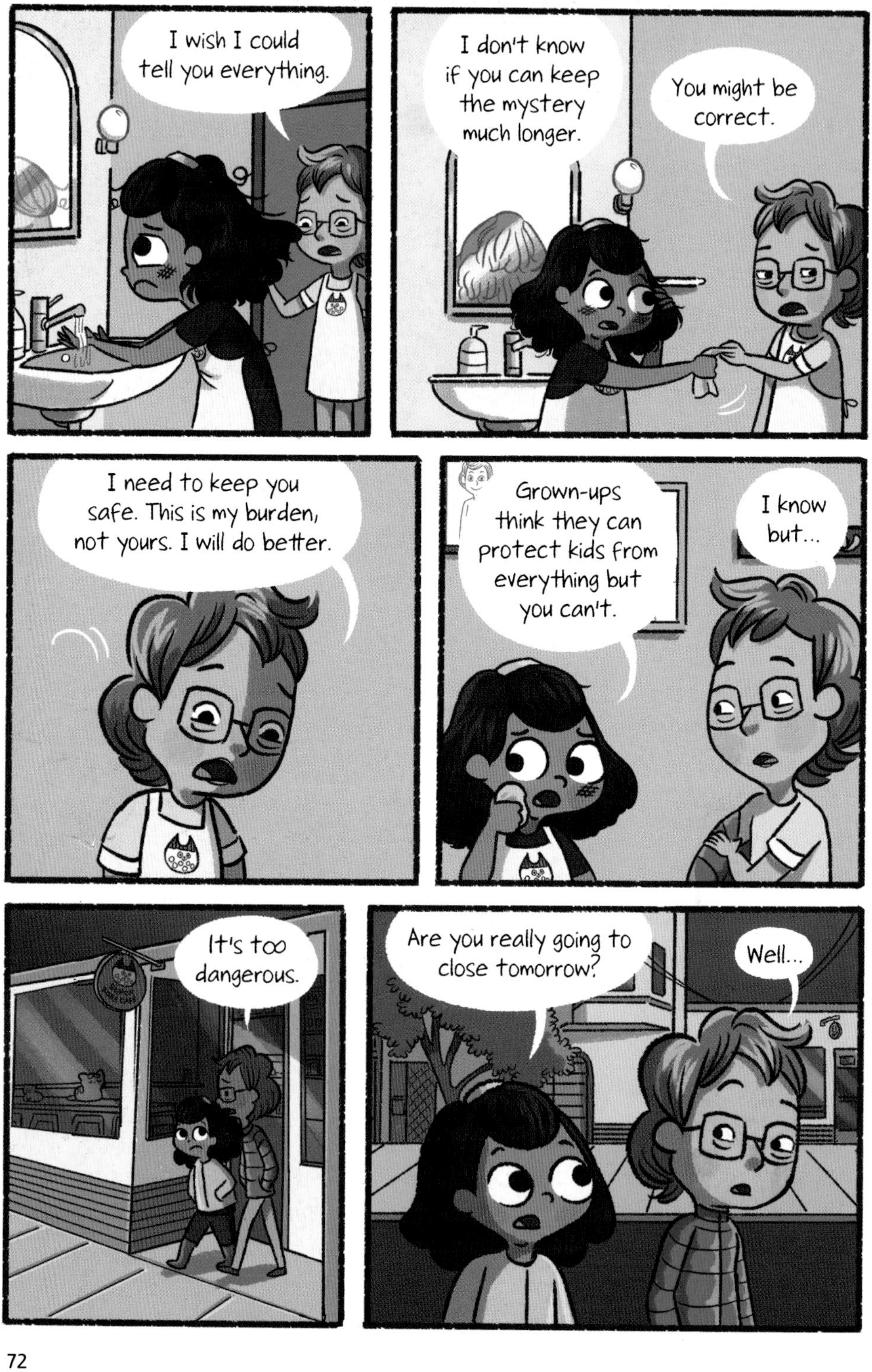
I wish I could tell you everything.
I don't know if you can keep the mystery much longer.
You might be correct.
I need to keep you safe. This is my burden, not yours. I will do better.
Grown-ups think they can protect kids from everything but you can't.
I know but...
It's too dangerous.
Are you really going to close tomorrow?
Well...

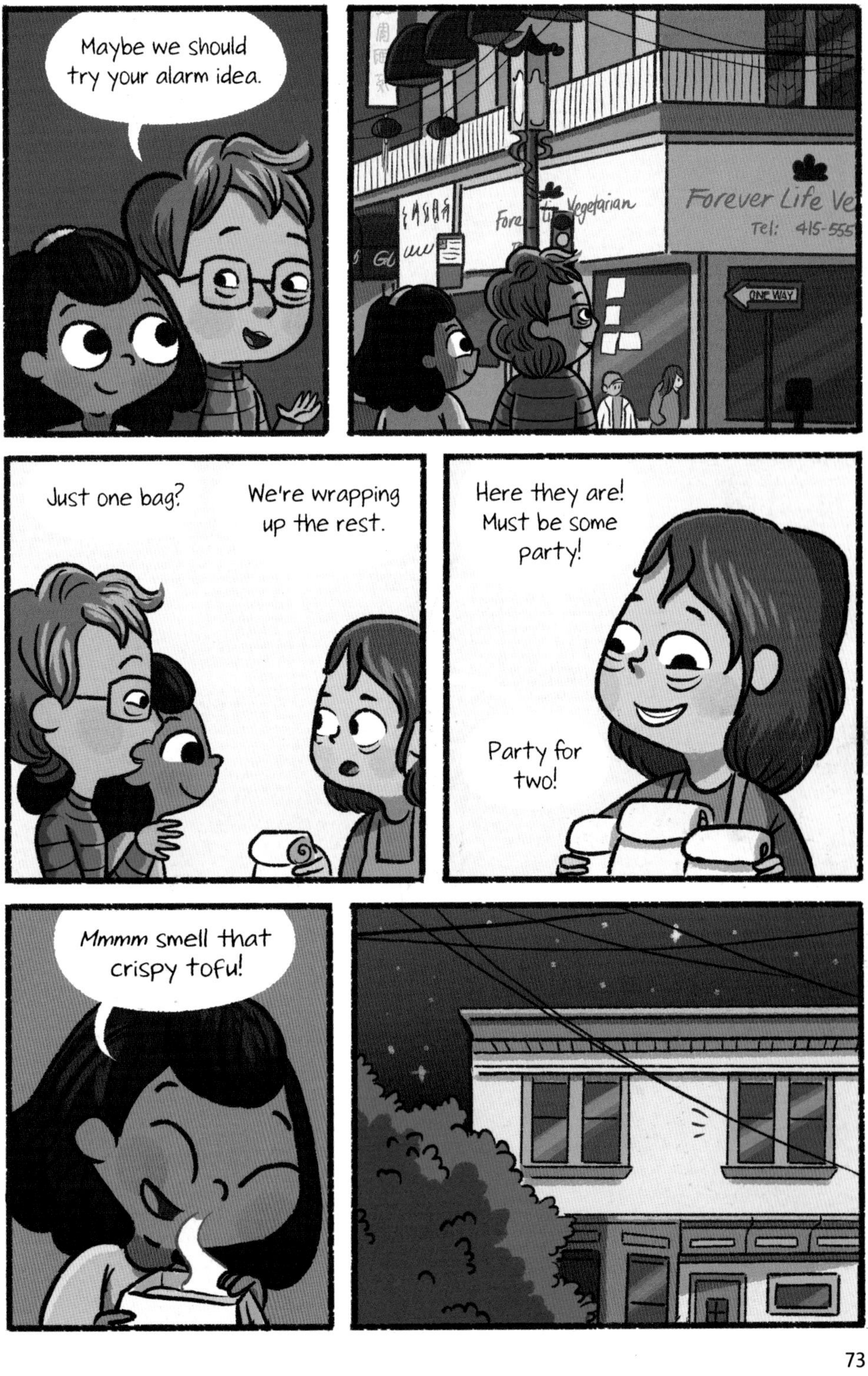
Maybe we should try your alarm idea.
Forever Life Vegetarian
Forever Life Ve
Tel: 415-555
ONE WAY
Just one bag?
We're wrapping up the rest.
Here they are! Must be some party!
Party for two!
Mmmm smell that crispy tofu!

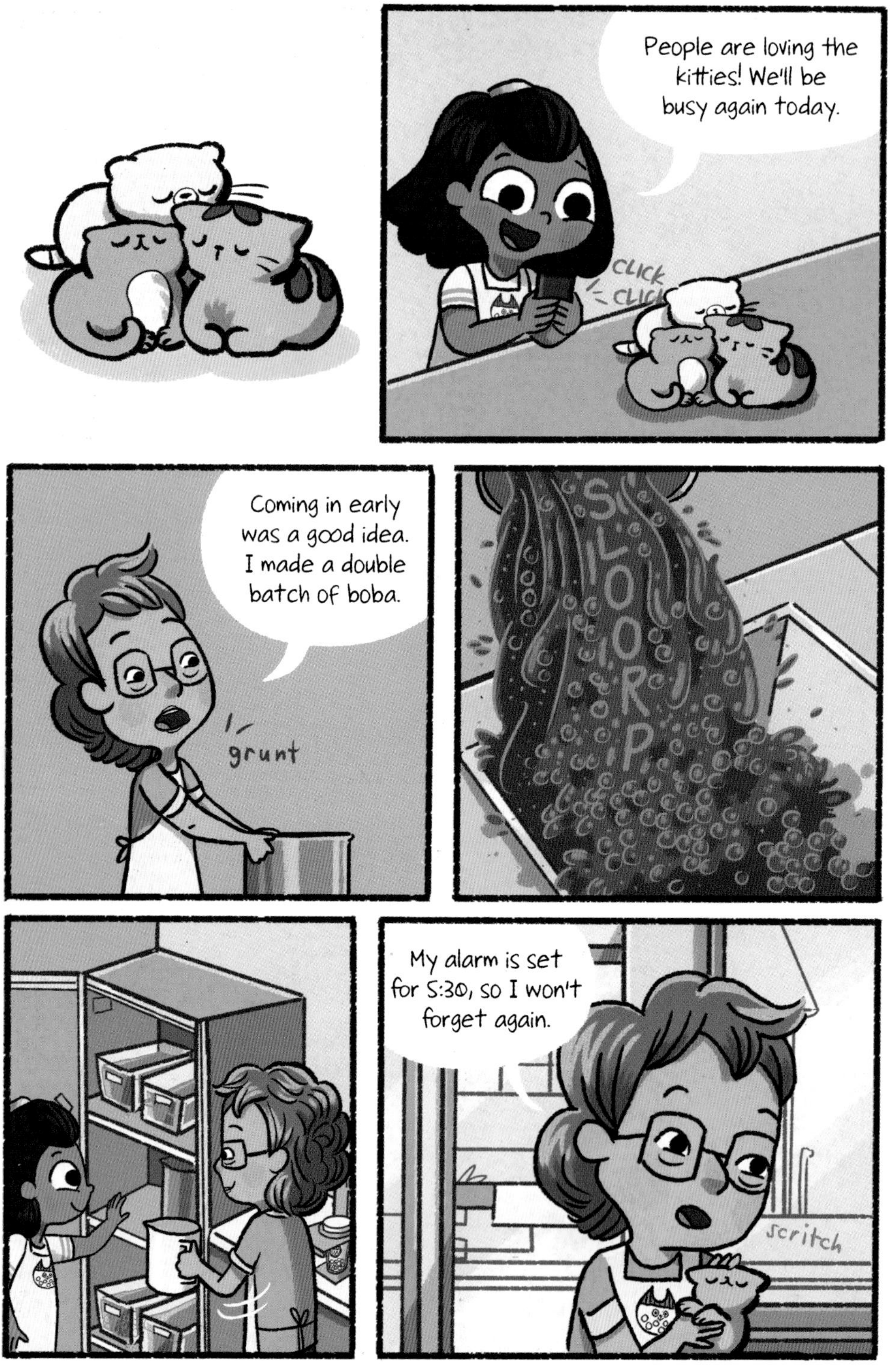
People are loving the kitties! We'll be busy again today.
CLICK
CLICK
Coming in early was a good idea. I made a double batch of boba.
grunt
SLOORP
My alarm is set for 5:30, so I won't forget again.
scritch

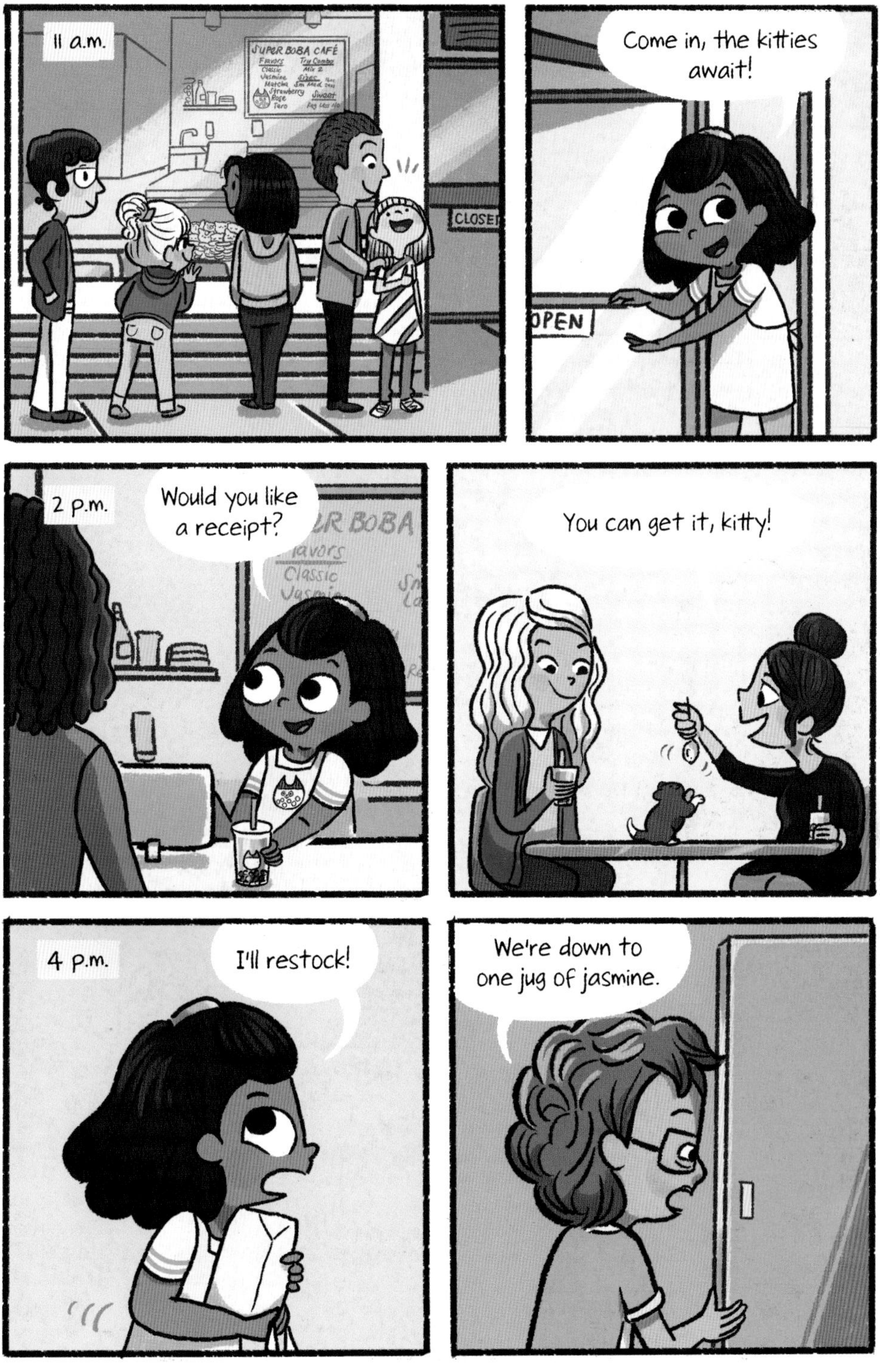
11 a.m.
SUPER BOBA CAFÉ
Come in, the kitties await!
OPEN
2 p.m.
Would you like a receipt?
You can get it, kitty!
4 p.m.
I'll restock!
We're down to one jug of jasmine.

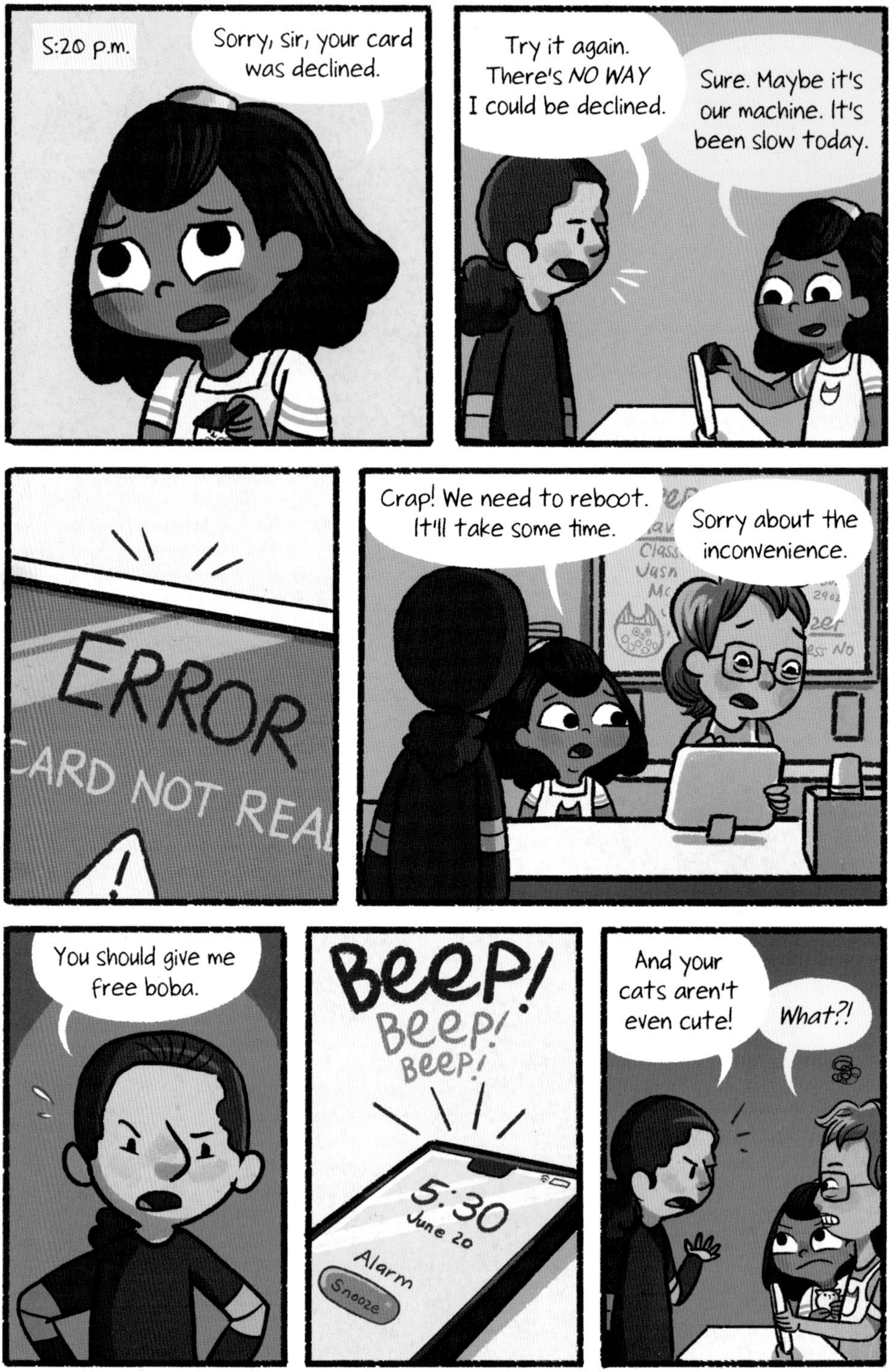
5:20 p.m.
Sorry, sir, your card was declined.
Try it again. There's NO WAY I could be declined.
Sure. Maybe it's our machine. It's been slow today.
ERROR
CARD NOT REAL
Crap! We need to reboot. It'll take some time.
Sorry about the inconvenience.
You should give me free boba.
BEEP!
BEEP!
BEEP!
5:30
June 20
Alarm
Snooze
And your cats aren't even cute!
What?!

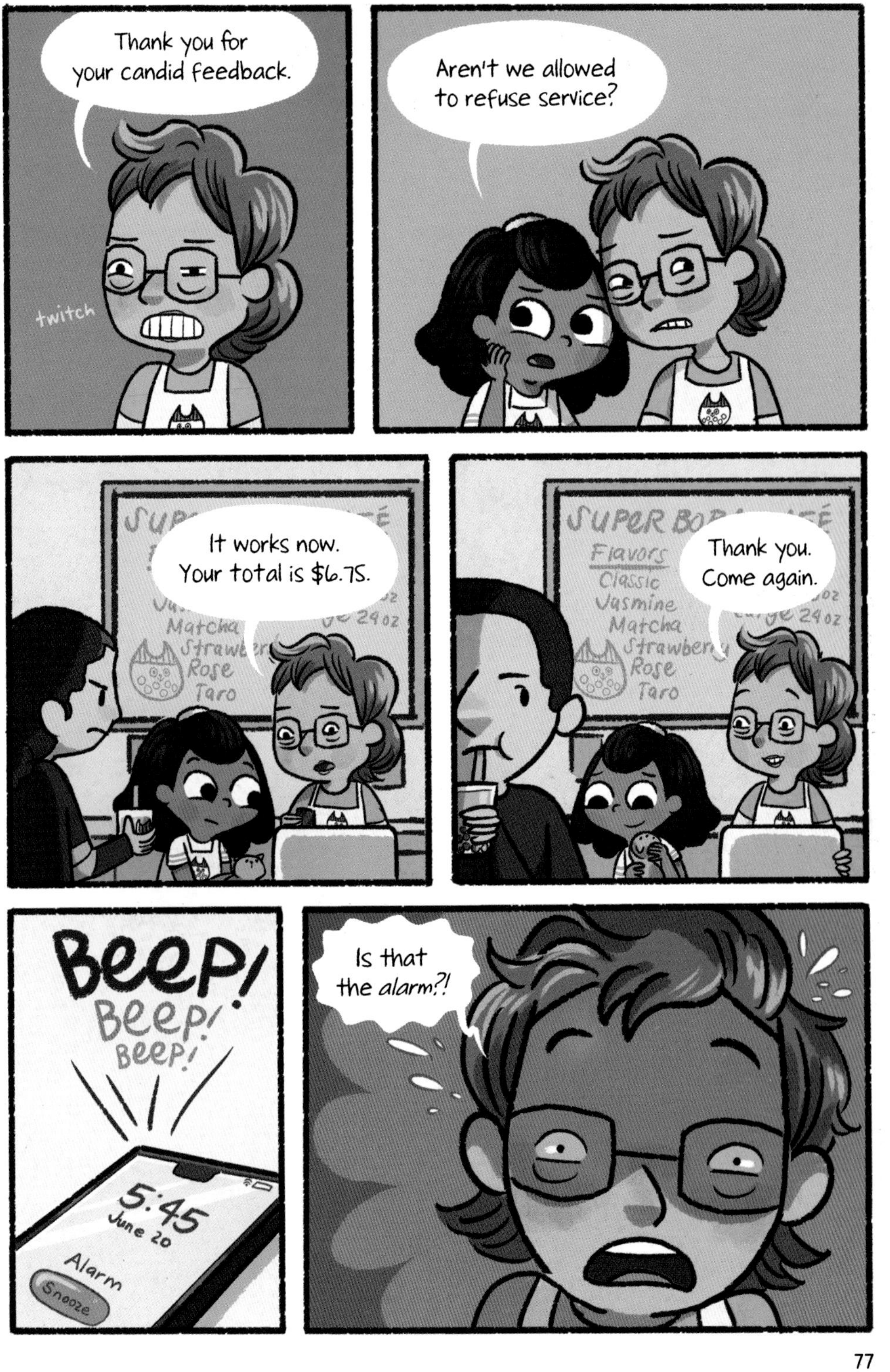

Thank you for your candid feedback.
twitch
Aren't we allowed to refuse service?
It works now. Your total is $6.75.
Thank you. Come again.
SUPER BOBA CAFÉ
Flavors
Classic
Jasmine
Matcha
Strawberry
Rose
Taro
BEEP! BEEP! BEEP!
5:45
June 20
Alarm
Snooze
Is that the *alarm*?!

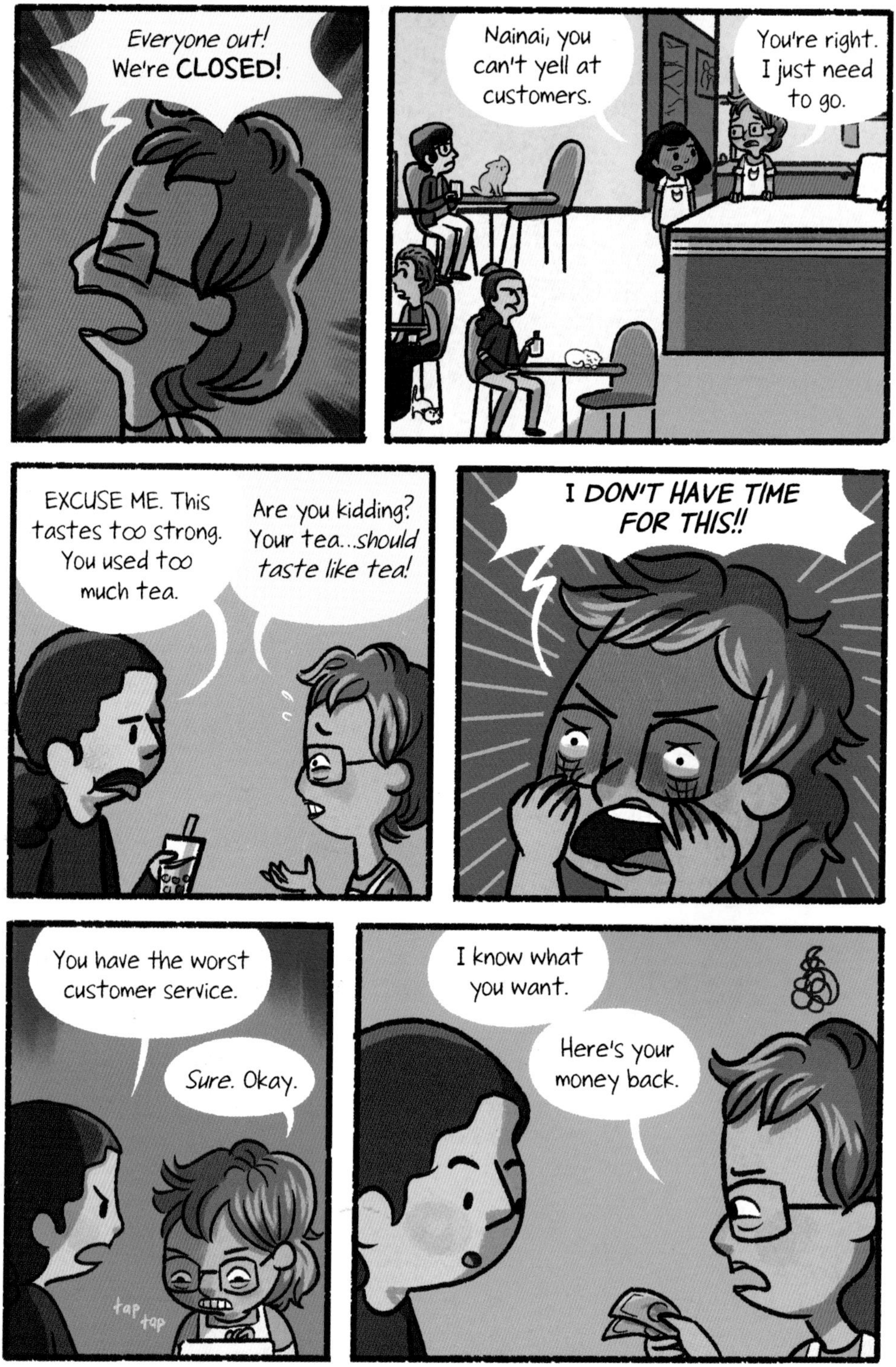
Everyone out! We're CLOSED!
Nainai, you can't yell at customers.
You're right. I just need to go.
EXCUSE ME. This tastes too strong. You used too much tea.
Are you kidding? Your tea...should taste like tea!
I DON'T HAVE TIME FOR THIS!!
You have the worst customer service.
Sure. Okay.
tap tap
I know what you want.
Here's your money back.

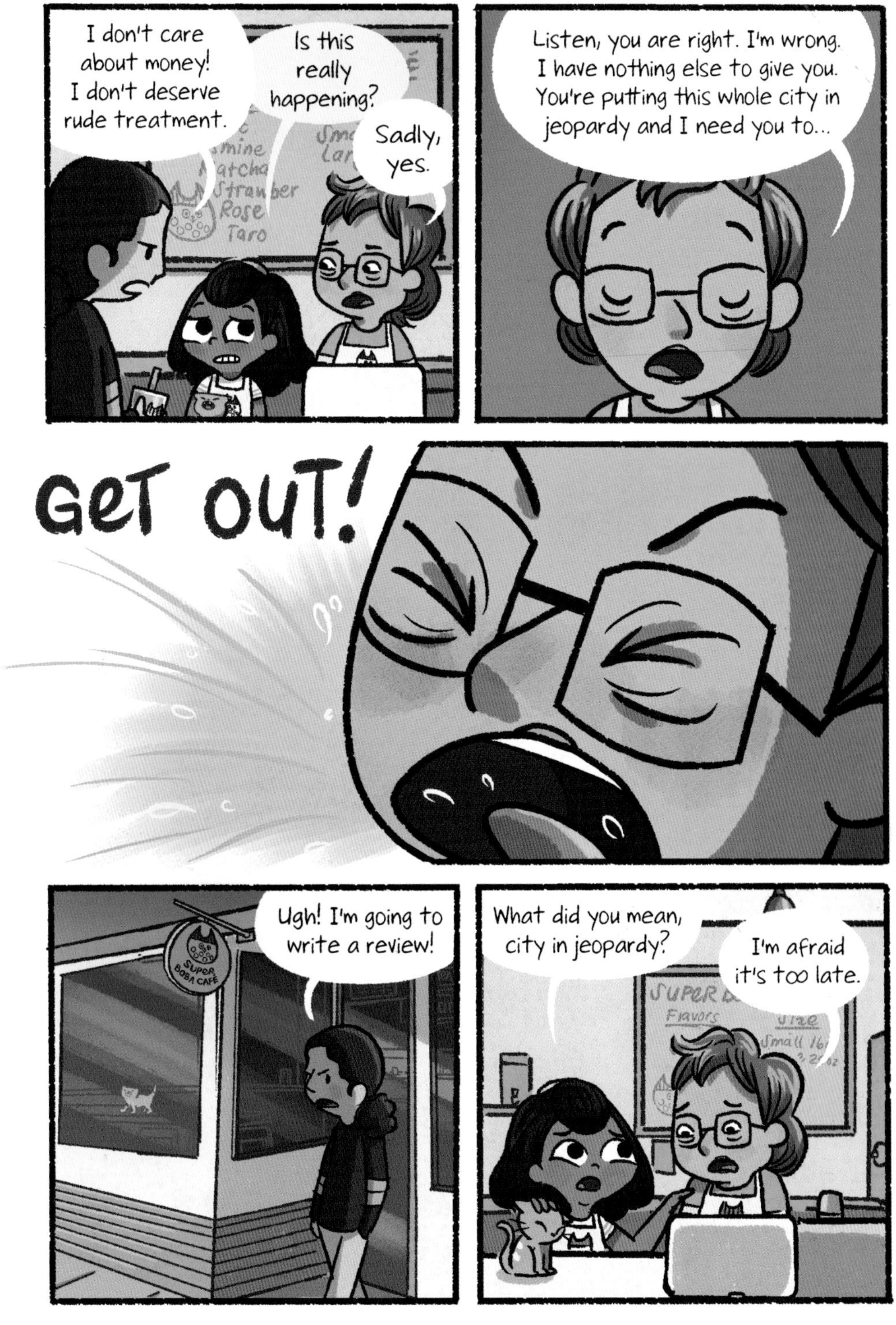
I don't care about money! I don't deserve rude treatment.
Is this really happening?
Sadly, yes.
Listen, you are right. I'm wrong. I have nothing else to give you. You're putting this whole city in jeopardy and I need you to...
GET OUT!
Ugh! I'm going to write a review!
SUPER BOBA CAFE
What did you mean, city in jeopardy?
I'm afraid it's too late.

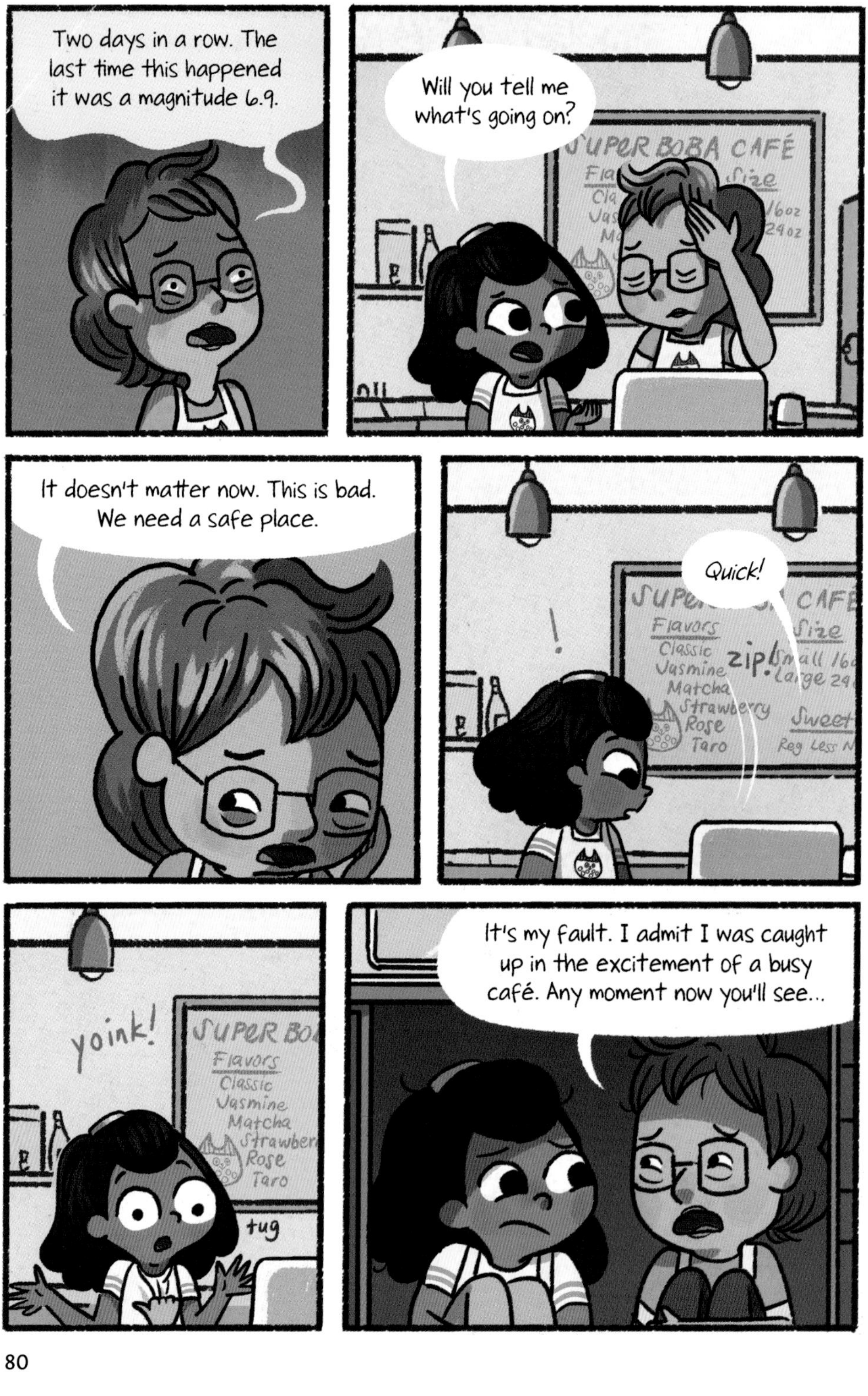
Two days in a row. The last time this happened it was a magnitude 6.9.
Will you tell me what's going on?
SUPER BOBA CAFÉ
It doesn't matter now. This is bad. We need a safe place.
Quick!
!
zip!
SUPER
CAFÉ
Flavors
Classic
Jasmine
Matcha
Strawberry
Rose
Taro
Size
Small 16
Large 24
Sweet
Reg Less
yoink!
SUPER BO
Flavors
Classic
Jasmine
Matcha
Strawber
Rose
Taro
tug
It's my fault. I admit I was caught up in the excitement of a busy café. Any moment now you'll see...

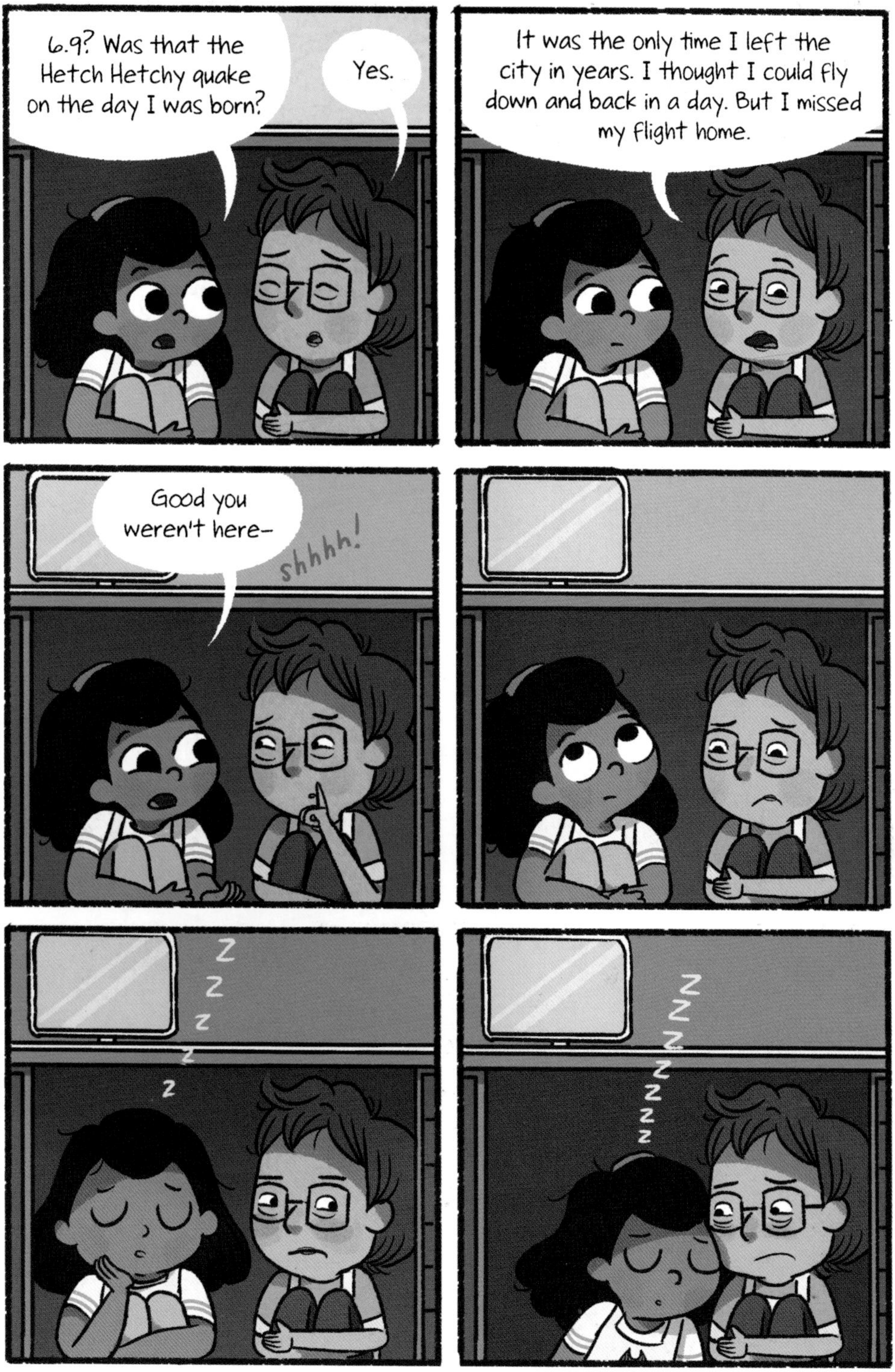
6.9? Was that the Hetch Hetchy quake on the day I was born?
Yes.
It was the only time I left the city in years. I thought I could fly down and back in a day. But I missed my flight home.
Good you weren't here-
shhhh!
Z
Z
Z
Z
Z
Z
Z
Z
Z
Z
Z
Z

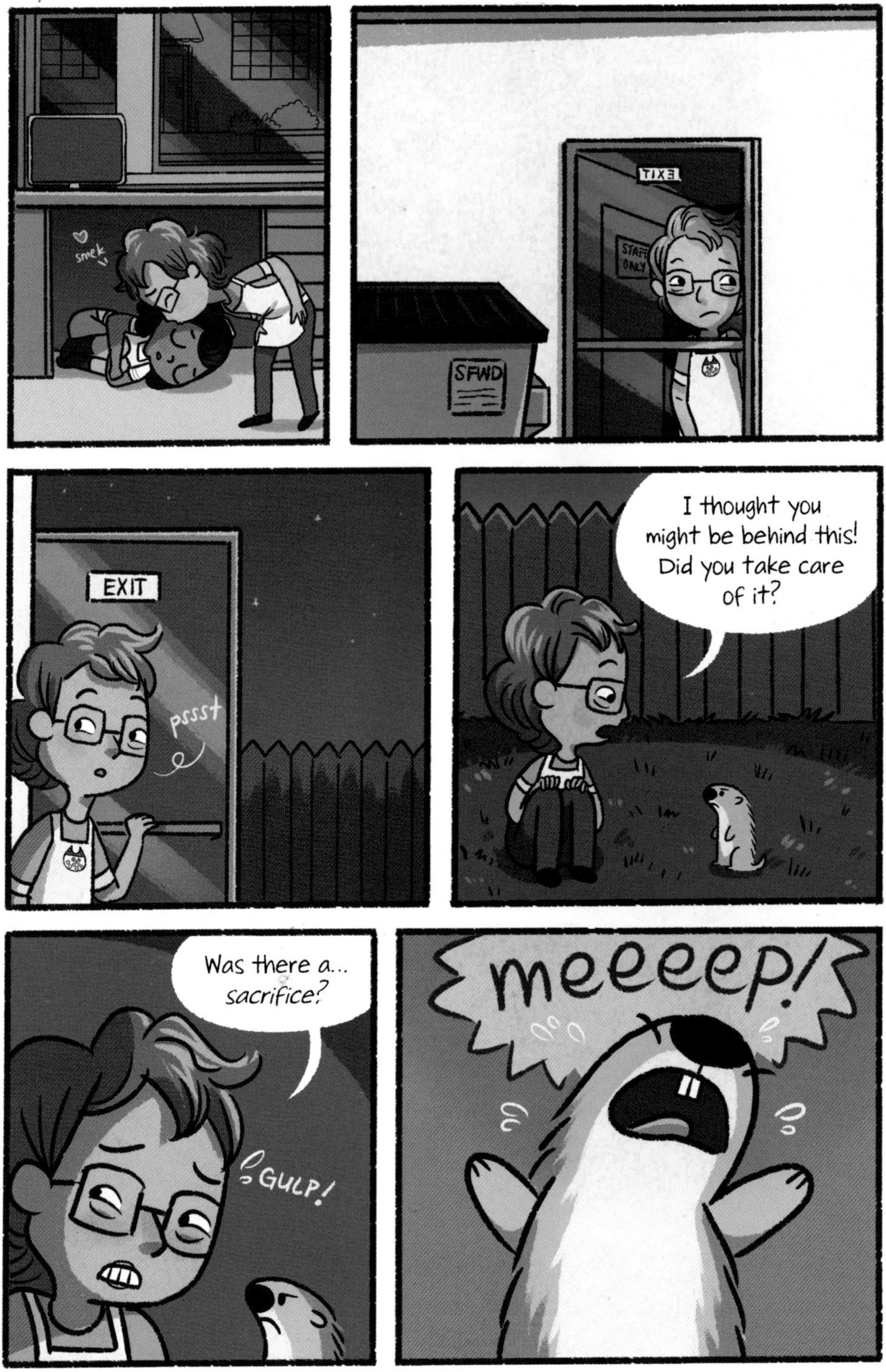
smek
EXIT
STAFF ONLY
SFWD
EXIT
pssst
I thought you might be behind this! Did you take care of it?
Was there a... sacrifice?
GULP!
meeeep!

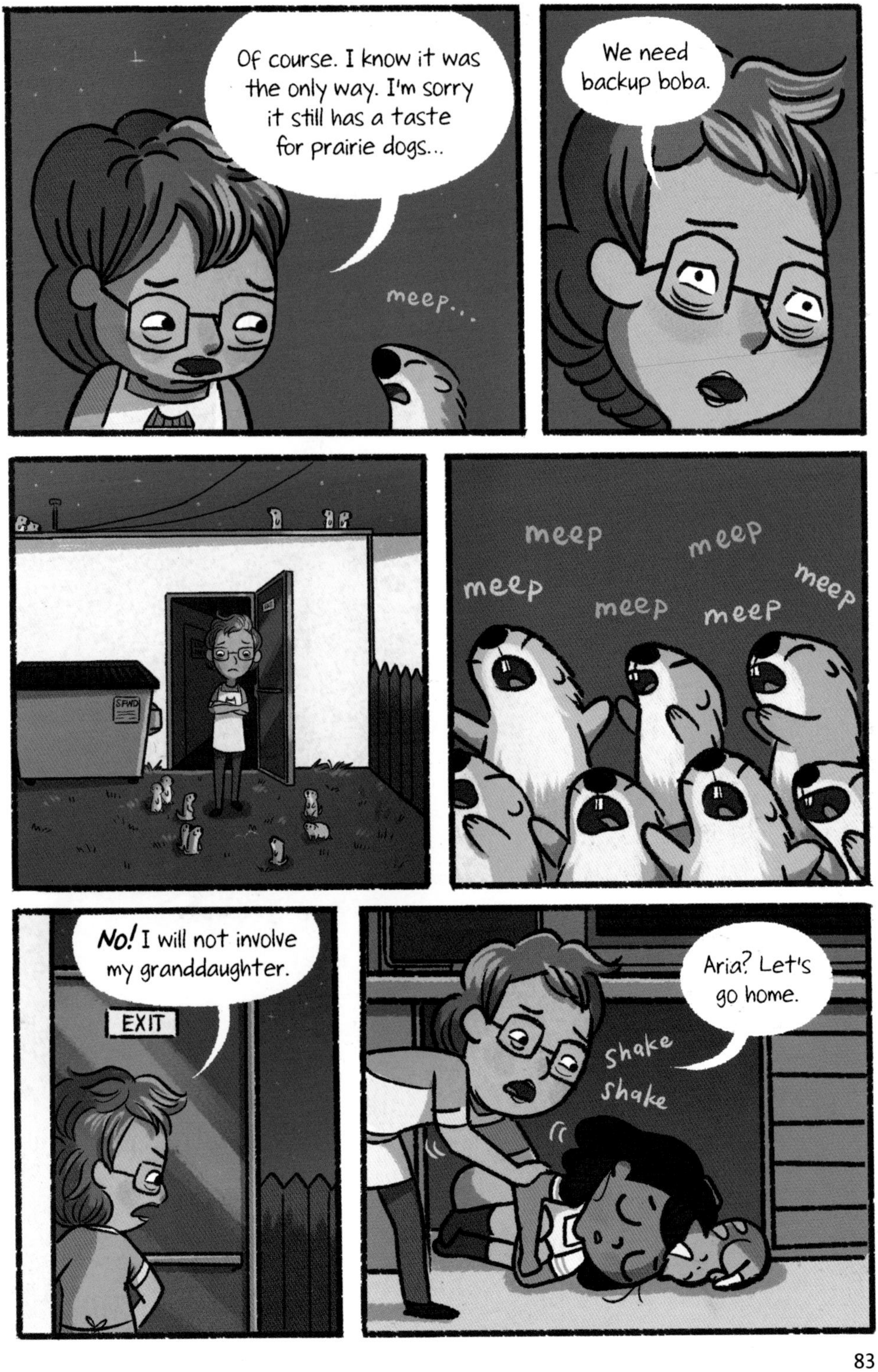
Of course. I know it was the only way. I'm sorry it still has a taste for prairie dogs...
meep...
We need backup boba.
meep
meep
meep
meep
meep
meep
No! I will not involve my granddaughter.
EXIT
Aria? Let's go home.
shake
shake

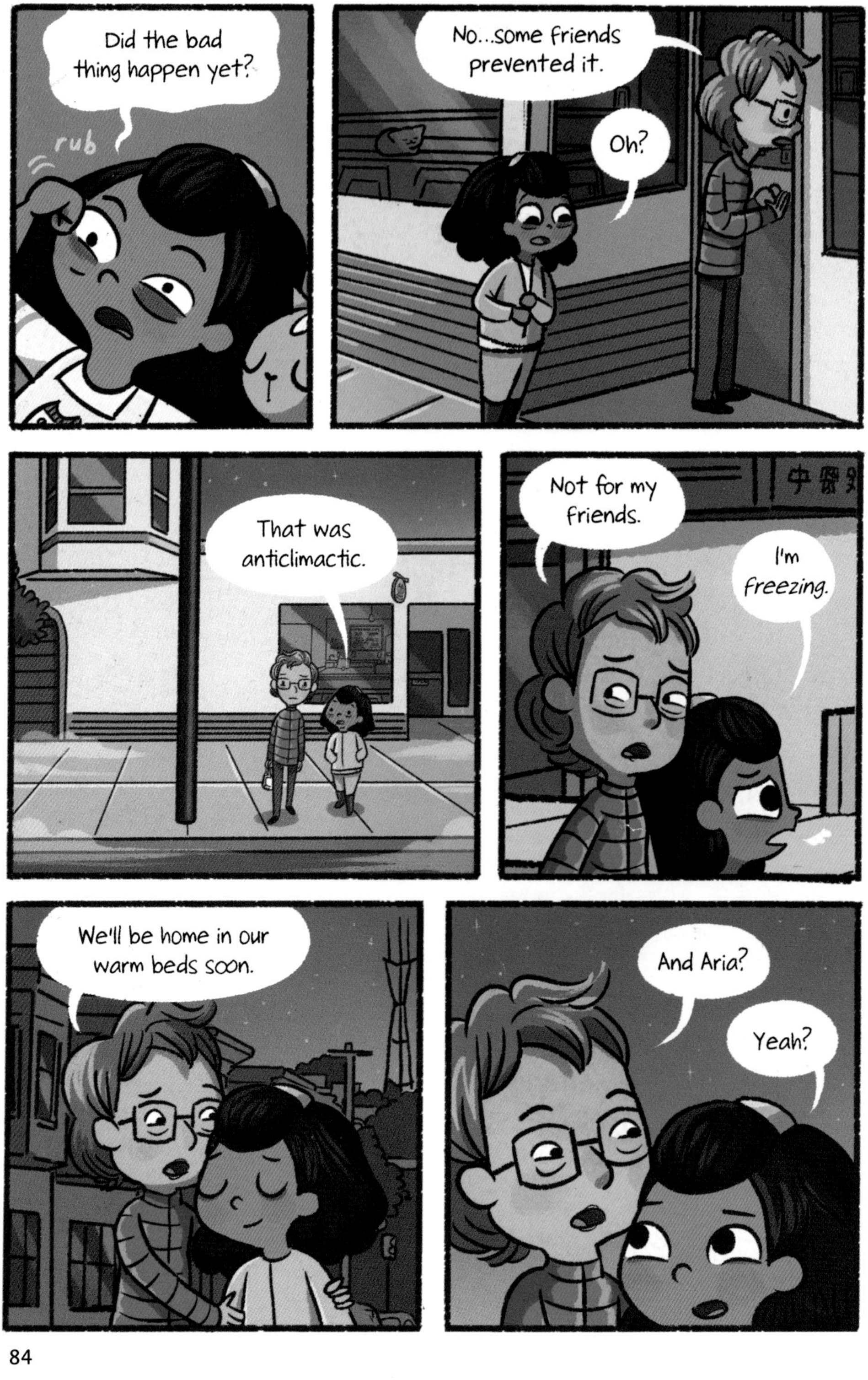
Did the bad thing happen yet?
rub
No...some friends prevented it.
Oh?
That was anticlimactic.
Not for my friends.
I'm freezing.
We'll be home in our warm beds soon.
And Aria?
Yeah?

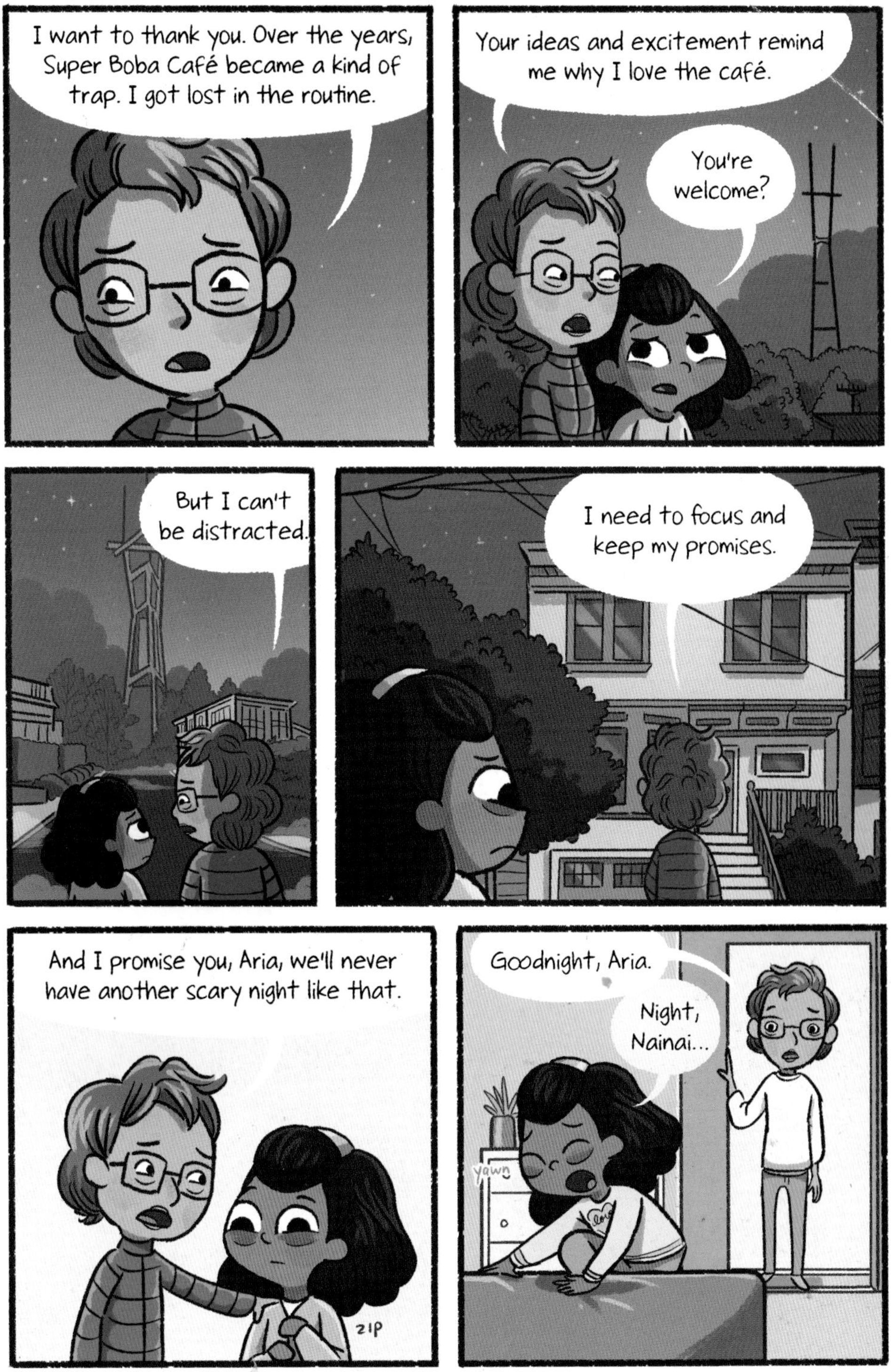
I want to thank you. Over the years, Super Boba Café became a kind of trap. I got lost in the routine.
Your ideas and excitement remind me why I love the café.
You're welcome?
But I can't be distracted.
I need to focus and keep my promises.
And I promise you, Aria, we'll never have another scary night like that.
zip
Goodnight, Aria.
Night, Nainai...
yawn

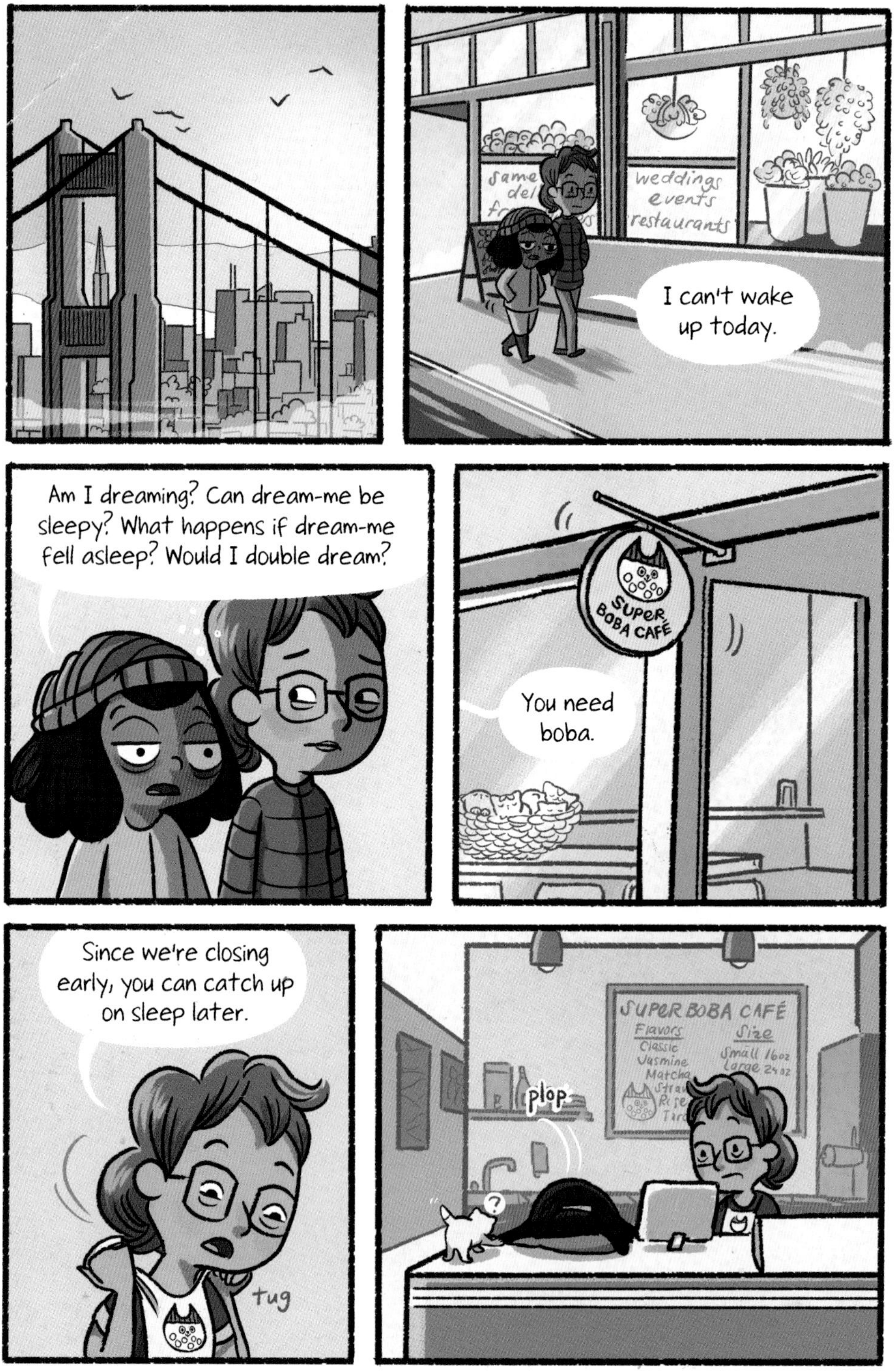
weddings
events
restaurants
I can't wake up today.
Am I dreaming? Can dream-me be sleepy? What happens if dream-me fell asleep? Would I double dream?
SUPER BOBA CAFÉ
You need boba.
Since we're closing early, you can catch up on sleep later.
tug
SUPER BOBA CAFÉ
Flavors
Classic
Jasmine
Matcha
Size
Small 16oz
Large 24oz
plop

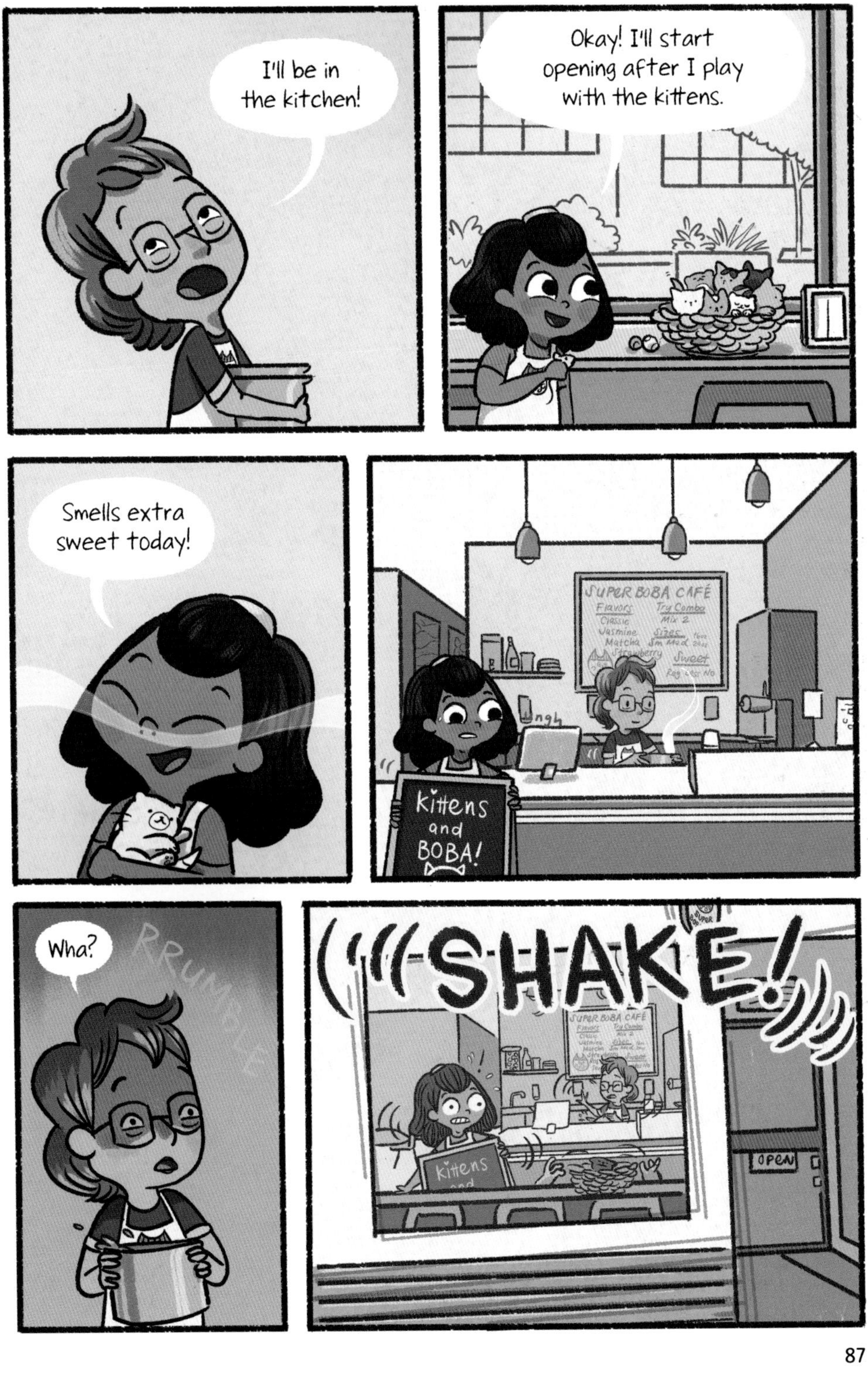
I'll be in the kitchen!
Okay! I'll start opening after I play with the kittens.
Smells extra sweet today!
SUPER BOBA CAFÉ
Flavors
Classic
Jasmine
Matcha
Strawberry
Try Combo
Mix 2
Sizes
Sm Med.
Sweet
Reg. Less No
Kittens and BOBA!
Wha?
RRUMBLE
SHAKE!
OPEN

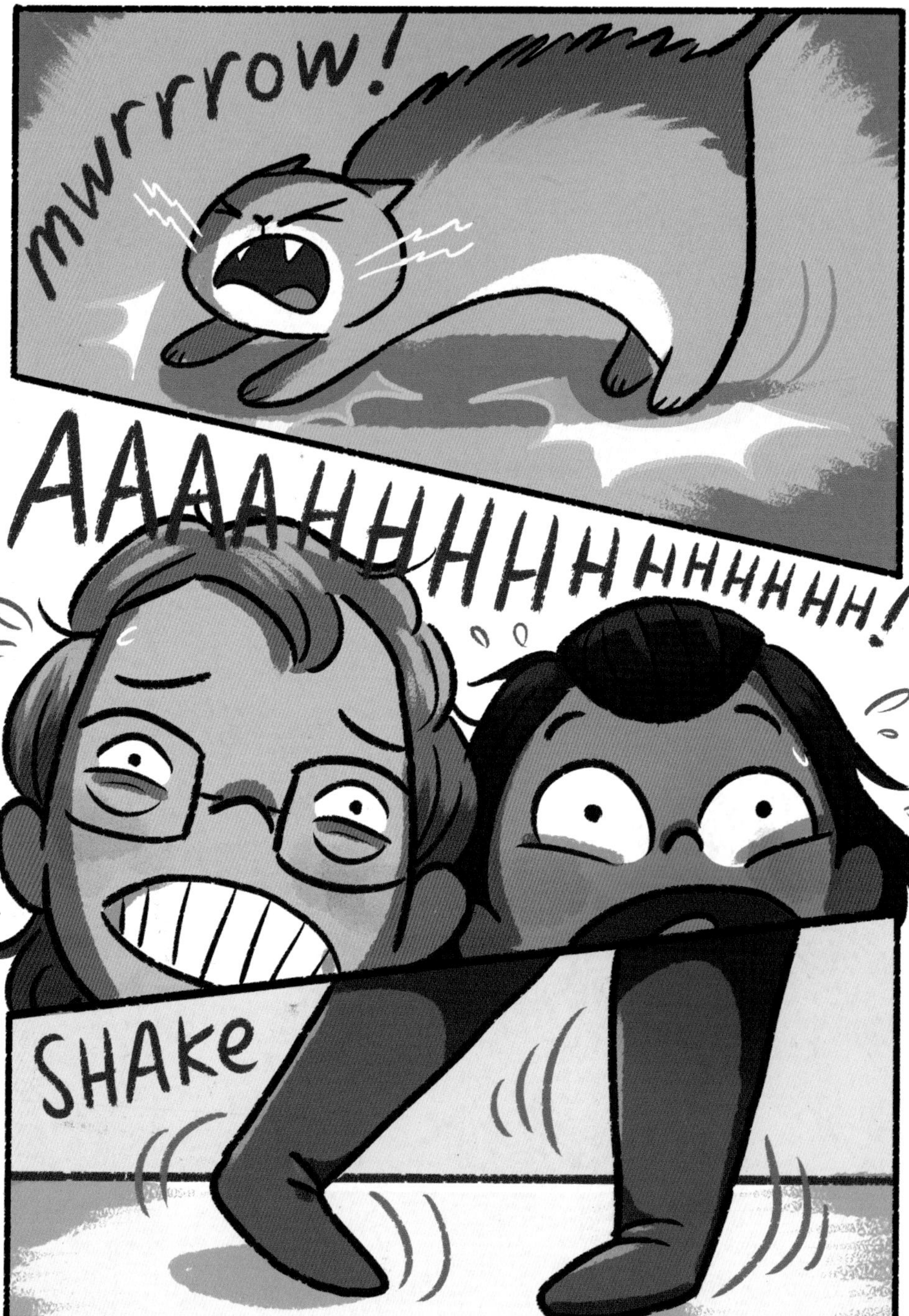
mwrrrow!
AAAAHHHHHHHHHHHH!
SHAKE

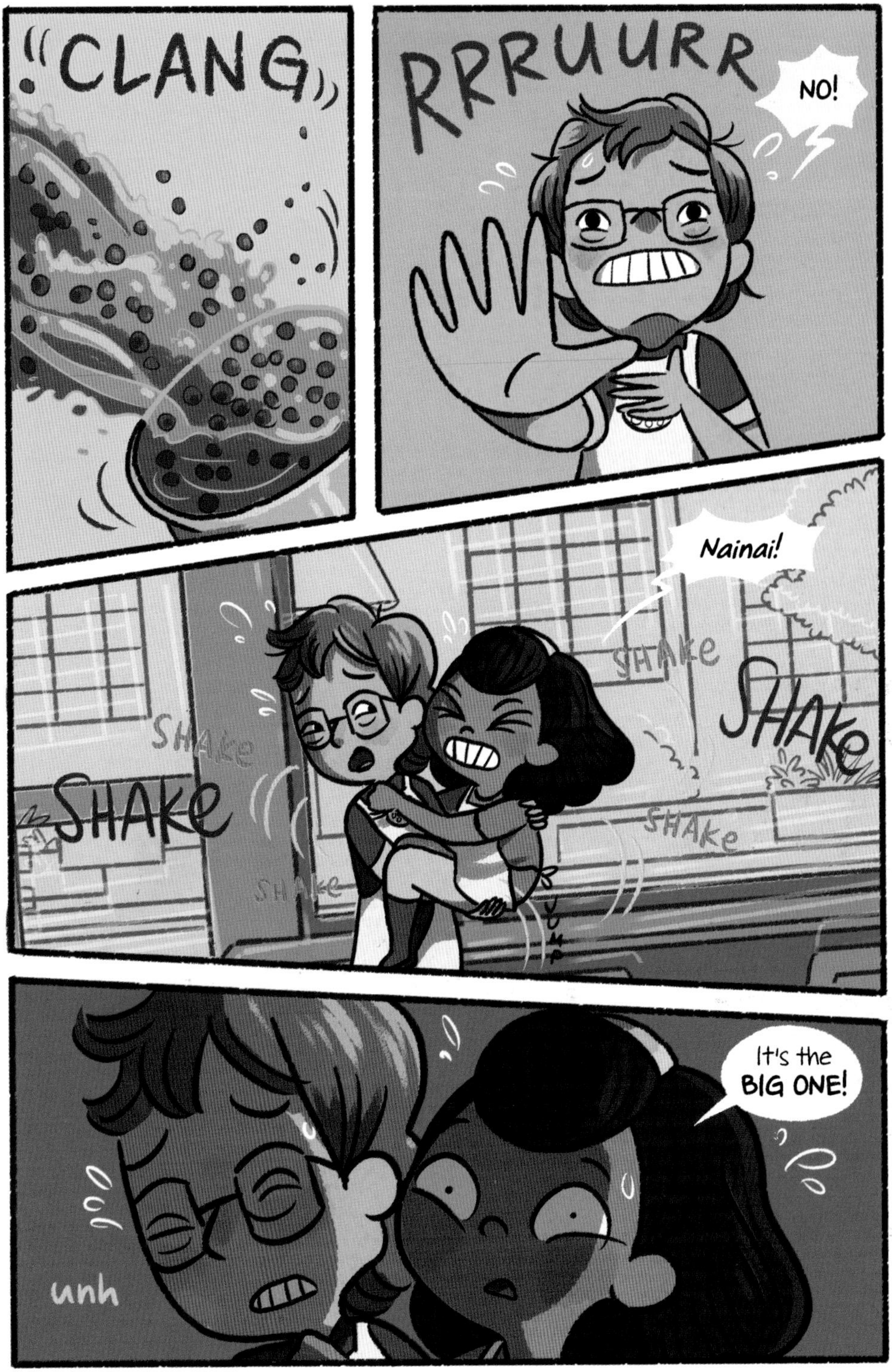
CLANG
RRRUURR
NO!
Nainai!
SHAKE
SHAKE
SHAKE
SHAKE
SHAKE
SHAKE
It's the BIG ONE!
unh

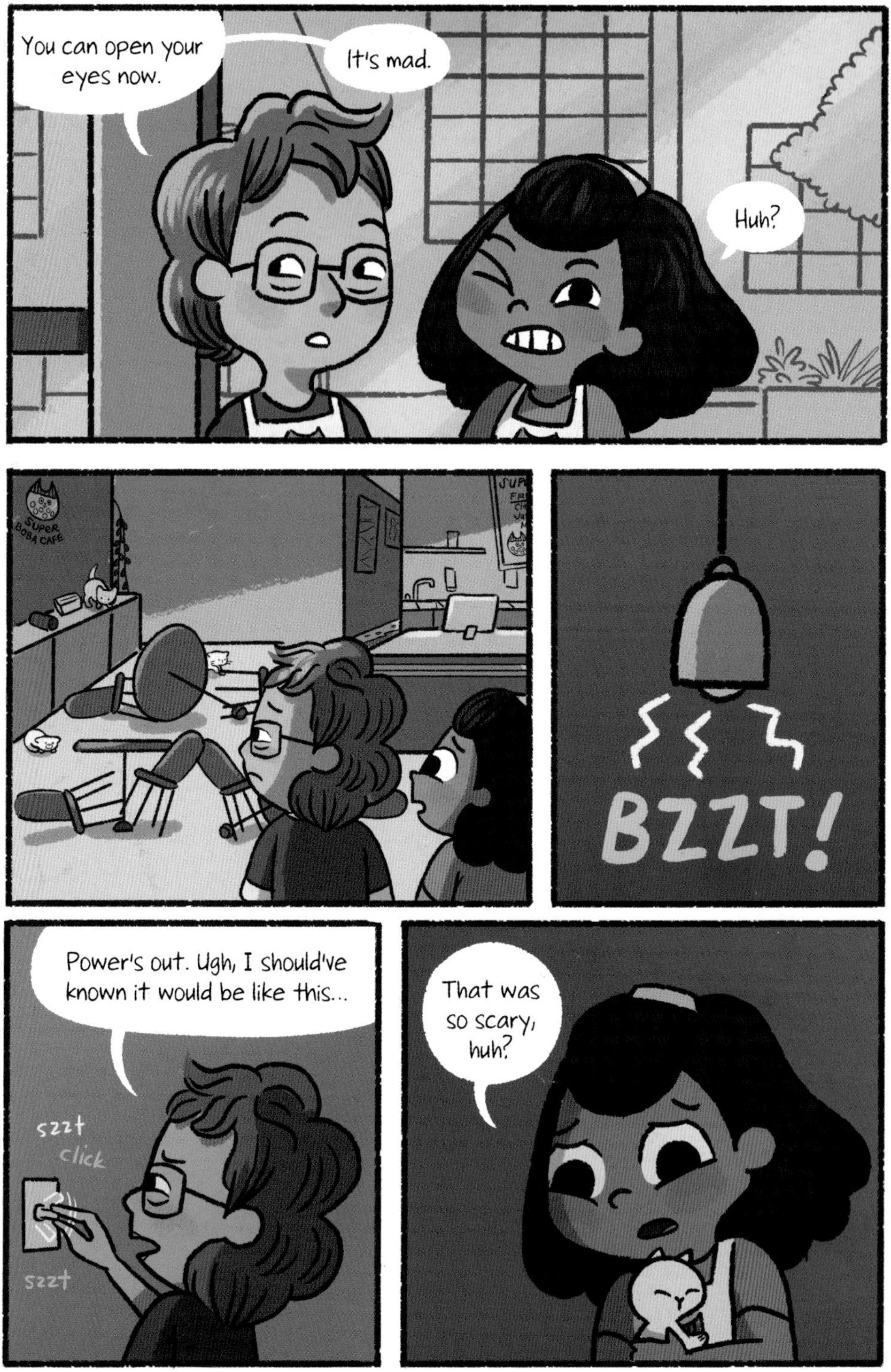
You can open your eyes now.
It's mad.
Huh?
SUPER BOBA CAFE
BZZT!
Power's out. Ugh, I should've known it would be like this...
szzt
click
szzt
That was so scary, huh?

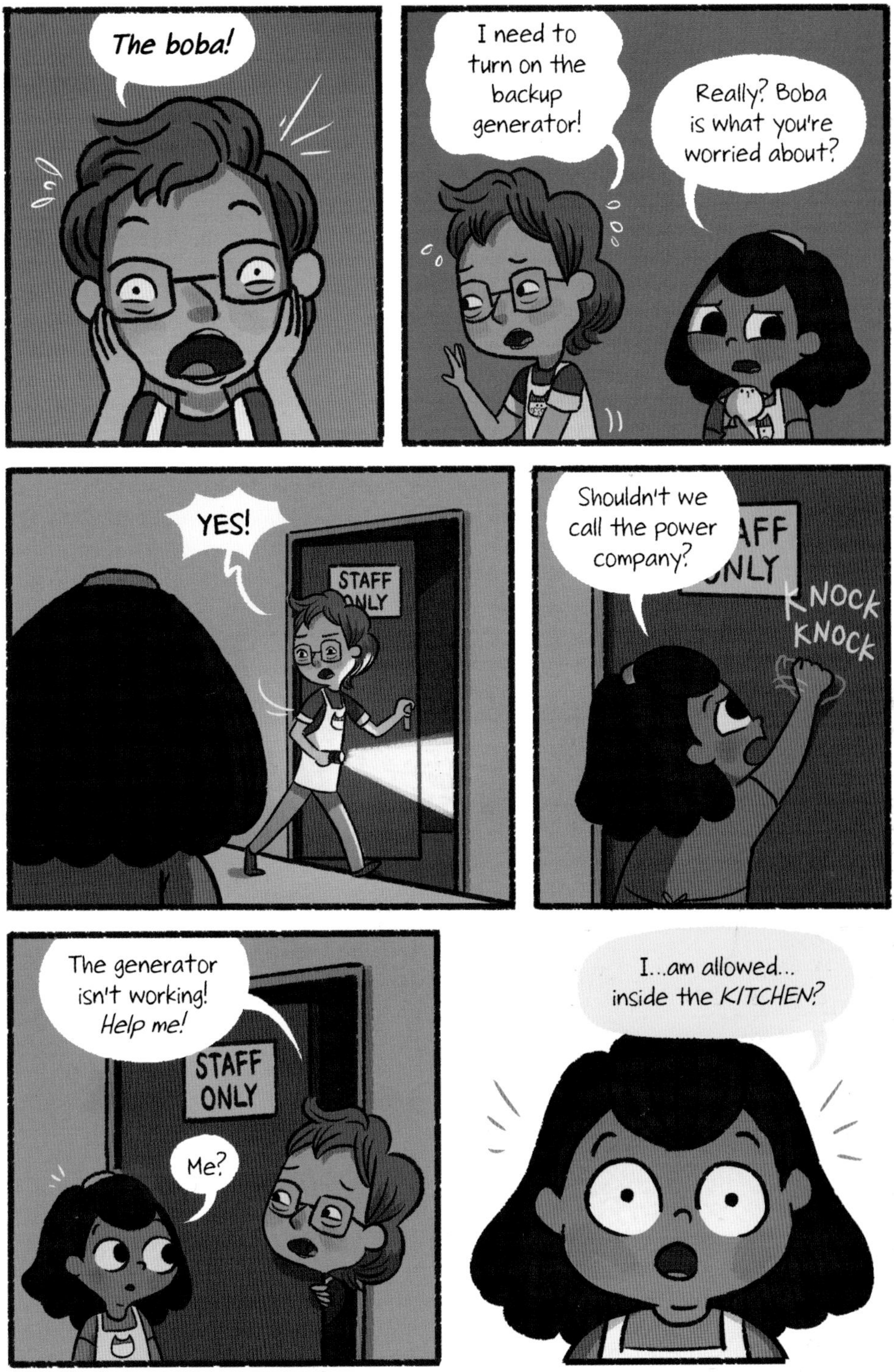
The boba!
I need to turn on the backup generator!
Really? Boba is what you're worried about?
YES!
STAFF ONLY
Shouldn't we call the power company?
KNOCK KNOCK
The generator isn't working! Help me!
STAFF ONLY
Me?
I...am allowed... inside the KITCHEN?

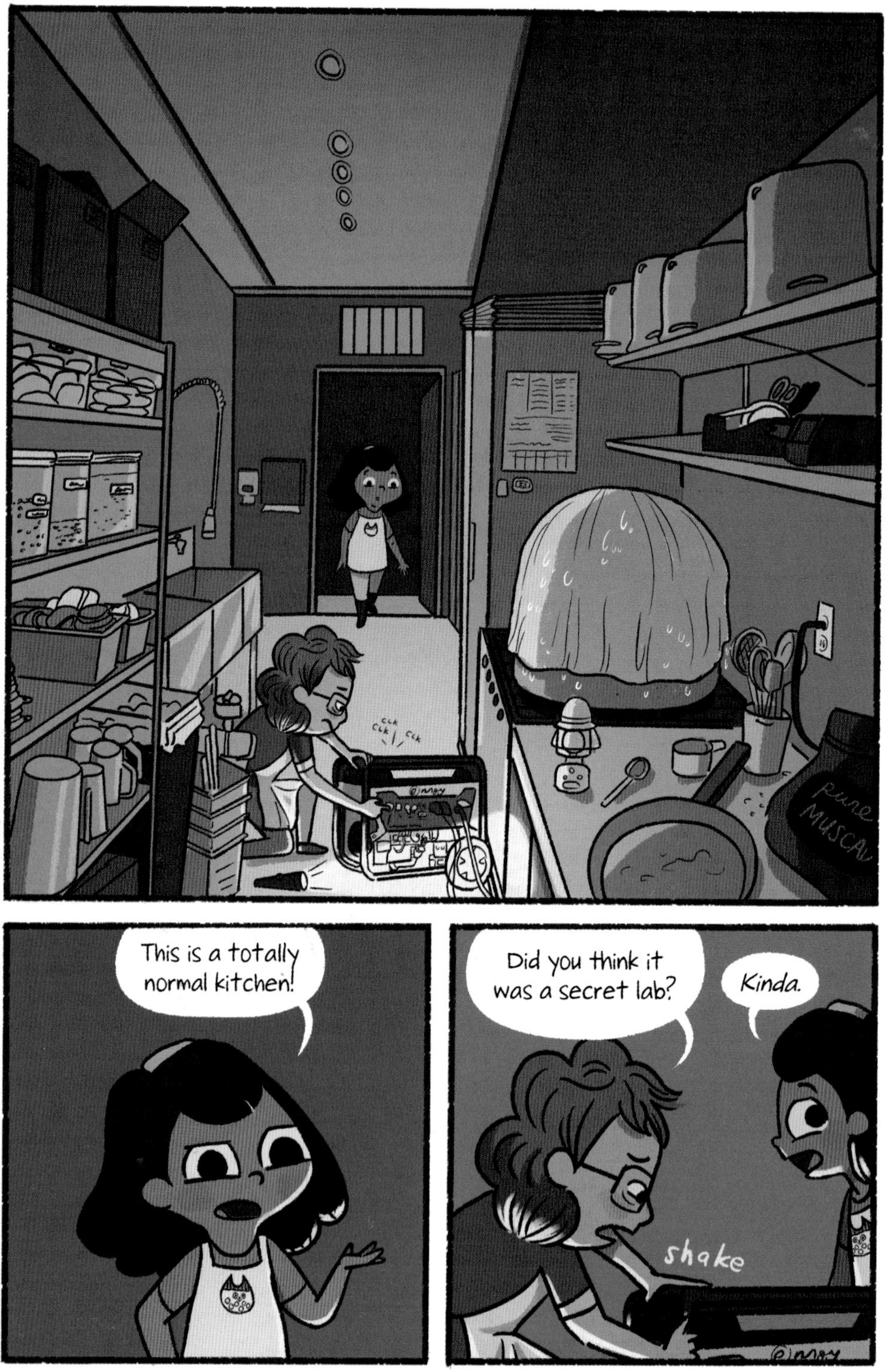
This is a totally normal kitchen!
Did you think it was a secret lab?
Kinda.
shake

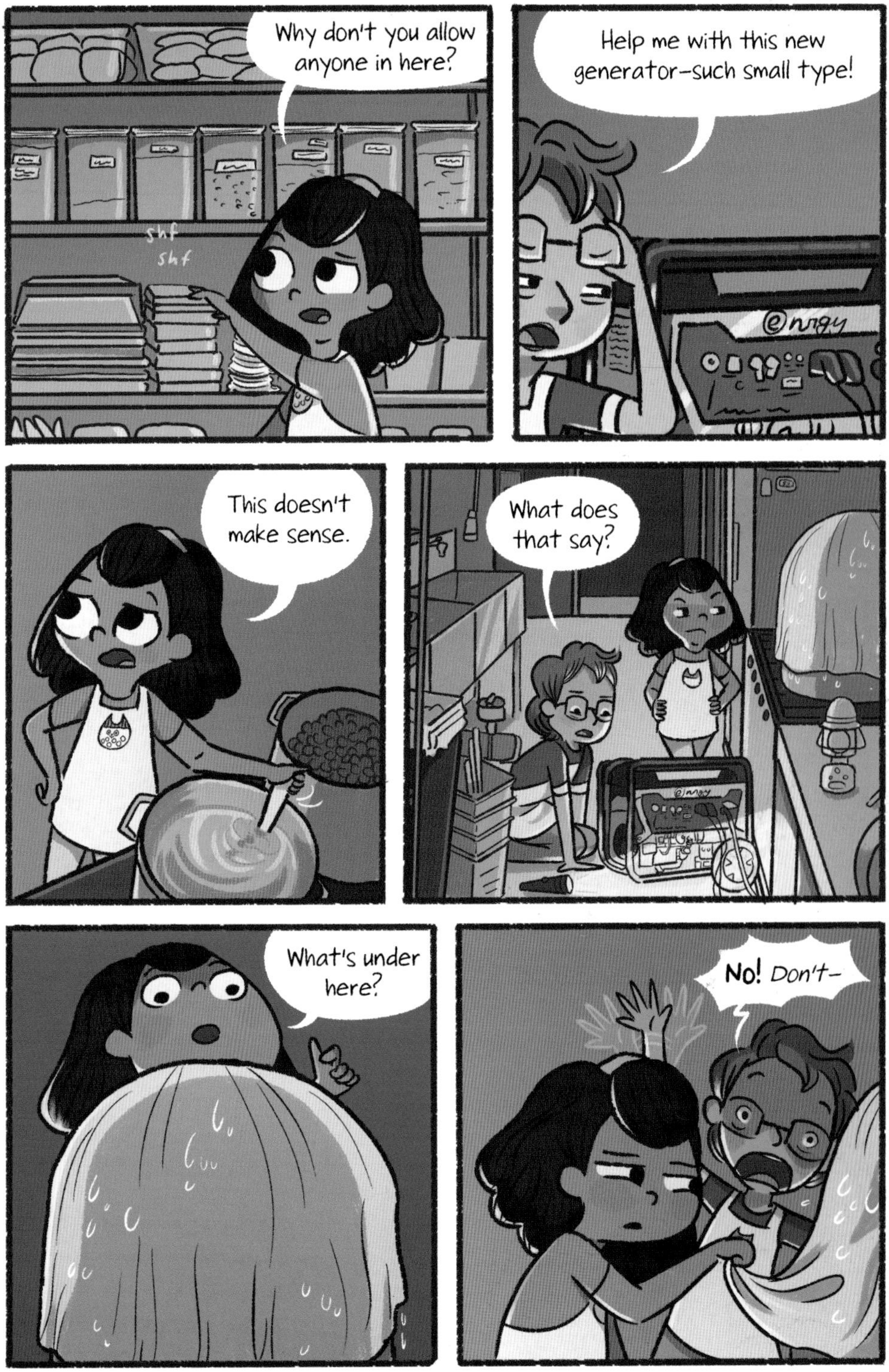
Why don't you allow anyone in here?
shf
shf
Help me with this new generator—such small type!
@nrgy
This doesn't make sense.
What does that say?
What's under here?
No! Don't—

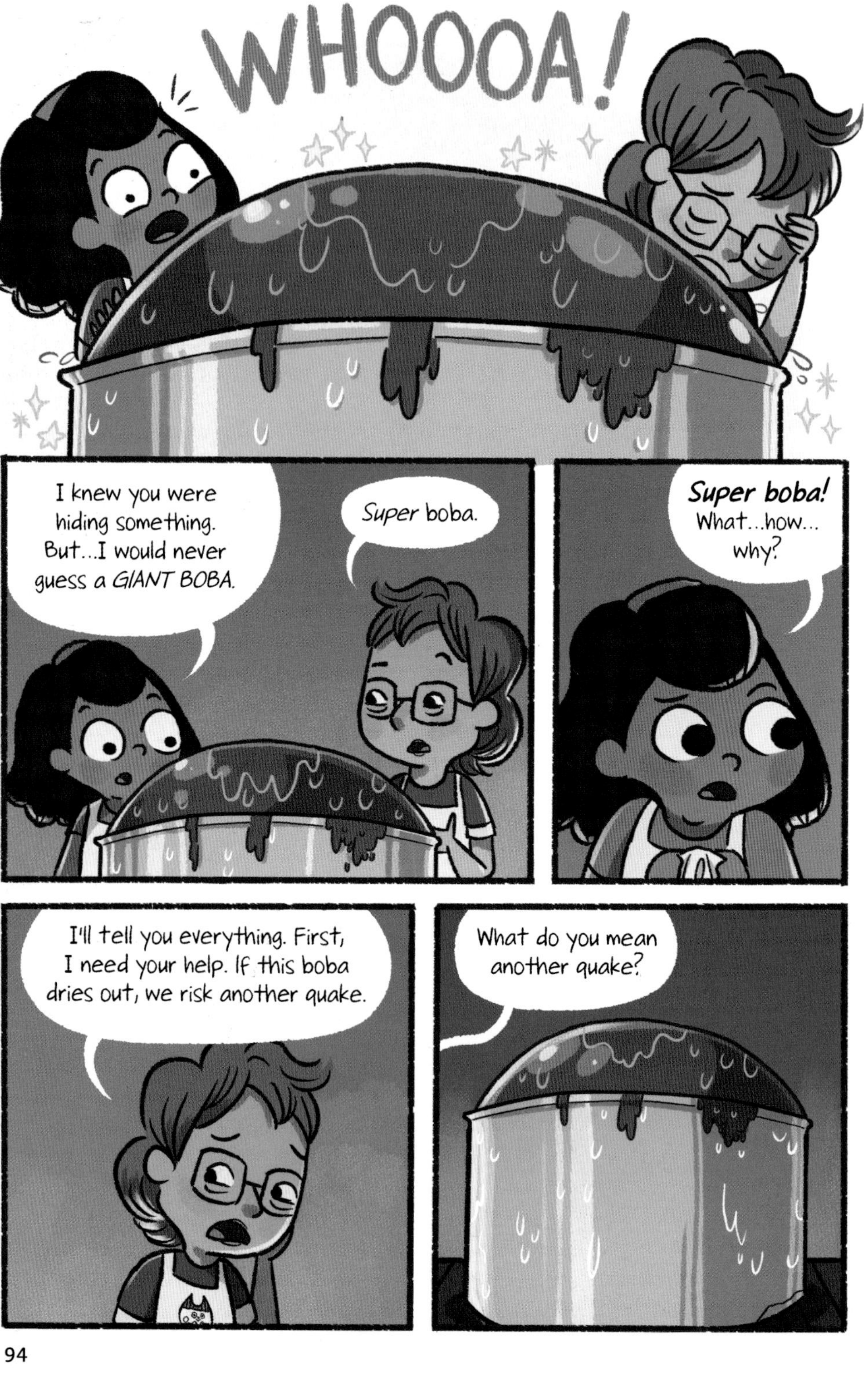
WHOOOA!
I knew you were hiding something. But...I would never guess a *GIANT BOBA*.
Super boba.
Super boba! What...how... why?
I'll tell you everything. First, I need your help. If this boba dries out, we risk another quake.
What do you mean another quake?

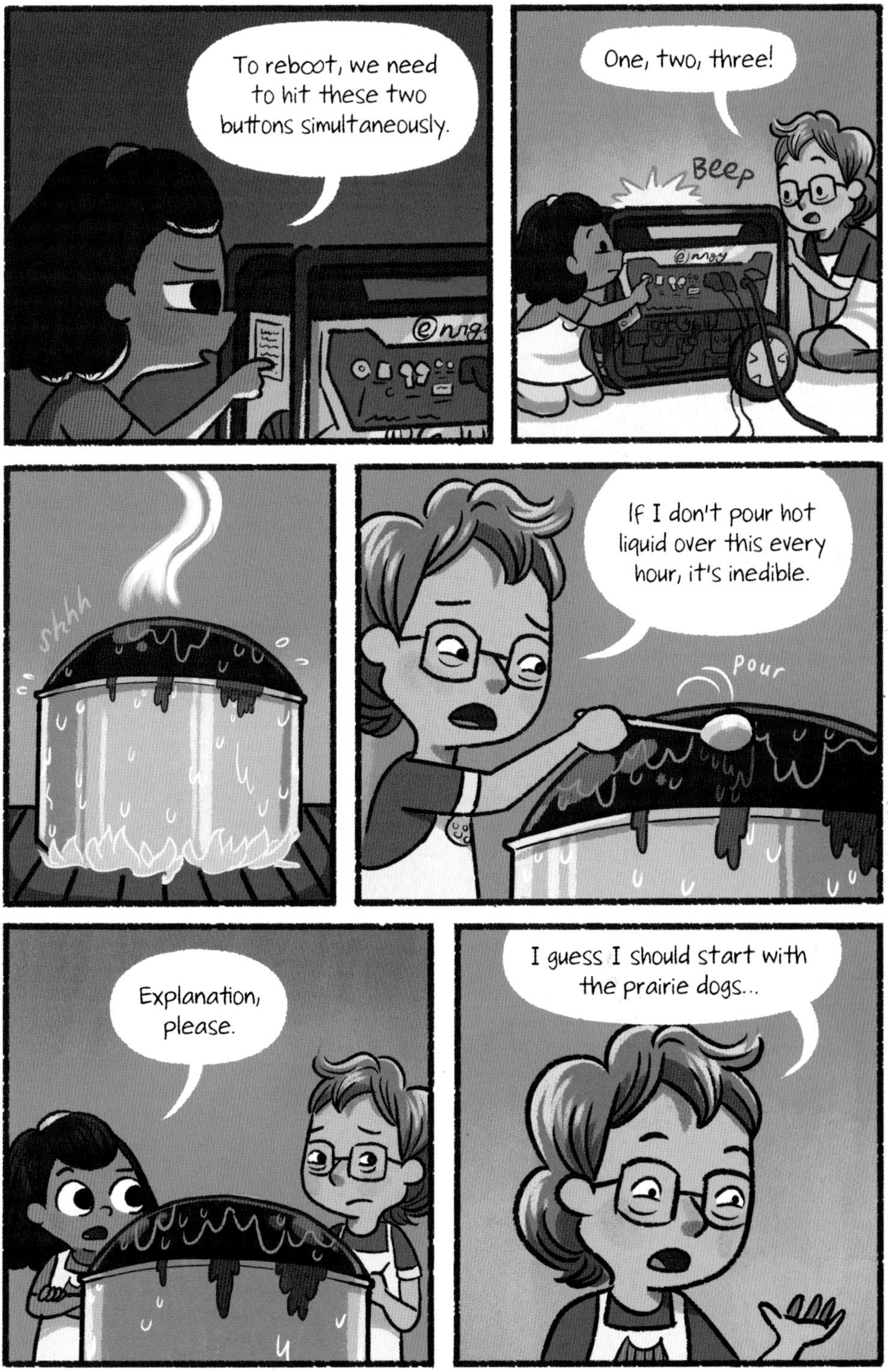
To reboot, we need to hit these two buttons simultaneously.
One, two, three!
Beep
shhh
If I don't pour hot liquid over this every hour, it's inedible.
pour
Explanation, please.
I guess I should start with the prairie dogs...

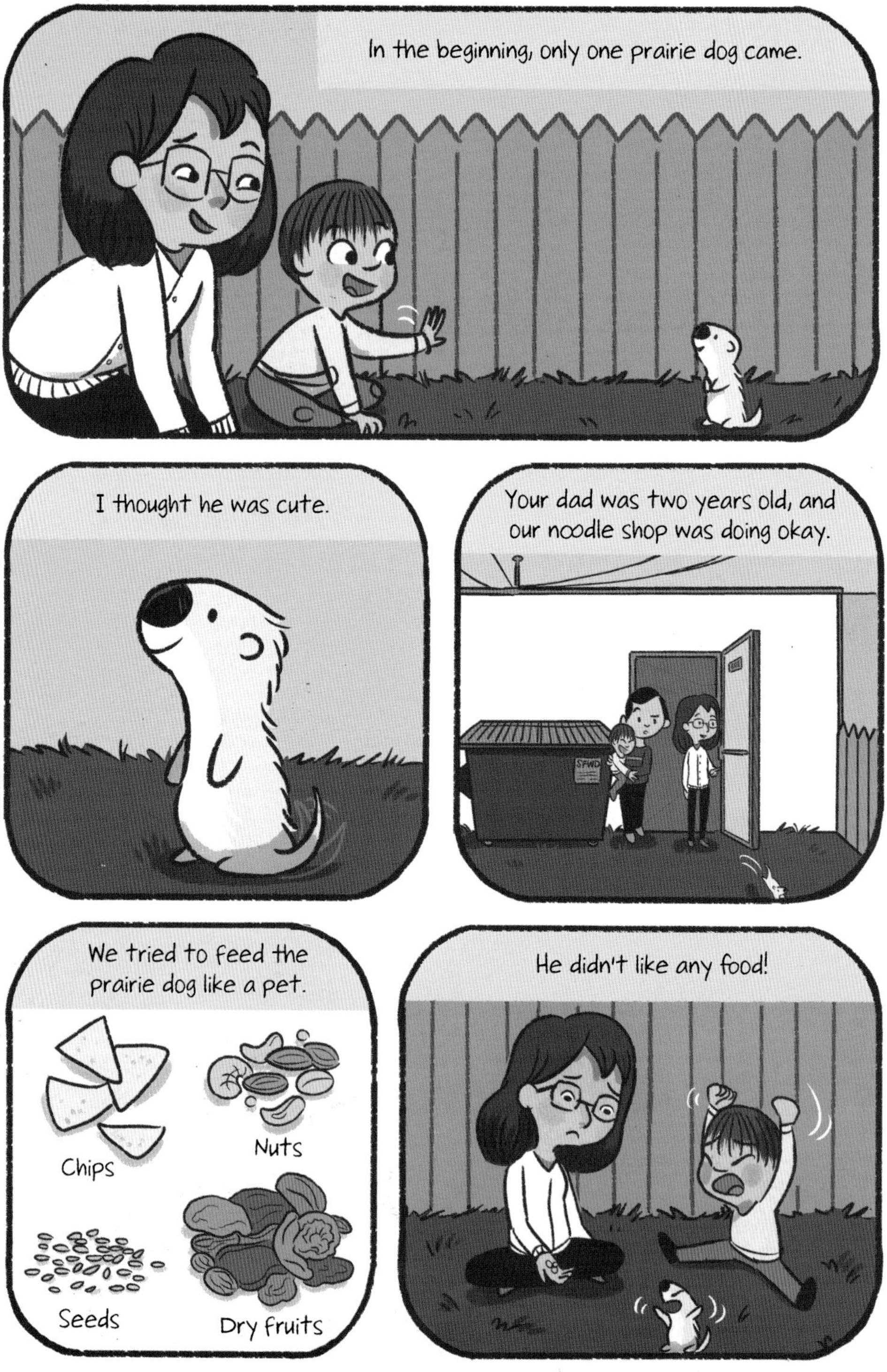
In the beginning, only one prairie dog came.
I thought he was cute.
Your dad was two years old, and our noodle shop was doing okay.
We tried to feed the prairie dog like a pet.
Chips
Nuts
Seeds
Dry fruits
He didn't like any food!

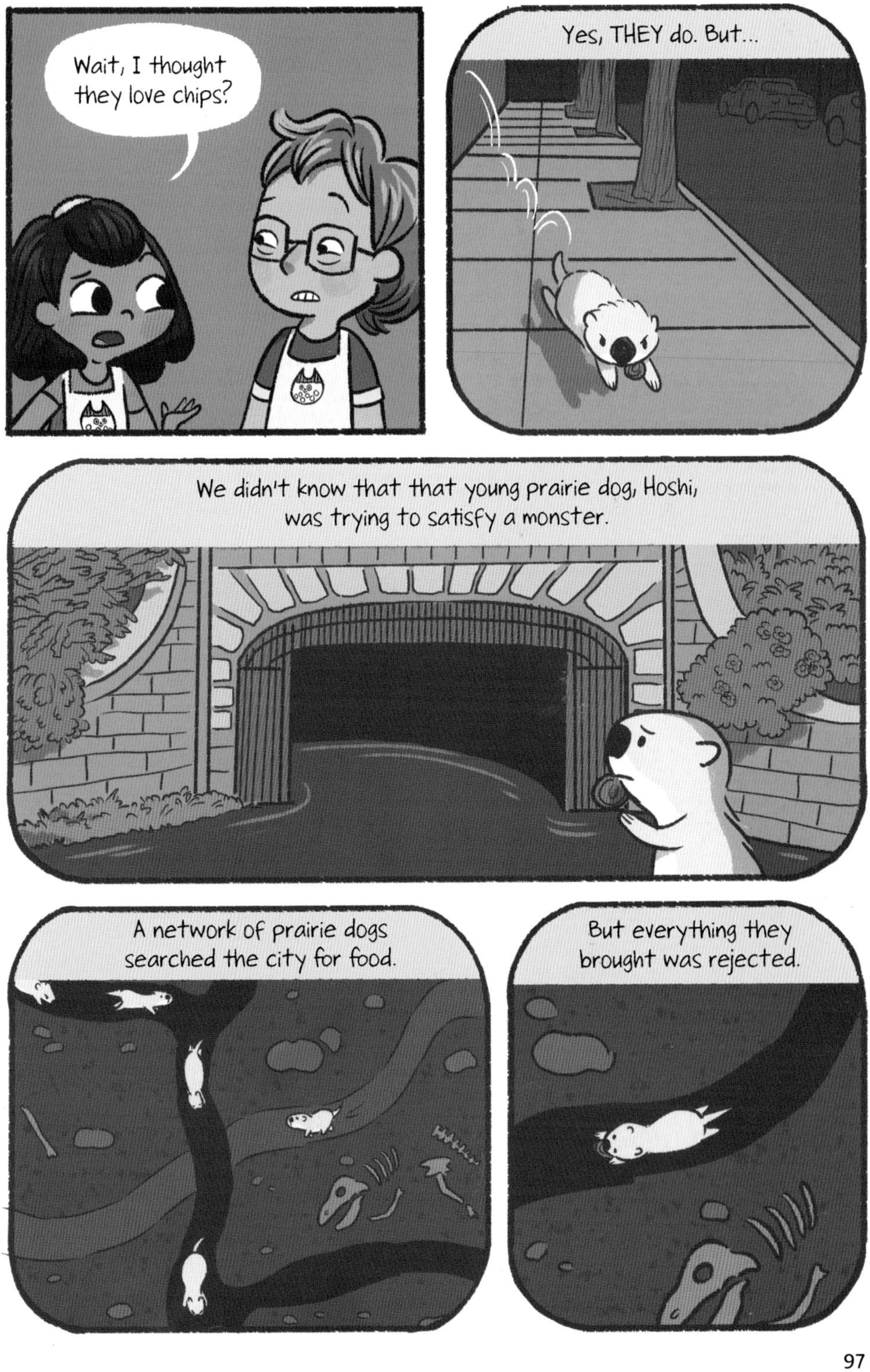
Wait, I thought they love chips?
Yes, THEY do. But...
We didn't know that that young prairie dog, Hoshi, was trying to satisfy a monster.
A network of prairie dogs searched the city for food.
But everything they brought was rejected.

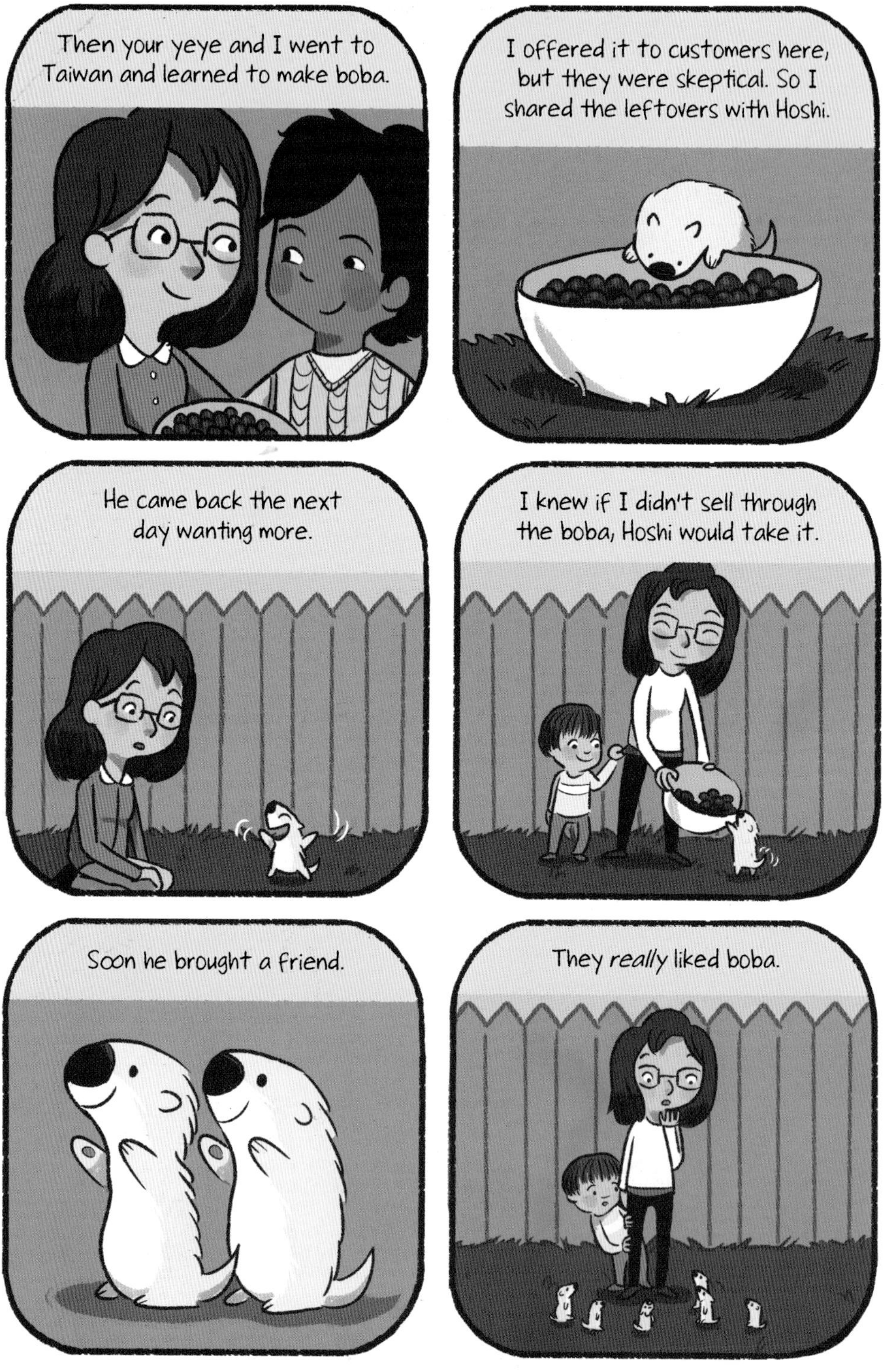
Then your yeye and I went to Taiwan and learned to make boba.
I offered it to customers here, but they were skeptical. So I shared the leftovers with Hoshi.
He came back the next day wanting more.
I knew if I didn't sell through the boba, Hoshi would take it.
Soon he brought a friend.
They *really* liked boba.

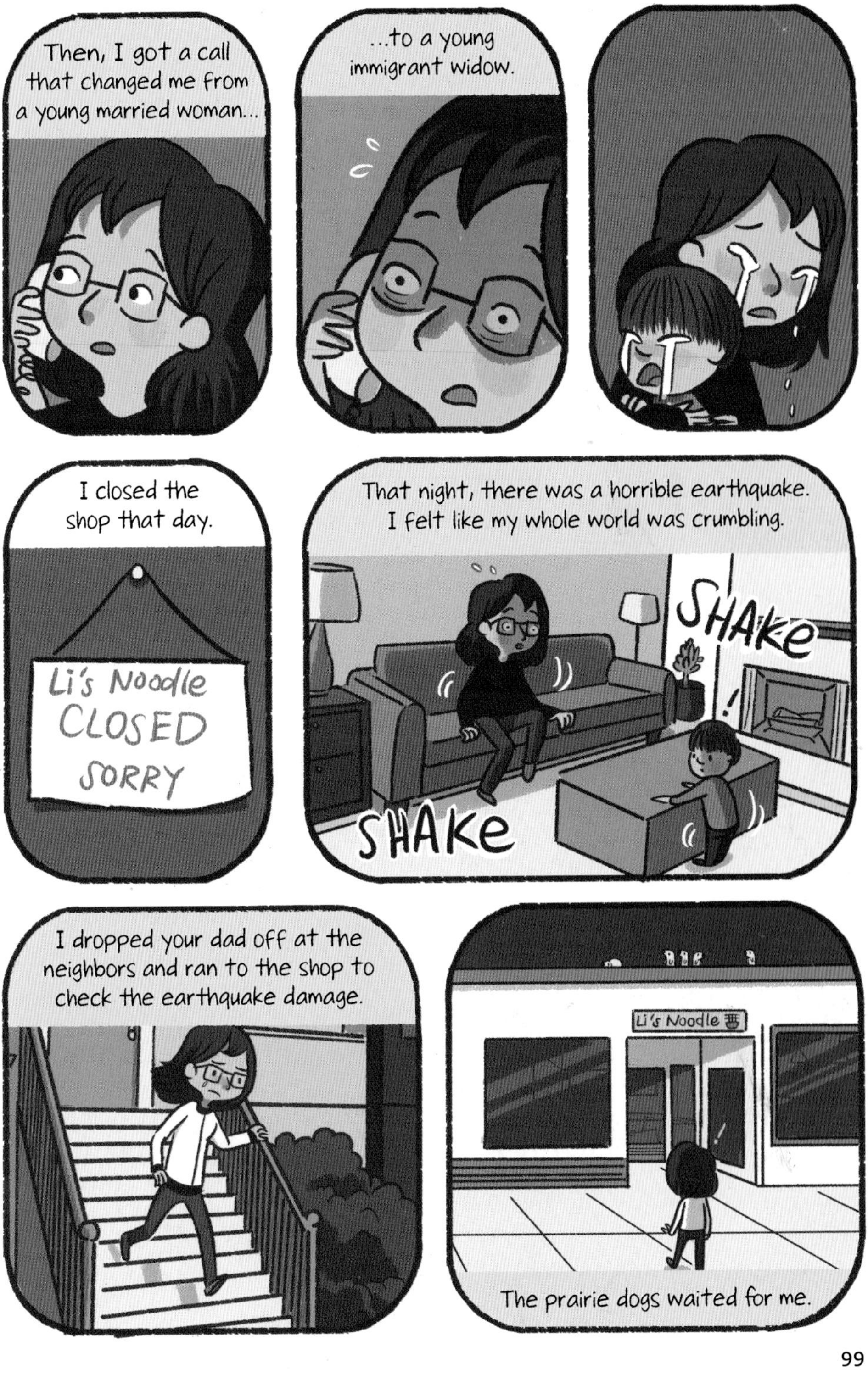
Then, I got a call that changed me from a young married woman...
...to a young immigrant widow.
I closed the shop that day.
Li's Noodle
CLOSED
SORRY
That night, there was a horrible earthquake. I felt like my whole world was crumbling.
SHAKE
SHAKE
I dropped your dad off at the neighbors and ran to the shop to check the earthquake damage.
Li's Noodle
The prairie dogs waited for me.

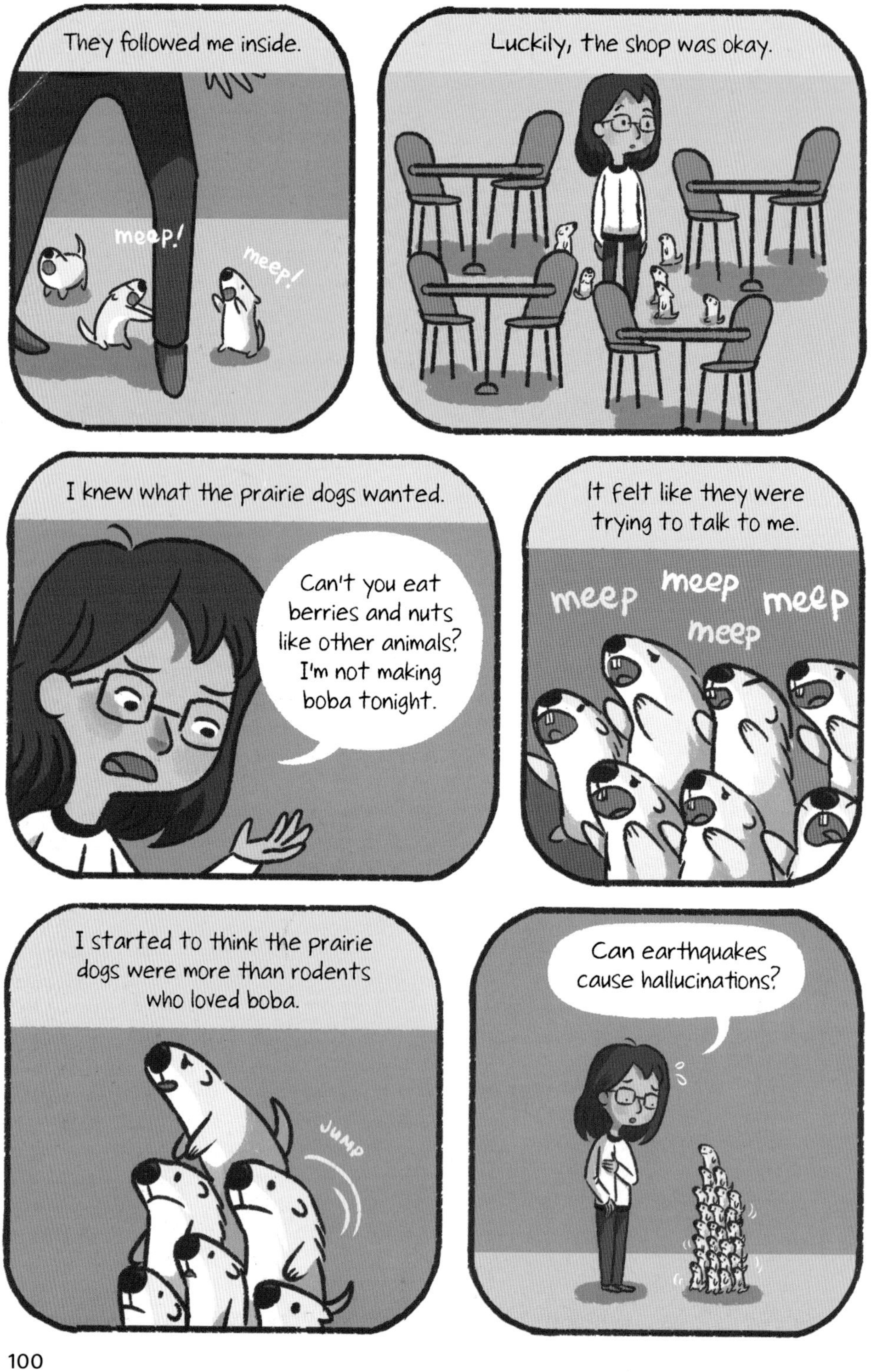
They followed me inside.
meep!
meep!
Luckily, the shop was okay.
I knew what the prairie dogs wanted.
Can't you eat berries and nuts like other animals? I'm not making boba tonight.
It felt like they were trying to talk to me.
meep
meep
meep
meep
I started to think the prairie dogs were more than rodents who loved boba.
JUMP
Can earthquakes cause hallucinations?

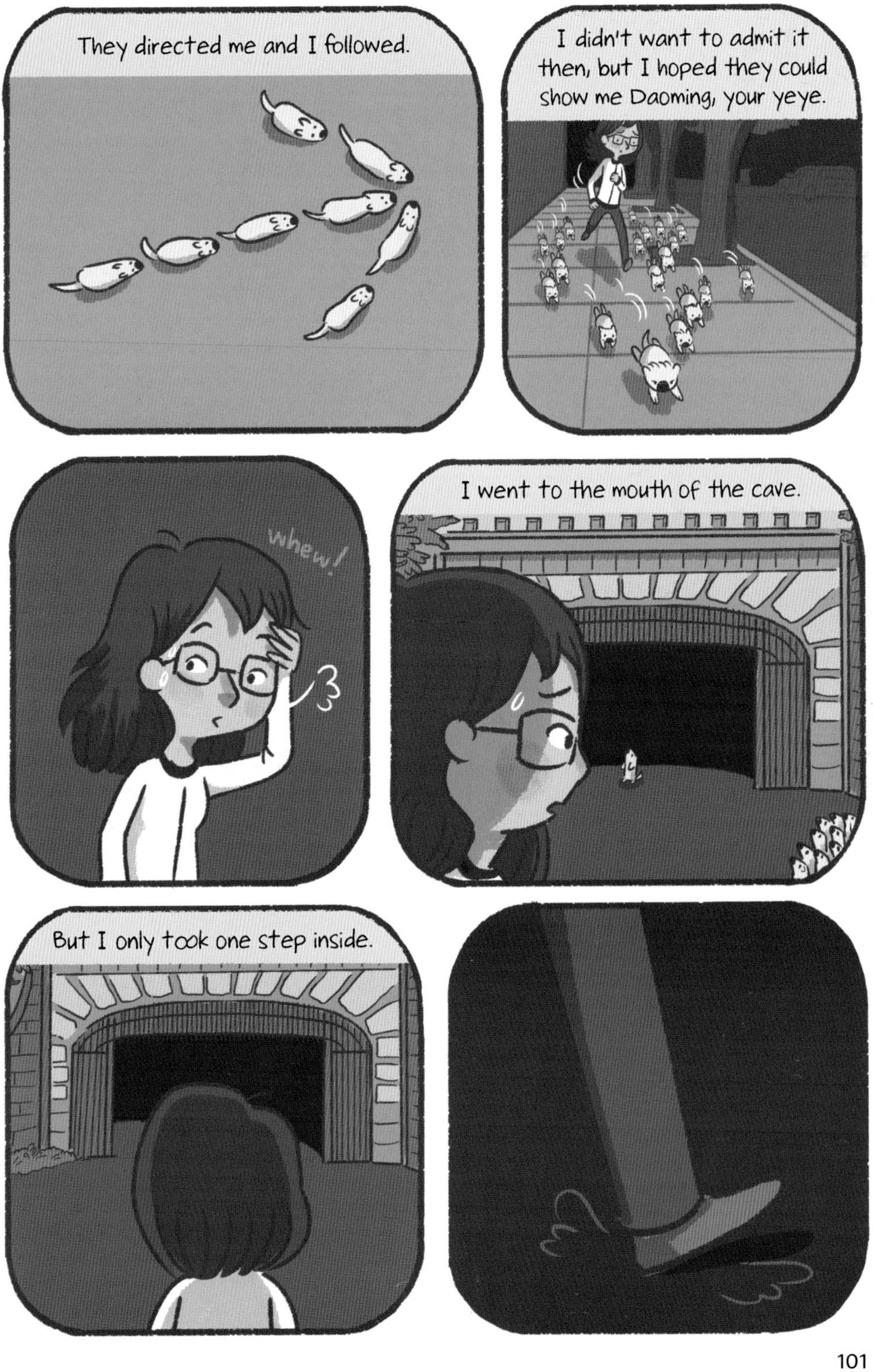
They directed me and I followed.
I didn't want to admit it then, but I hoped they could show me Daoming, your yeye.
whew!
I went to the mouth of the cave.
But I only took one step inside.

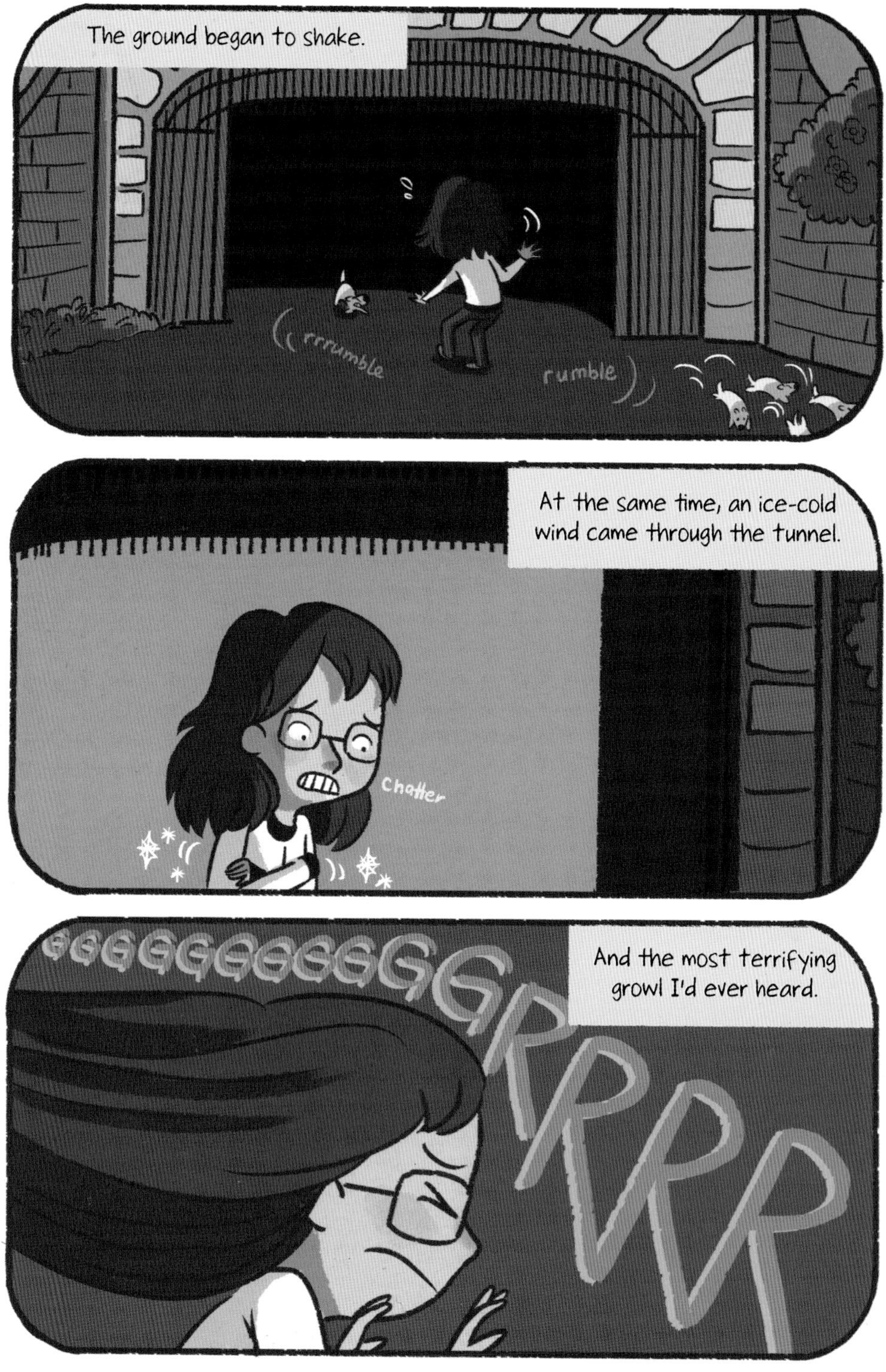
The ground began to shake.
rrrumble
rumble
At the same time, an ice-cold wind came through the tunnel.
chatter
And the most terrifying growl I'd ever heard.
GGGGGGGGGGGGRRRRR

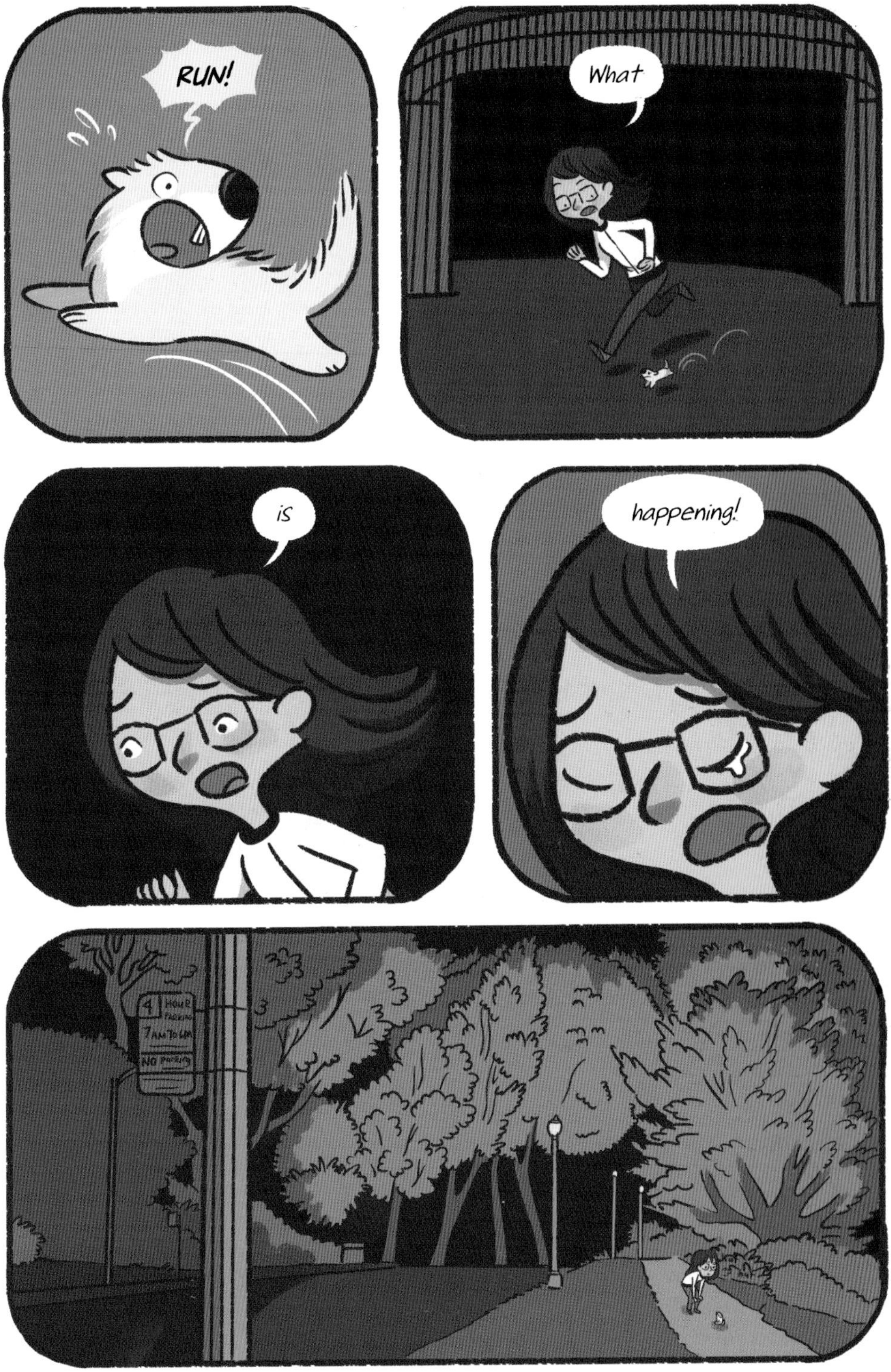
RUN!
What
is
happening!

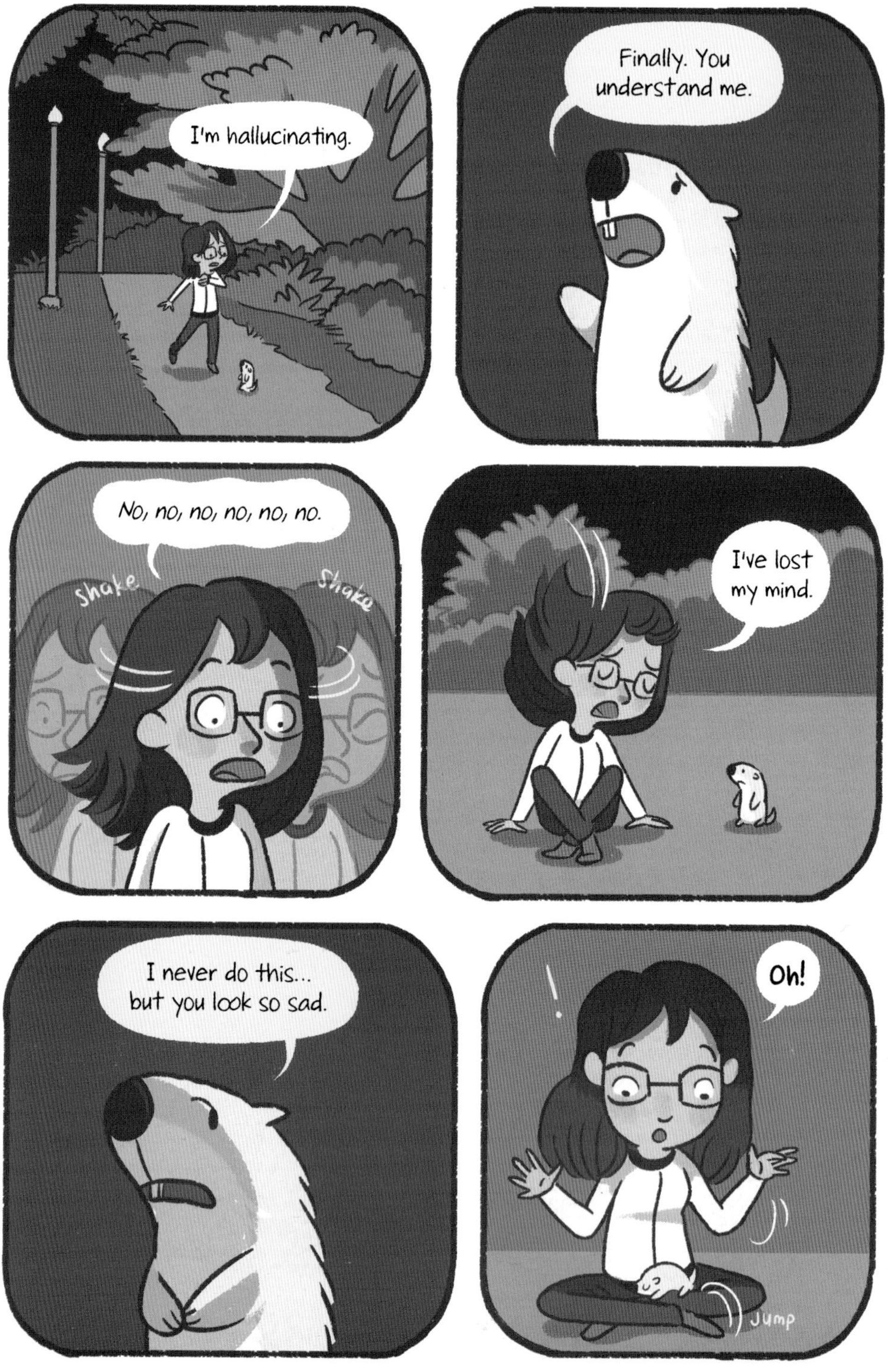
I'm hallucinating.
Finally. You understand me.
No, no, no, no, no, no.
shake
shake
I've lost my mind.
I never do this... but you look so sad.
!
Oh!
JUMP

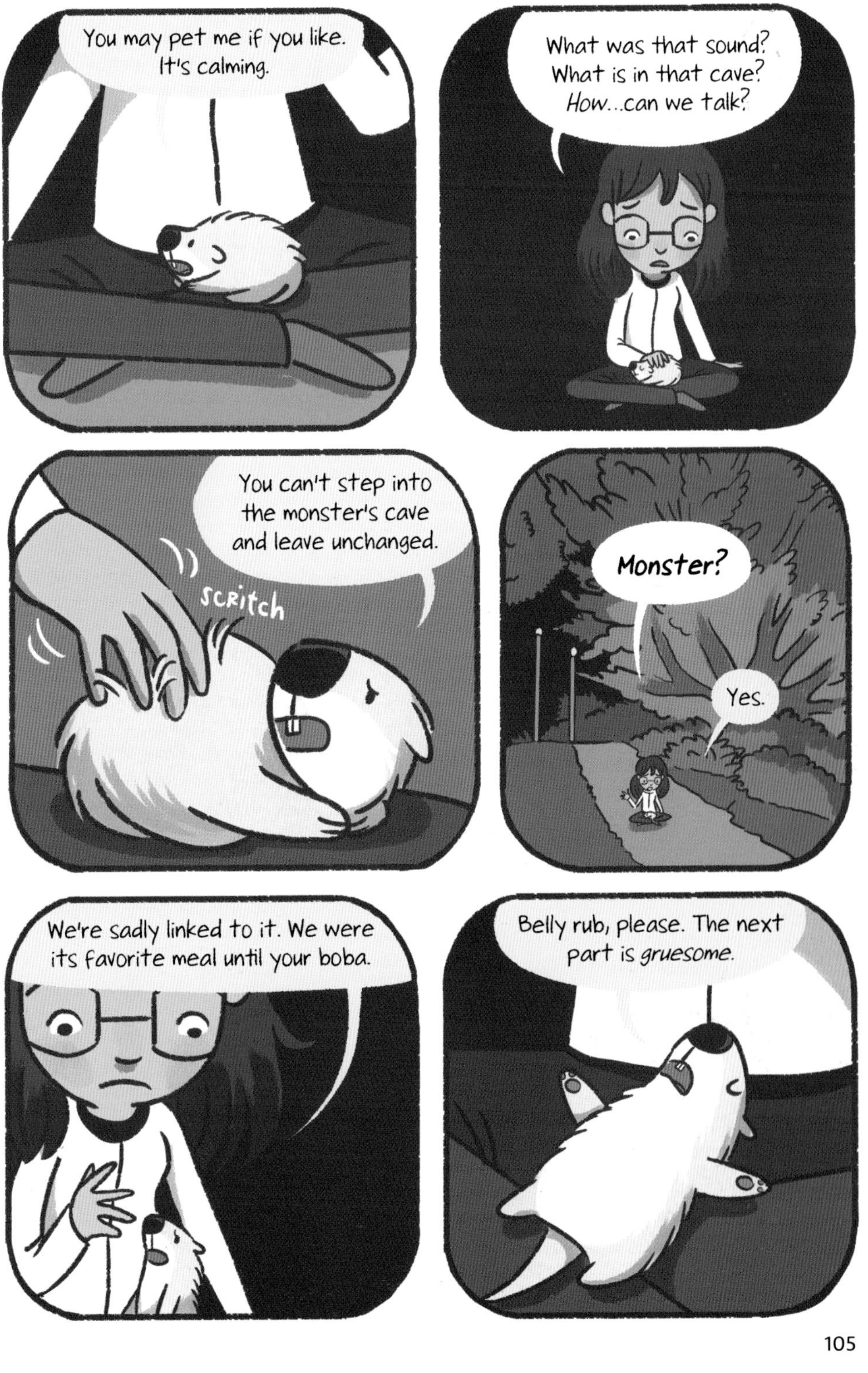
You may pet me if you like. It's calming.
What was that sound? What is in that cave? *How*...can we talk?
You can't step into the monster's cave and leave unchanged.
SCRITCH
Monster?
Yes.
We're sadly linked to it. We were its favorite meal until your boba.
Belly rub, please. The next part is *gruesome*.

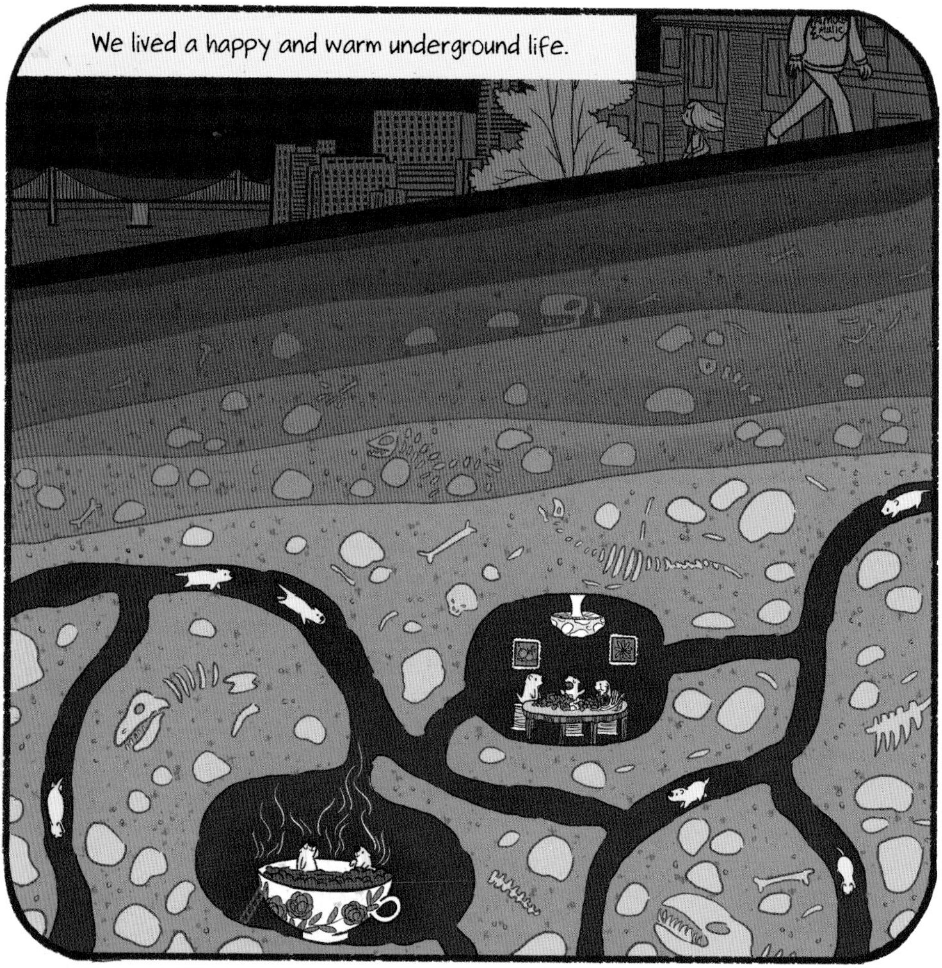
We lived a happy and warm underground life.

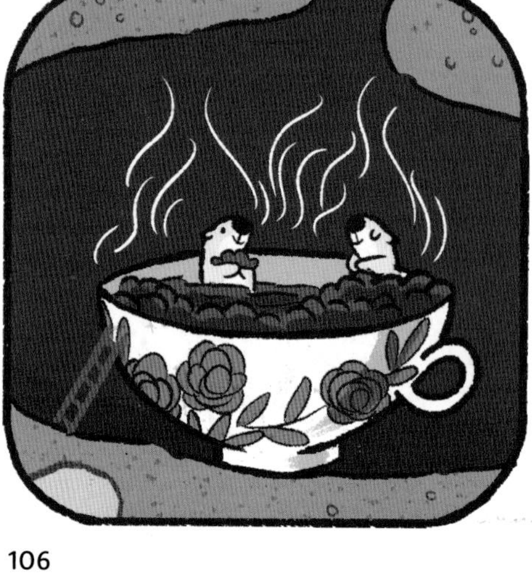

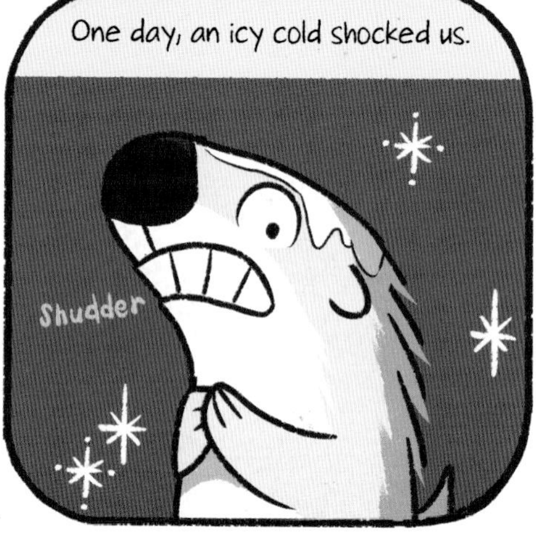
One day, an icy cold shocked us.
Shudder

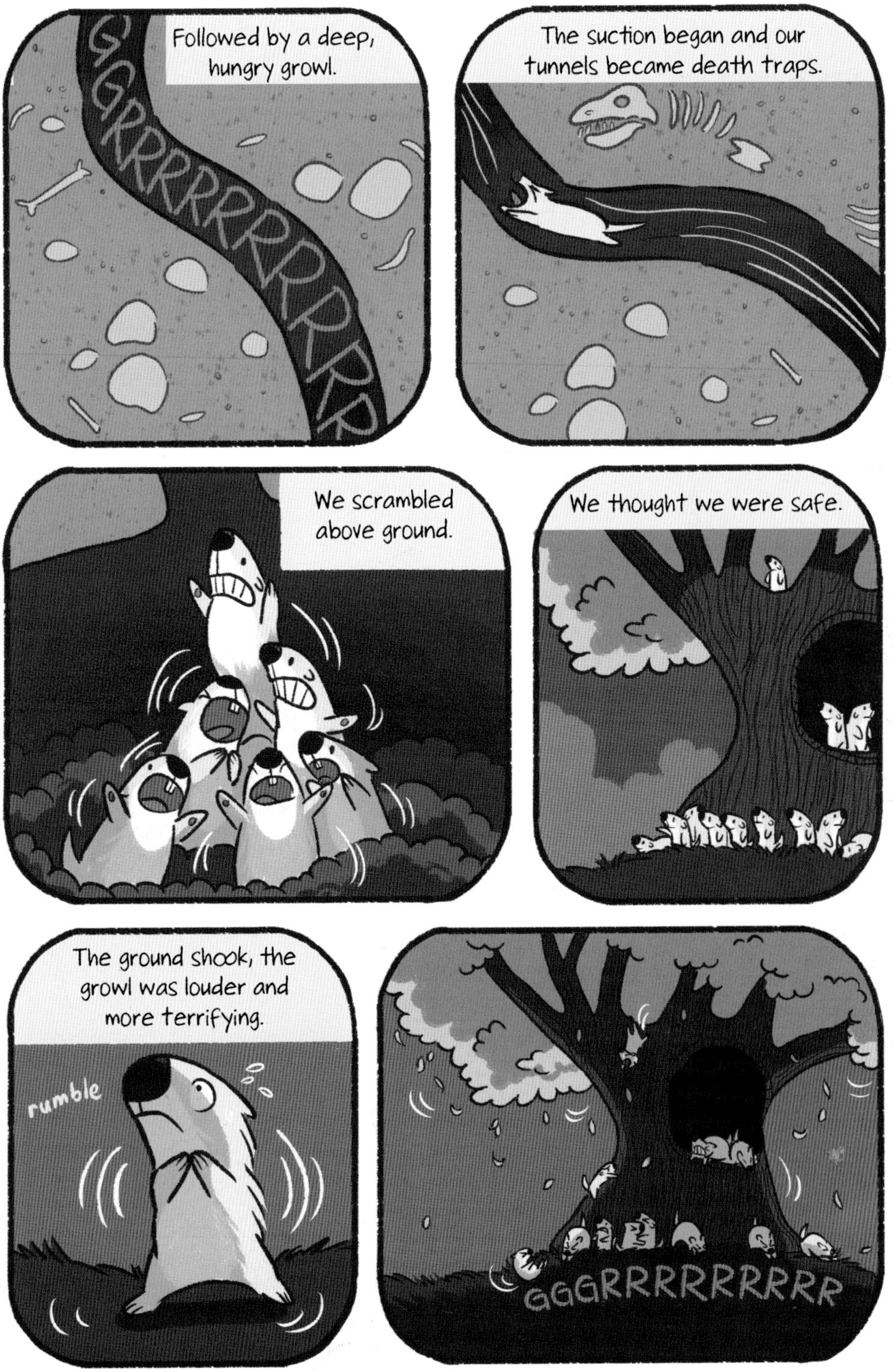
Followed by a deep, hungry growl.
GGRRRRRRRRRRR
The suction began and our tunnels became death traps.
We scrambled above ground.
We thought we were safe.
The ground shook, the growl was louder and more terrifying.
rumble
GGGRRRRRRRRRR

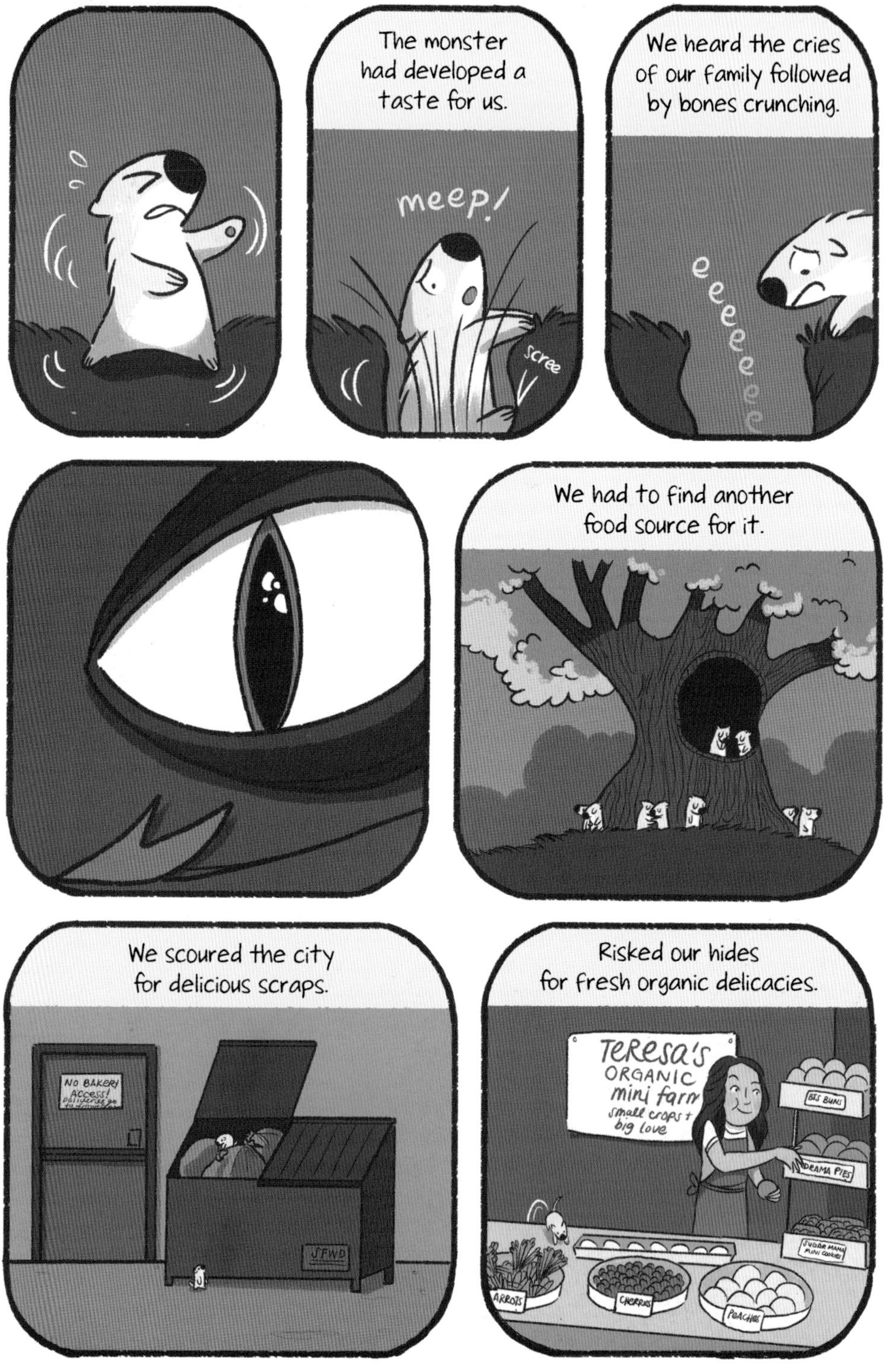
The monster had developed a taste for us.
meep!
scree
We heard the cries of our family followed by bones crunching.
eeeeeee
We had to find another food source for it.
We scoured the city for delicious scraps.
NO BAKERY Access!
SFWD
Risked our hides for fresh organic delicacies.
Teresa's ORGANIC mini farm small crops + big love
BIG BUNS
DRAMA PIES
SUGAR MAMA MINI COOKIES
ARROTS
CHERRIES
PEACHES

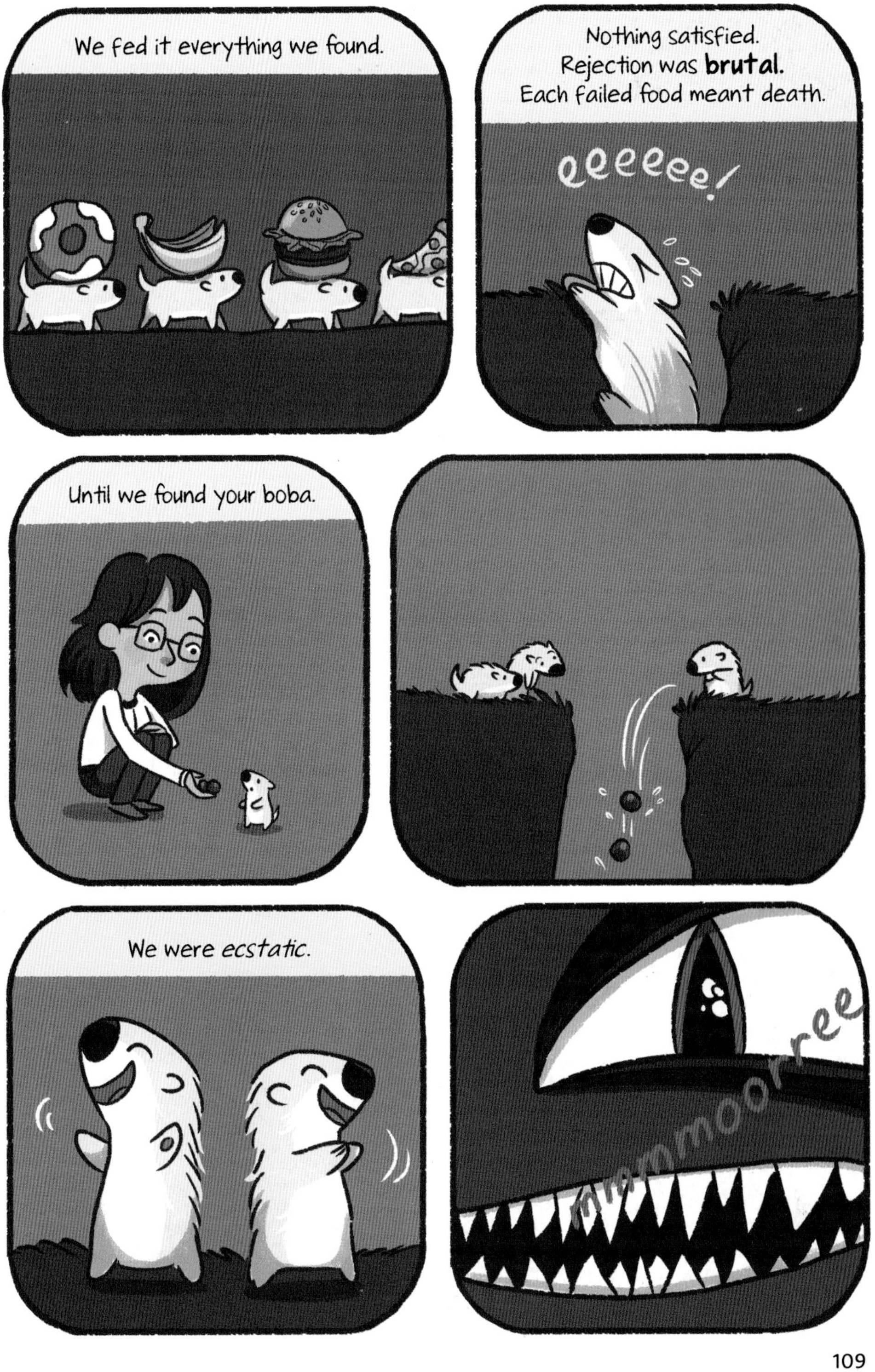
We fed it everything we found.
Nothing satisfied.
Rejection was **brutal.**
Each failed food meant death.
eeeeee!
Until we found your boba.
We were *ecstatic.*
mmmoorree

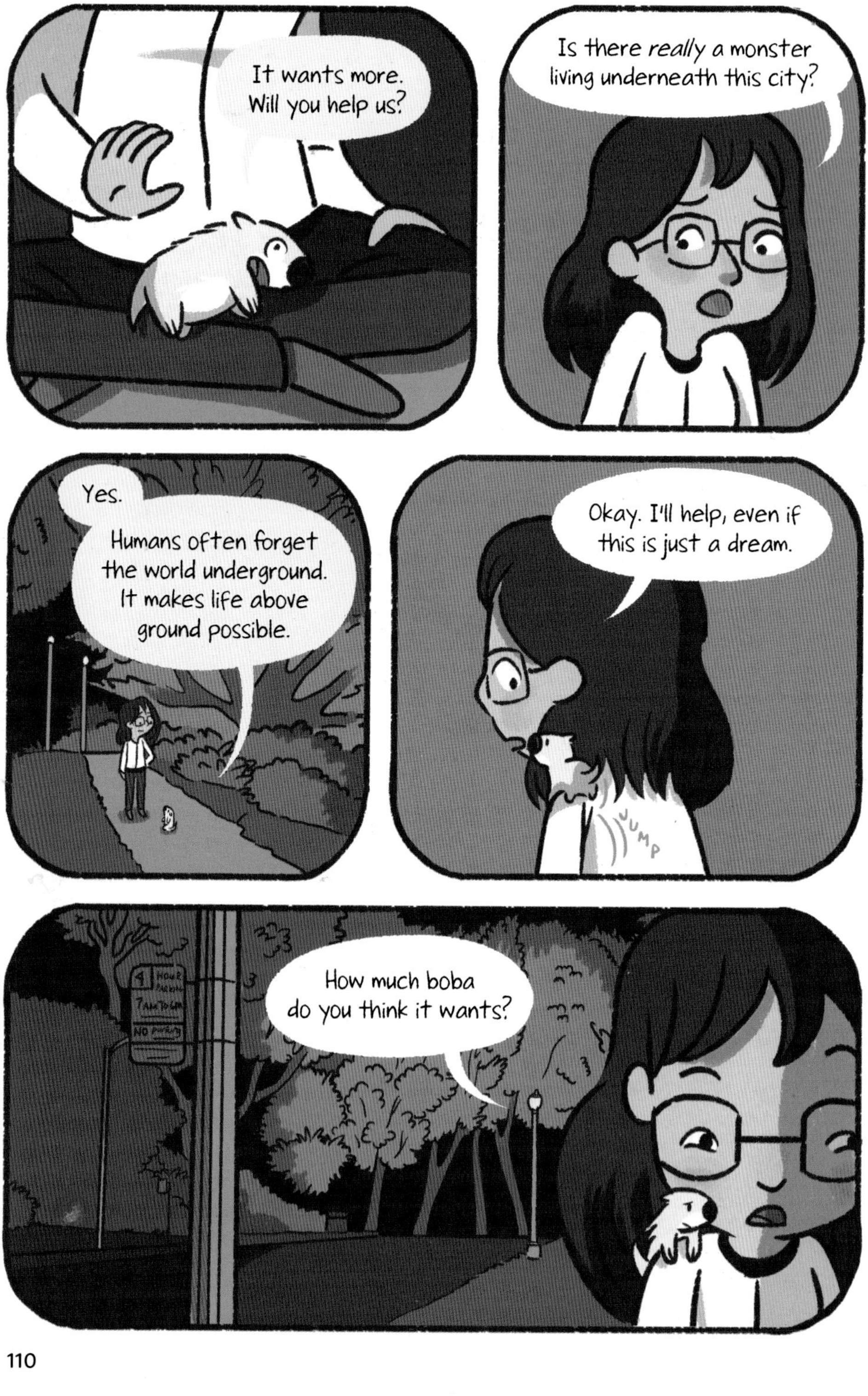
It wants more. Will you help us?
Is there *really* a monster living underneath this city?
Yes.
Humans often forget the world underground. It makes life above ground possible.
Okay. I'll help, even if this is just a dream.
JUMP
How much boba do you think it wants?

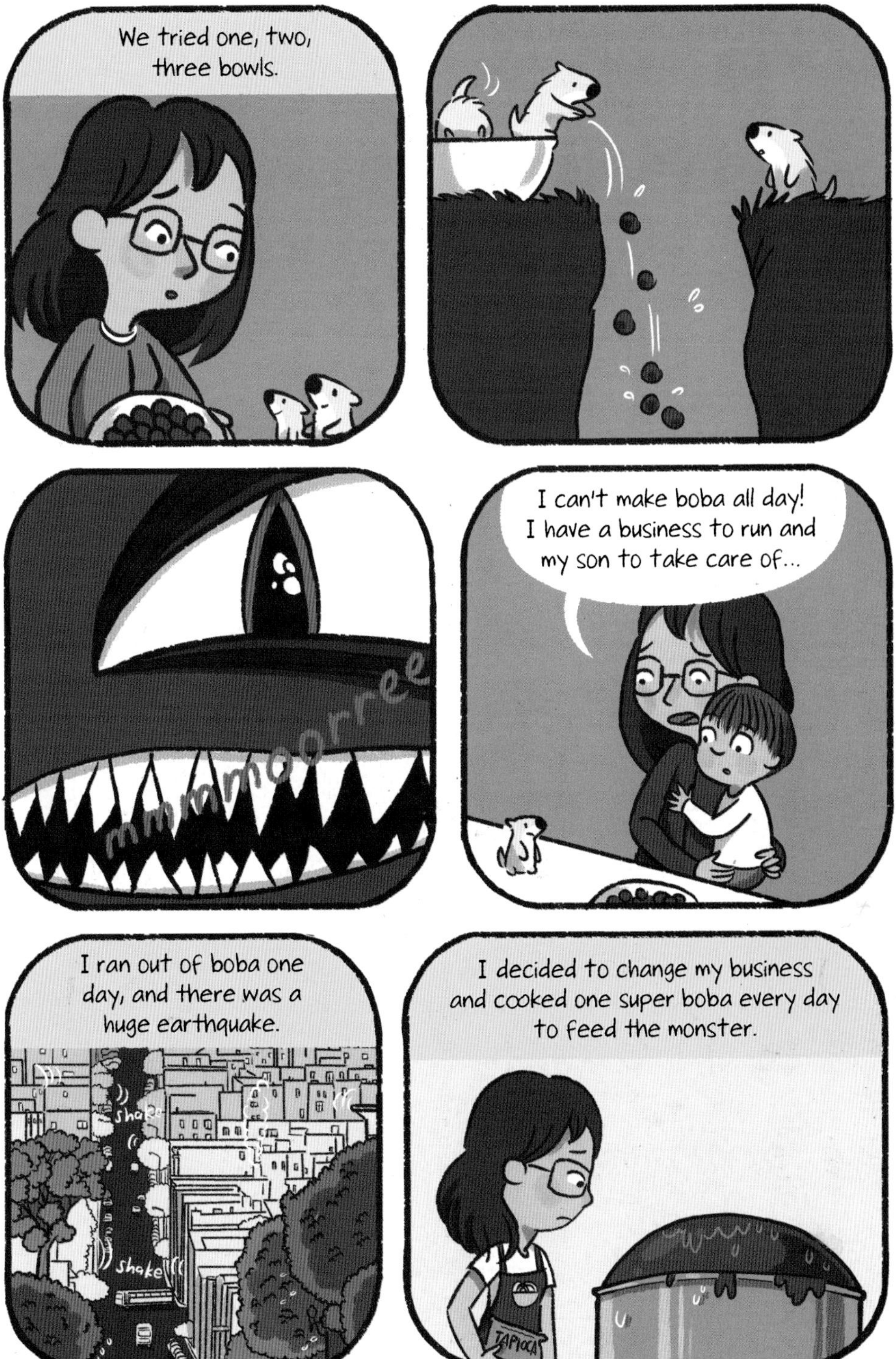
We tried one, two, three bowls.
mmmoorree
I can't make boba all day! I have a business to run and my son to take care of...
I ran out of boba one day, and there was a huge earthquake.
shake
shake
I decided to change my business and cooked one super boba every day to feed the monster.
TAPIOCA

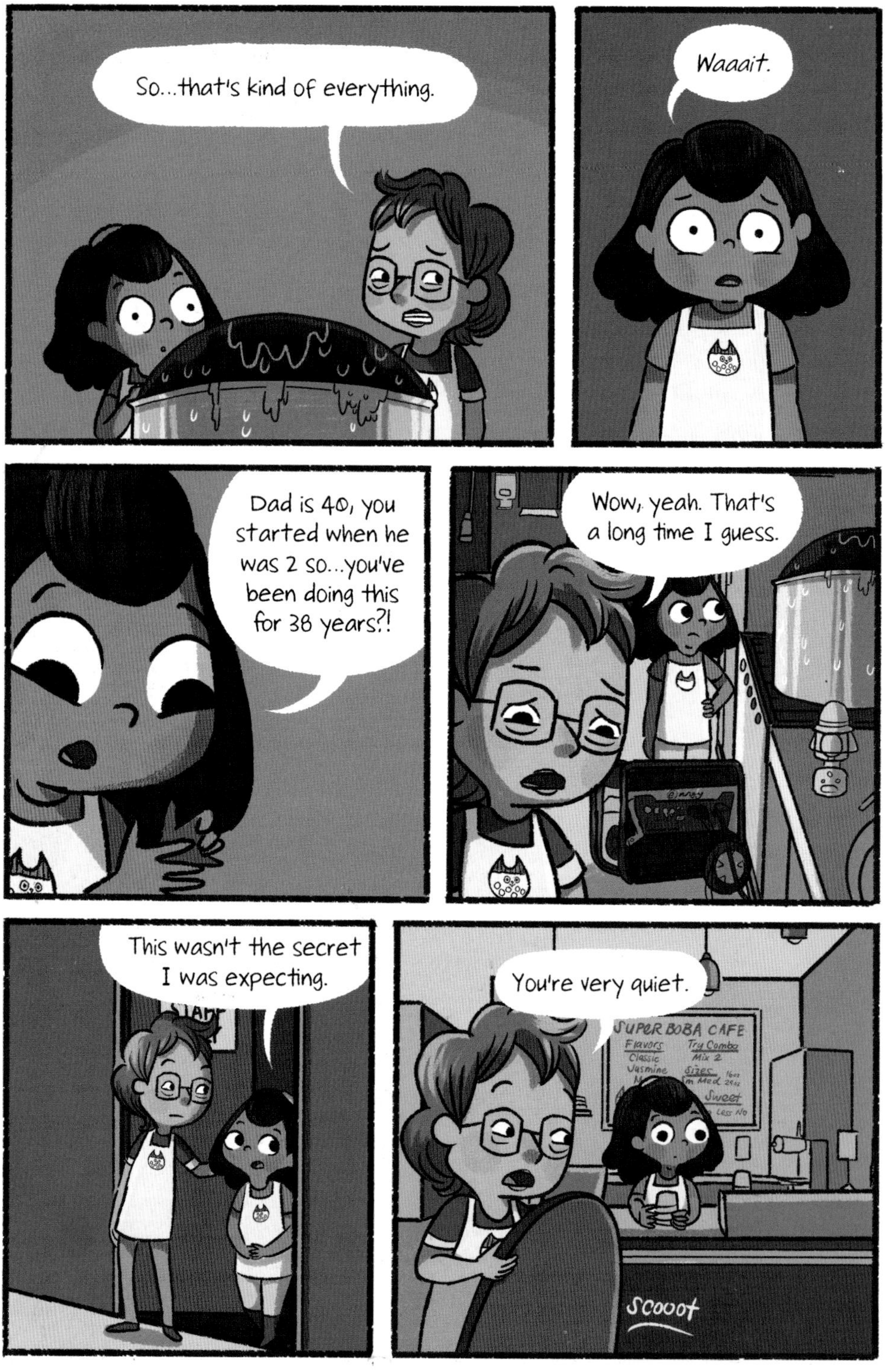
So...that's kind of everything.
Waaait.
Dad is 40, you started when he was 2 so...you've been doing this for 38 years?!
Wow, yeah. That's a long time I guess.
This wasn't the secret I was expecting.
You're very quiet.
SUPER BOBA CAFE
Flavors
Classic
Try Combo
Mix 2
Sizes
Sweet
scooot

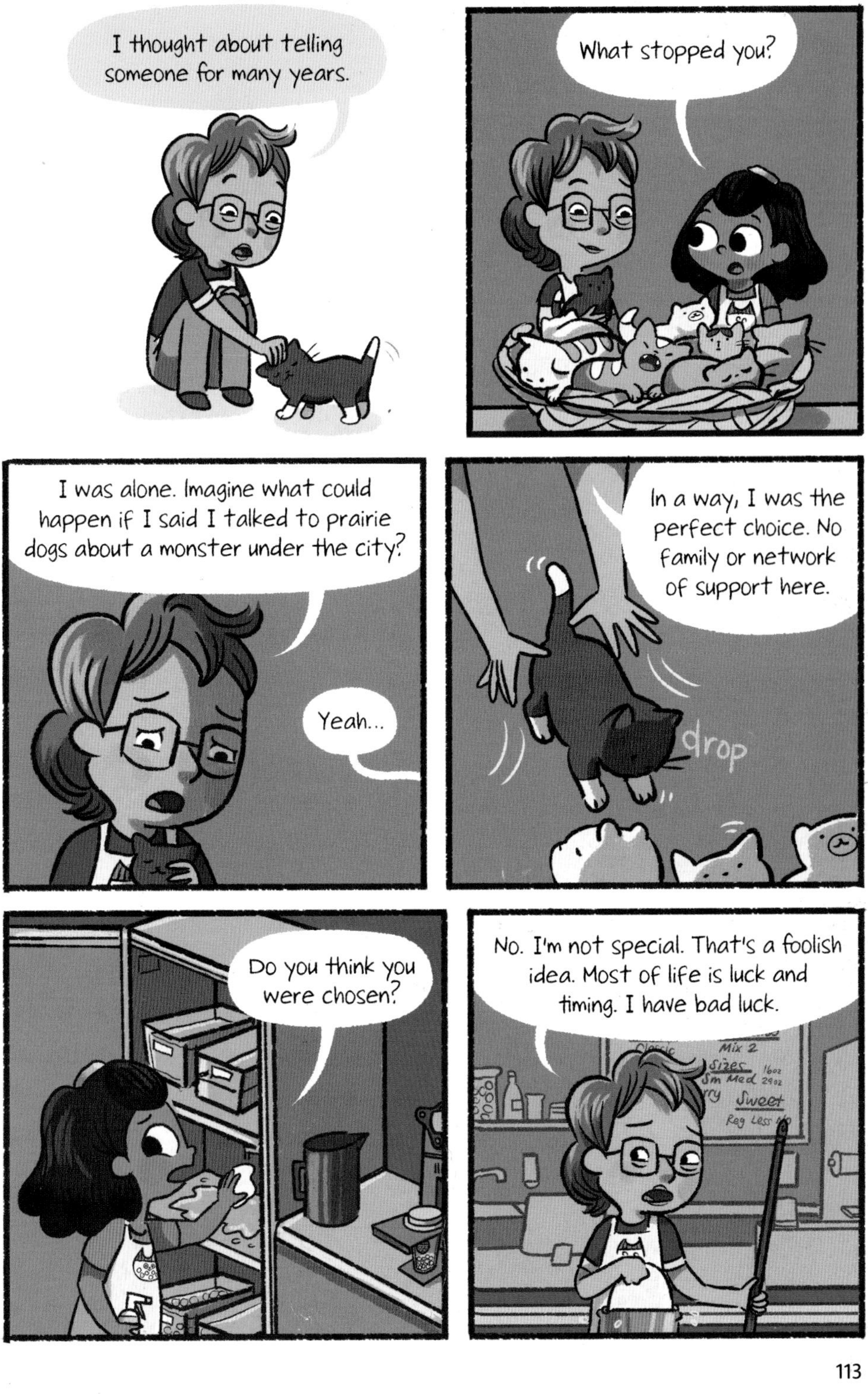

I thought about telling someone for many years.
What stopped you?
I was alone. Imagine what could happen if I said I talked to prairie dogs about a monster under the city?
Yeah...
In a way, I was the perfect choice. No family or network of support here.
drop
Do you think you were chosen?
No. I'm not special. That's a foolish idea. Most of life is luck and timing. I have bad luck.

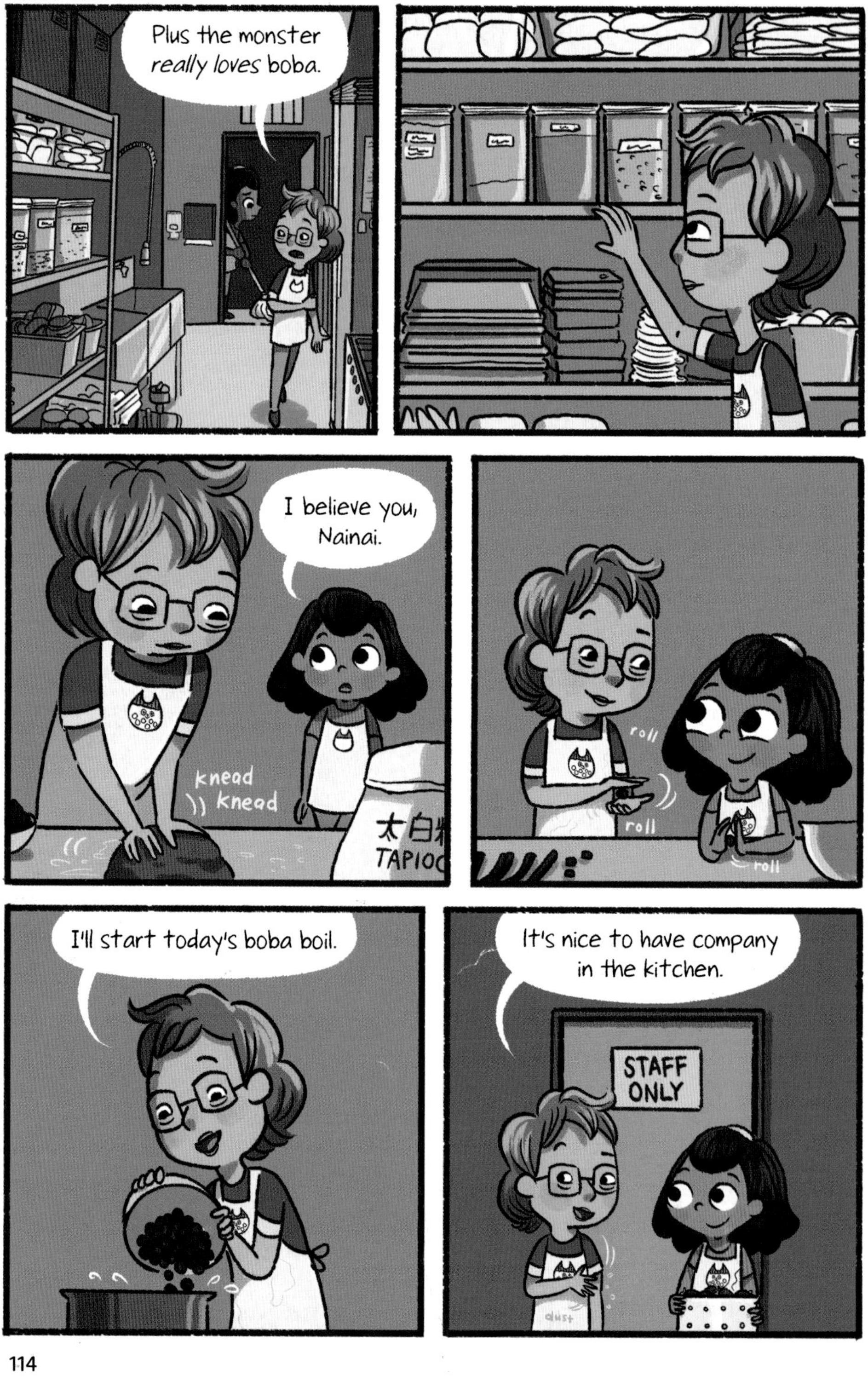
Plus the monster *really loves* boba.
I believe you, Nainai.
knead
knead
太白粉
TAPIOC
roll
roll
roll
I'll start today's boba boil.
It's nice to have company in the kitchen.
STAFF ONLY

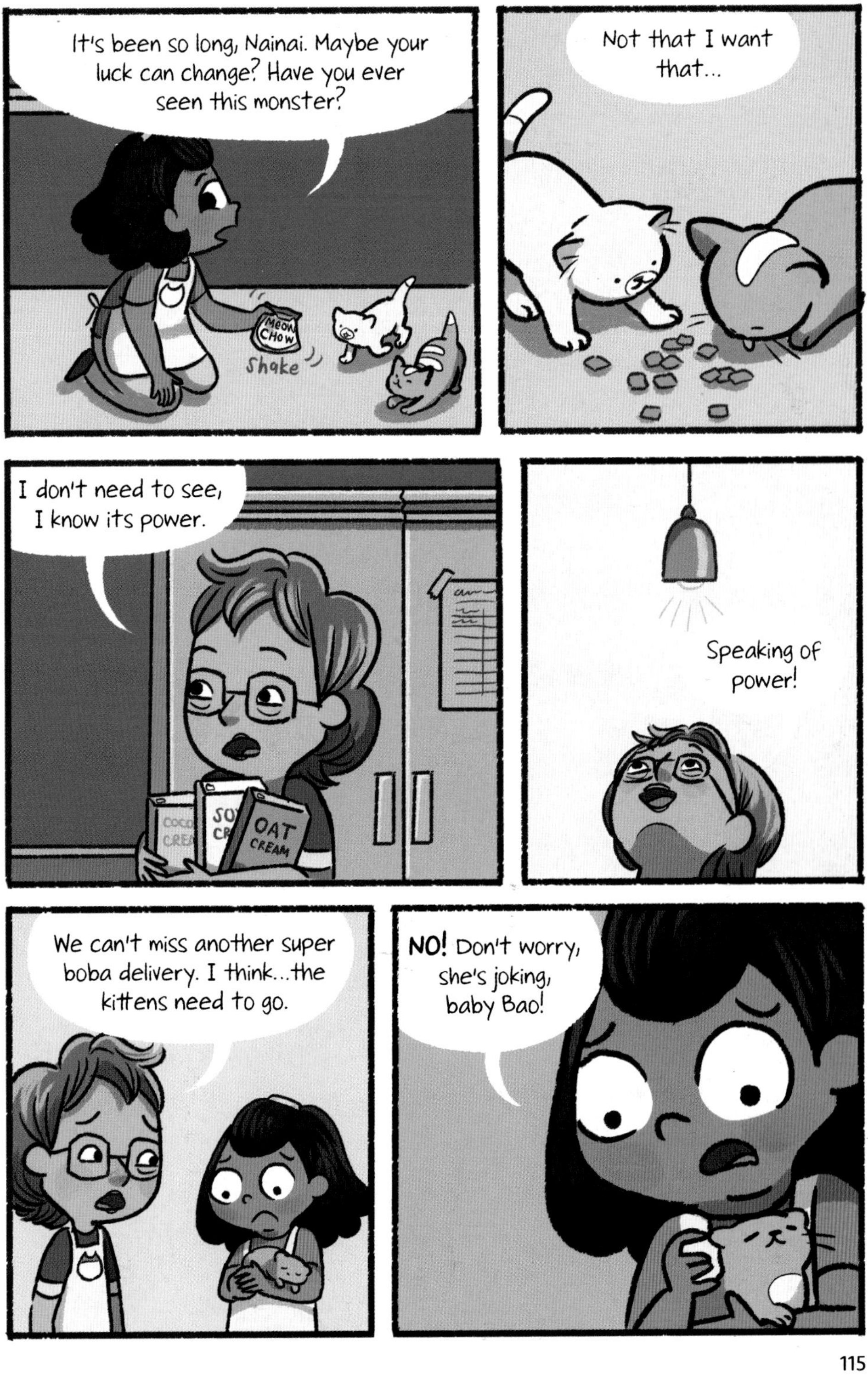
It's been so long, Nainai. Maybe your luck can change? Have you ever seen this monster?
MEOW CHOW
Shake
Not that I want that...
I don't need to see, I know its power.
COCO CREA
SOY CR
OAT CREAM
Speaking of power!
We can't miss another super boba delivery. I think...the kittens need to go.
NO! Don't worry, she's joking, baby Bao!

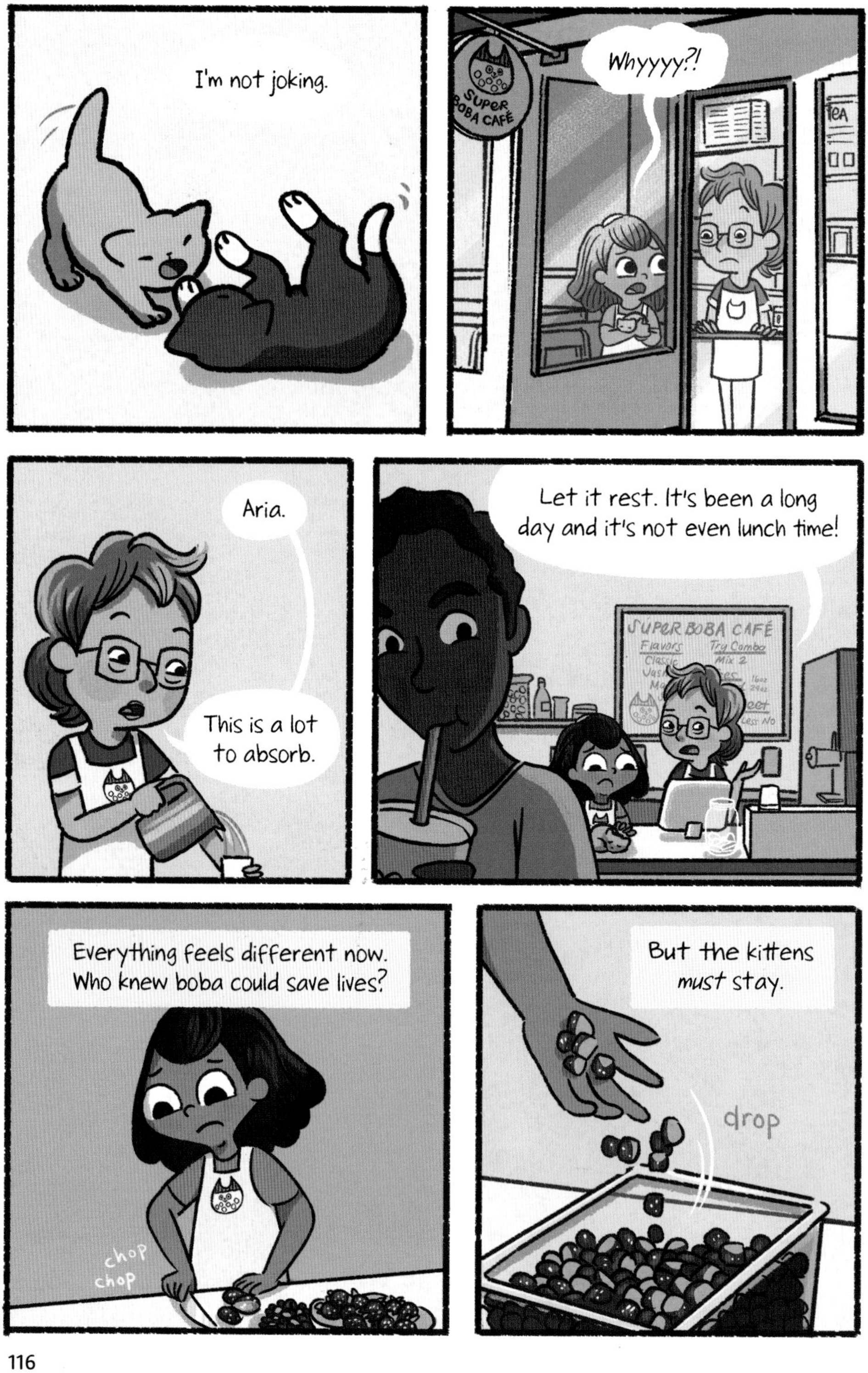
I'm not joking.
SUPER BOBA CAFÉ
Whyyyy?!
TEA
Aria.
This is a lot to absorb.
Let it rest. It's been a long day and it's not even lunch time!
SUPER BOBA CAFÉ
Flavors
Try Combo
Classic
Mix 2
16oz
24oz
Less No
Everything feels different now. Who knew boba could save lives?
chop chop
But the kittens *must* stay.
drop

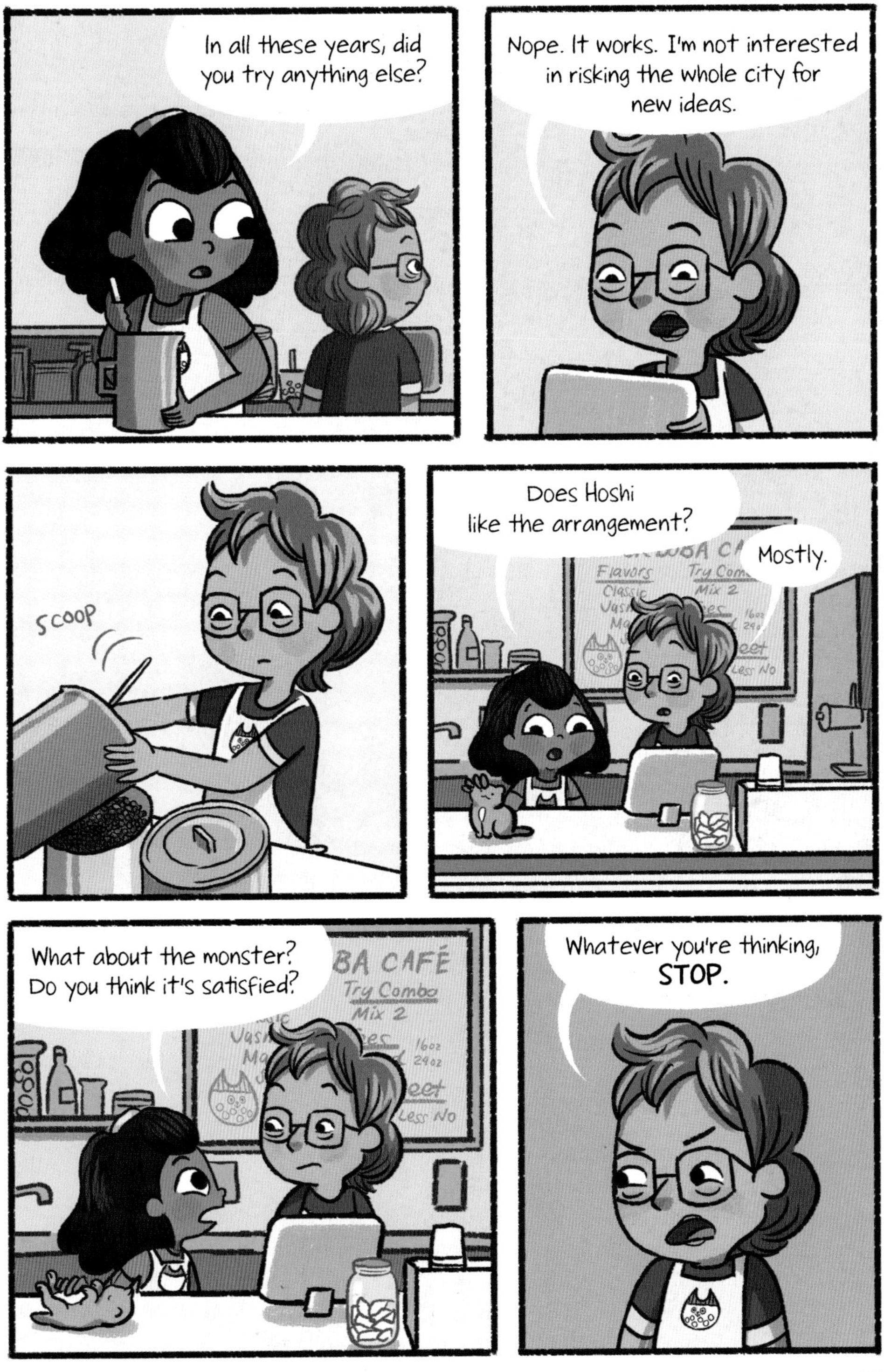
In all these years, did you try anything else?
Nope. It works. I'm not interested in risking the whole city for new ideas.
SCOOP
Does Hoshi like the arrangement?
Mostly.
Flavors
Classic
Try Combo
Mix 2
What about the monster? Do you think it's satisfied?
BA CAFÉ
Try Combo
Mix 2
16oz
24oz
Less No
Whatever you're thinking, **STOP.**

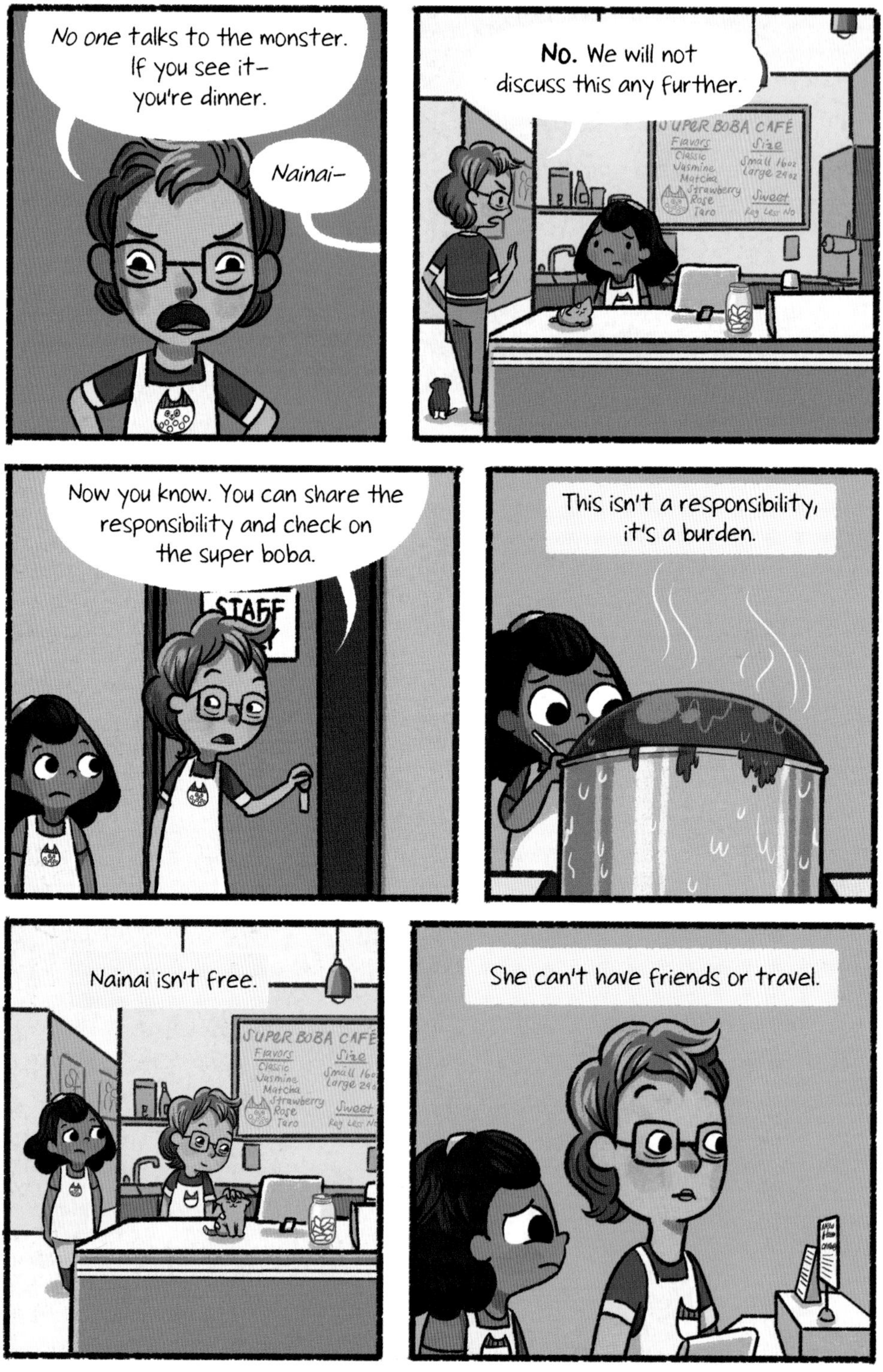
No one talks to the monster. If you see it— you're dinner.
Nainai—
No. We will not discuss this any further.
SUPER BOBA CAFÉ
Now you know. You can share the responsibility and check on the super boba.
STAFF
This isn't a responsibility, it's a burden.
Nainai isn't free.
SUPER BOBA CAFÉ
She can't have friends or travel.

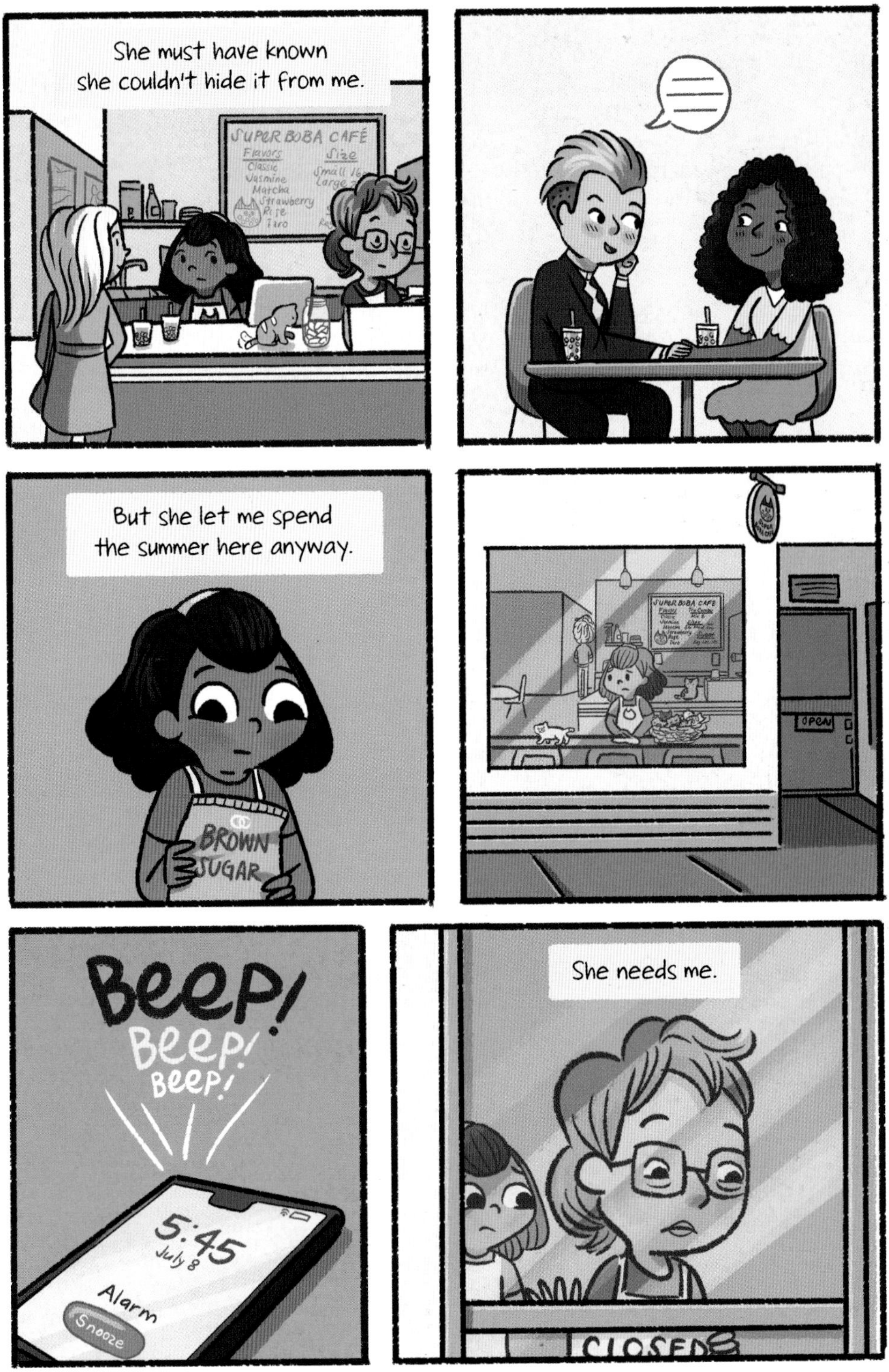
She must have known
she couldn't hide it from me.
SUPER BOBA CAFÉ
But she let me spend
the summer here anyway.
BROWN
SUGAR
SUPER BOBA CAFÉ
OPEN
BEEP!
BEEP!
BEEP!
5:45
July 8
Alarm
Snooze
She needs me.
CLOSED

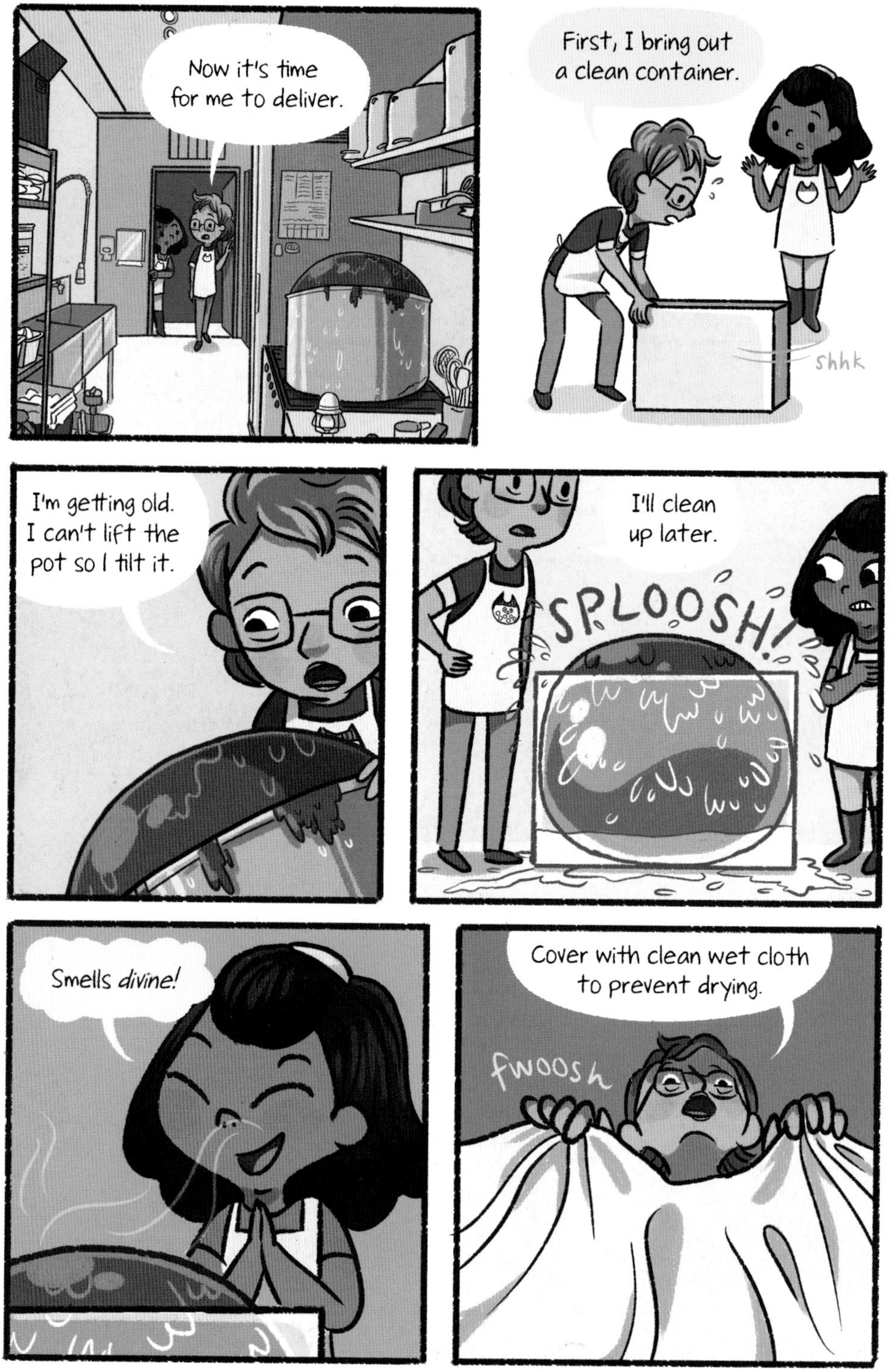
Now it's time for me to deliver.
First, I bring out a clean container.
shhk
I'm getting old. I can't lift the pot so I tilt it.
I'll clean up later.
SPLOOSH!
Smells *divine!*
Cover with clean wet cloth to prevent drying.
fwoosh

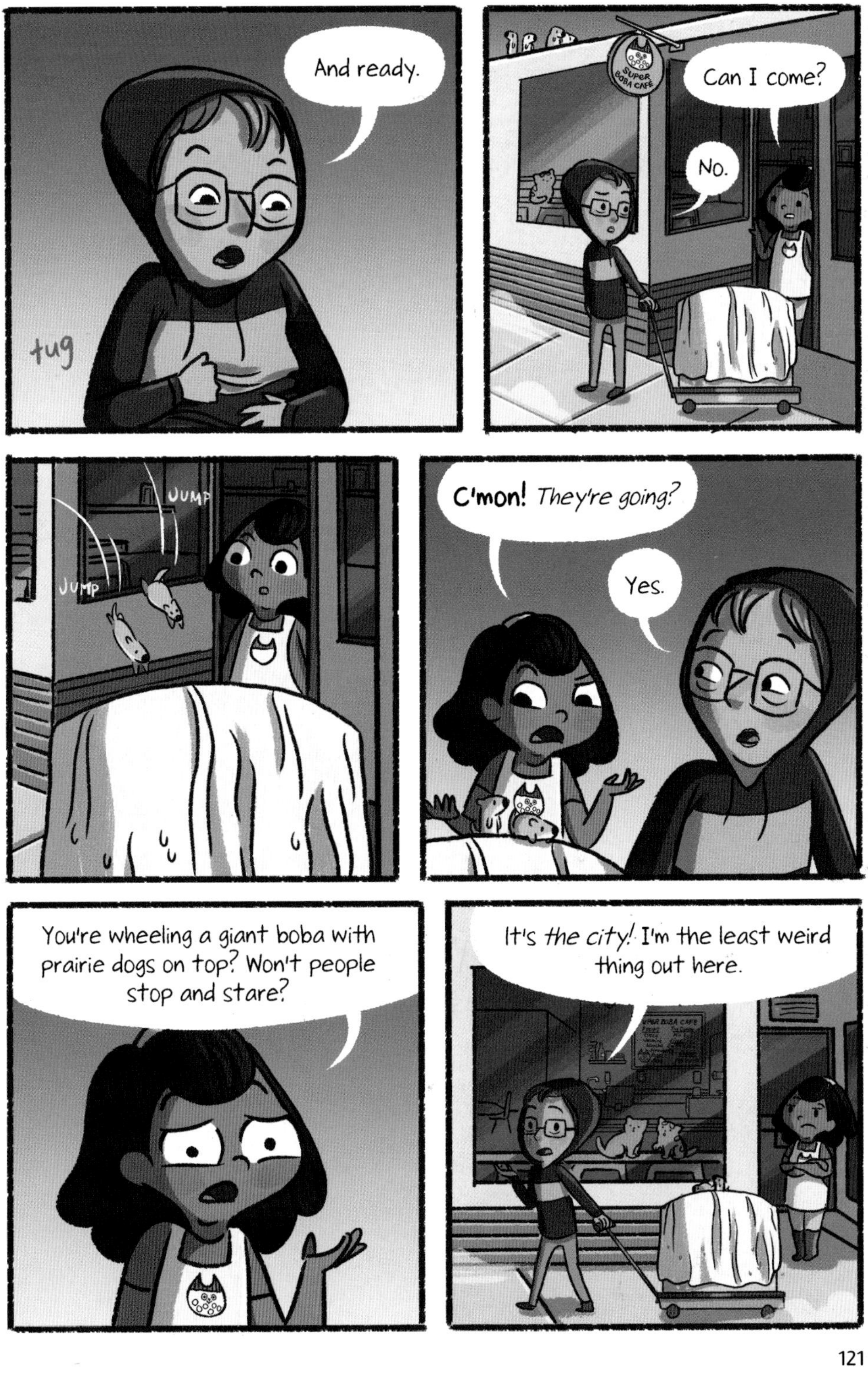
And ready.
tug
SUPER BOBA CAFE
Can I come?
No.
JUMP
JUMP
C'mon! *They're going?*
Yes.
You're wheeling a giant boba with prairie dogs on top? Won't people stop and stare?
It's *the city!* I'm the least weird thing out here.
SUPER BOBA CAFE

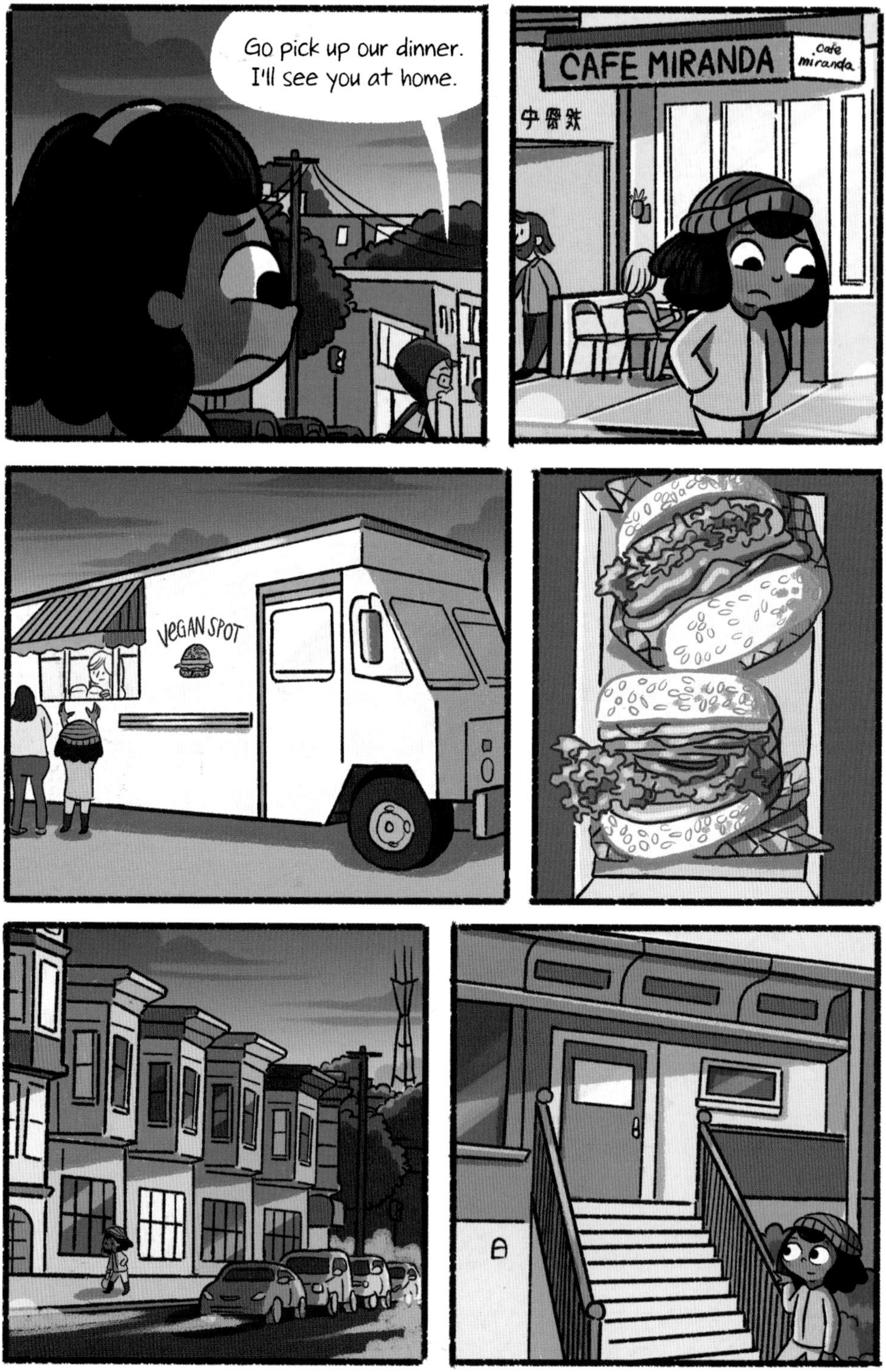
Go pick up our dinner. I'll see you at home.
CAFE MIRANDA
cafe miranda
VEGAN SPOT

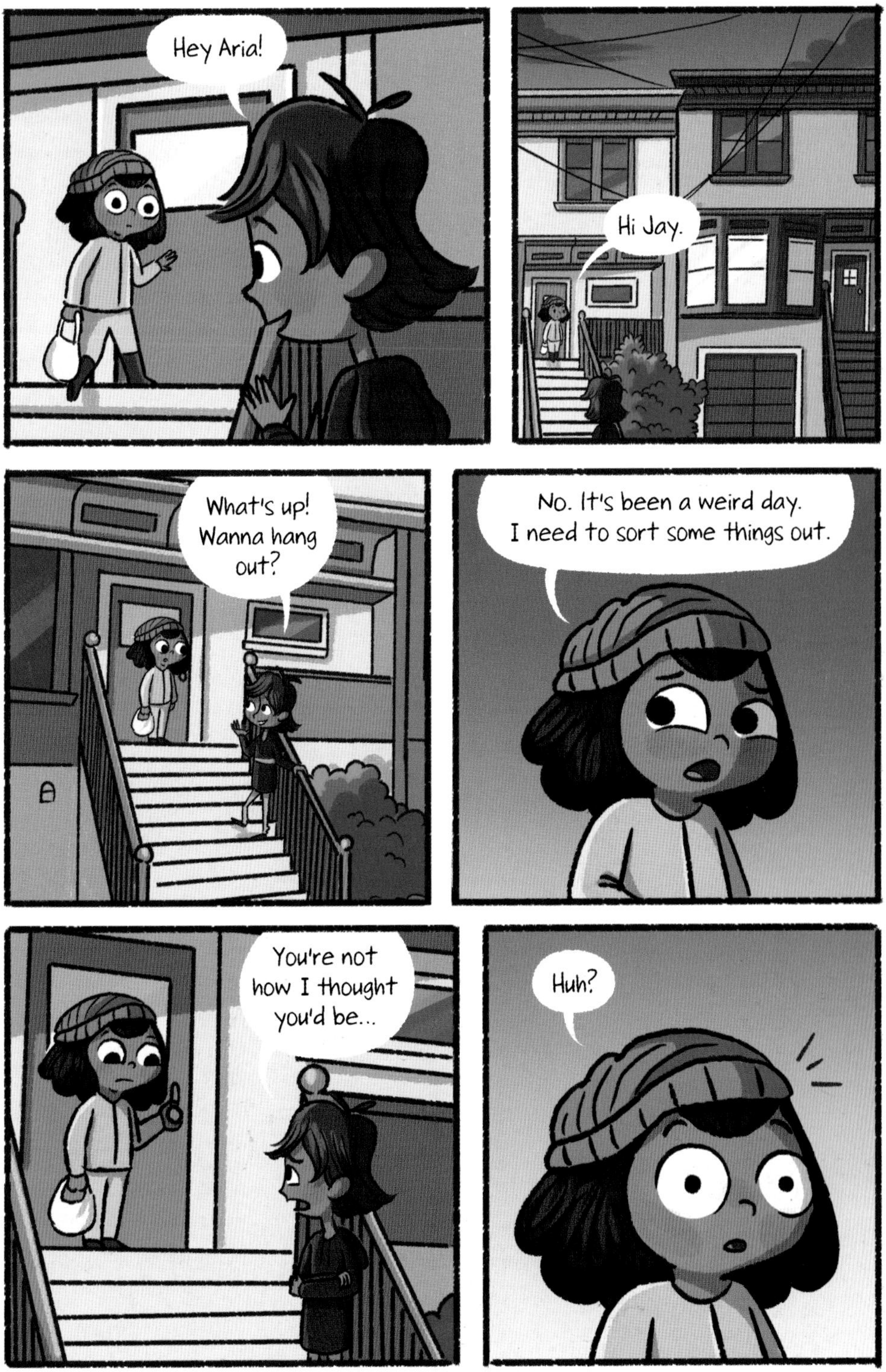
Hey Aria!
Hi Jay.
What's up! Wanna hang out?
No. It's been a weird day. I need to sort some things out.
You're not how I thought you'd be...
Huh?

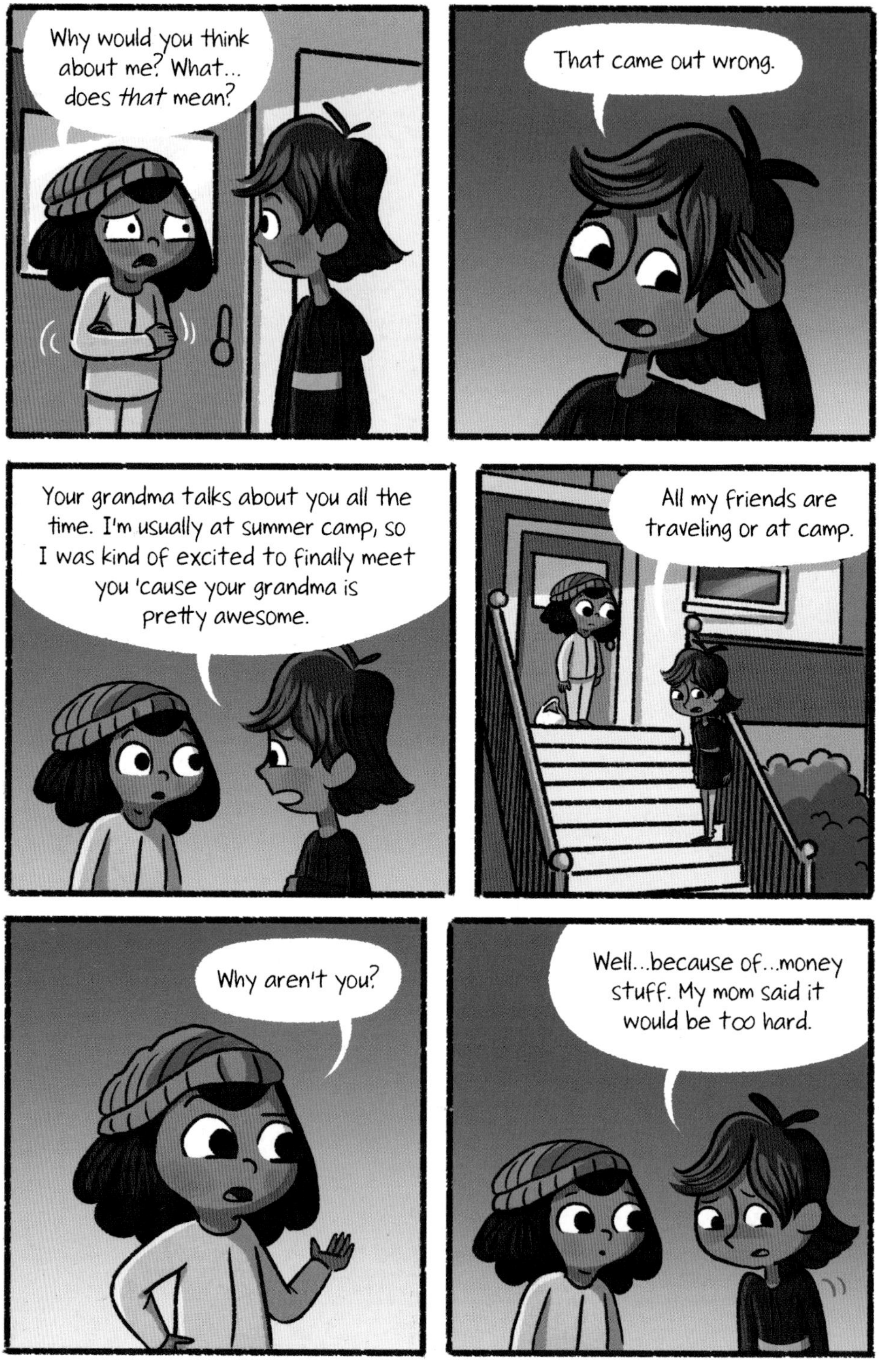
Why would you think about me? What... does *that* mean?
That came out wrong.
Your grandma talks about you all the time. I'm usually at summer camp, so I was kind of excited to finally meet you 'cause your grandma is pretty awesome.
All my friends are traveling or at camp.
Why aren't you?
Well...because of...money stuff. My mom said it would be too hard.

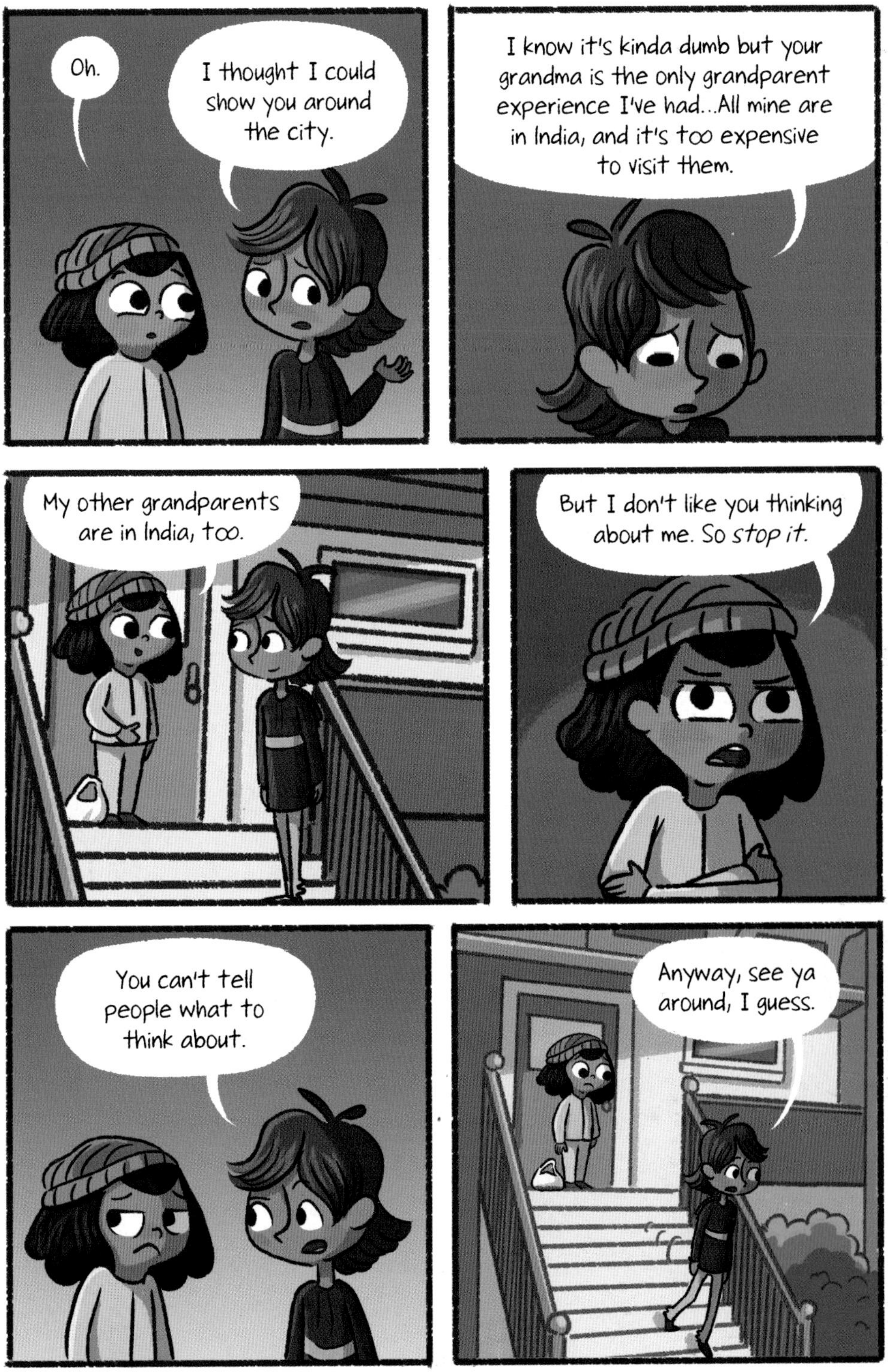
Oh.
I thought I could show you around the city.
I know it's kinda dumb but your grandma is the only grandparent experience I've had...All mine are in India, and it's too expensive to visit them.
My other grandparents are in India, too.
But I don't like you thinking about me. So *stop it*.
You can't tell people what to think about.
Anyway, see ya around, I guess.

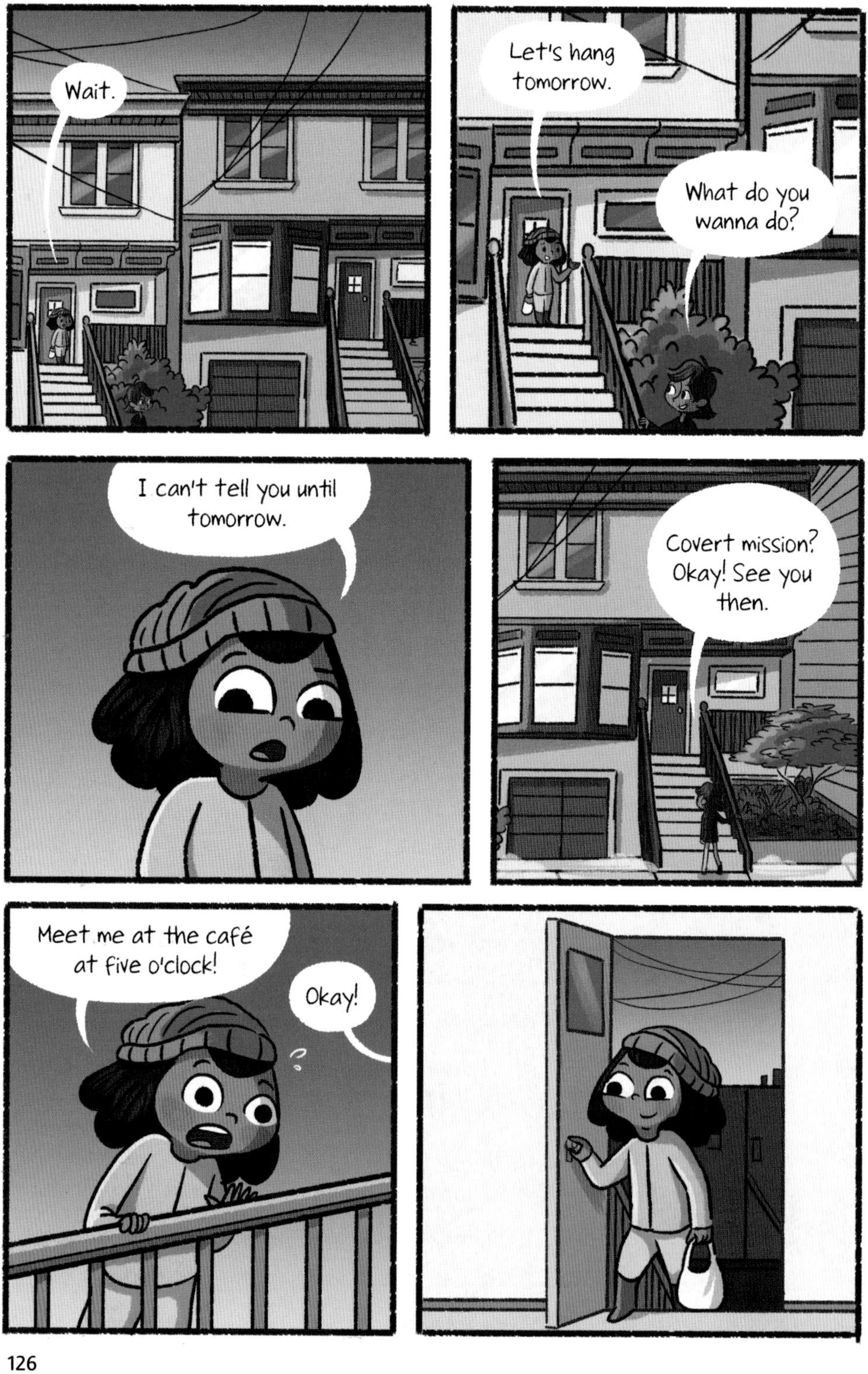
Wait.
Let's hang tomorrow.
What do you wanna do?
I can't tell you until tomorrow.
Covert mission? Okay! See you then.
Meet me at the café at five o'clock!
Okay!

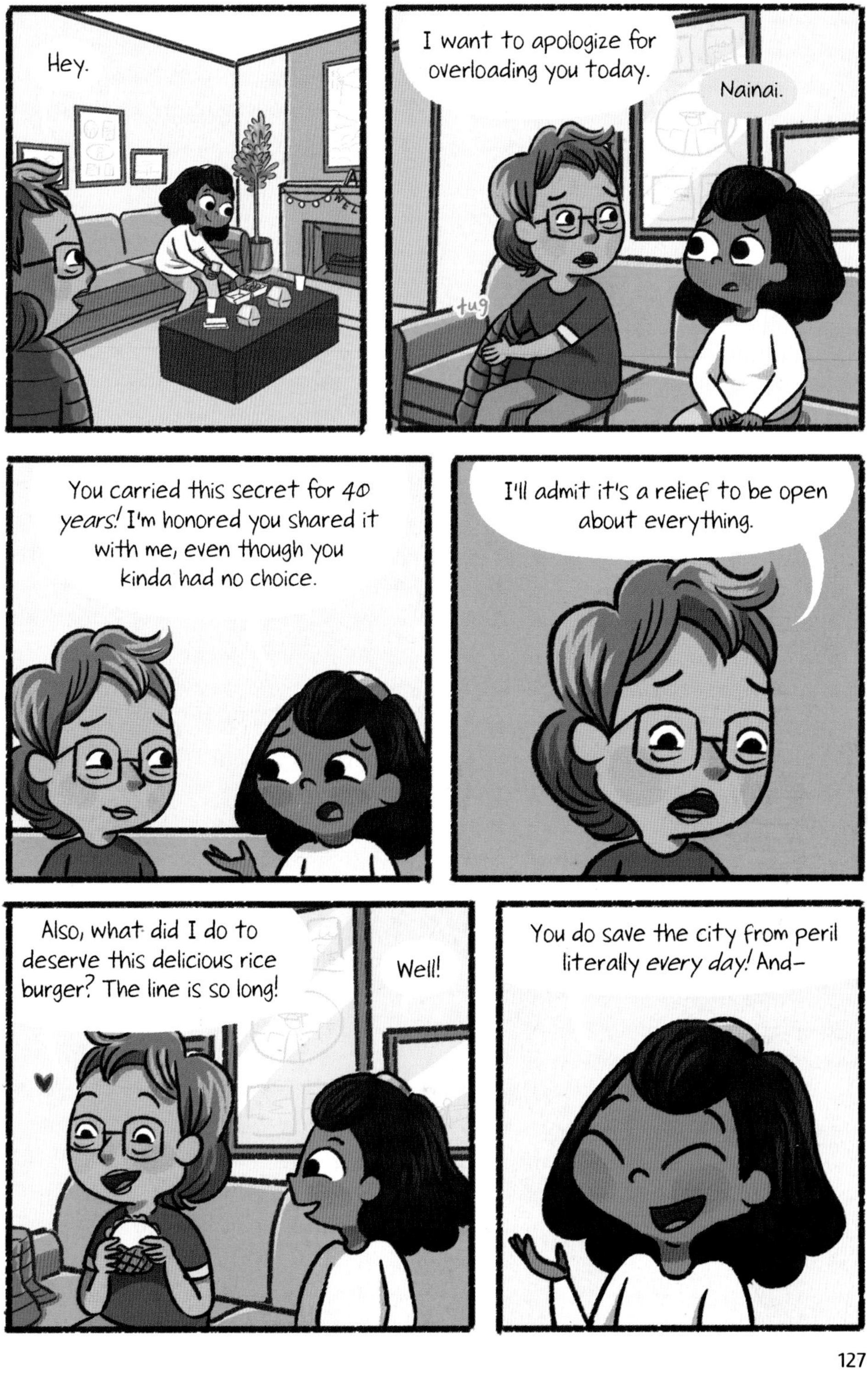
Hey.
I want to apologize for overloading you today.
Nainai.
tug
You carried this secret for 40 *years!* I'm honored you shared it with me, even though you kinda had no choice.
I'll admit it's a relief to be open about everything.
Also, what did I do to deserve this delicious rice burger? The line is so long!
Well!
You do save the city from peril literally *every day!* And–

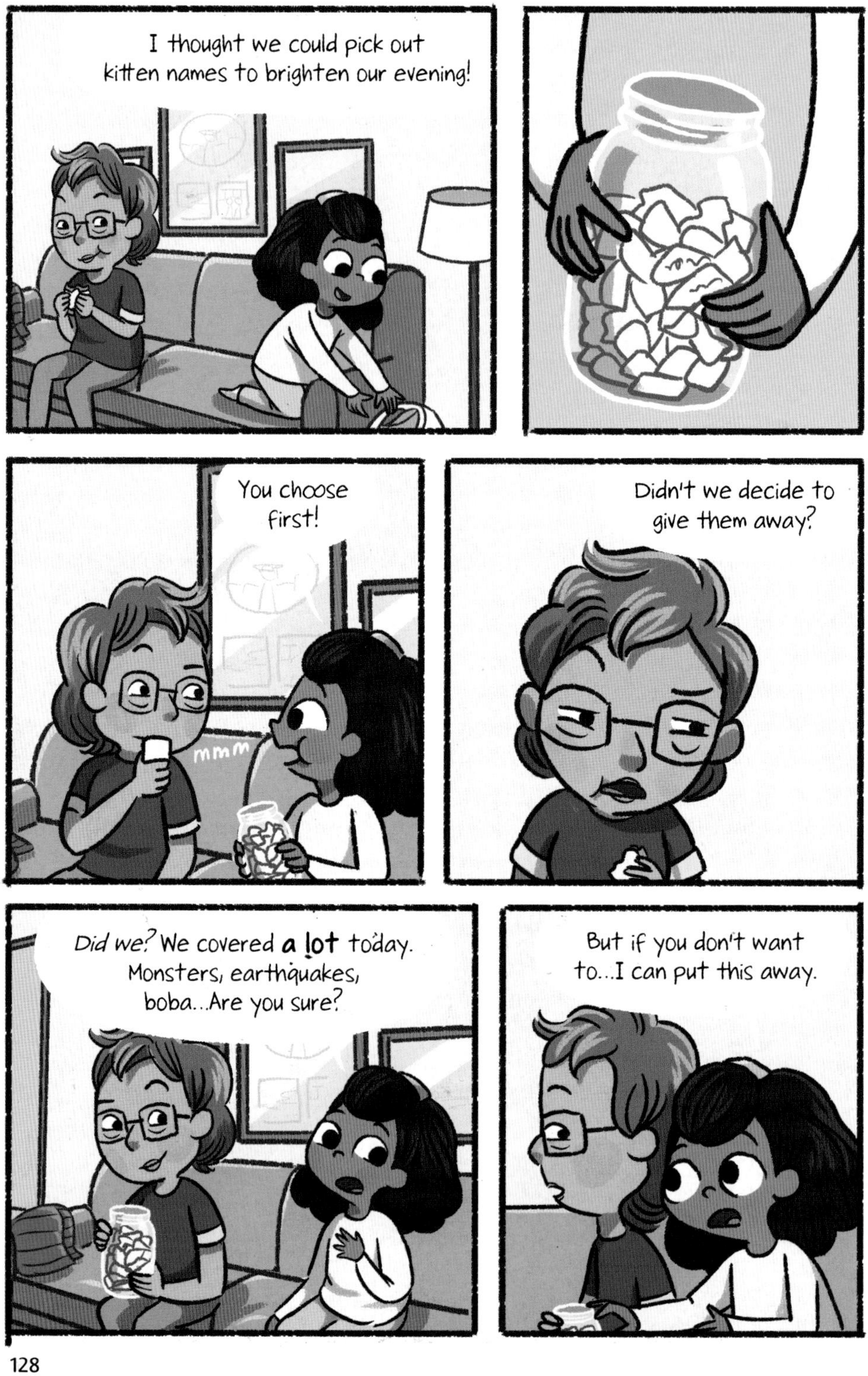
I thought we could pick out kitten names to brighten our evening!
You choose first!
mmm
Didn't we decide to give them away?
Did we? We covered **a lot** today. Monsters, earthquakes, boba...Are you sure?
But if you don't want to...I can put this away.

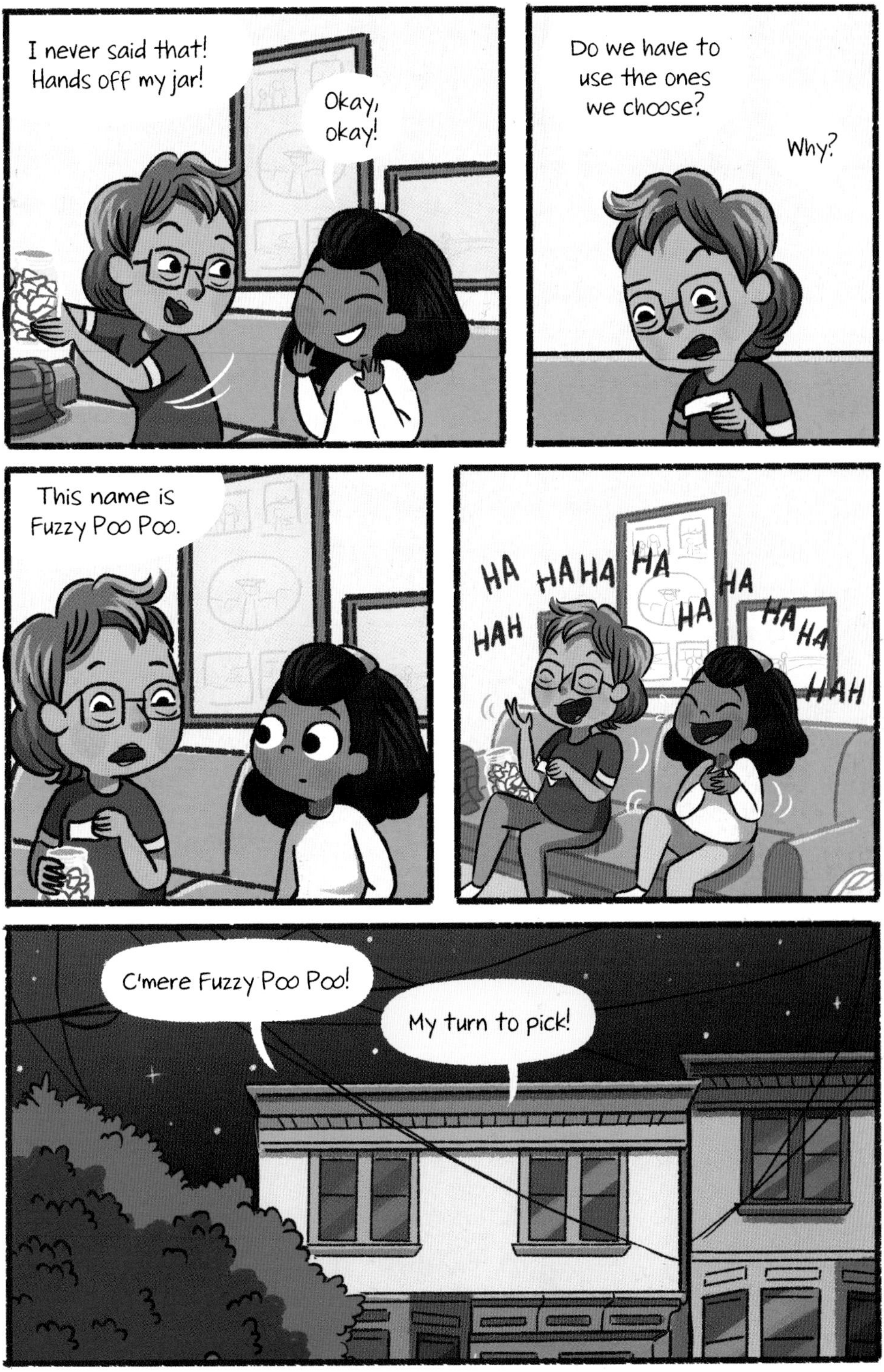

I never said that! Hands off my jar!
Okay, okay!
Do we have to use the ones we choose?
Why?
This name is Fuzzy Poo Poo.
HA HAHAHA HA HA HA HAH HA HA HA HAH
C'mere Fuzzy Poo Poo!
My turn to pick!

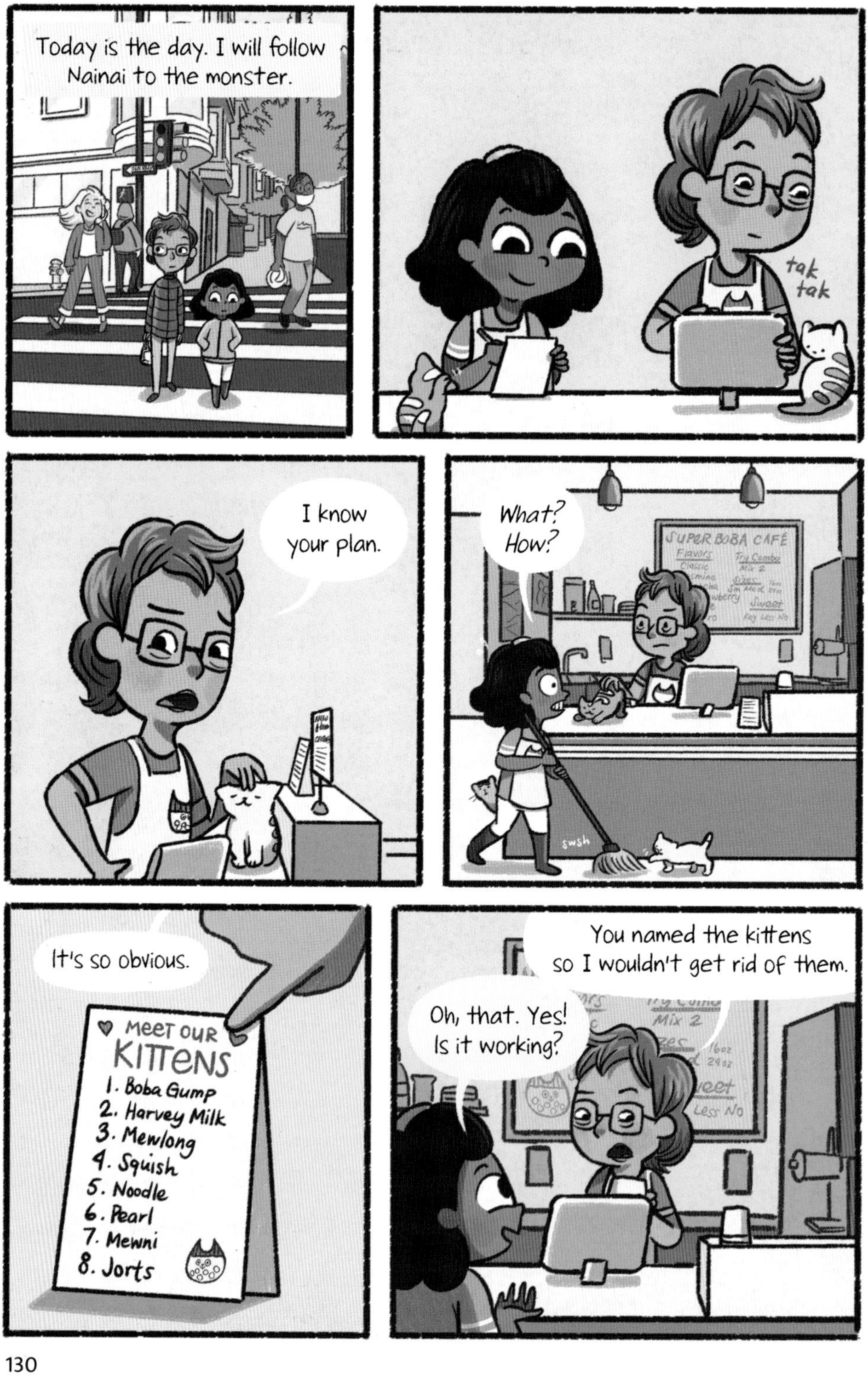
Today is the day. I will follow Nainai to the monster.
tak tak
I know your plan.
What? How?
SUPER BOBA CAFÉ
Flavors
Try Combo
Mix 2
Sizes
Sweet
swsh
It's so obvious.
MEET OUR KITTENS
1. Boba Gump
2. Harvey Milk
3. Mewlong
4. Squish
5. Noodle
6. Pearl
7. Mewni
8. Jorts
You named the kittens so I wouldn't get rid of them.
Oh, that. Yes! Is it working?

The names **are** pretty great.

So are the kitties!

Mewni is your sous chef!

No animals in the kitchen, Mewni!

STAFF ONLY

Plus we're changing our hours. There's no reason to kick the kittens out now.

skrch

NEW HOURS

I'm here for my free boba. I suggested the name Boba Gump!

Of course! Here it is and thank you!

BOBA CAFÉ
Jasmine
Matcha
Strawberry
Reg Less No

Hmmmm.

131

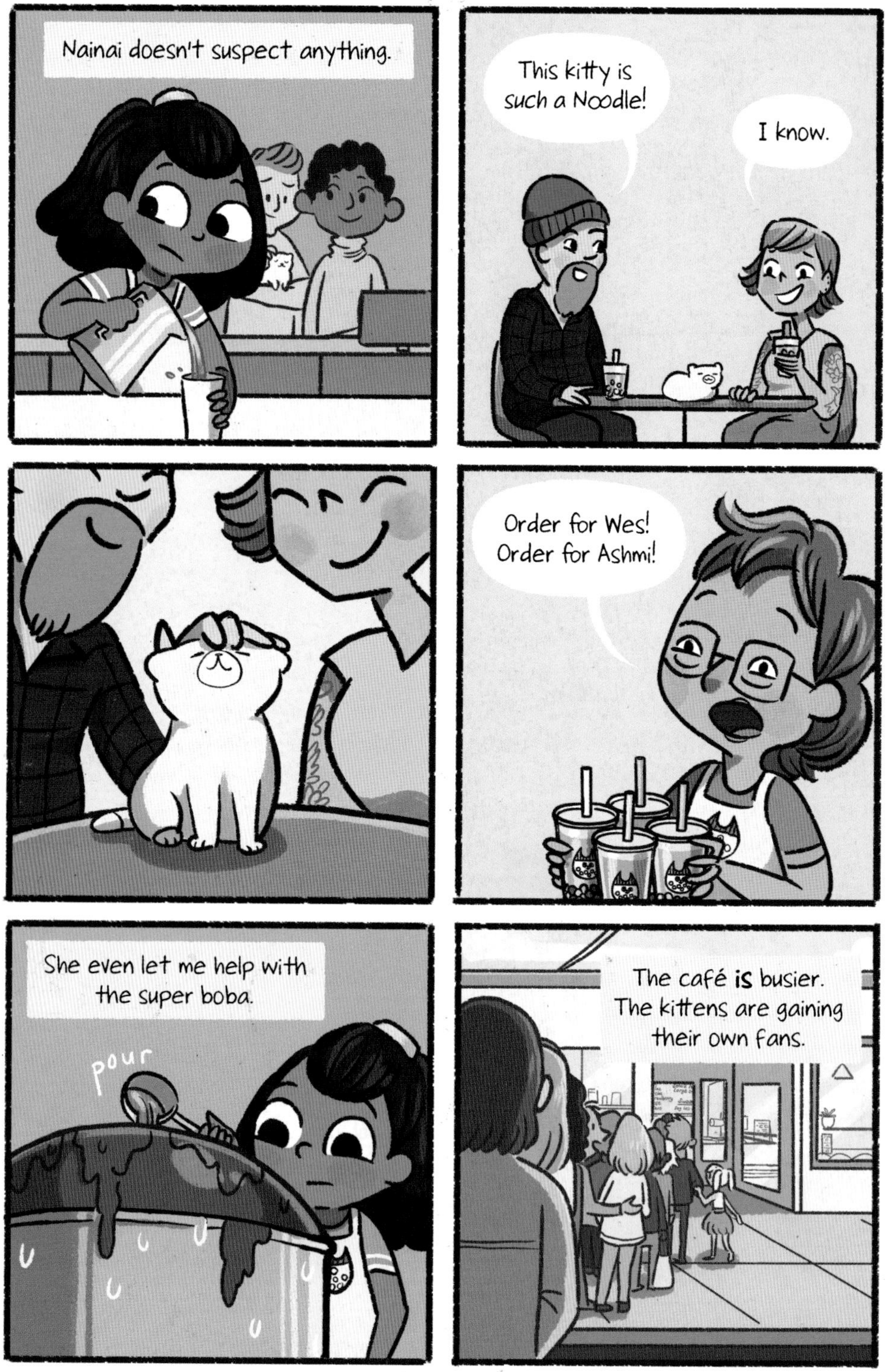
Nainai doesn't suspect anything.
This kitty is such a Noodle!
I know.
Order for Wes! Order for Ashmi!
She even let me help with the super boba.
pour
The café **is** busier. The kittens are gaining their own fans.

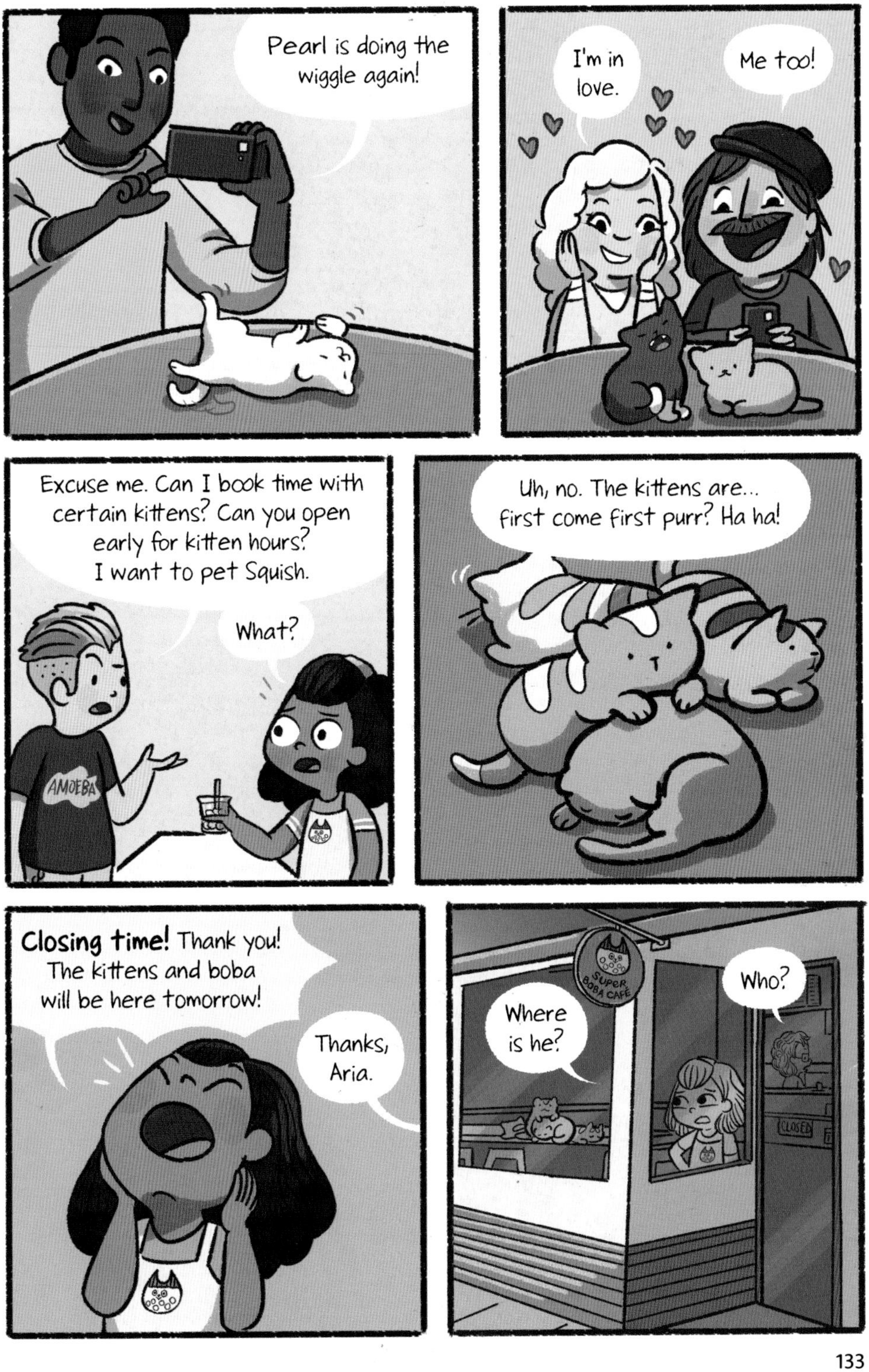
Pearl is doing the wiggle again!
I'm in love.
Me too!
Excuse me. Can I book time with certain kittens? Can you open early for kitten hours? I want to pet Squish.
What?
AMOEBA
Uh, no. The kittens are... first come first purr? Ha ha!
Closing time! Thank you! The kittens and boba will be here tomorrow!
Thanks, Aria.
SUPER BOBA CAFÉ
Where is he?
Who?
CLOSED

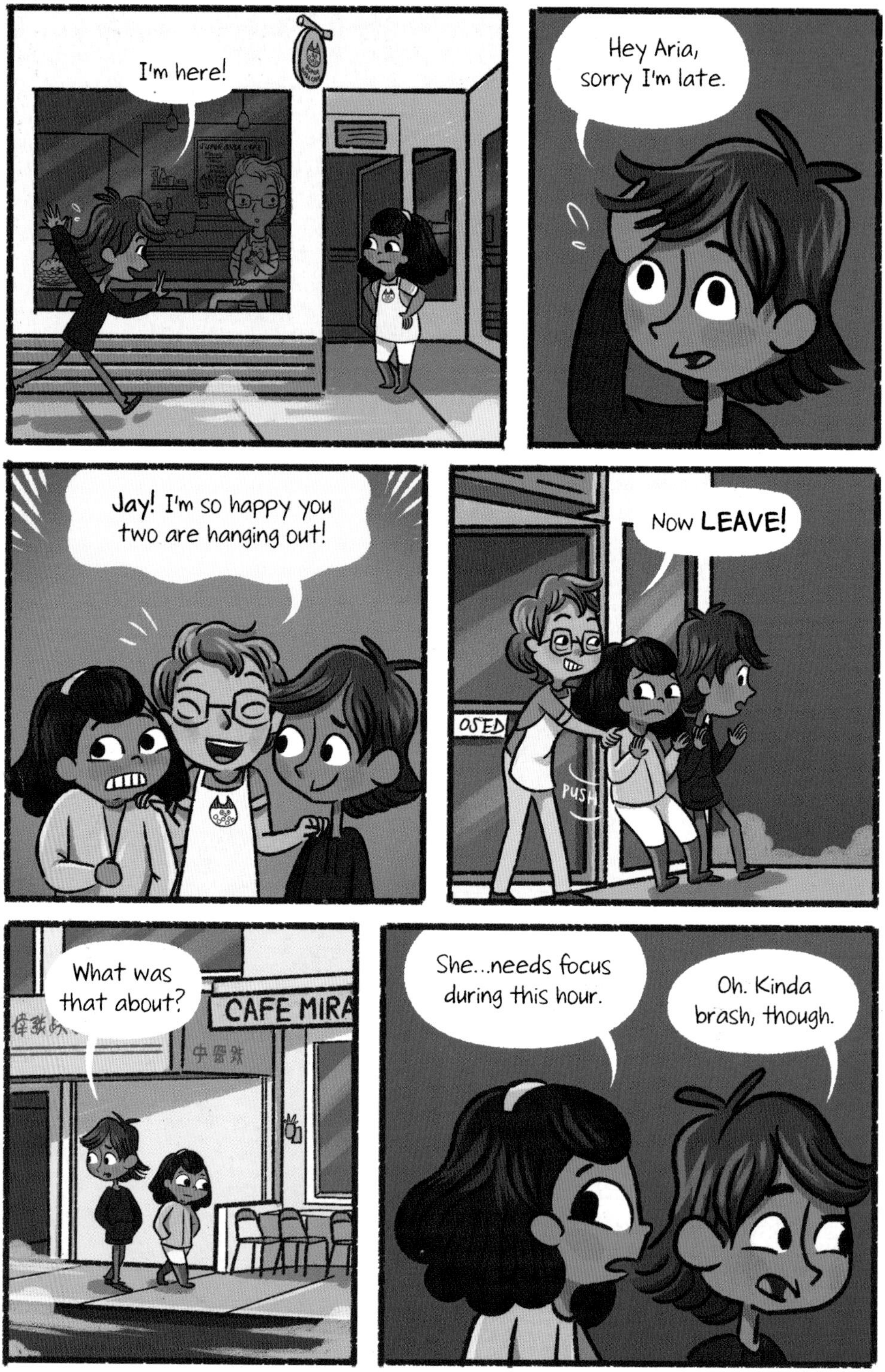
I'm here!
Hey Aria, sorry I'm late.
Jay! I'm so happy you two are hanging out!
Now LEAVE!
OSED
PUSH
What was that about?
CAFE MIRA
She...needs focus during this hour.
Oh. Kinda brash, though.

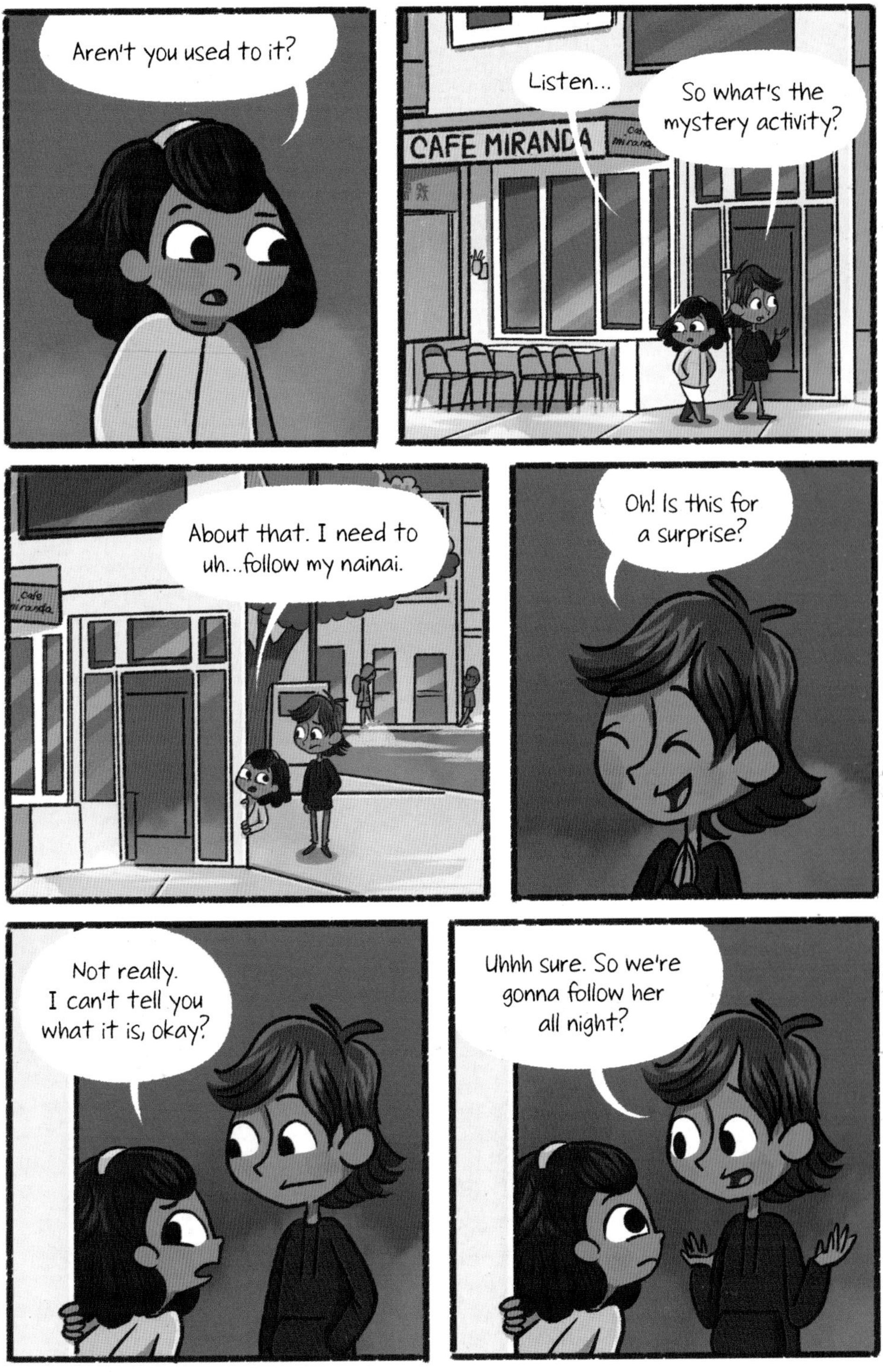
Aren't you used to it?
Listen...
So what's the mystery activity?
CAFE MIRANDA
About that. I need to uh...follow my nainai.
Oh! Is this for a surprise?
Not really. I can't tell you what it is, okay?
Uhhh sure. So we're gonna follow her all night?

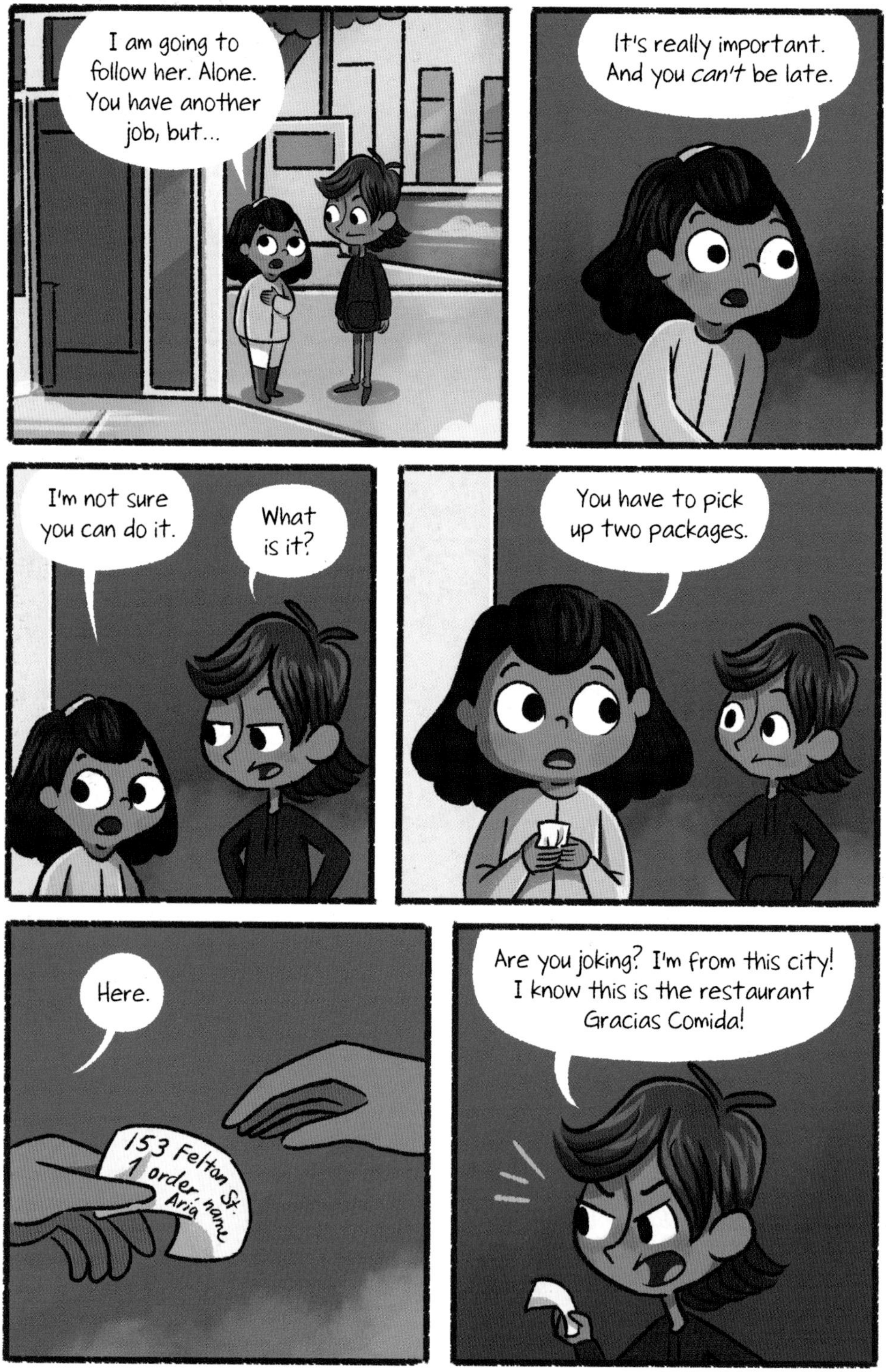
I am going to follow her. Alone. You have another job, but...
It's really important. And you *can't* be late.
I'm not sure you can do it.
What is it?
You have to pick up two packages.
Here.
153 Felton St. 1 order, name Aria
Are you joking? I'm from this city! I know this is the restaurant Gracias Comida!

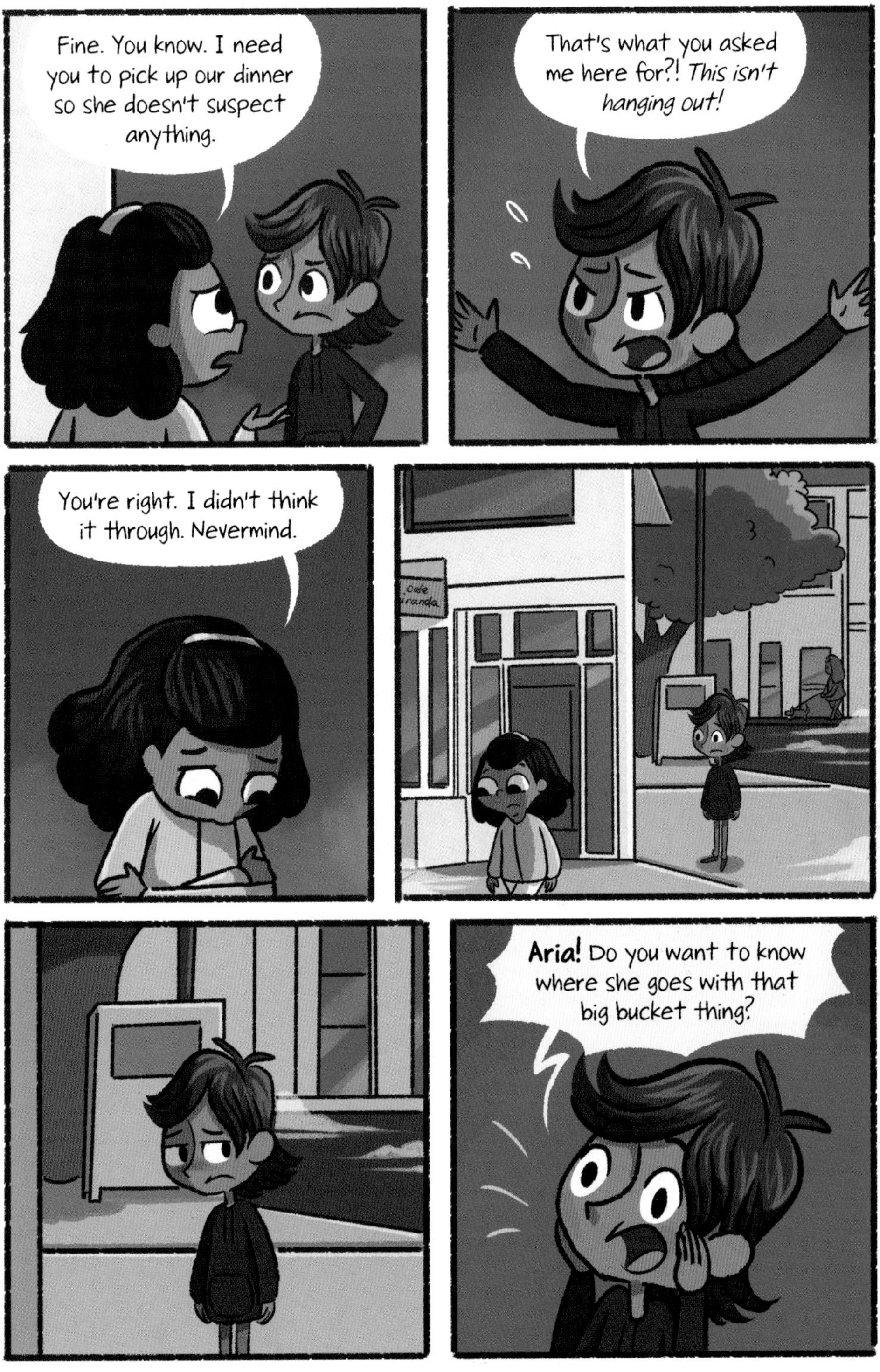
Fine. You know. I need you to pick up our dinner so she doesn't suspect anything.
That's what you asked me here for?! *This isn't hanging out!*
You're right. I didn't think it through. Nevermind.
Cafe Miranda
Aria! Do you want to know where she goes with that big bucket thing?

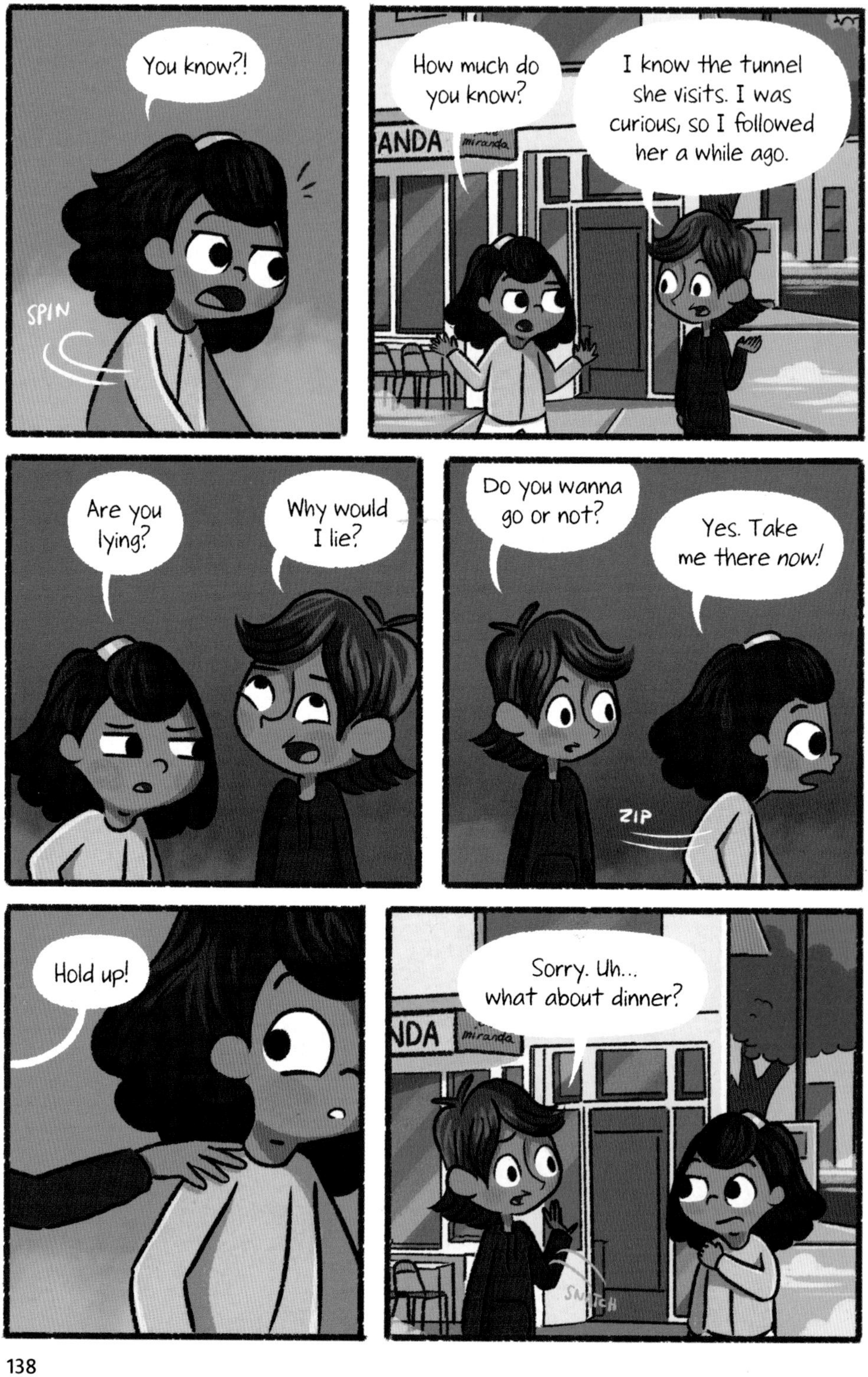
You know?!
SPIN
How much do you know?
I know the tunnel she visits. I was curious, so I followed her a while ago.
ANDA
miranda
Are you lying?
Why would I lie?
Do you wanna go or not?
Yes. Take me there *now!*
ZIP
Hold up!
Sorry. Uh... what about dinner?
NDA
miranda
SNATCH

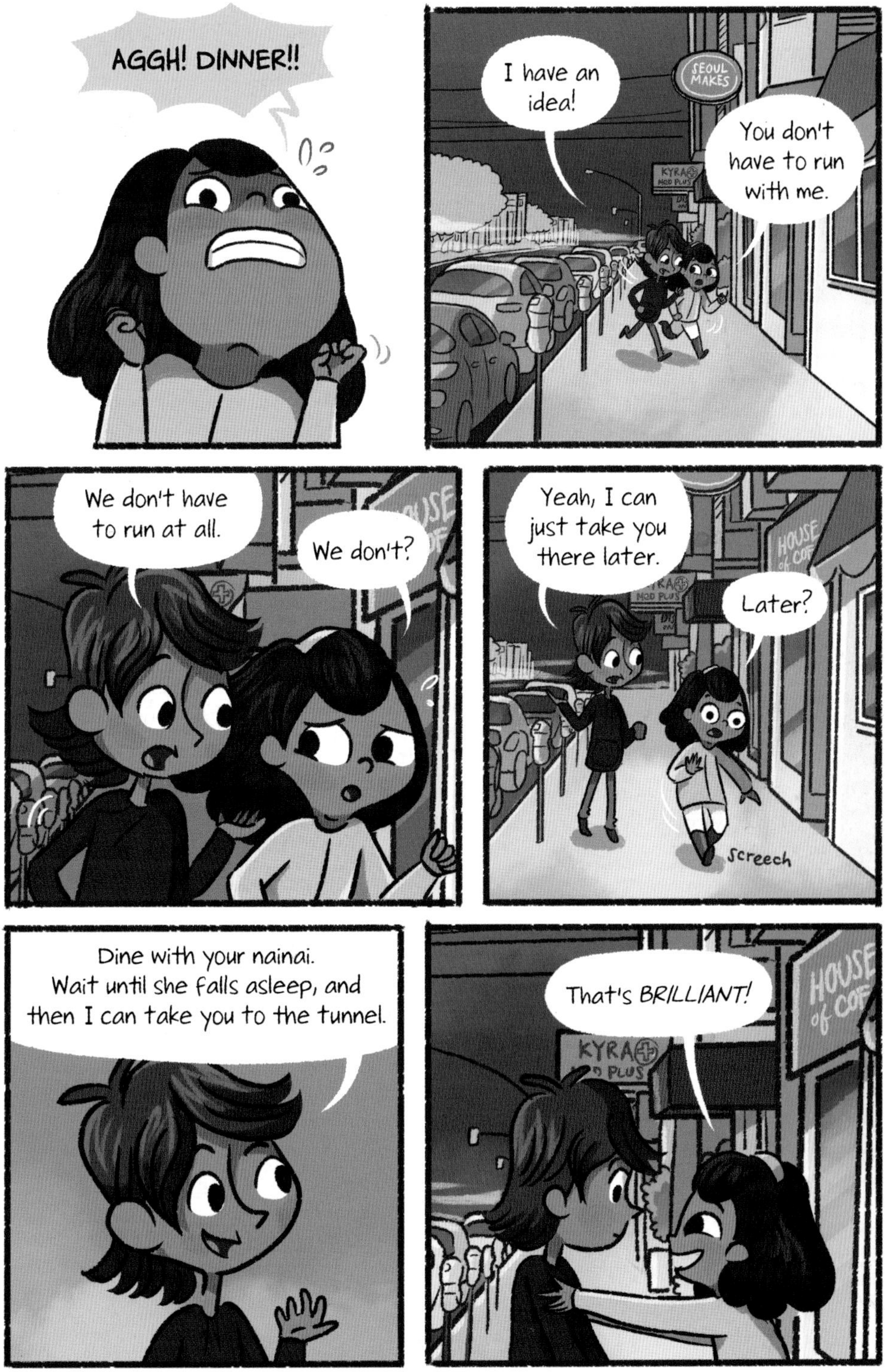

AGGH! DINNER!!
I have an idea!
SEOUL MAKES
You don't have to run with me.
We don't have to run at all.
We don't?
Yeah, I can just take you there later.
Later?
Screech
Dine with your nainai. Wait until she falls asleep, and then I can take you to the tunnel.
That's BRILLIANT!

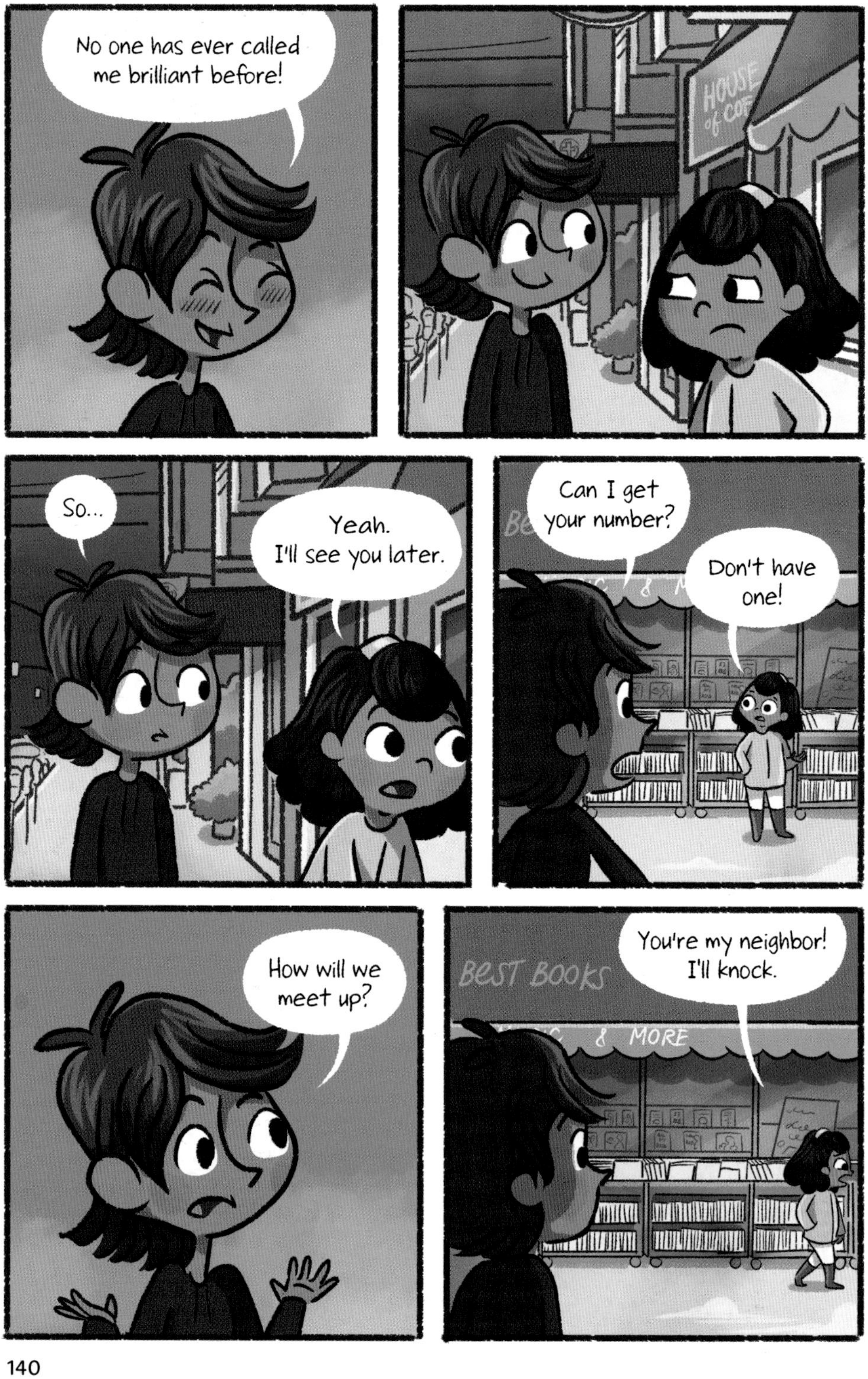
No one has ever called me brilliant before!
HOUSE of COF
So...
Yeah. I'll see you later.
Can I get your number?
Don't have one!
How will we meet up?
BEST BOOKS
& MORE
You're my neighbor! I'll knock.

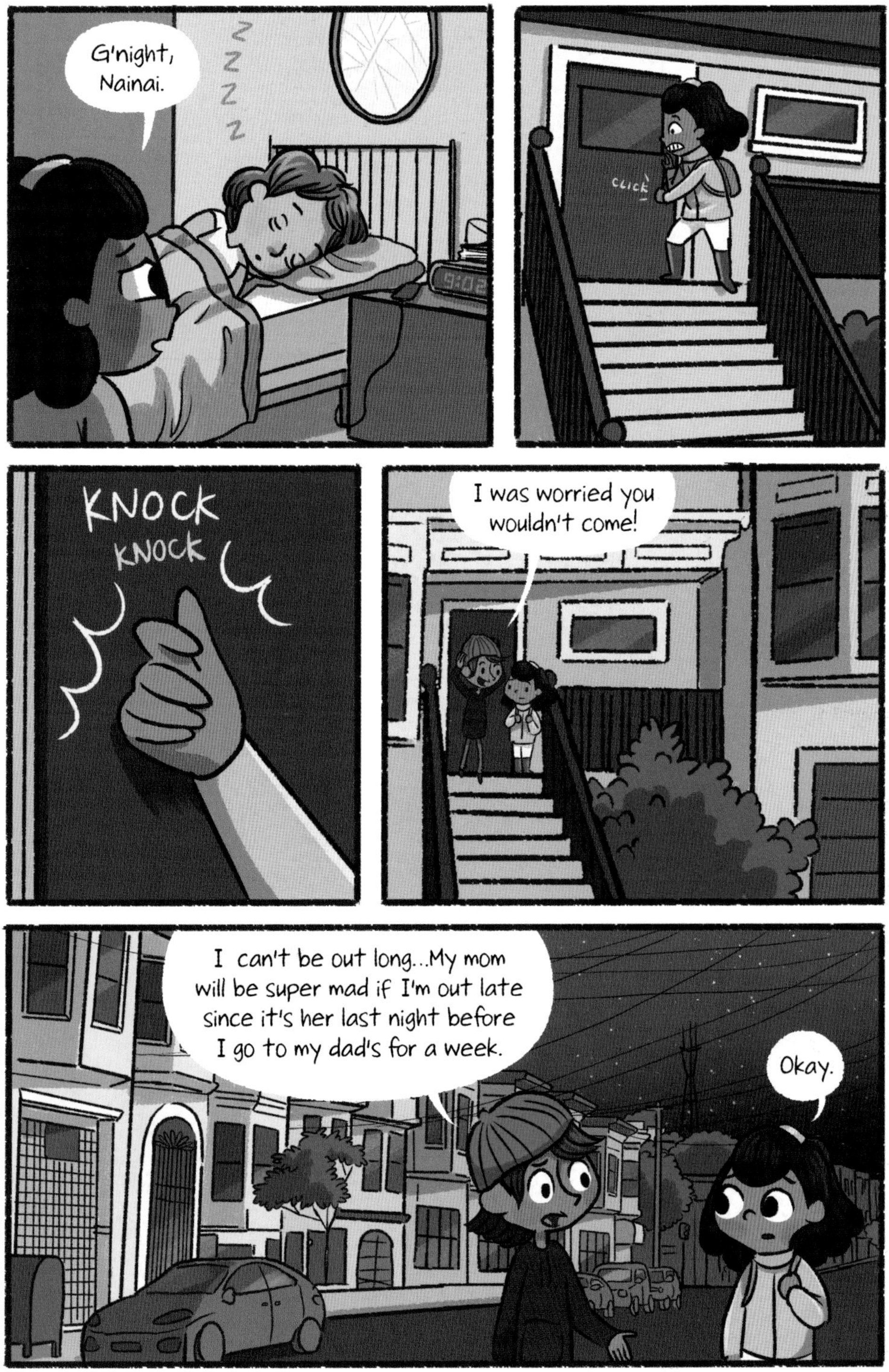
G'night, Nainai.
Z Z Z Z
CLICK
KNOCK KNOCK
I was worried you wouldn't come!
I can't be out long...My mom will be super mad if I'm out late since it's her last night before I go to my dad's for a week.
Okay.

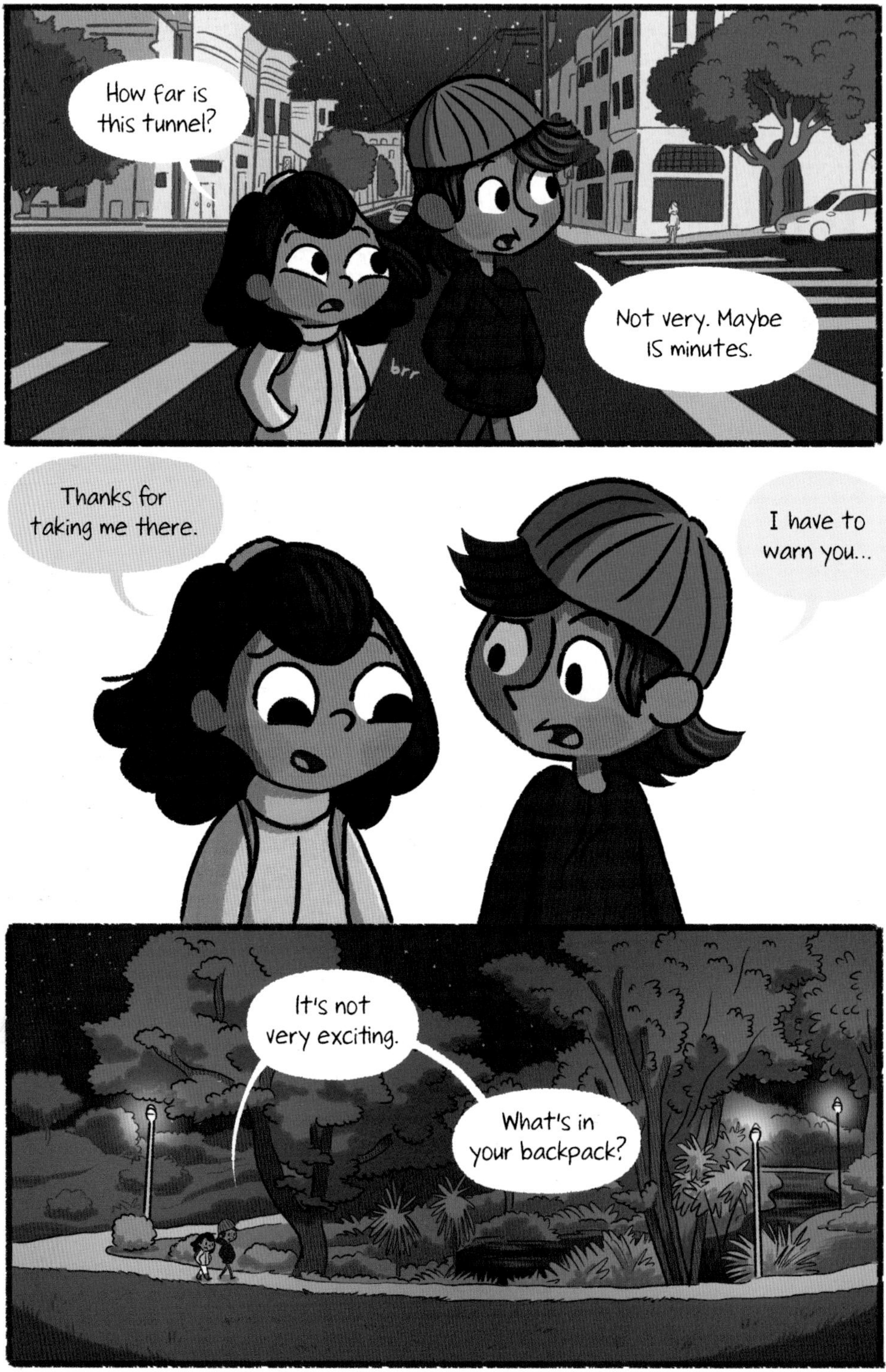
How far is this tunnel?
Not very. Maybe 15 minutes.
brr
Thanks for taking me there.
I have to warn you...
It's not very exciting.
What's in your backpack?

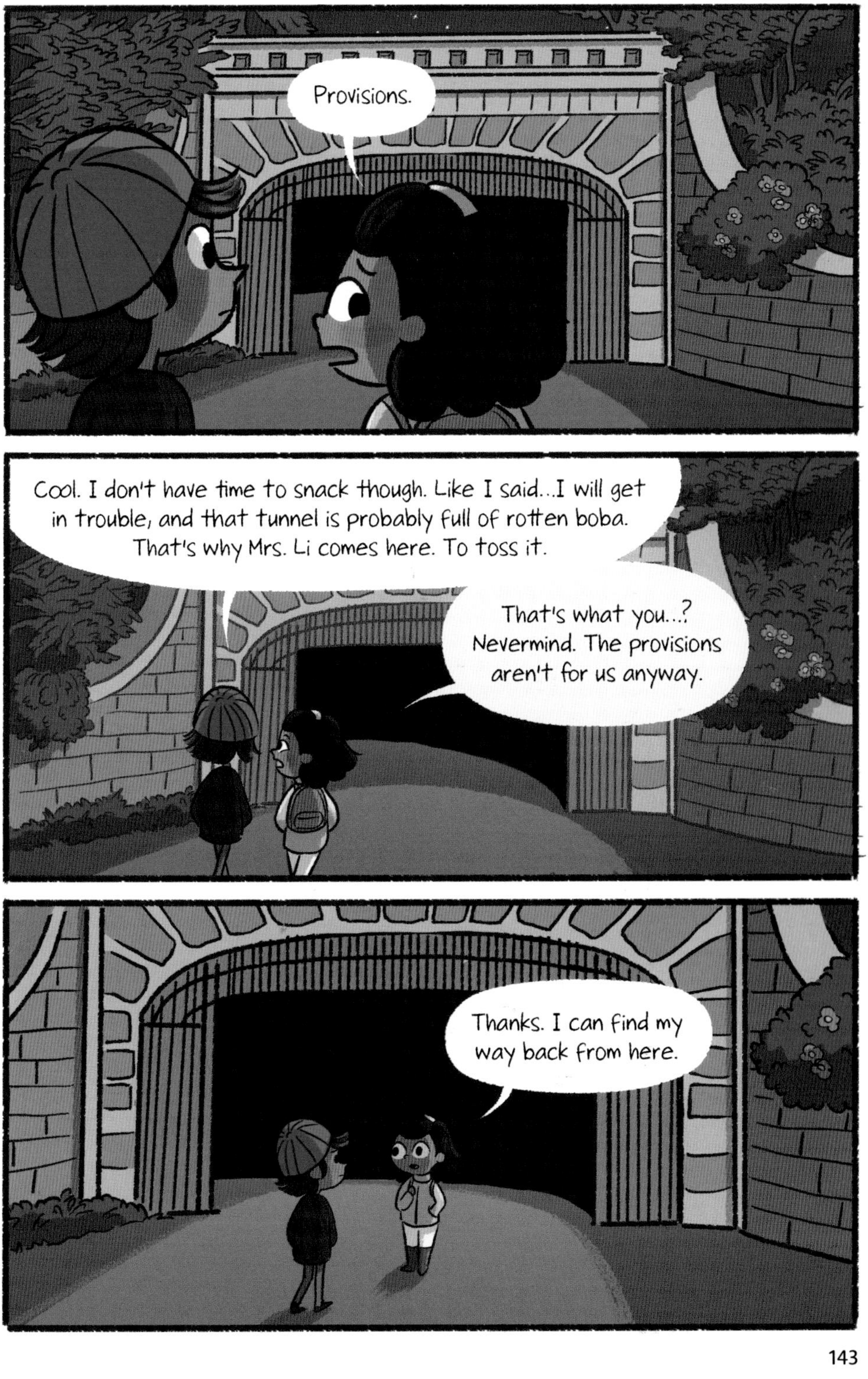
Provisions.
Cool. I don't have time to snack though. Like I said...I will get in trouble, and that tunnel is probably full of rotten boba. That's why Mrs. Li comes here. To toss it.
That's what you...? Nevermind. The provisions aren't for us anyway.
Thanks. I can find my way back from here.

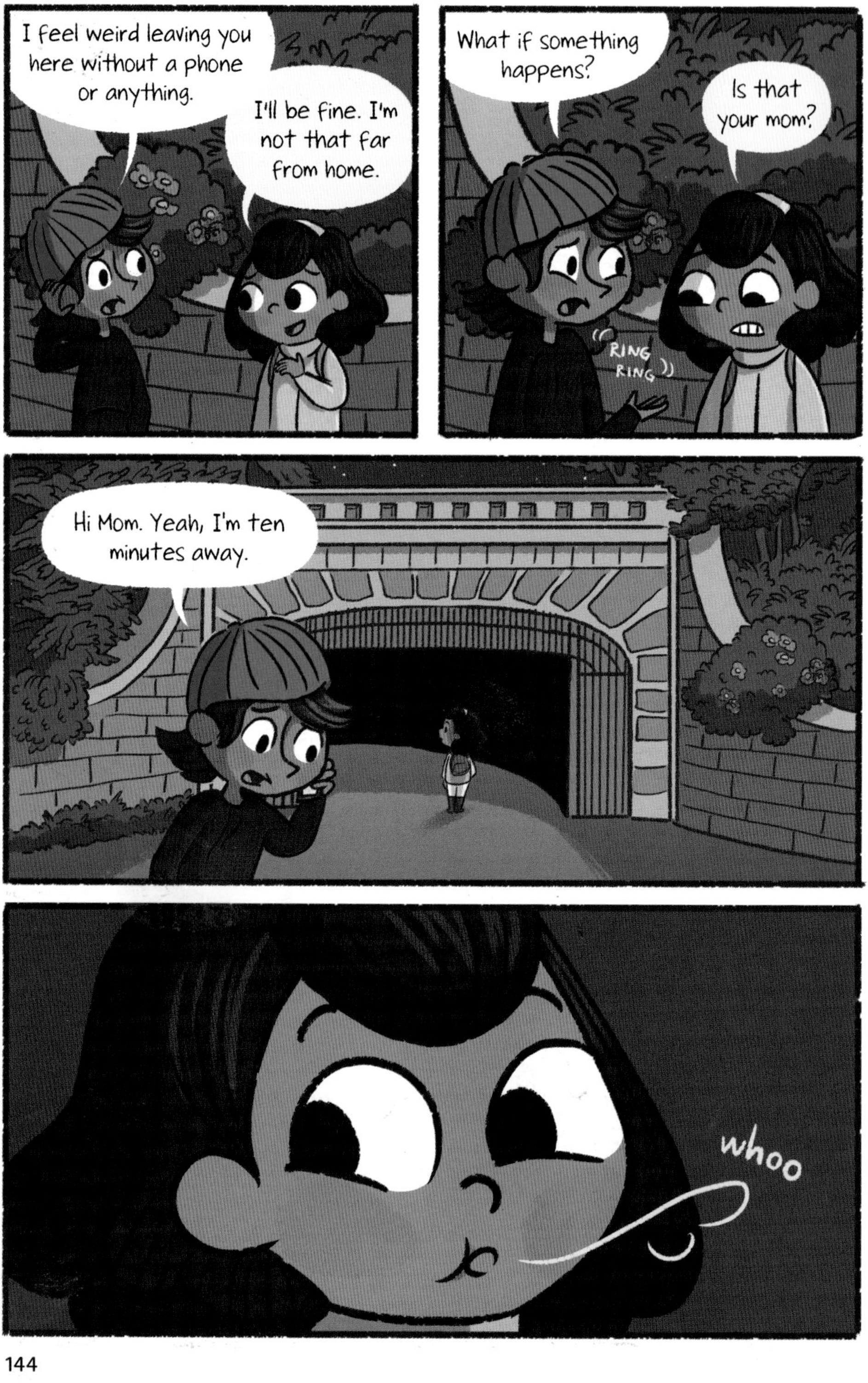
I feel weird leaving you here without a phone or anything.
I'll be fine. I'm not that far from home.
What if something happens?
RING RING
Is that your mom?
Hi Mom. Yeah, I'm ten minutes away.
whoo

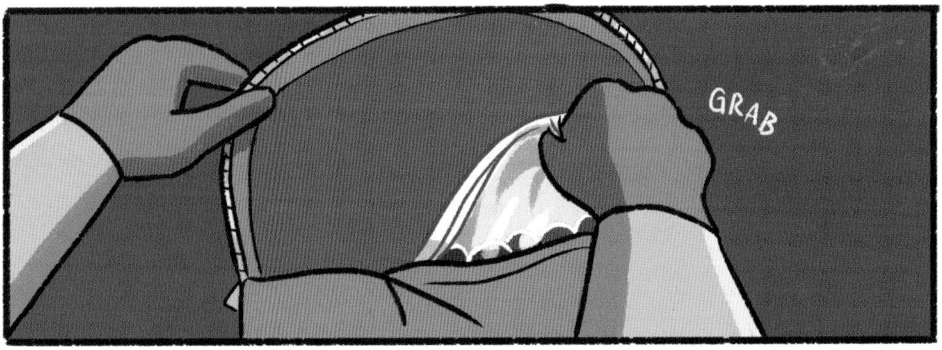
GRAB

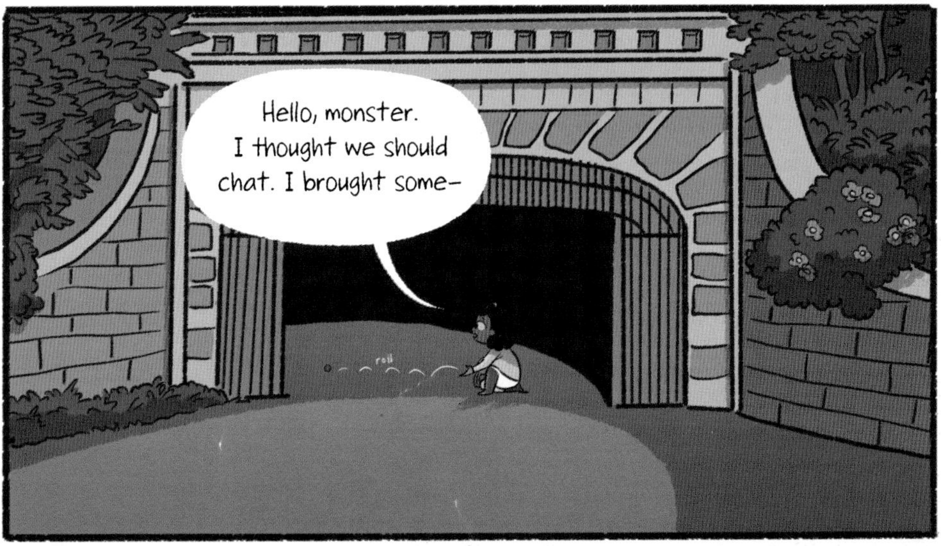
Hello, monster.
I thought we should
chat. I brought some-
roll

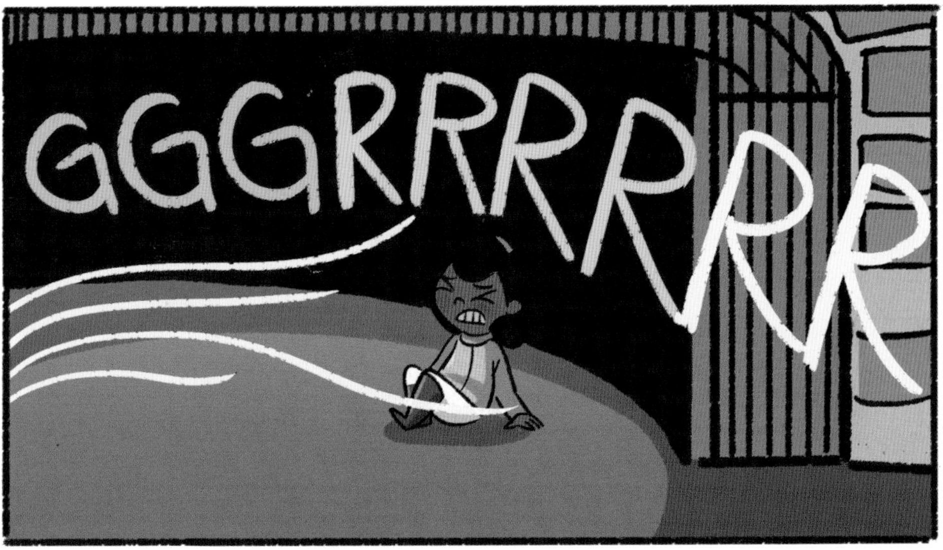
GGGRRRRRR

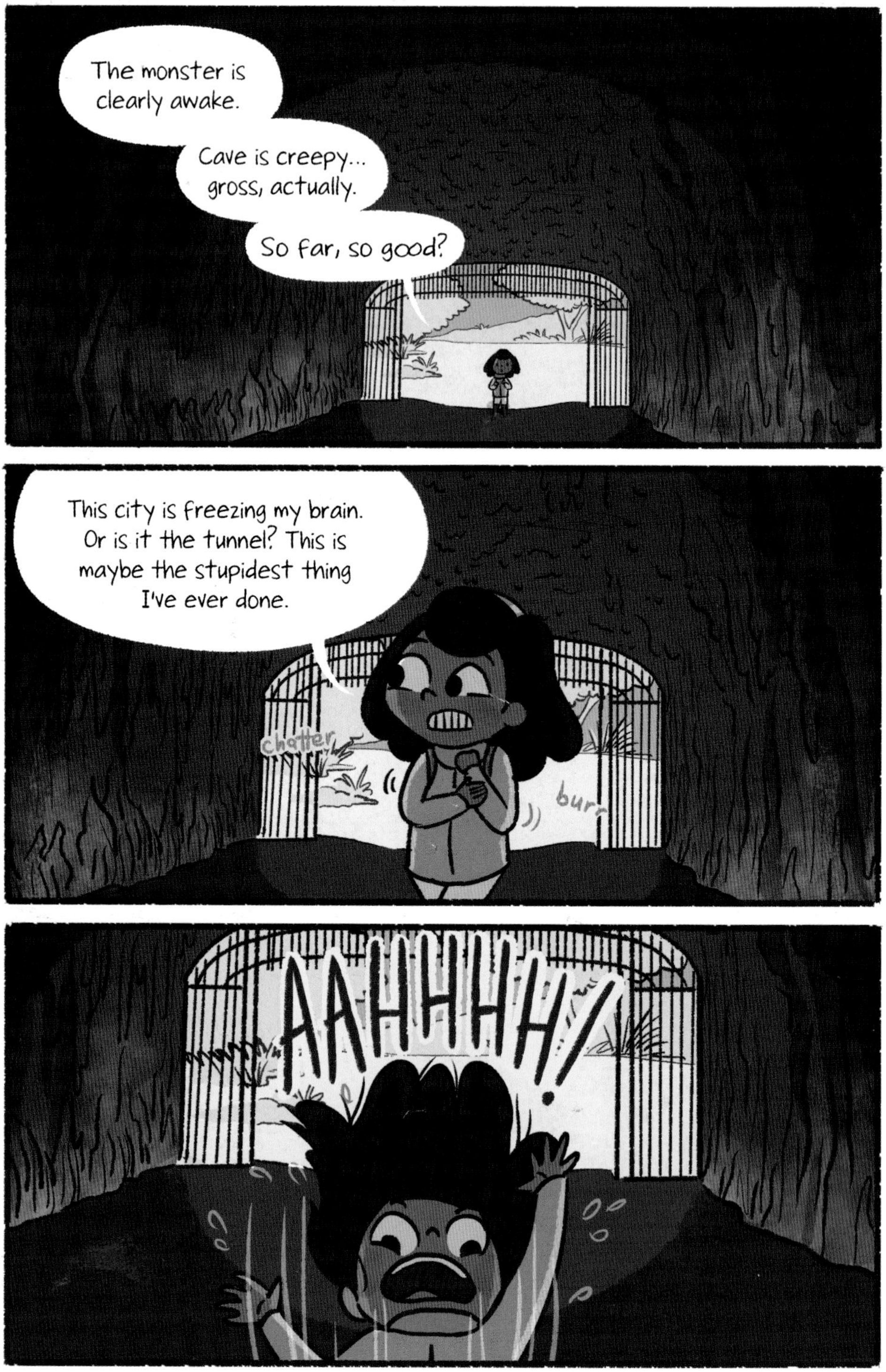
The monster is clearly awake.
Cave is creepy... gross, actually.
So far, so good?
This city is freezing my brain. Or is it the tunnel? This is maybe the stupidest thing I've ever done.
chatter
burr
AAHHHH!

NOOOO
OOOAAHHH
Help!

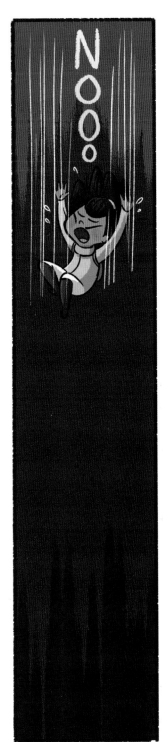

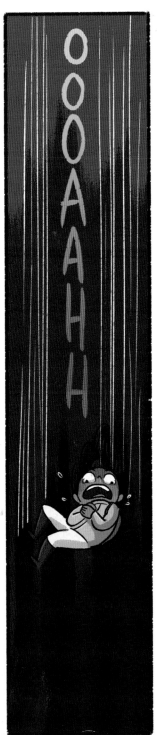

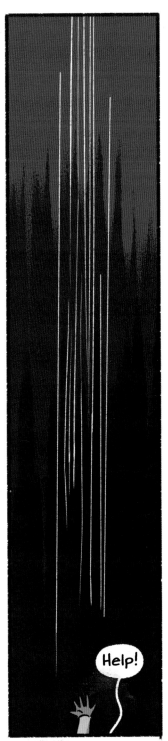

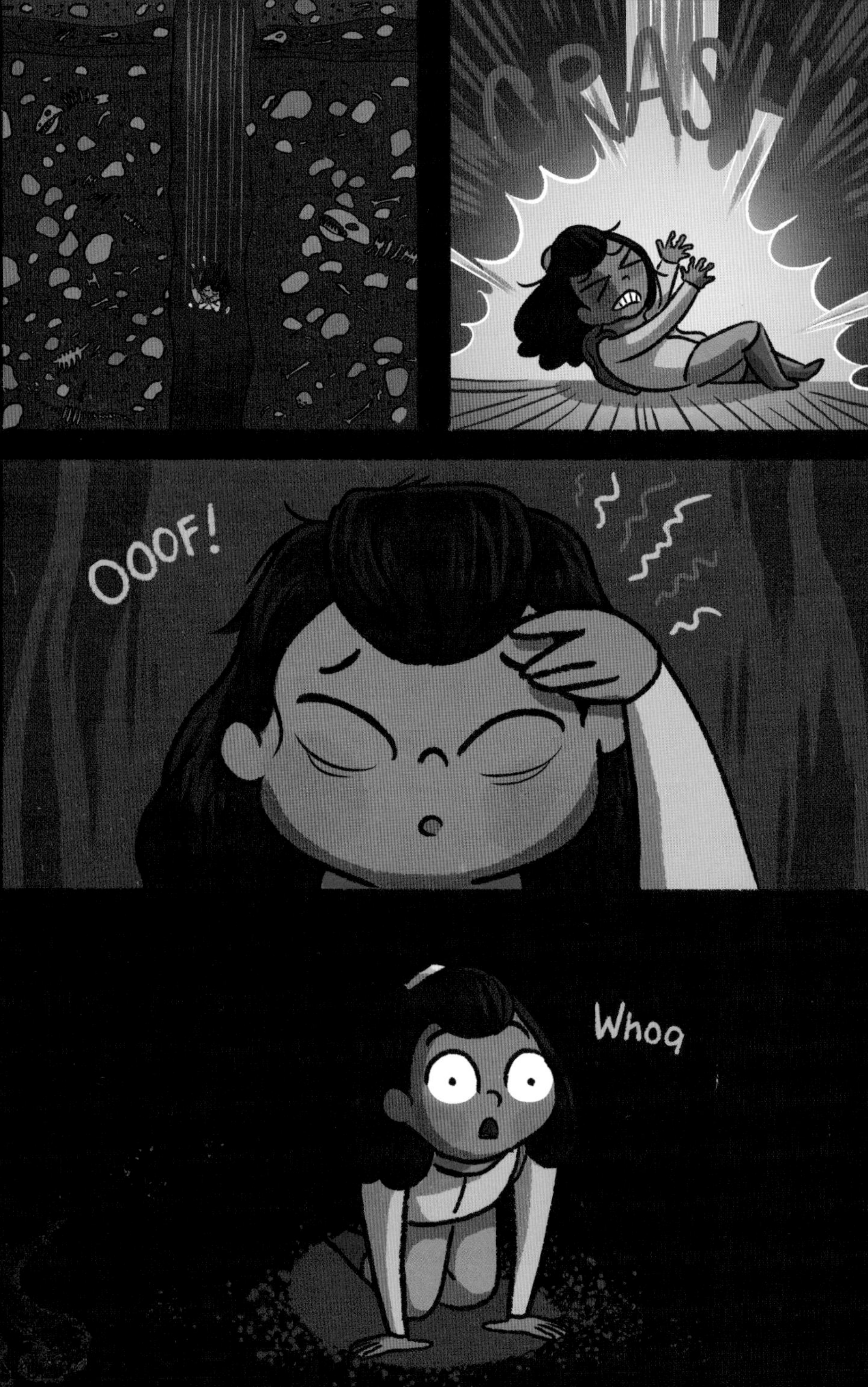
CRASH!
OOOF!
Whoa

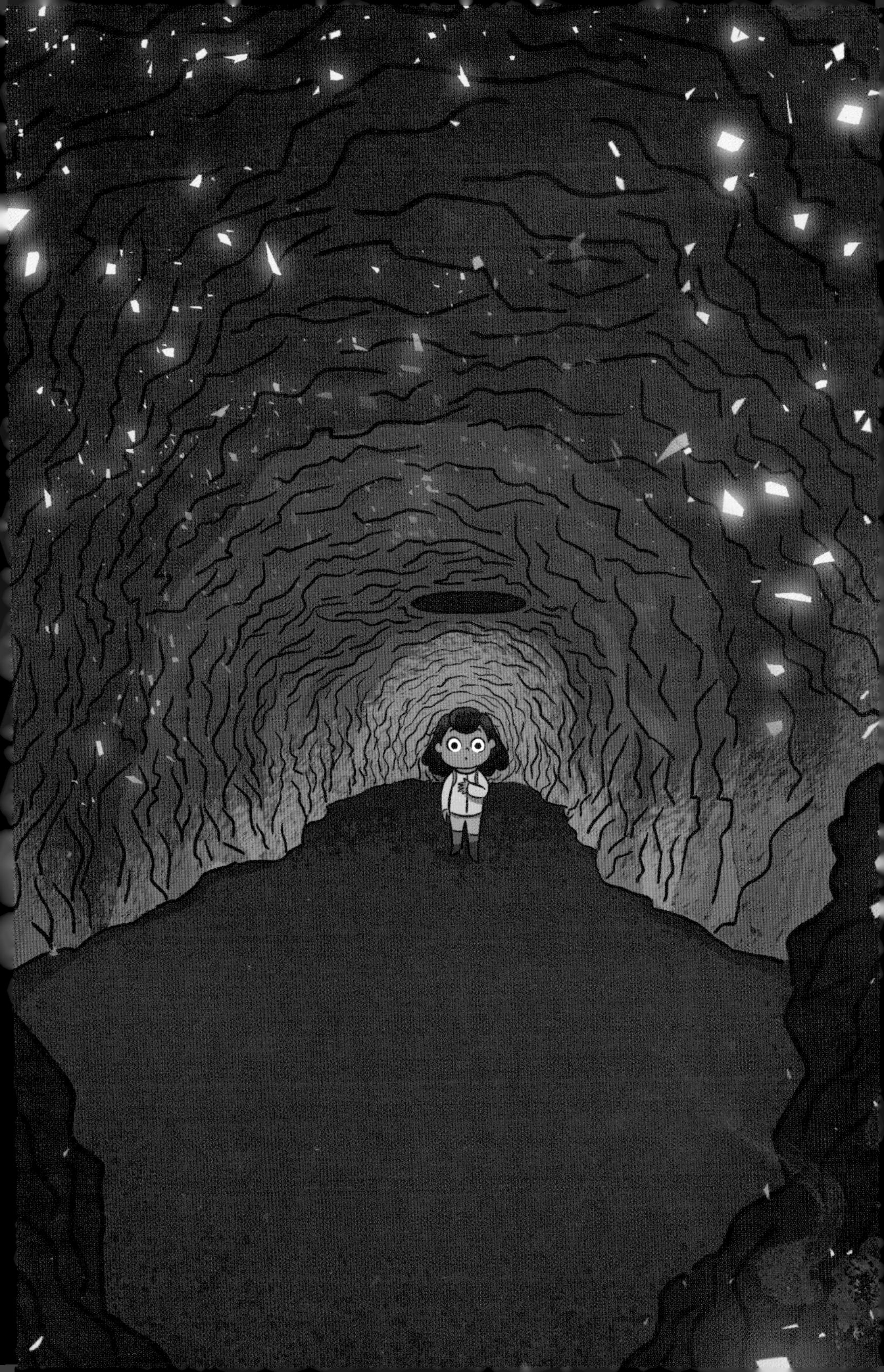

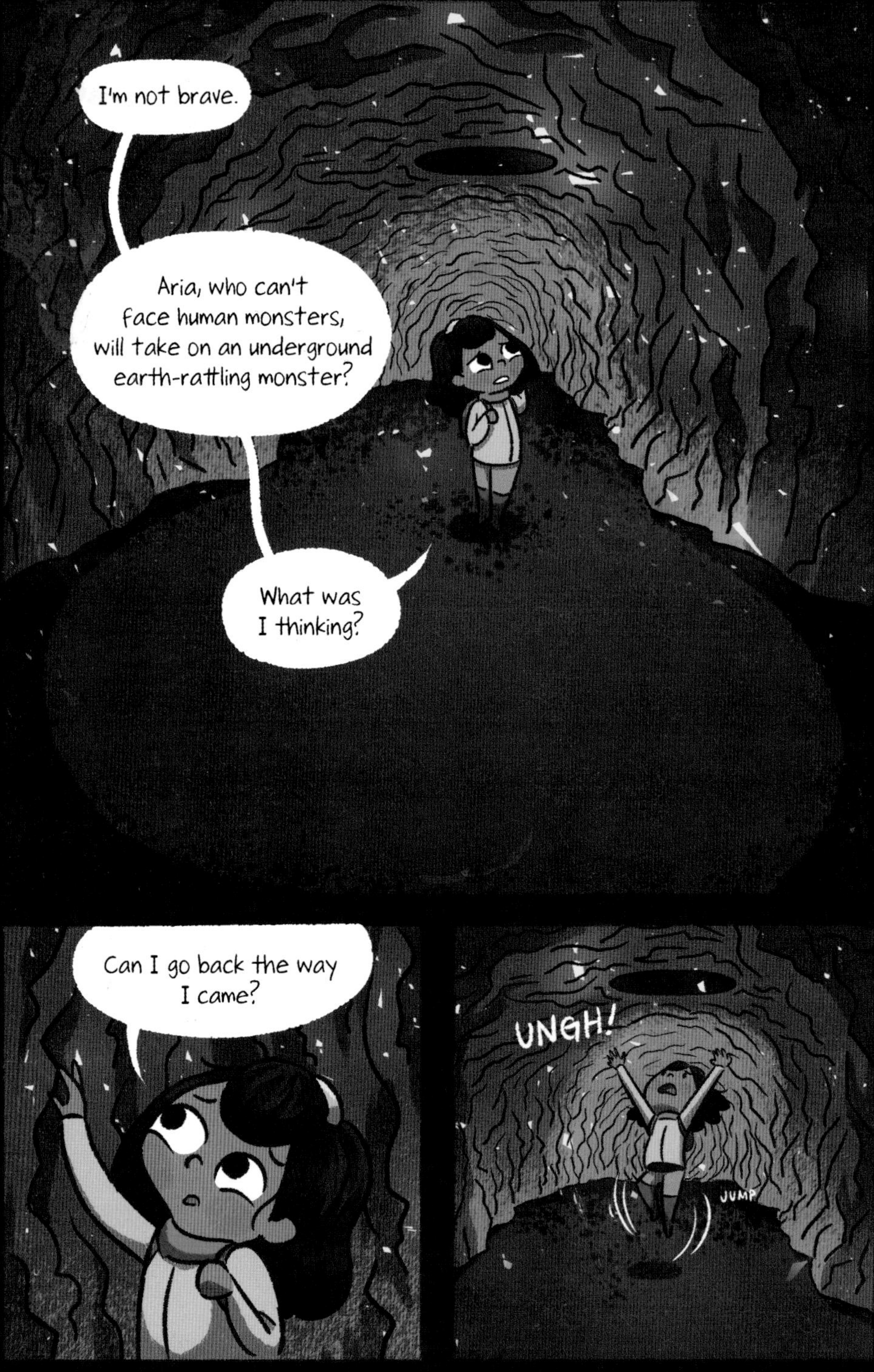

I'm not brave.
Aria, who can't face human monsters, will take on an underground earth-rattling monster?
What was I thinking?
Can I go back the way I came?
UNGH!
JUMP

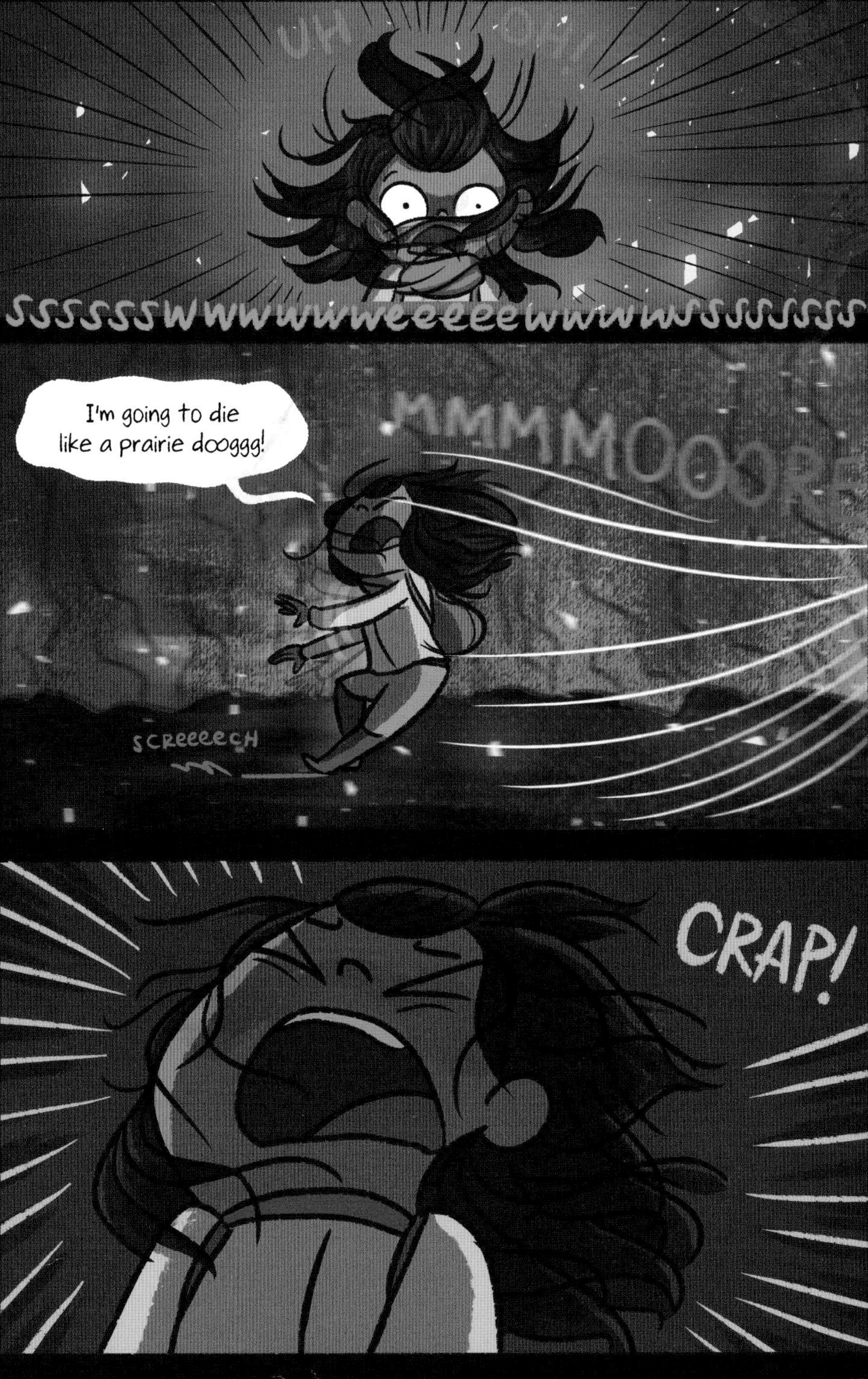
UH
SSSSSSWWWWWWeeeeeewwwwwSSSSSSSS
I'm going to die like a prairie dooggg!
MMMMOOOR
SCREEEECH
CRAP!

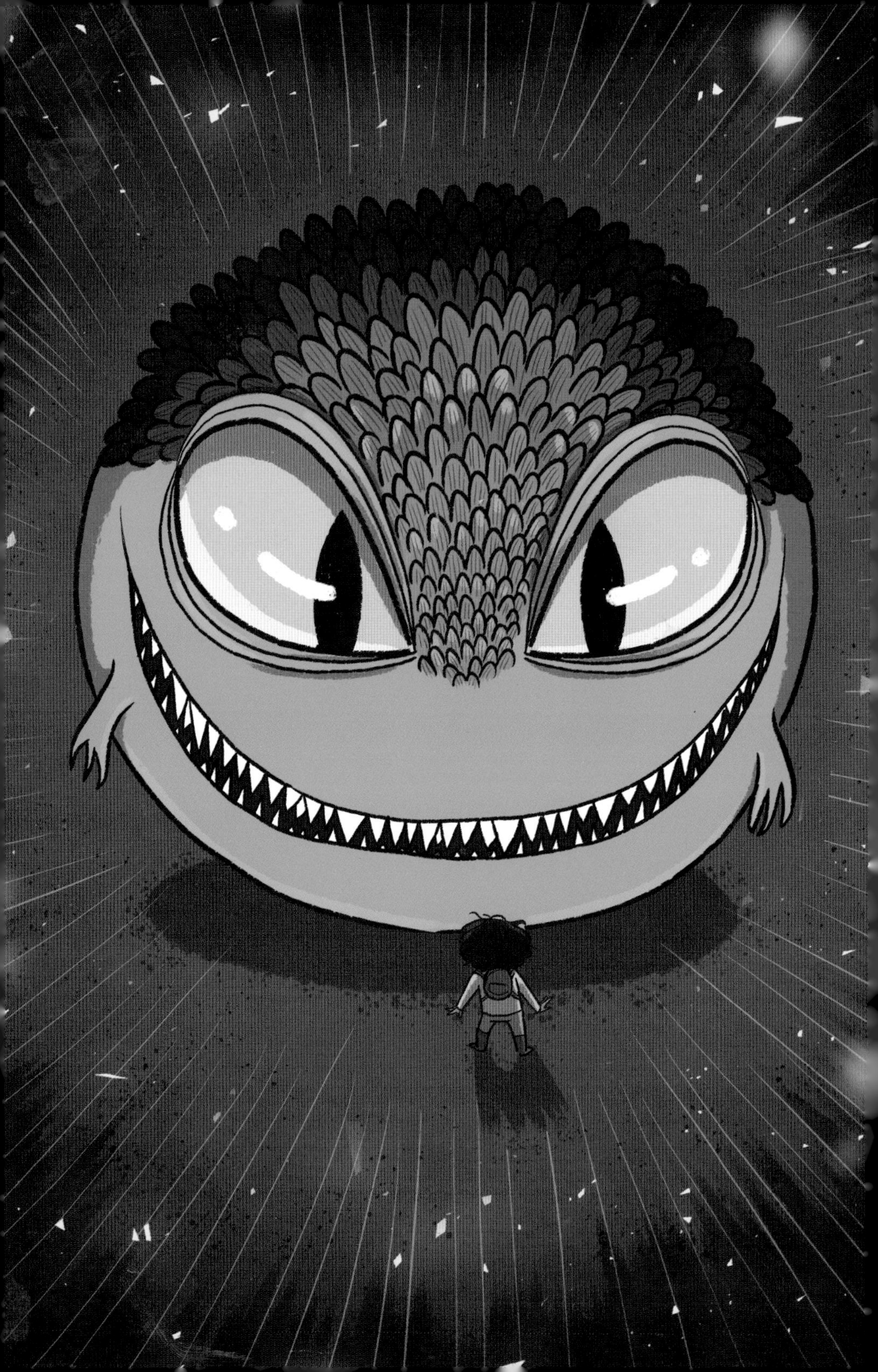

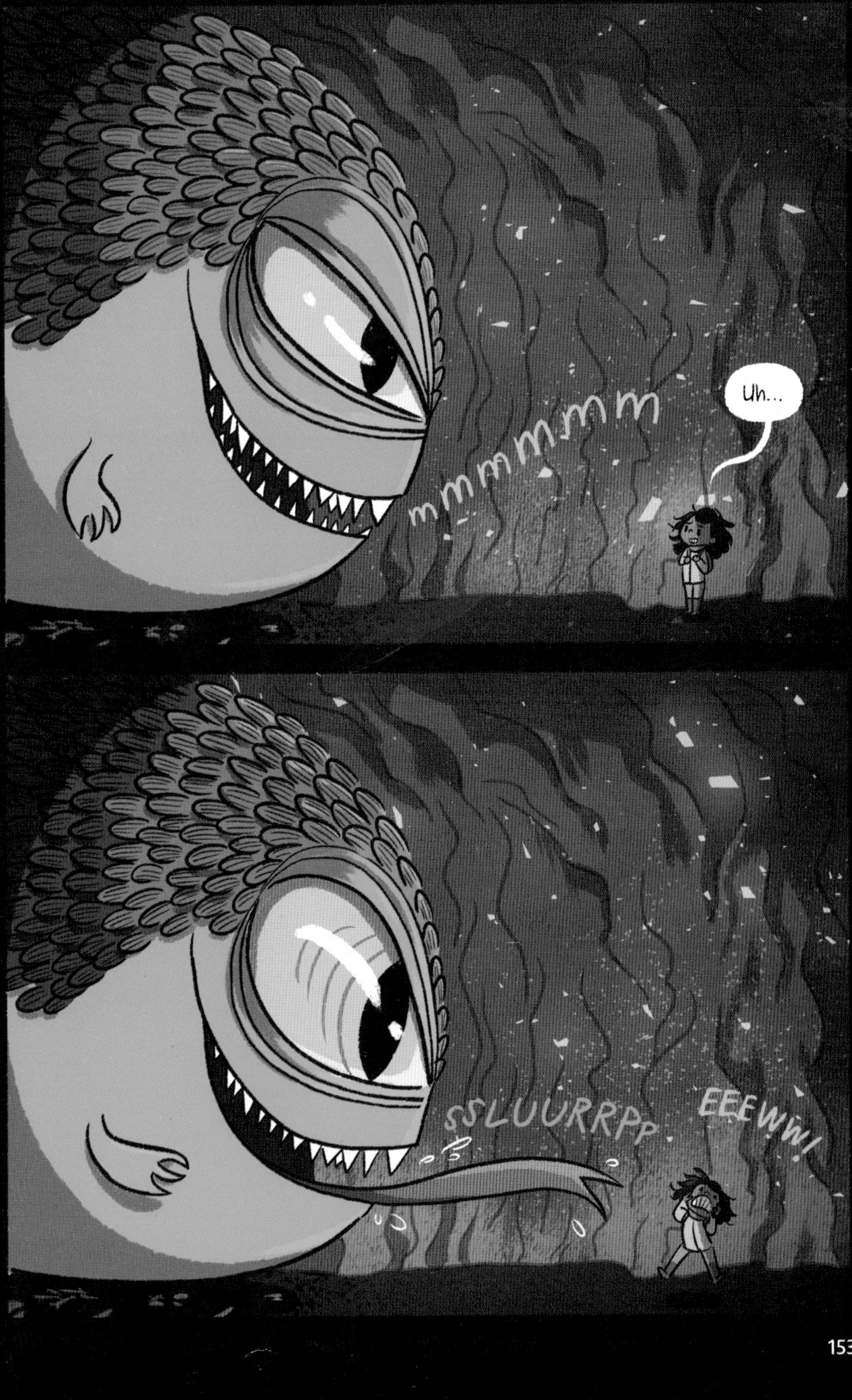
mmmmmmmm
Uh...
SSLUURRPP
EEEWW!

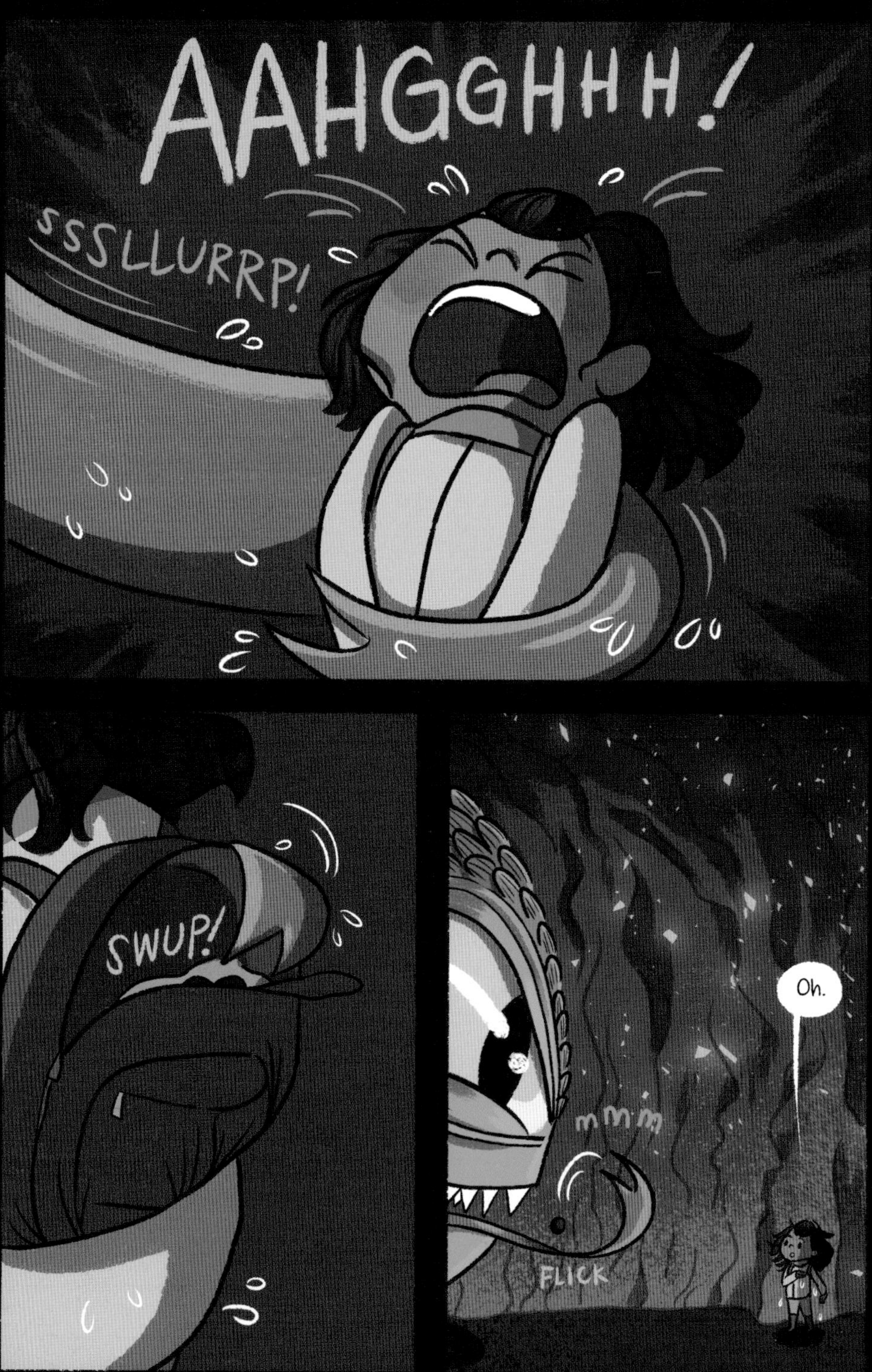
AAHGGHHH!
SSSLLURRP!
SWUP!
MMM
FLICK
Oh.

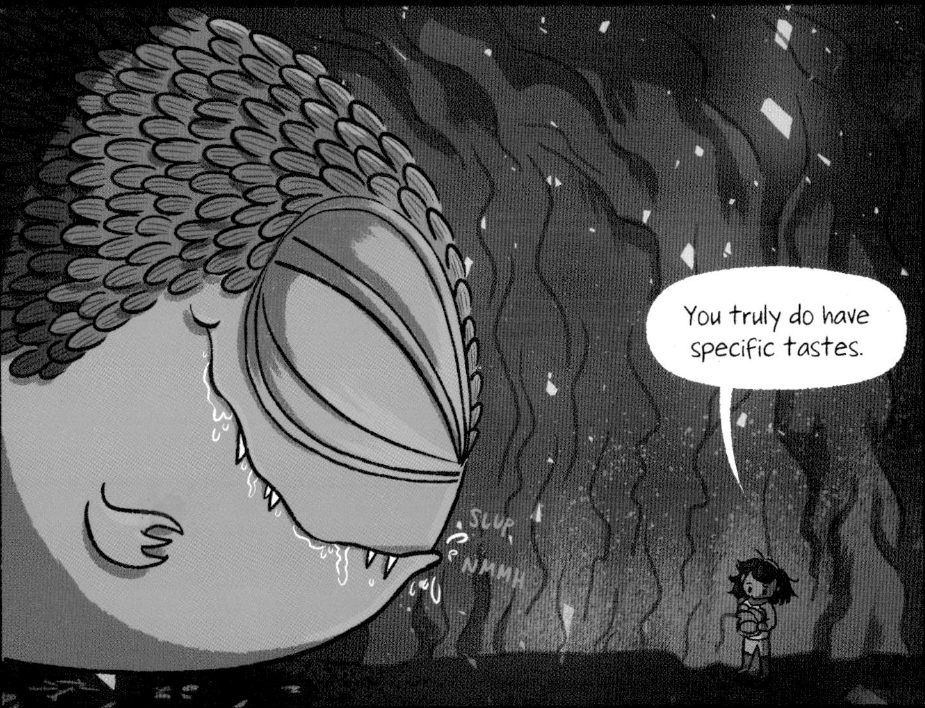
SLUP
NMMH
You truly do have specific tastes.

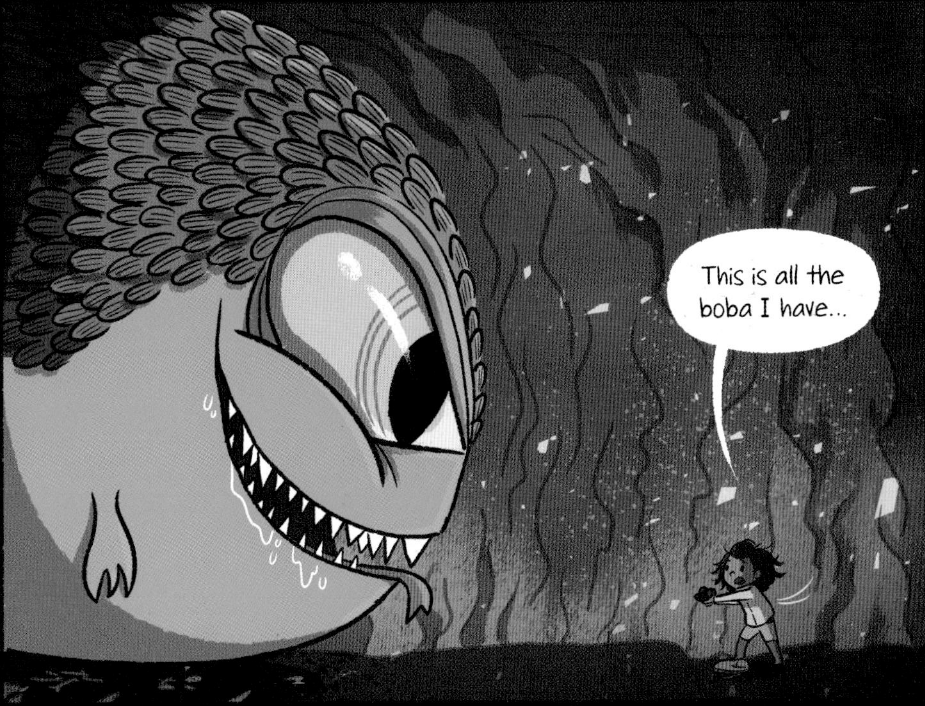
This is all the boba I have...

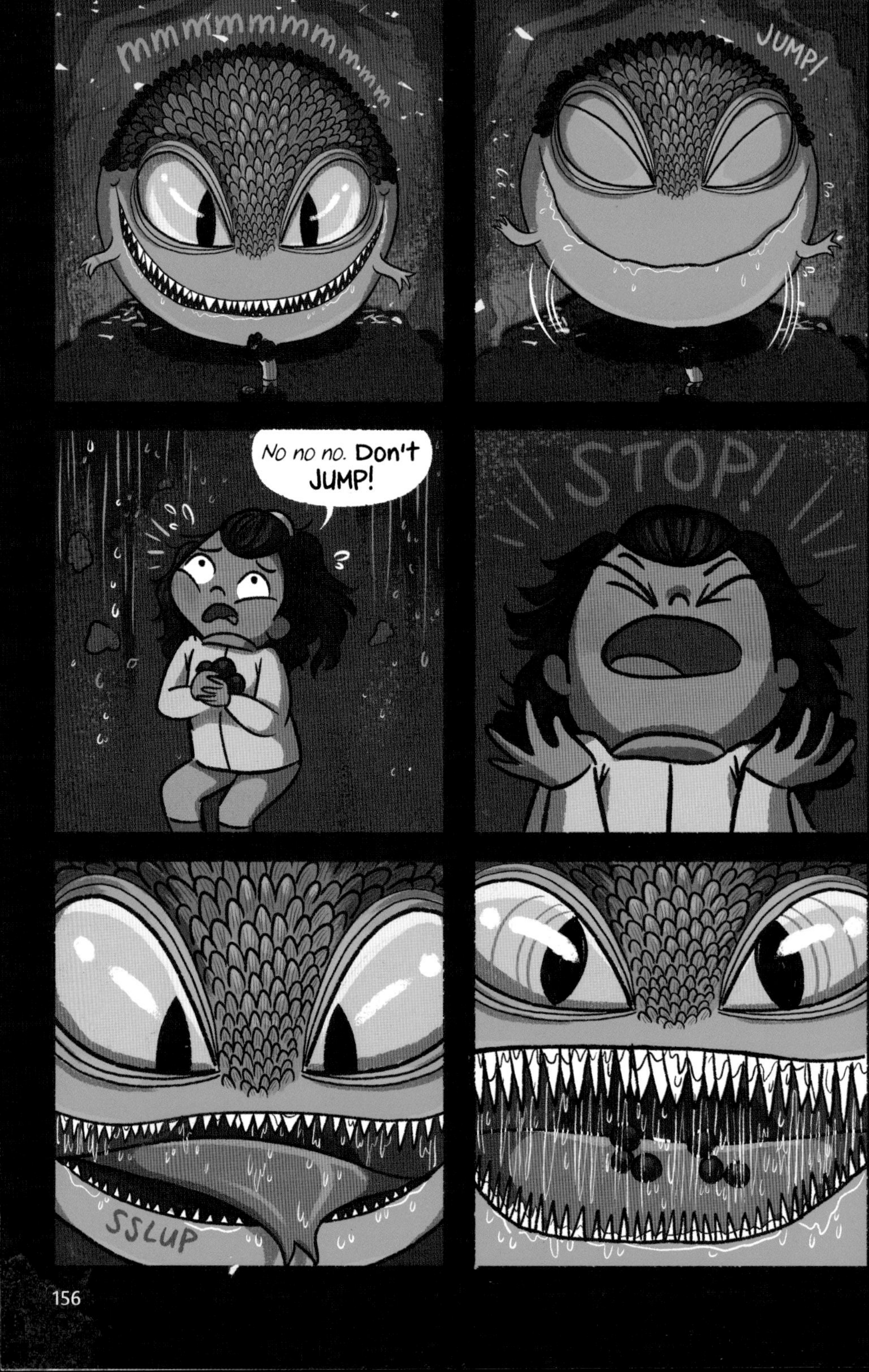
mmmmmmmmmmmm
JUMP!
No no no. Don't JUMP!
STOP!
SSLUP

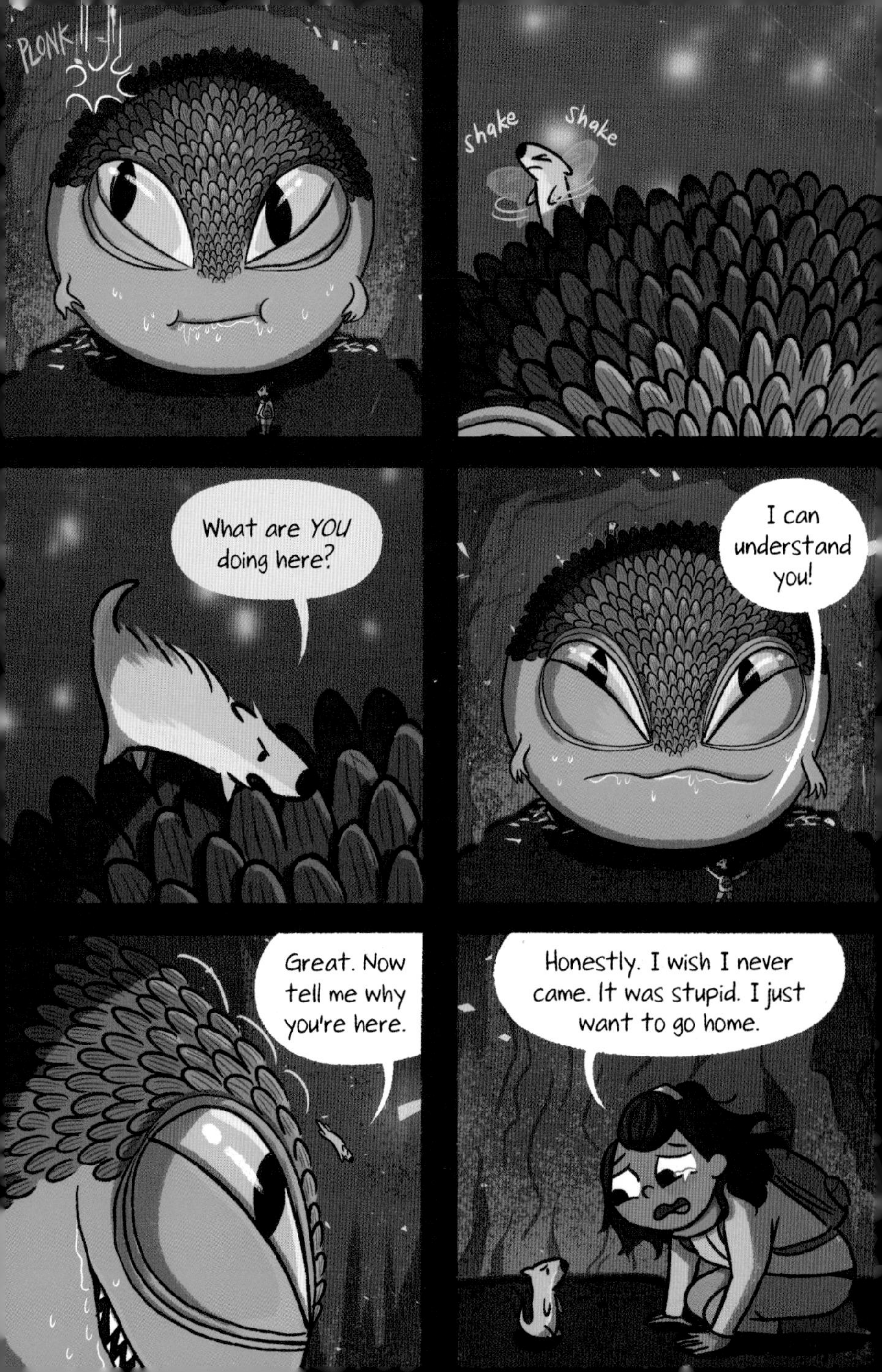
PLONK
shake shake
What are YOU doing here?
I can understand you!
Great. Now tell me why you're here.
Honestly. I wish I never came. It was stupid. I just want to go home.

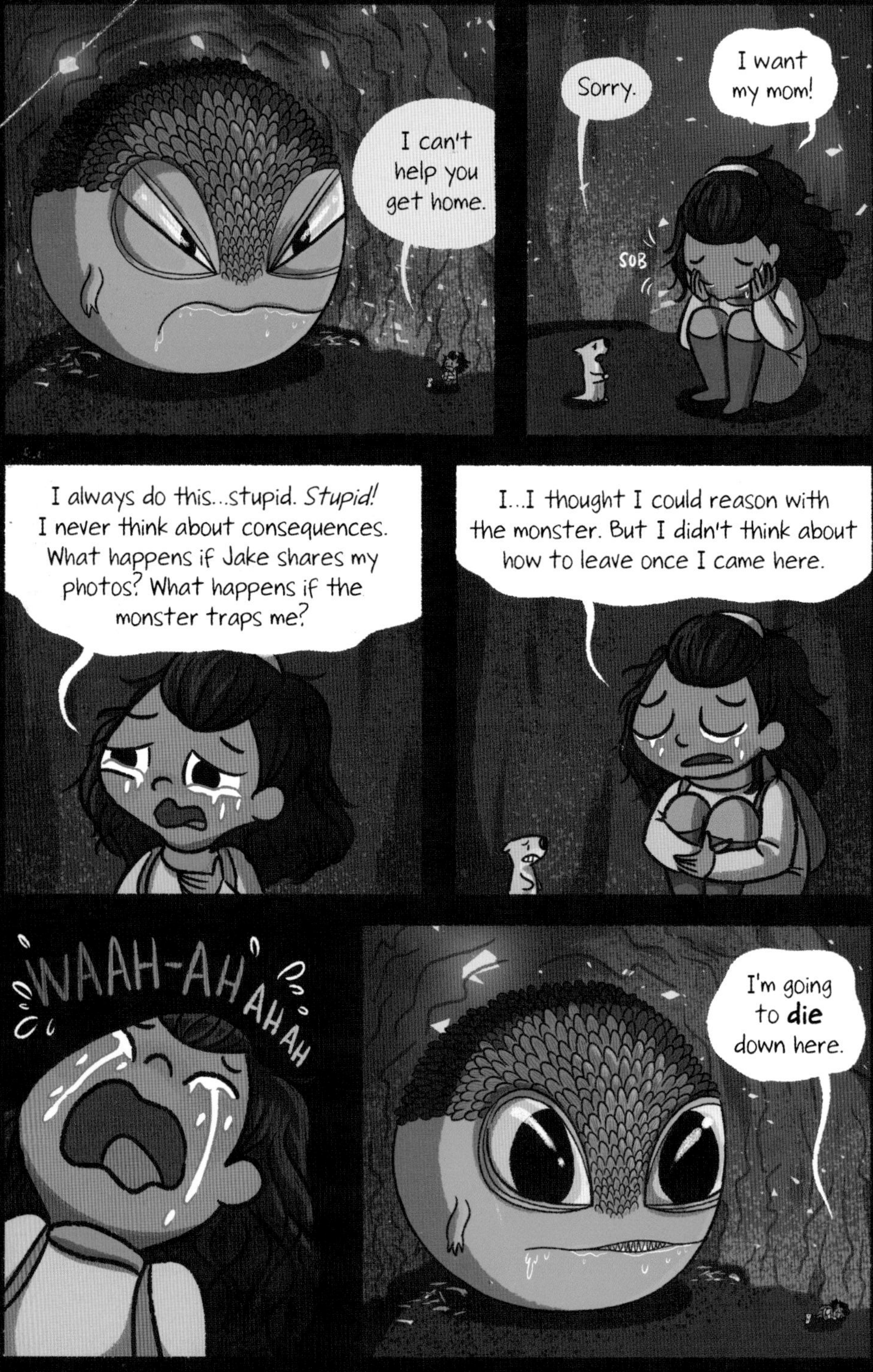
I can't help you get home.
Sorry.
I want my mom!
SOB
I always do this...stupid. *Stupid!* I never think about consequences. What happens if Jake shares my photos? What happens if the monster traps me?
I...I thought I could reason with the monster. But I didn't think about how to leave once I came here.
WAAH-AH AH AH AH
I'm going to **die** down here.

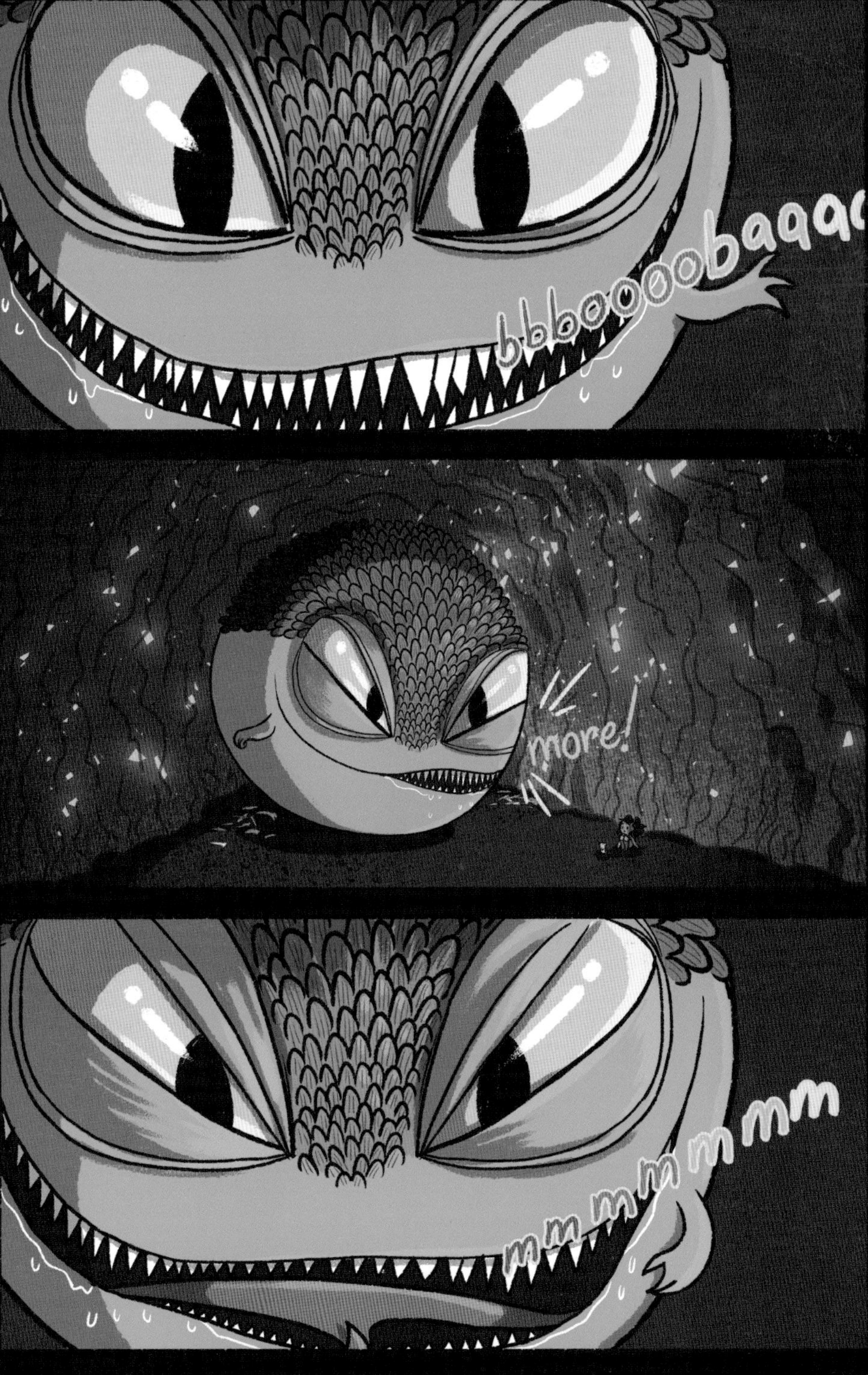
bbbooooobaaa
more!
mmmmmmm

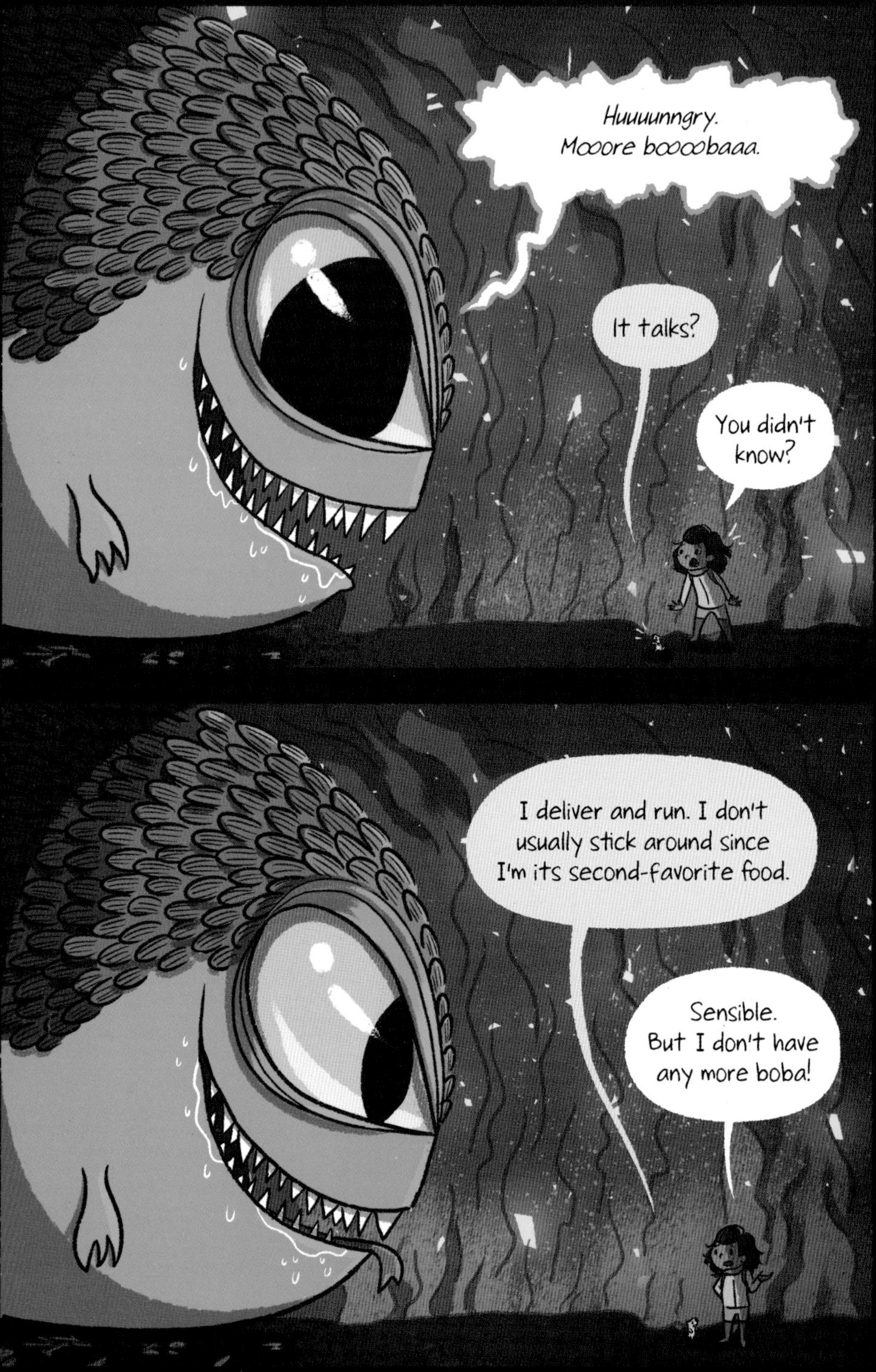
Huuuunngry. Mooore booooobaaa.
It talks?
You didn't know?
I deliver and run. I don't usually stick around since I'm its second-favorite food.
Sensible. But I don't have any more boba!

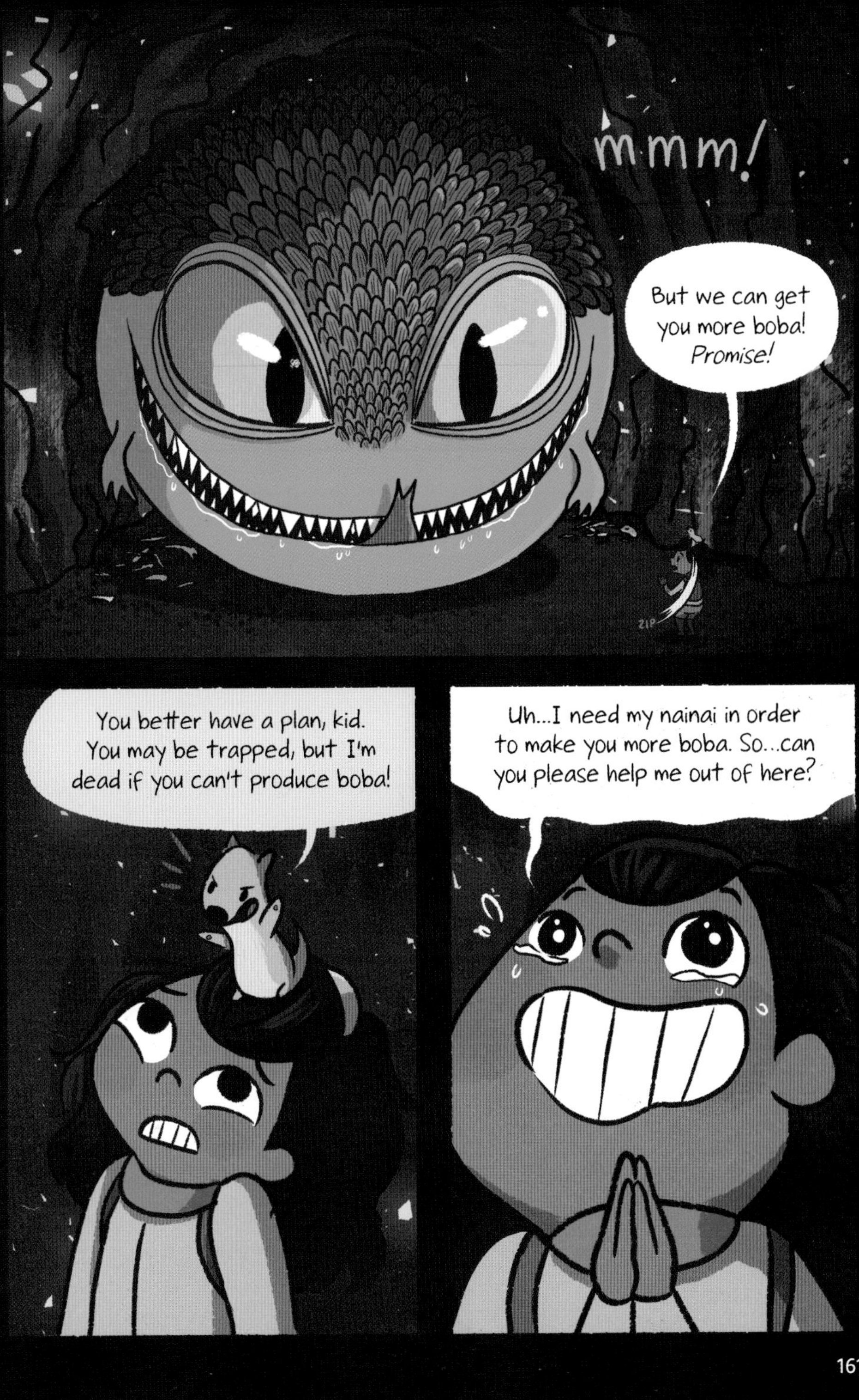
mmm!
But we can get you more boba! *Promise!*
ZIP
You better have a plan, kid. You may be trapped, but I'm dead if you can't produce boba!
Uh...I need my nainai in order to make you more boba. So...can you please help me out of here?

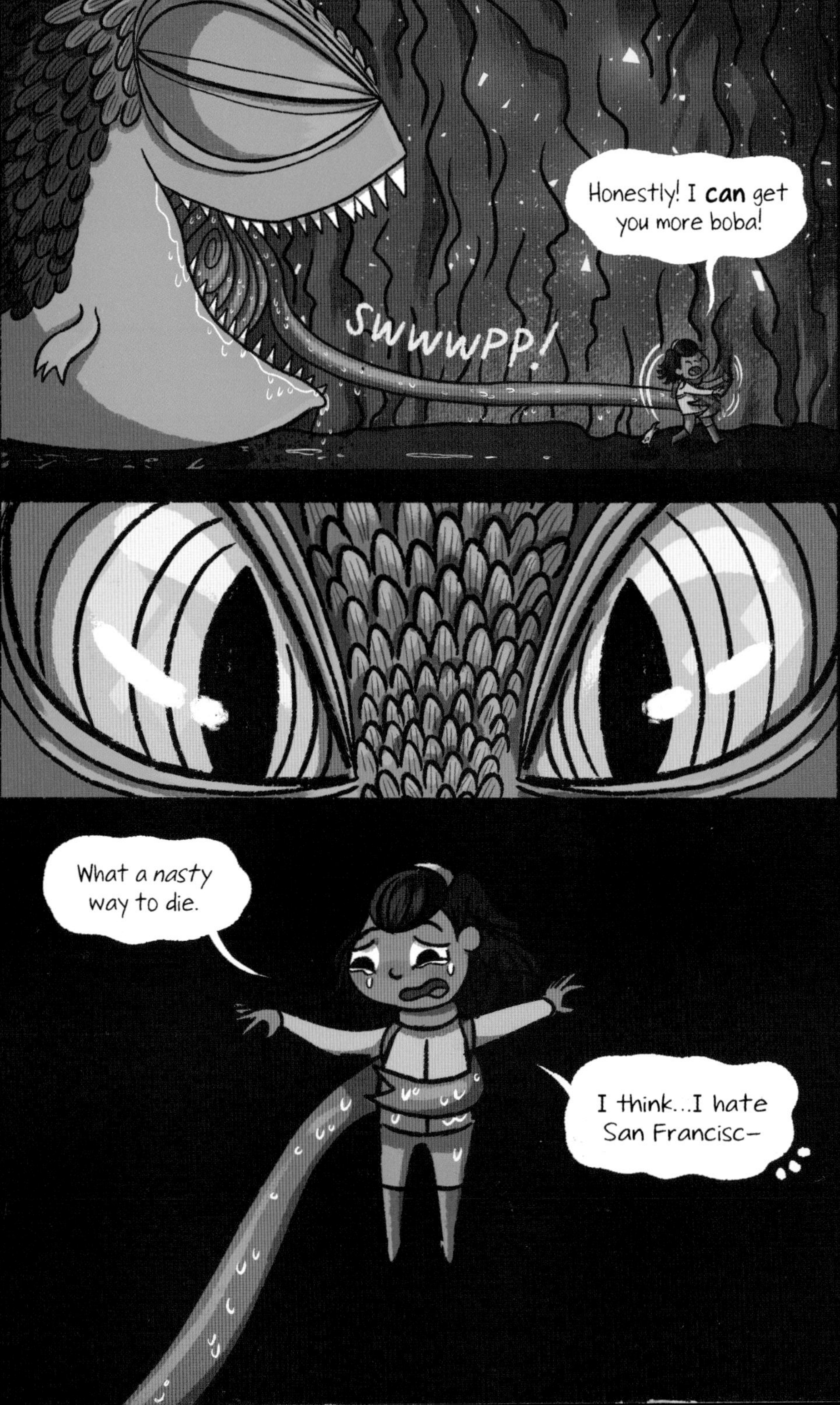
Honestly! I **can** get you more boba!
SWWWPP!
What a nasty way to die.
I think...I hate San Francisc–

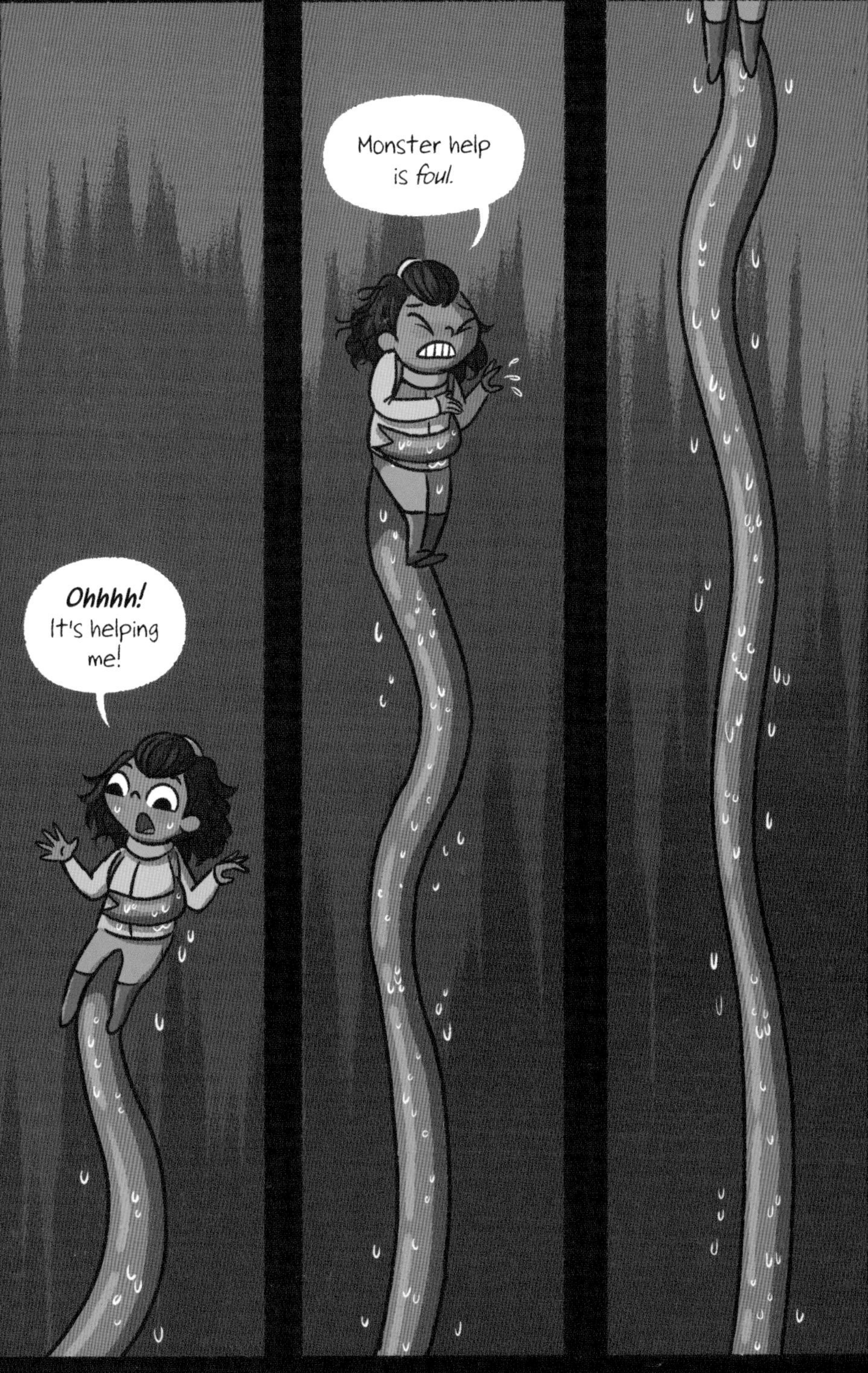
Ohhhh! It's helping me!
Monster help is *foul.*

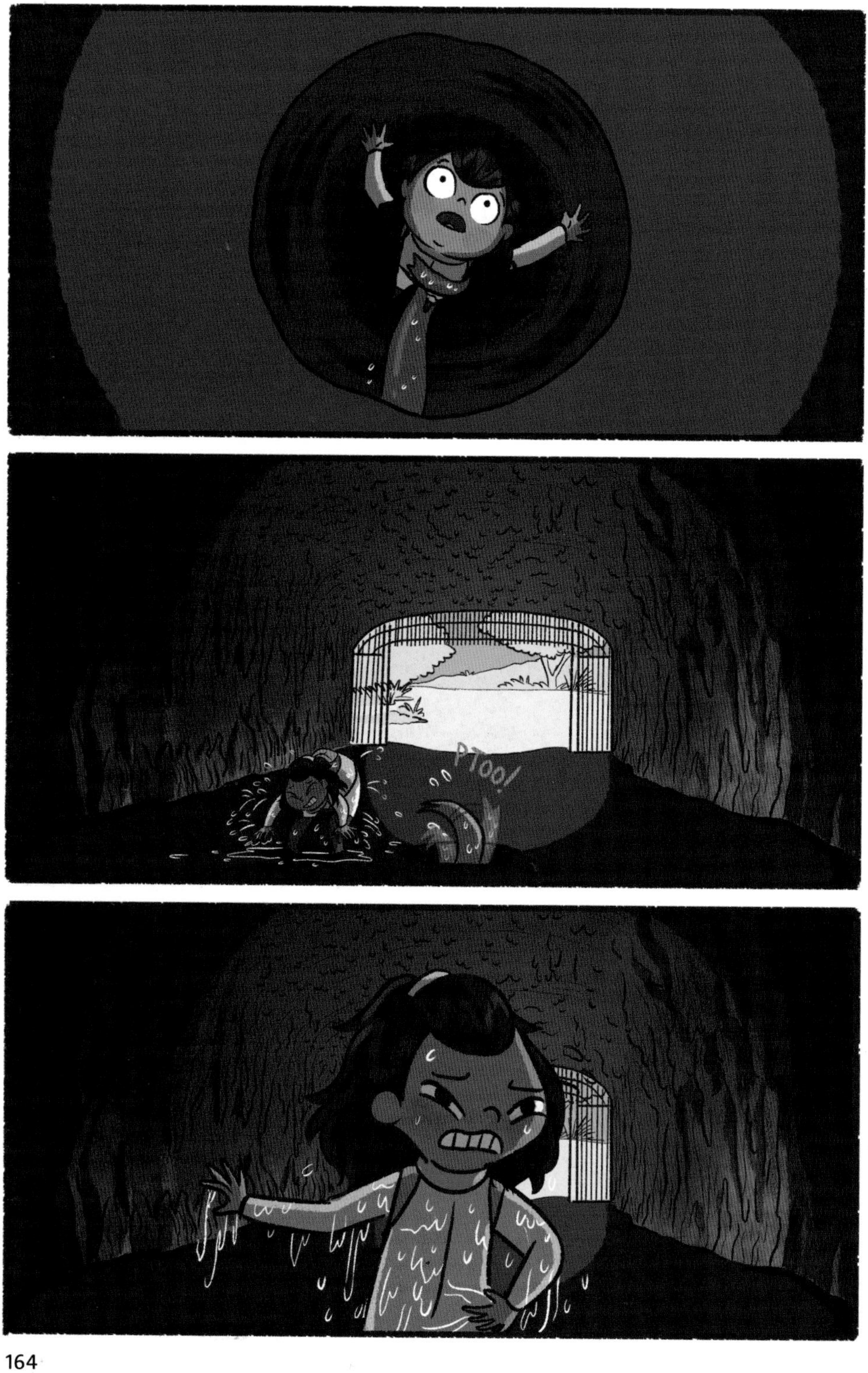
PTOO!

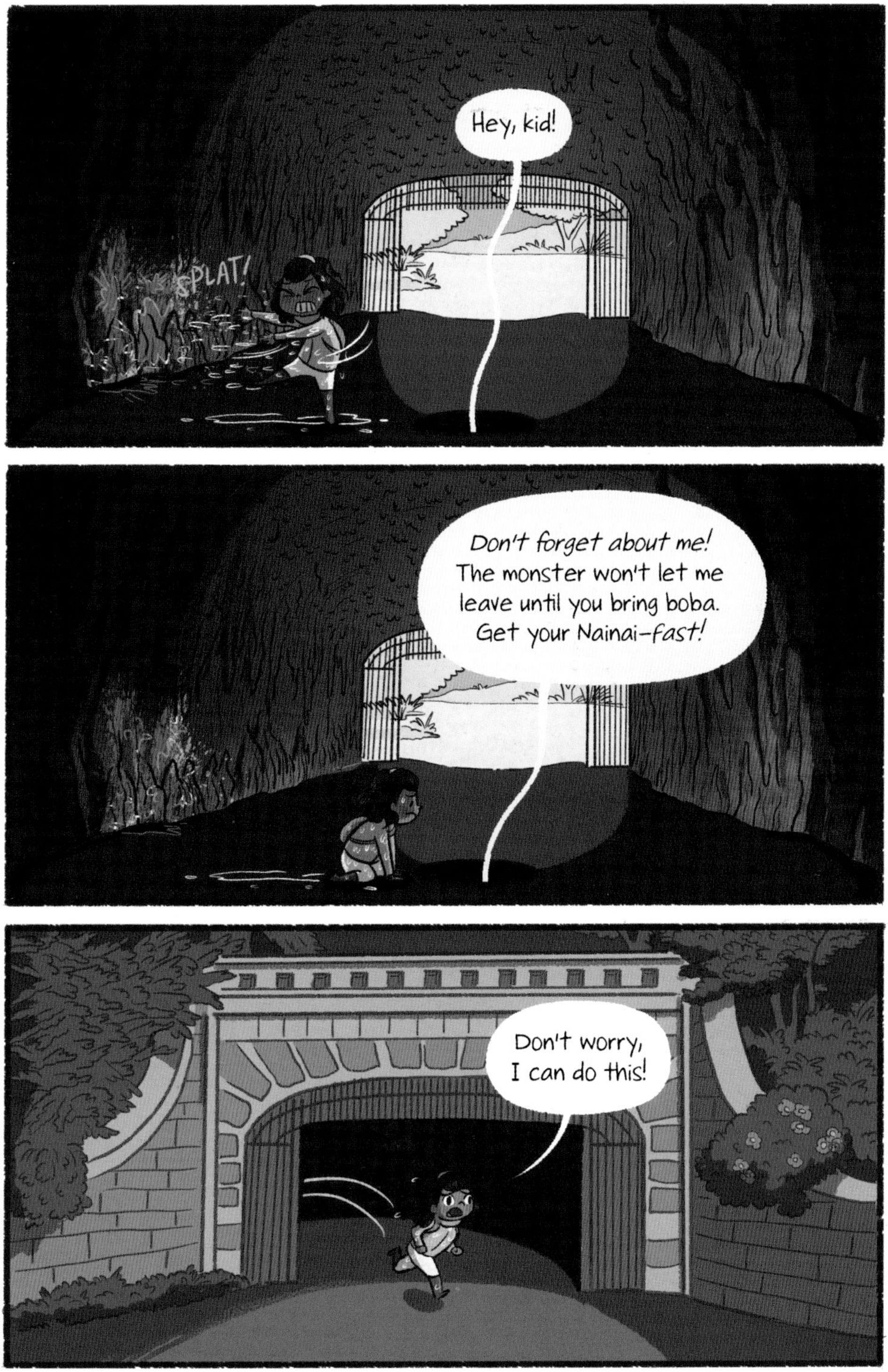
SPLAT!
Hey, kid!
Don't forget about me! The monster won't let me leave until you bring boba. Get your Nainai-fast!
Don't worry, I can do this!

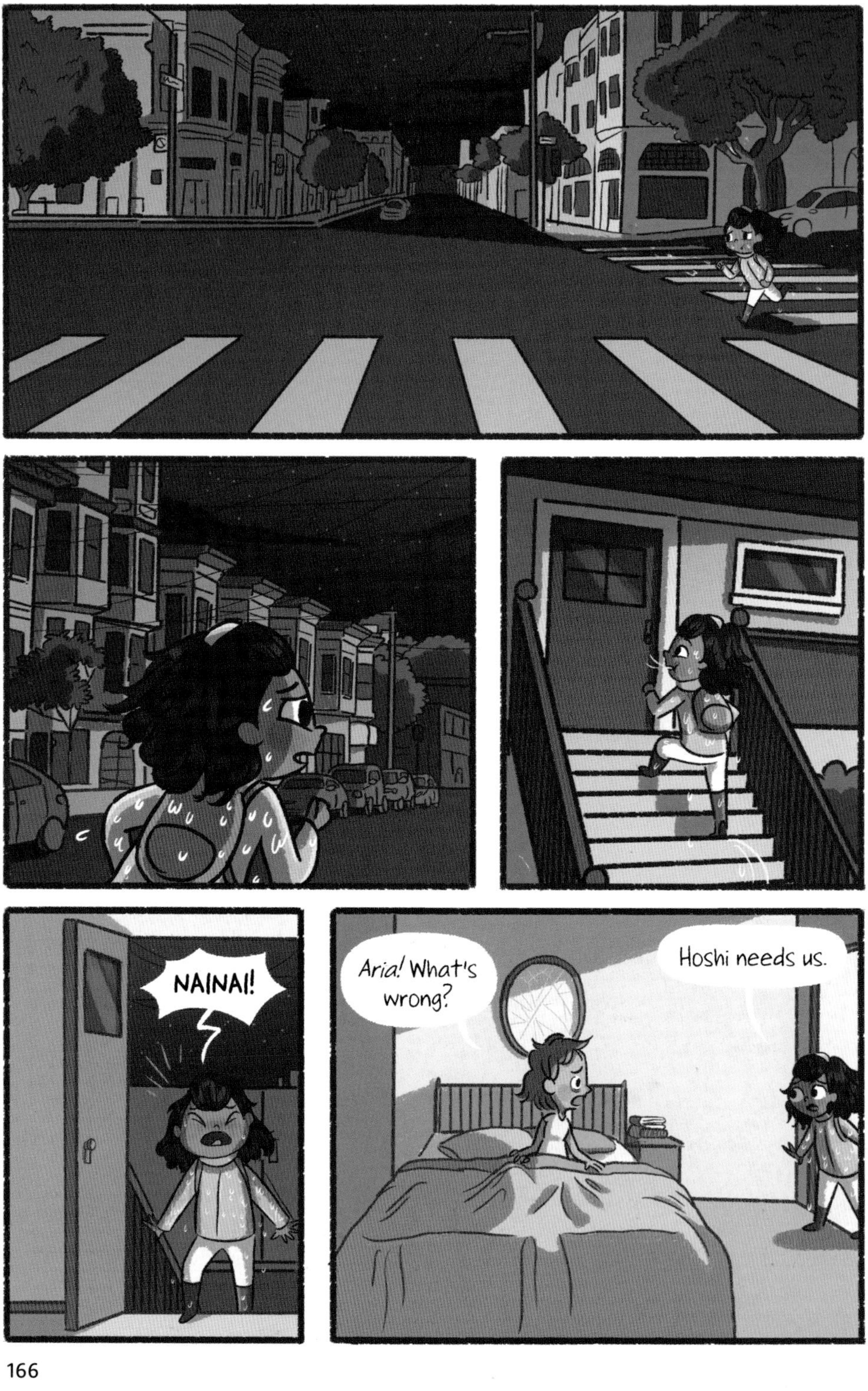
NAINAI!
Aria! What's wrong?
Hoshi needs us.

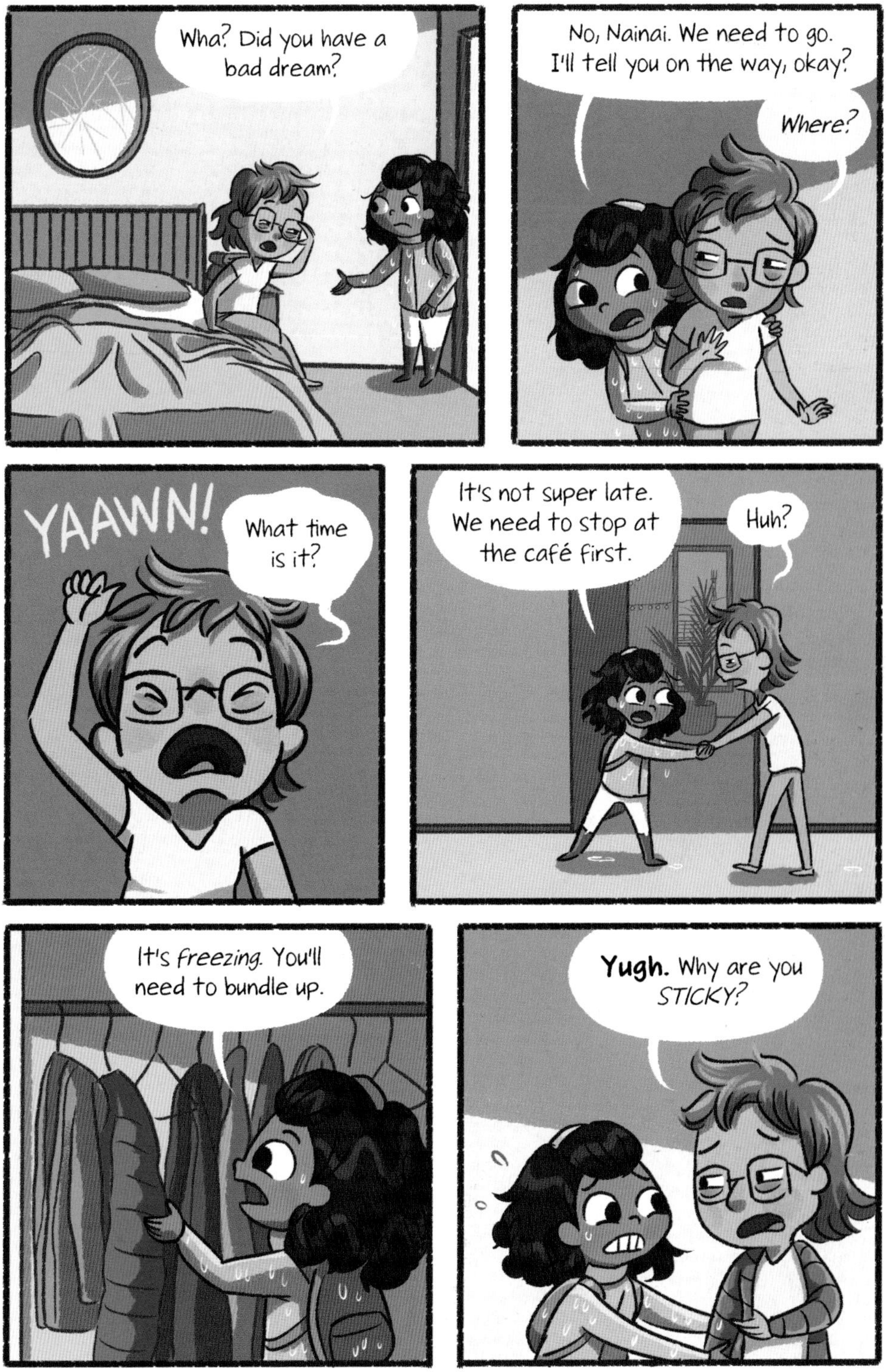
Wha? Did you have a bad dream?
No, Nainai. We need to go. I'll tell you on the way, okay?
Where?
YAAWN!
What time is it?
It's not super late. We need to stop at the café first.
Huh?
It's *freezing*. You'll need to bundle up.
Yugh. Why are you *STICKY?*

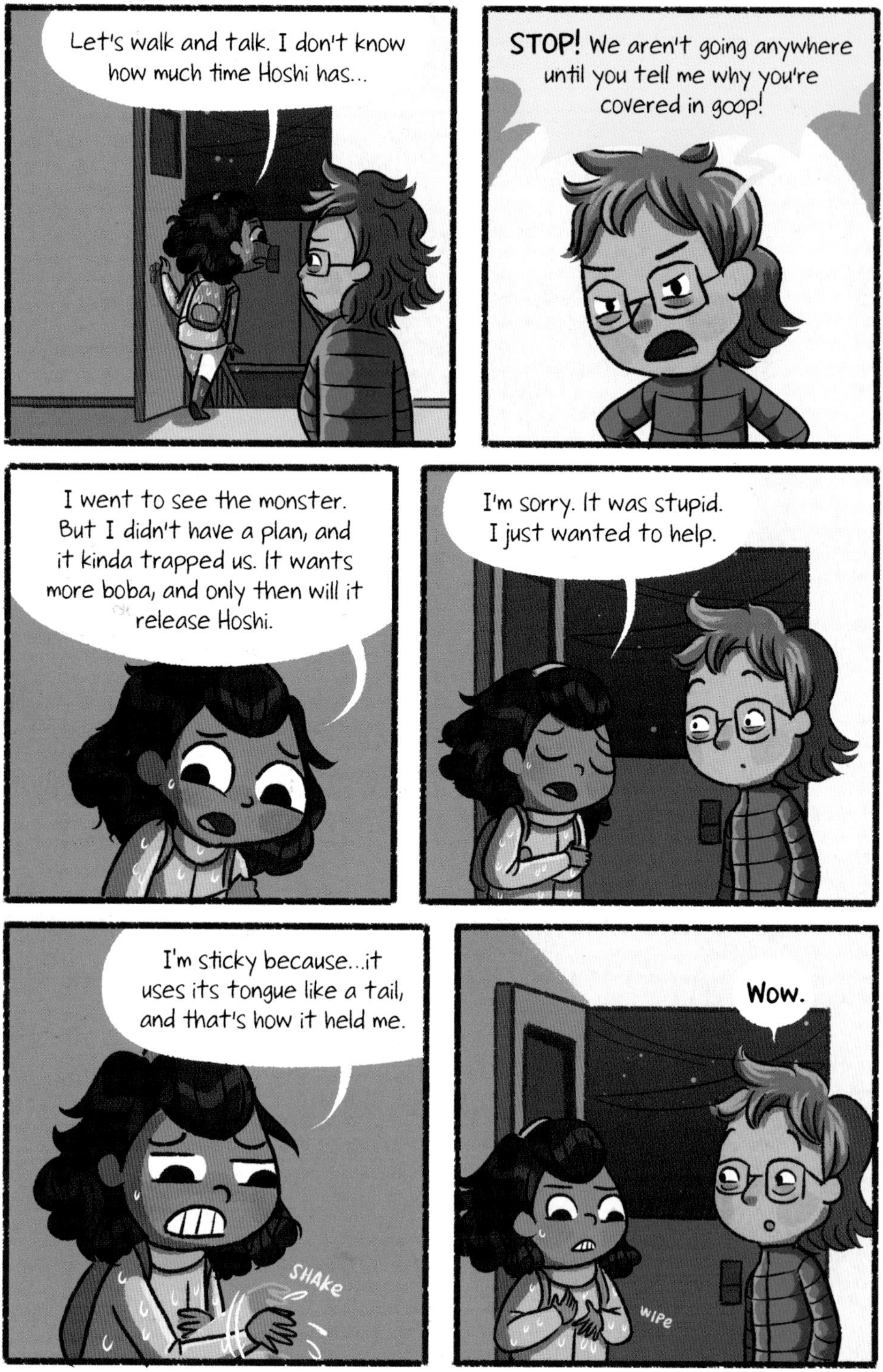
Let's walk and talk. I don't know how much time Hoshi has...
STOP! We aren't going anywhere until you tell me why you're covered in goop!
I went to see the monster. But I didn't have a plan, and it kinda trapped us. It wants more boba, and only then will it release Hoshi.
I'm sorry. It was stupid. I just wanted to help.
I'm sticky because...it uses its tongue like a tail, and that's how it held me.
SHAKE
Wow.
WIPE

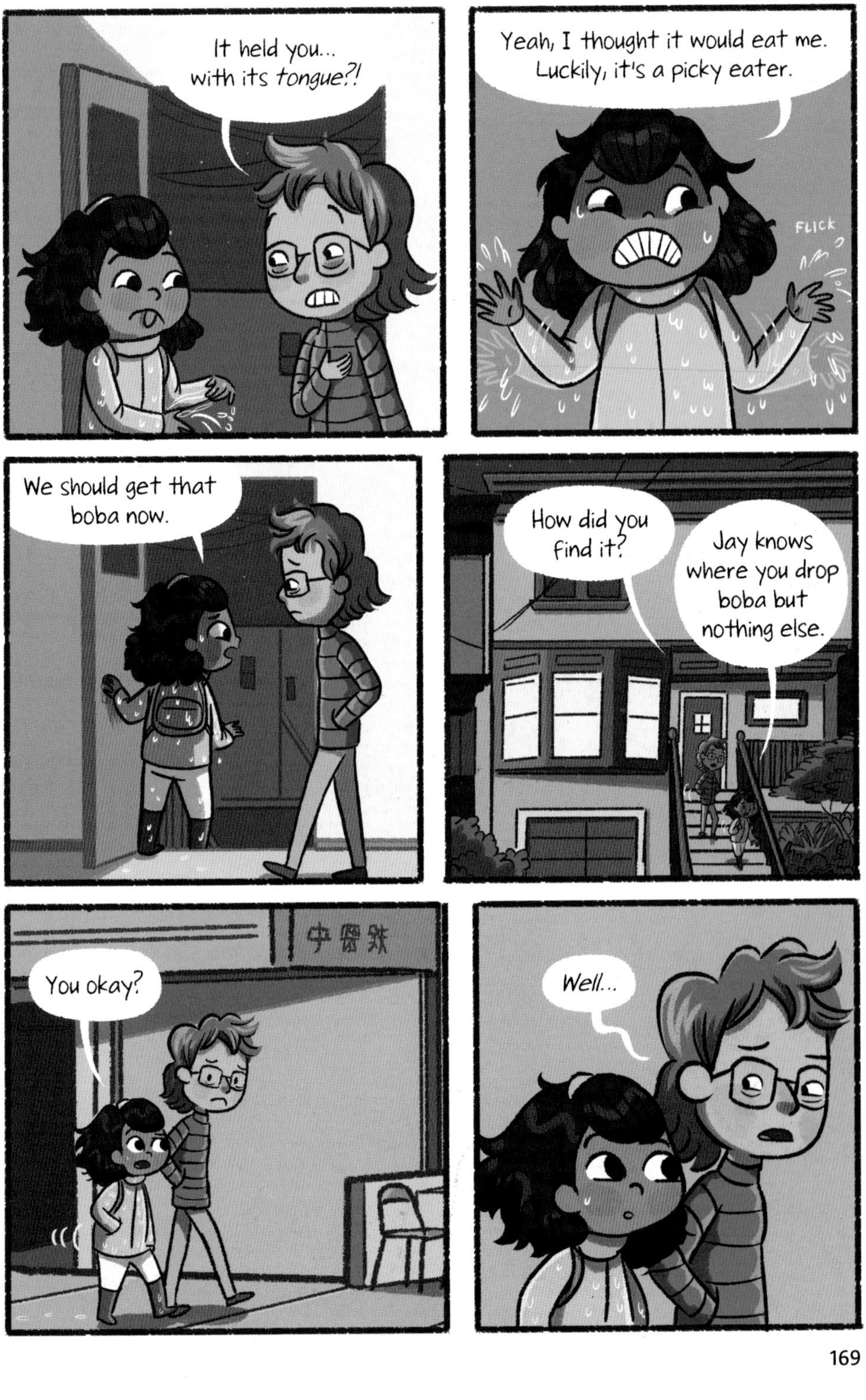
It held you... with its *tongue?!*
Yeah, I thought it would eat me. Luckily, it's a picky eater.
FLICK
We should get that boba now.
How did you find it?
Jay knows where you drop boba but nothing else.
You okay?
Well...

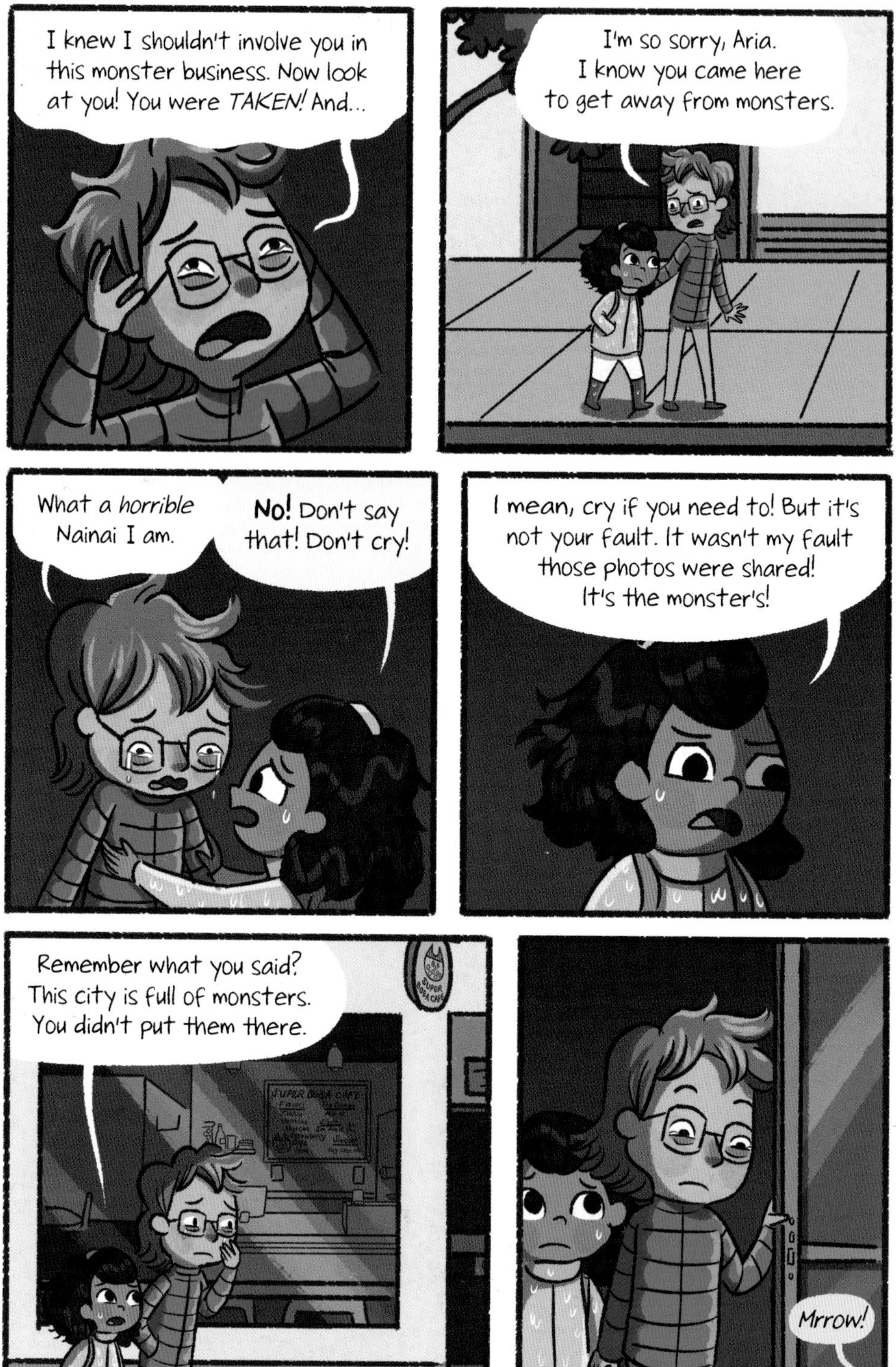
I knew I shouldn't involve you in this monster business. Now look at you! You were *TAKEN!* And...
I'm so sorry, Aria. I know you came here to get away from monsters.
What a *horrible* Nainai I am.
No! Don't say that! Don't cry!
I mean, cry if you need to! But it's not your fault. It wasn't my fault those photos were shared! It's the monster's!
Remember what you said? This city is full of monsters. You didn't put them there.
SUPER BOBA CAFE
Mrrow!

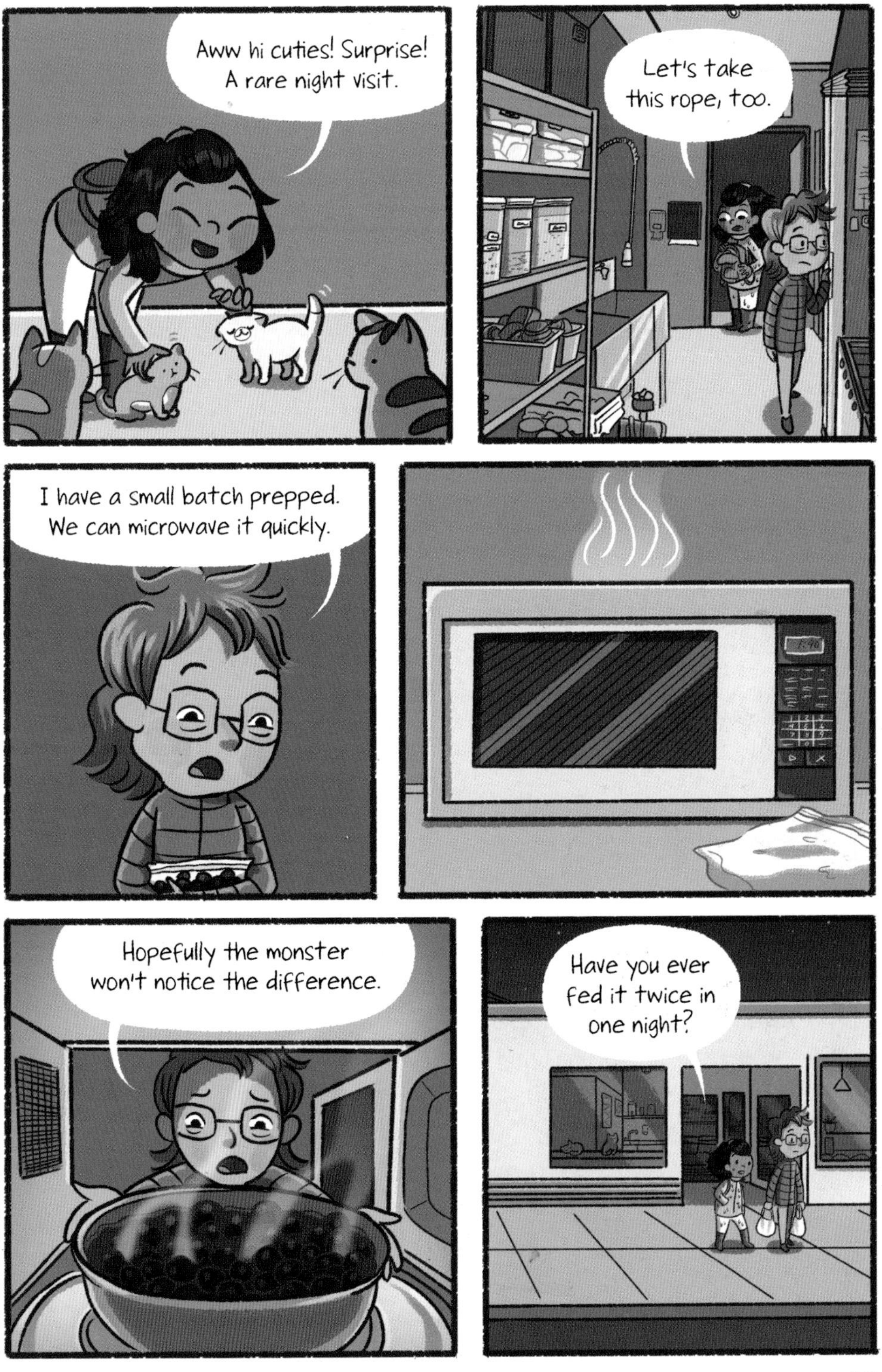

Aww hi cuties! Surprise! A rare night visit.
Let's take this rope, too.
I have a small batch prepped. We can microwave it quickly.
Hopefully the monster won't notice the difference.
Have you ever fed it twice in one night?

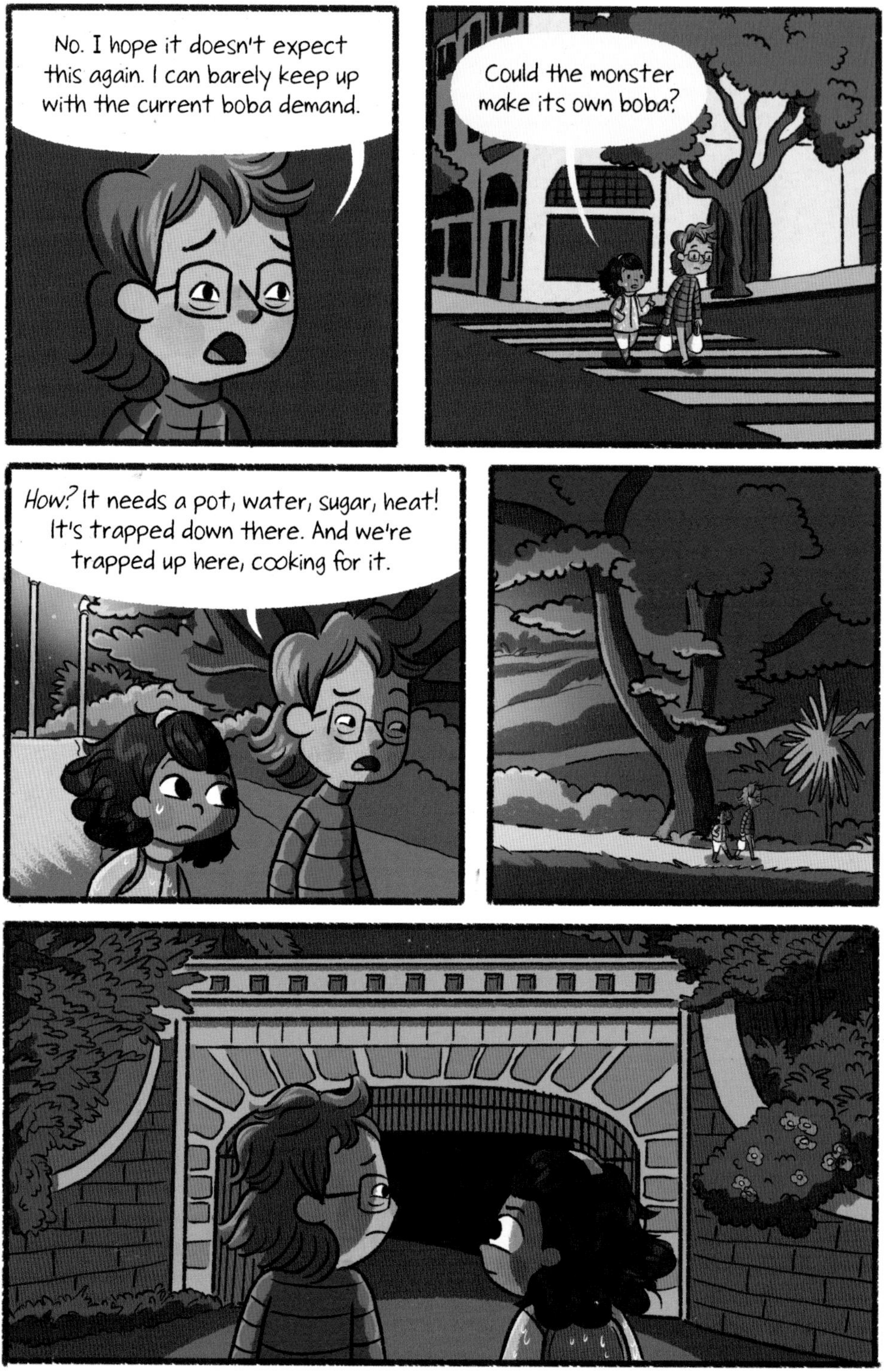
No. I hope it doesn't expect this again. I can barely keep up with the current boba demand.
Could the monster make its own boba?
How? It needs a pot, water, sugar, heat! It's trapped down there. And we're trapped up here, cooking for it.

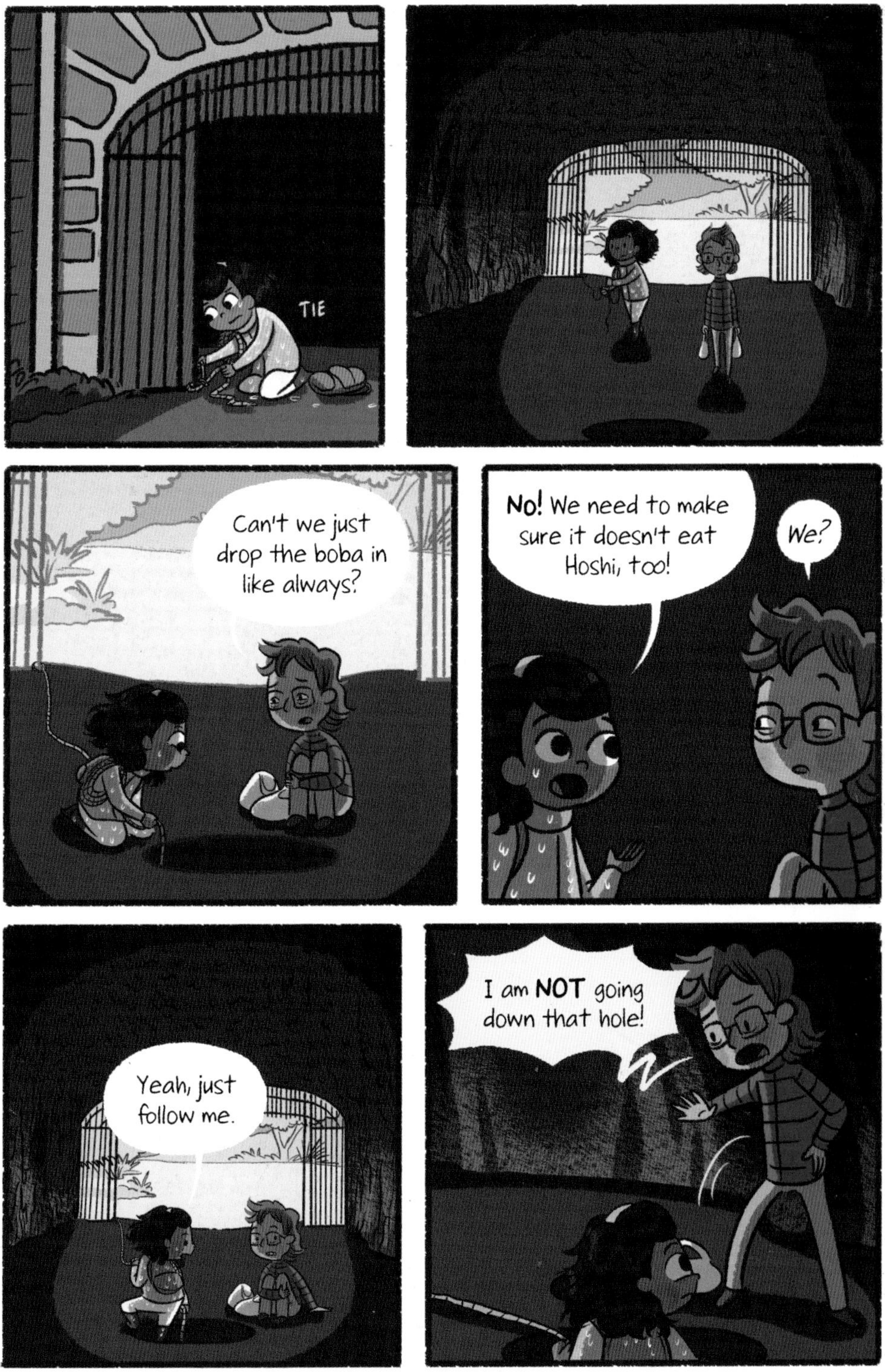
TIE
Can't we just drop the boba in like always?
No! We need to make sure it doesn't eat Hoshi, too!
We?
Yeah, just follow me.
I am NOT going down that hole!

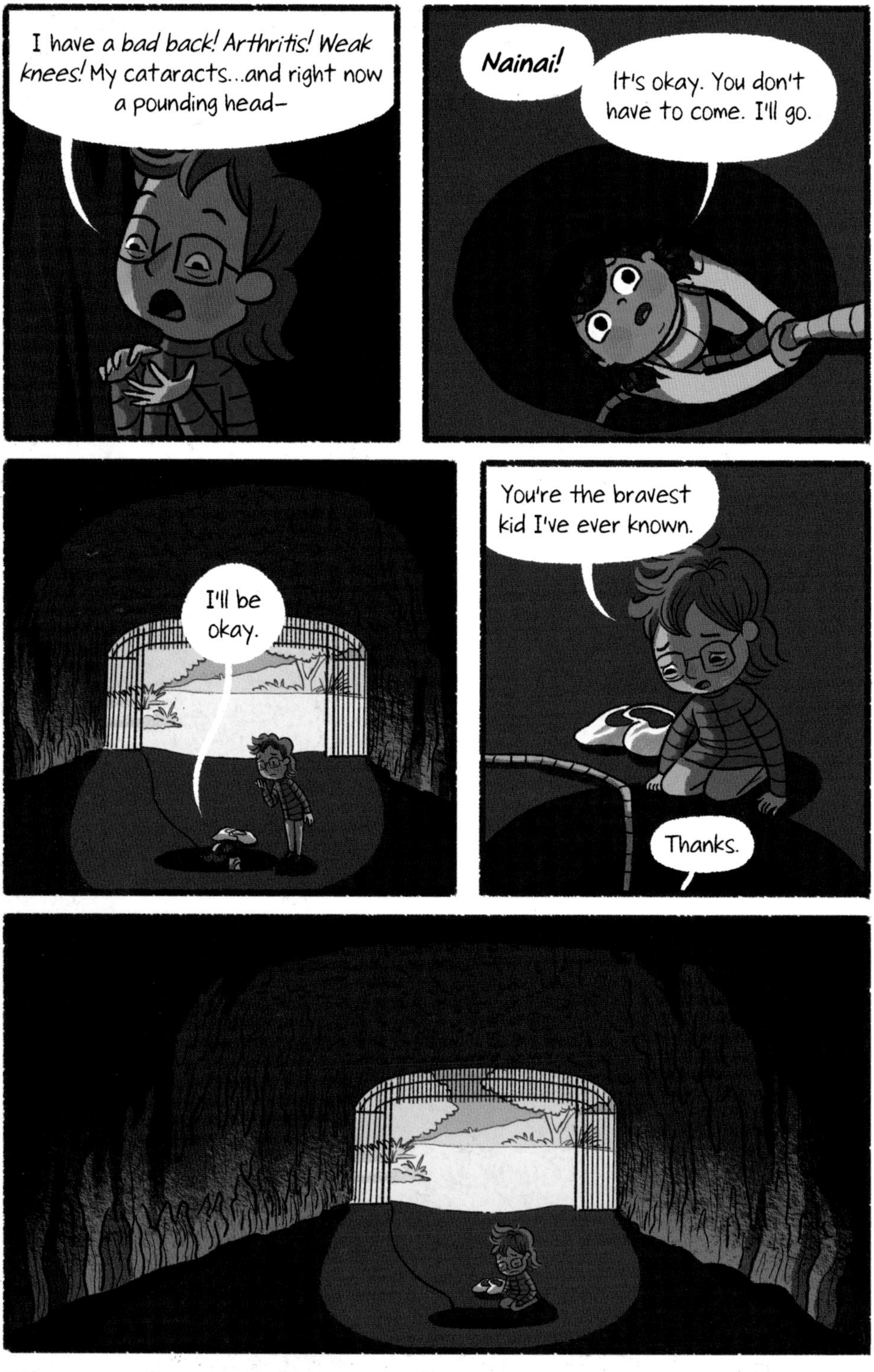
I have a *bad back!* Arthritis! Weak *knees!* My cataracts...and right now a pounding head–
Nainai!
It's okay. You don't have to come. I'll go.
I'll be okay.
You're the bravest kid I've ever known.
Thanks.

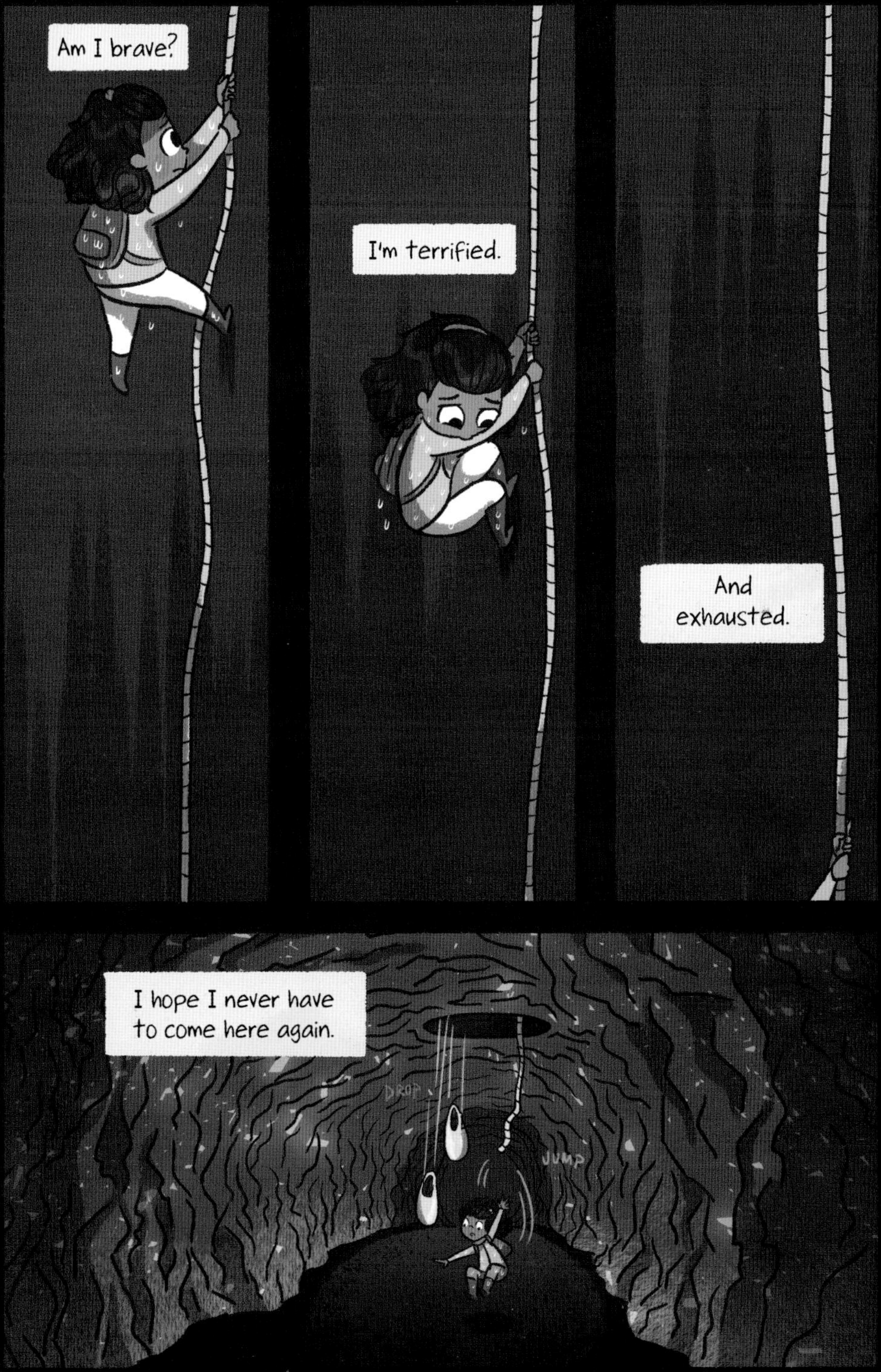
Am I brave?
I'm terrified.
And exhausted.
I hope I never have to come here again.
DROP
JUMP

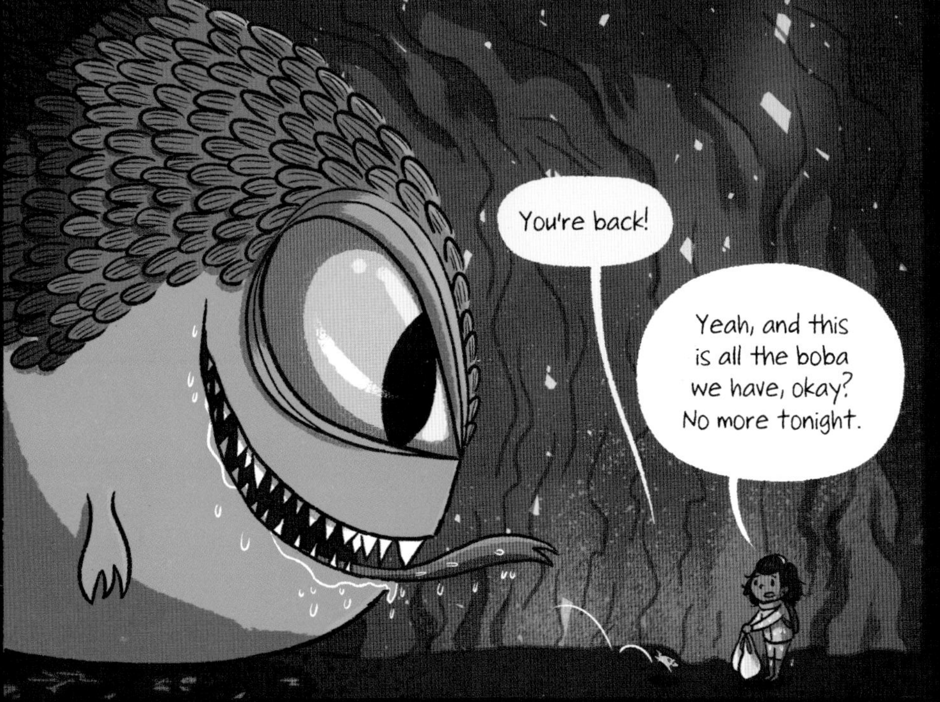
You're back!
Yeah, and this is all the boba we have, okay? No more tonight.

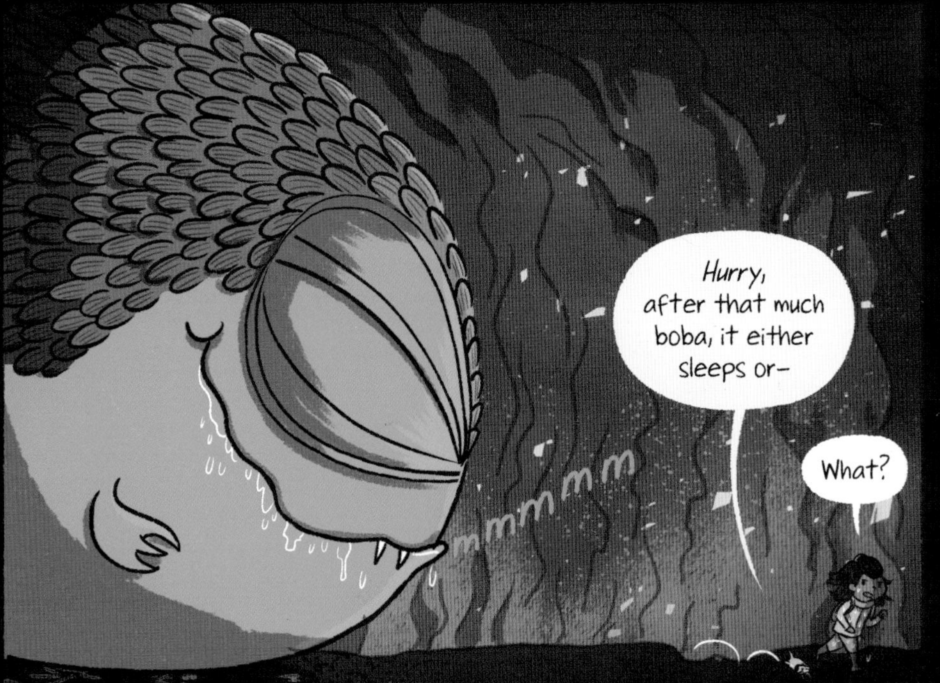
Hurry, after that much boba, it either sleeps or–
What?
mmmmmm

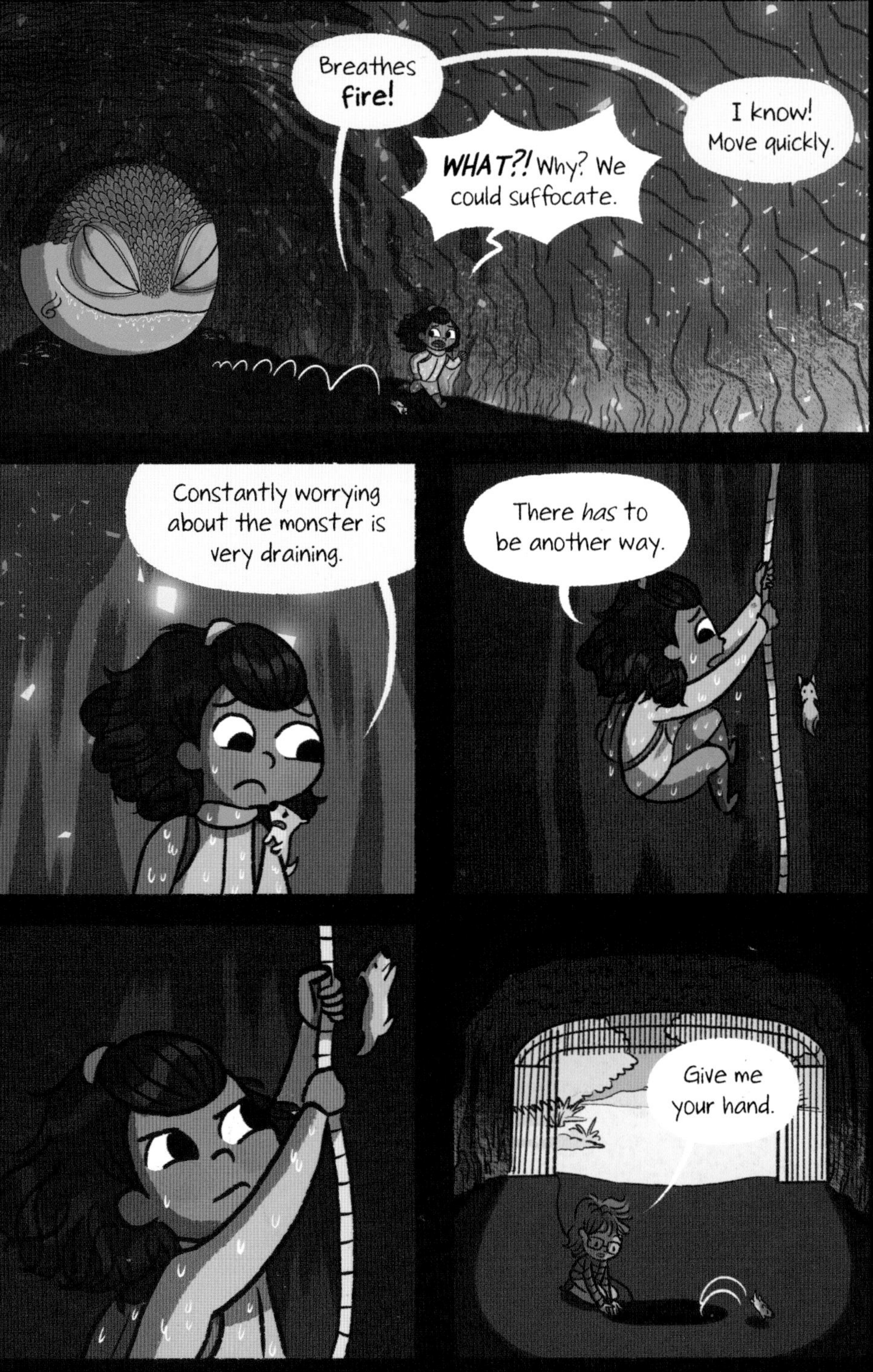
Breathes fire!
WHAT?! Why? We could suffocate.
I know! Move quickly.
Constantly worrying about the monster is very draining.
There has to be another way.
Give me your hand.

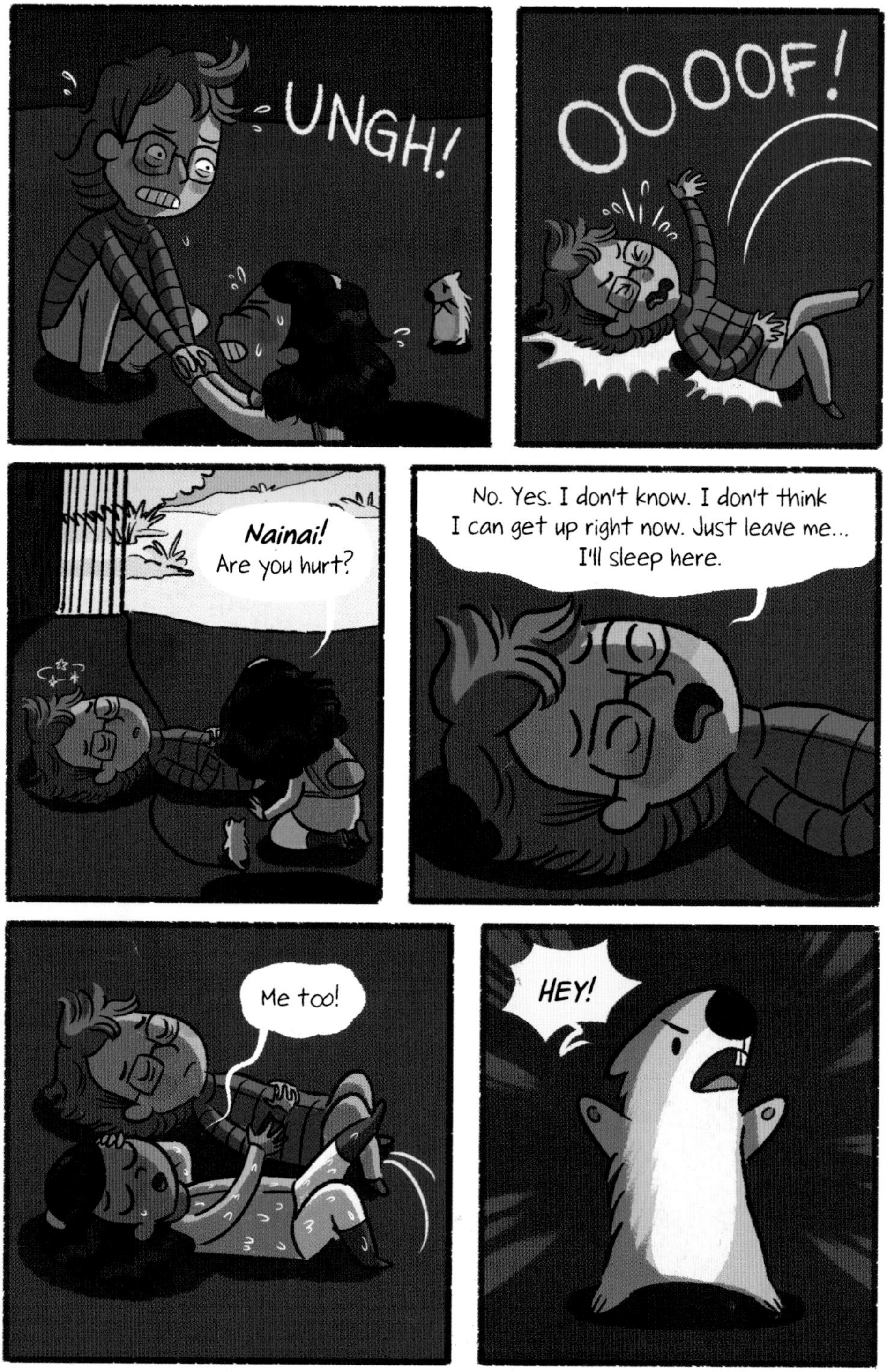
UNGH!
OOOOF!
Nainai! Are you hurt?
No. Yes. I don't know. I don't think I can get up right now. Just leave me... I'll sleep here.
Me too!
HEY!

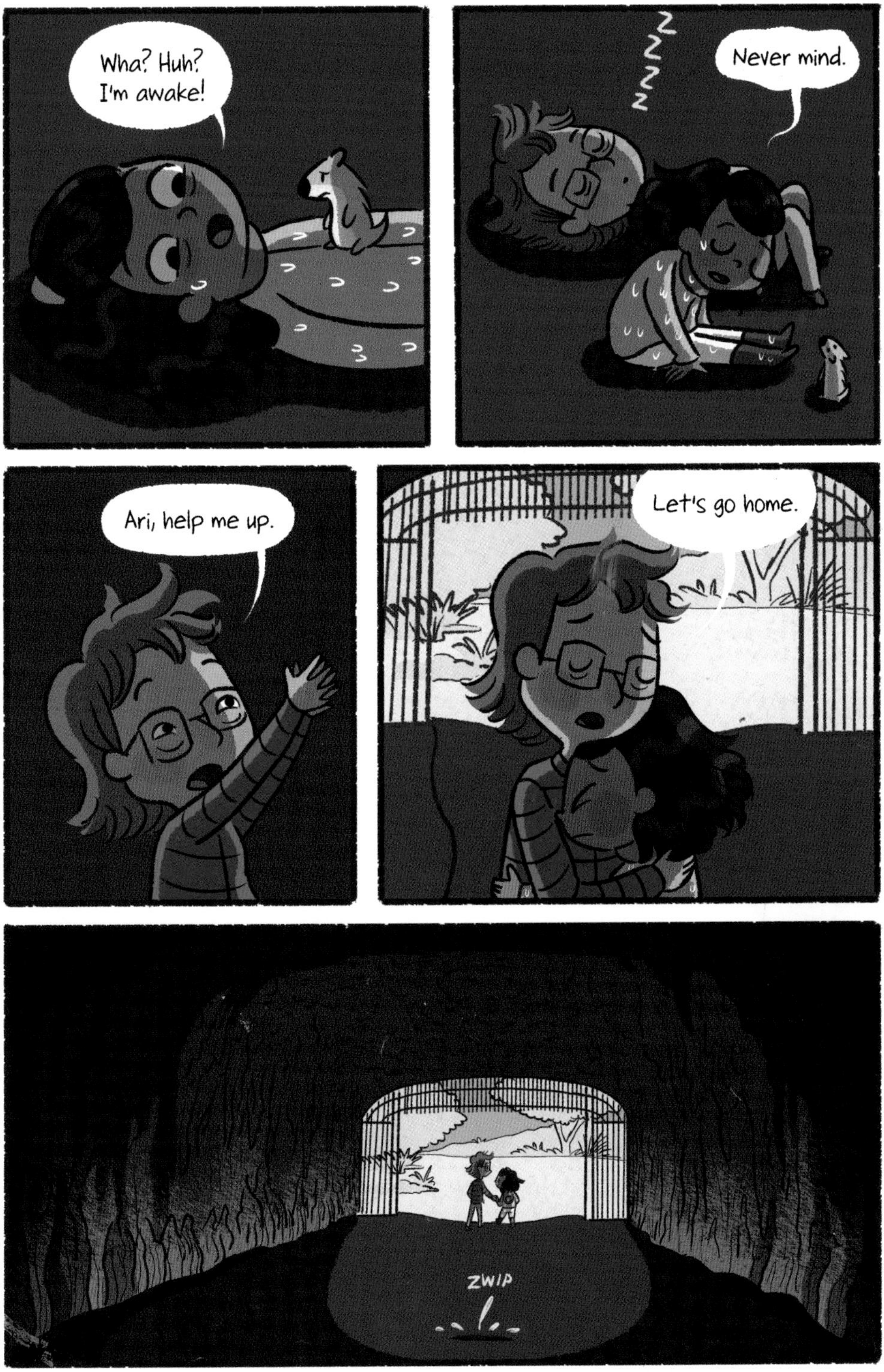
Wha? Huh?
I'm awake!
Z Z Z Z
Never mind.
Ari, help me up.
Let's go home.
ZWIP

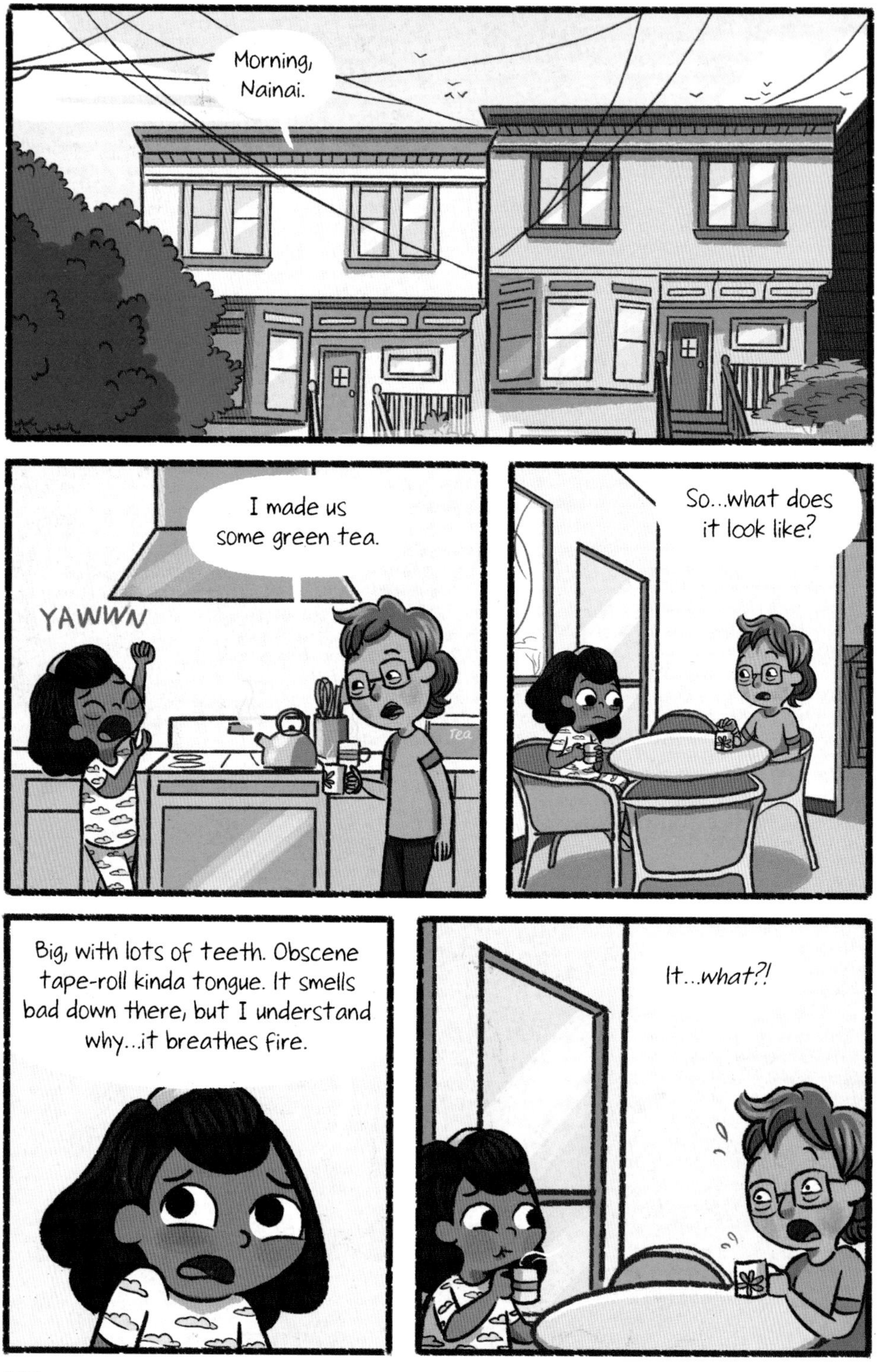
Morning, Nainai.
I made us some green tea.
YAWWN
TEA
So...what does it look like?
Big, with lots of teeth. Obscene tape-roll kinda tongue. It smells bad down there, but I understand why...it breathes fire.
It...what?!

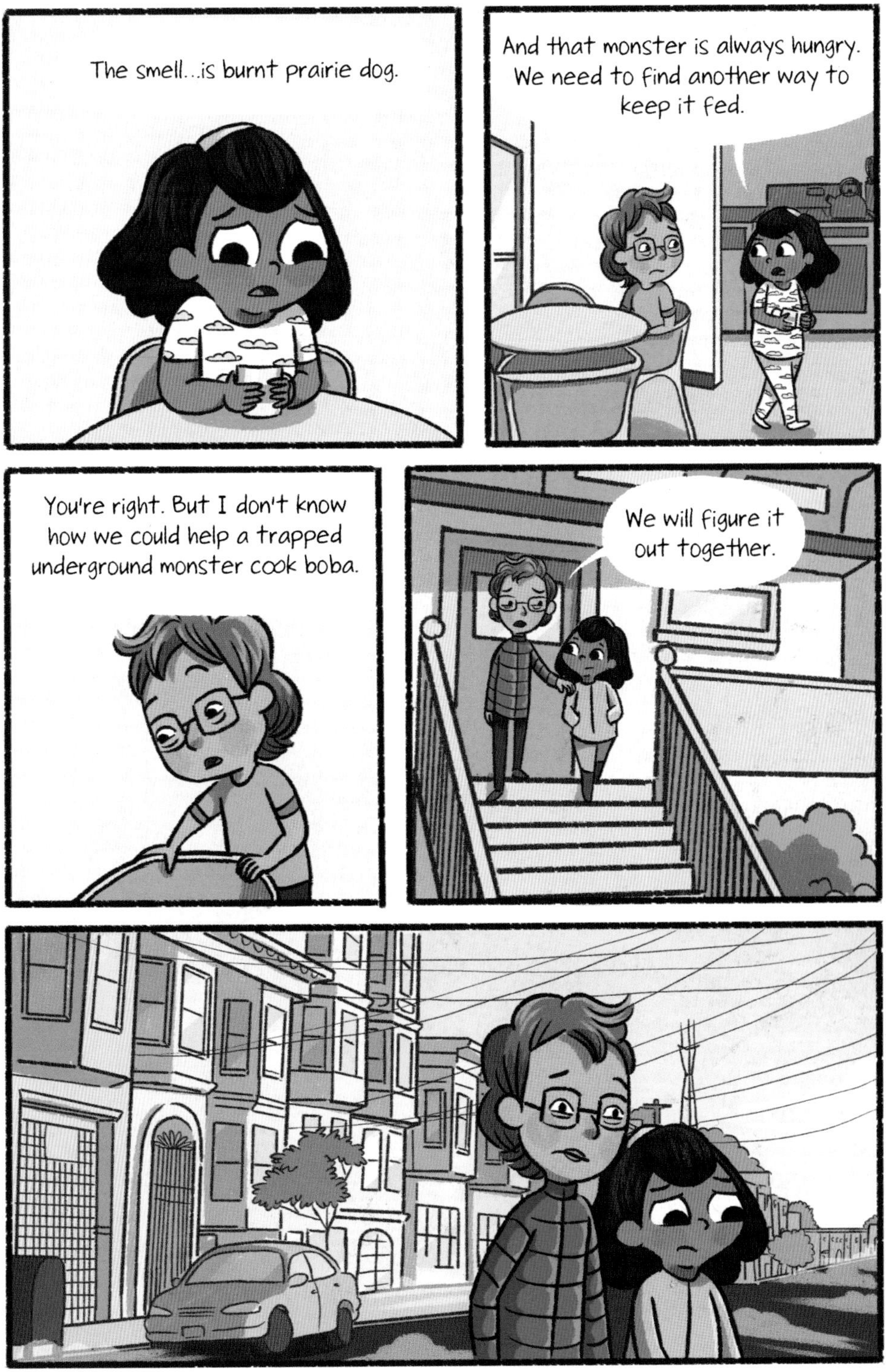
The smell...is burnt prairie dog.
And that monster is always hungry. We need to find another way to keep it fed.
You're right. But I don't know how we could help a trapped underground monster cook boba.
We will figure it out together.

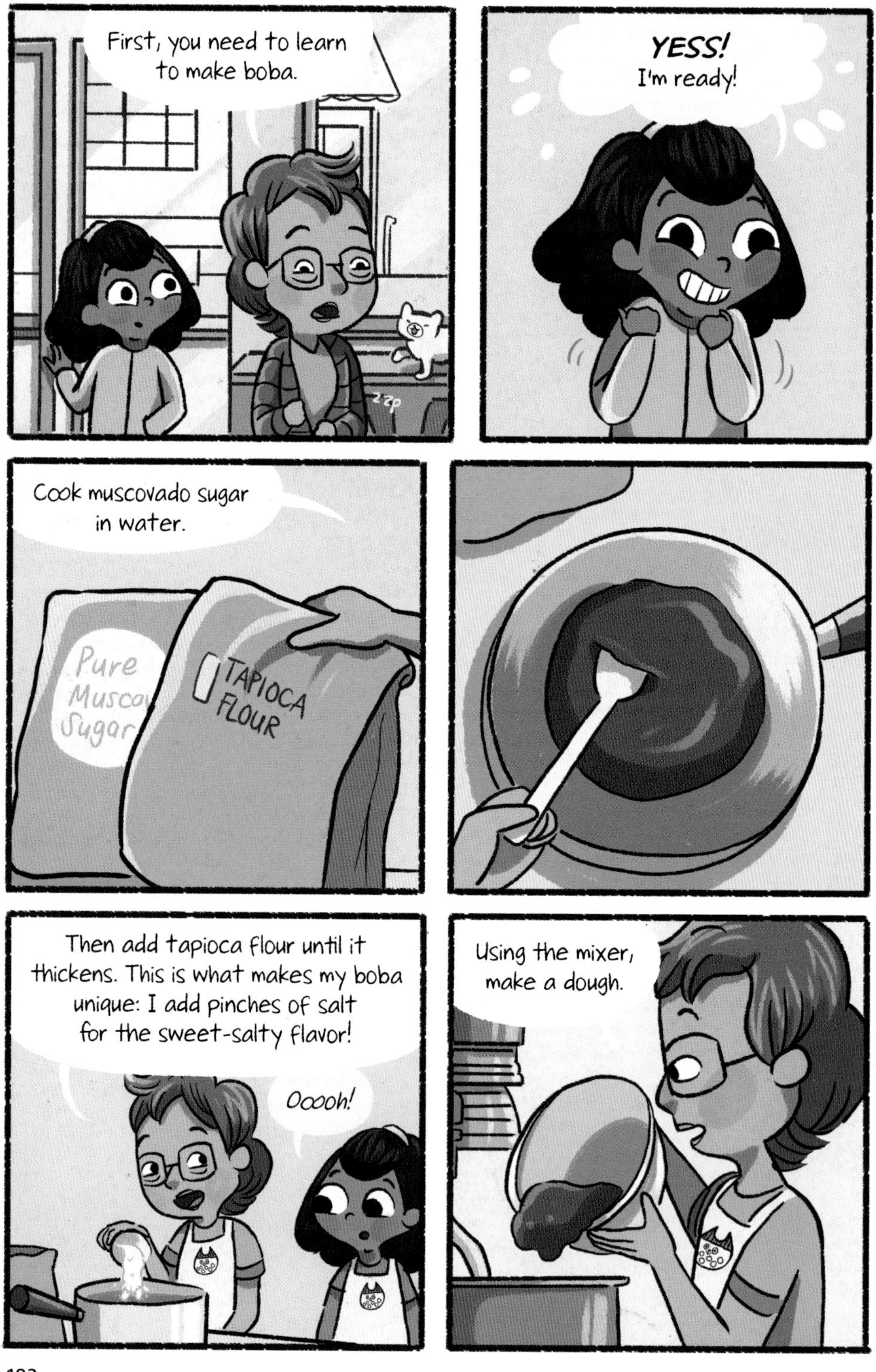
First, you need to learn to make boba.
zzp
YESS! I'm ready!
Cook muscovado sugar in water.
Pure Musca Sugar
TAPIOCA FLOUR
Then add tapioca flour until it thickens. This is what makes my boba unique: I add pinches of salt for the sweet-salty flavor!
Ooooh!
Using the mixer, make a dough.

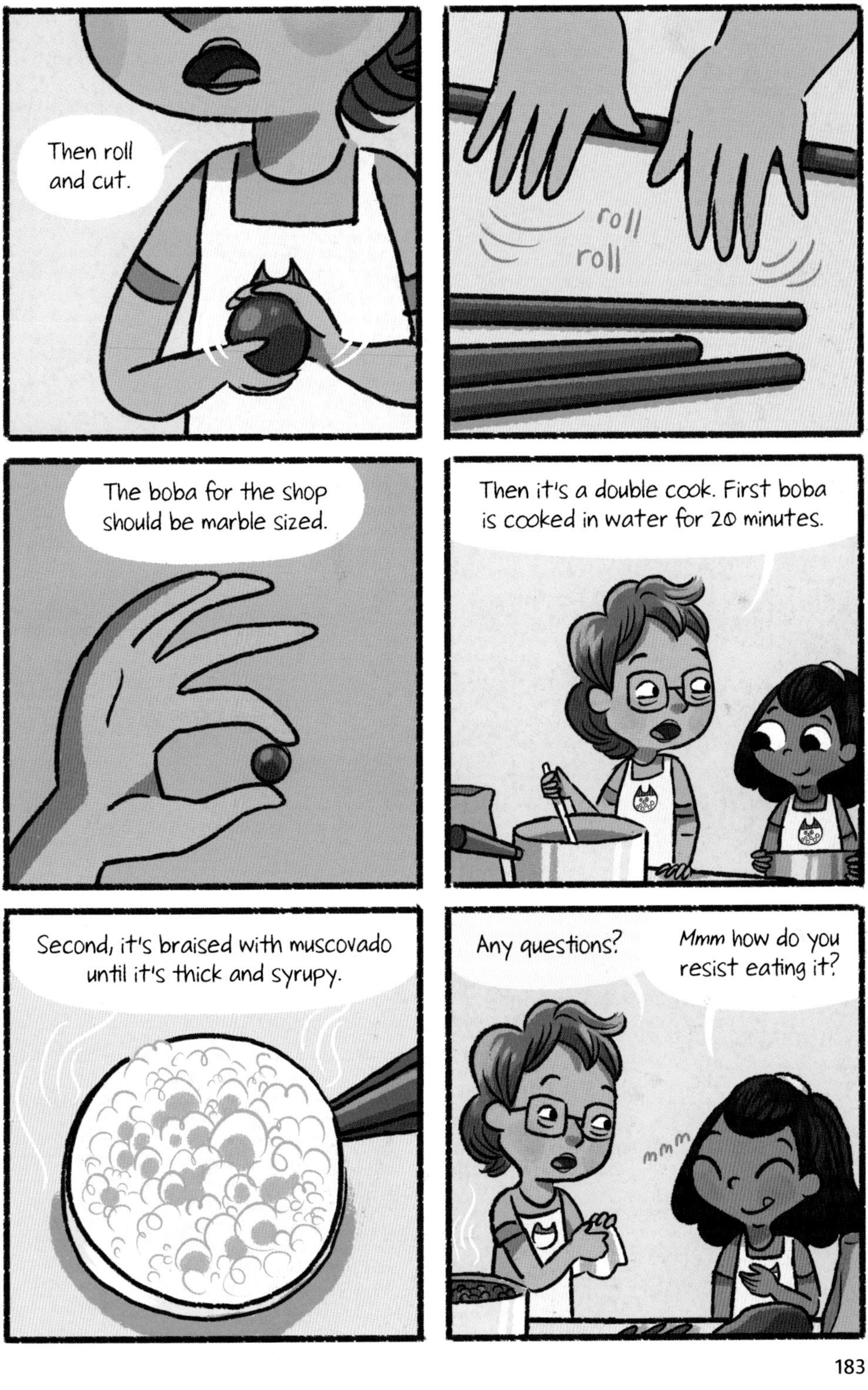
Then roll and cut.
roll
roll
The boba for the shop should be marble sized.
Then it's a double cook. First boba is cooked in water for 20 minutes.
Second, it's braised with muscovado until it's thick and syrupy.
Any questions?
Mmm how do you resist eating it?
mmm

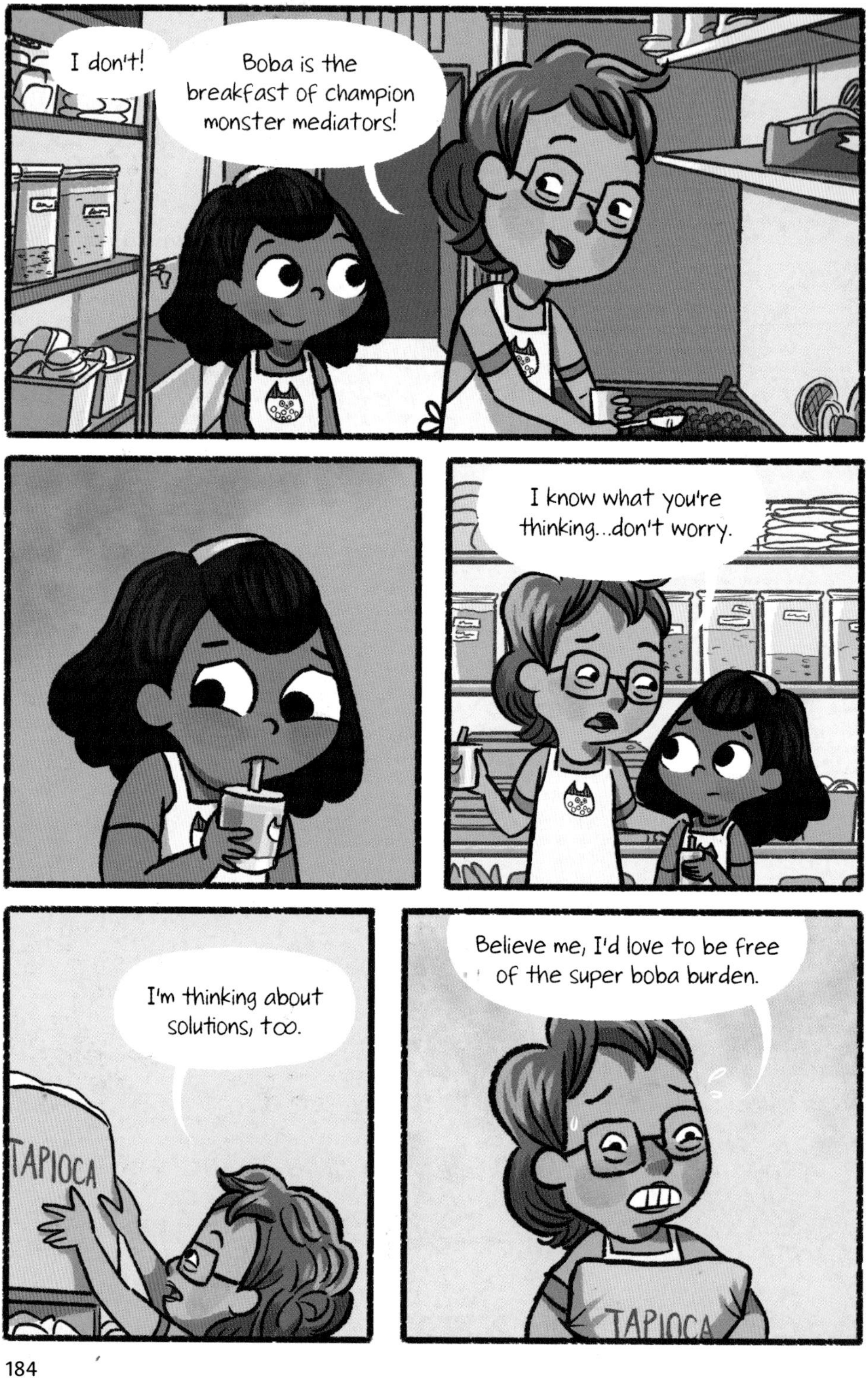
I don't!
Boba is the breakfast of champion monster mediators!
I know what you're thinking...don't worry.
I'm thinking about solutions, too.
TAPIOCA
Believe me, I'd love to be free of the super boba burden.
TAPIOCA

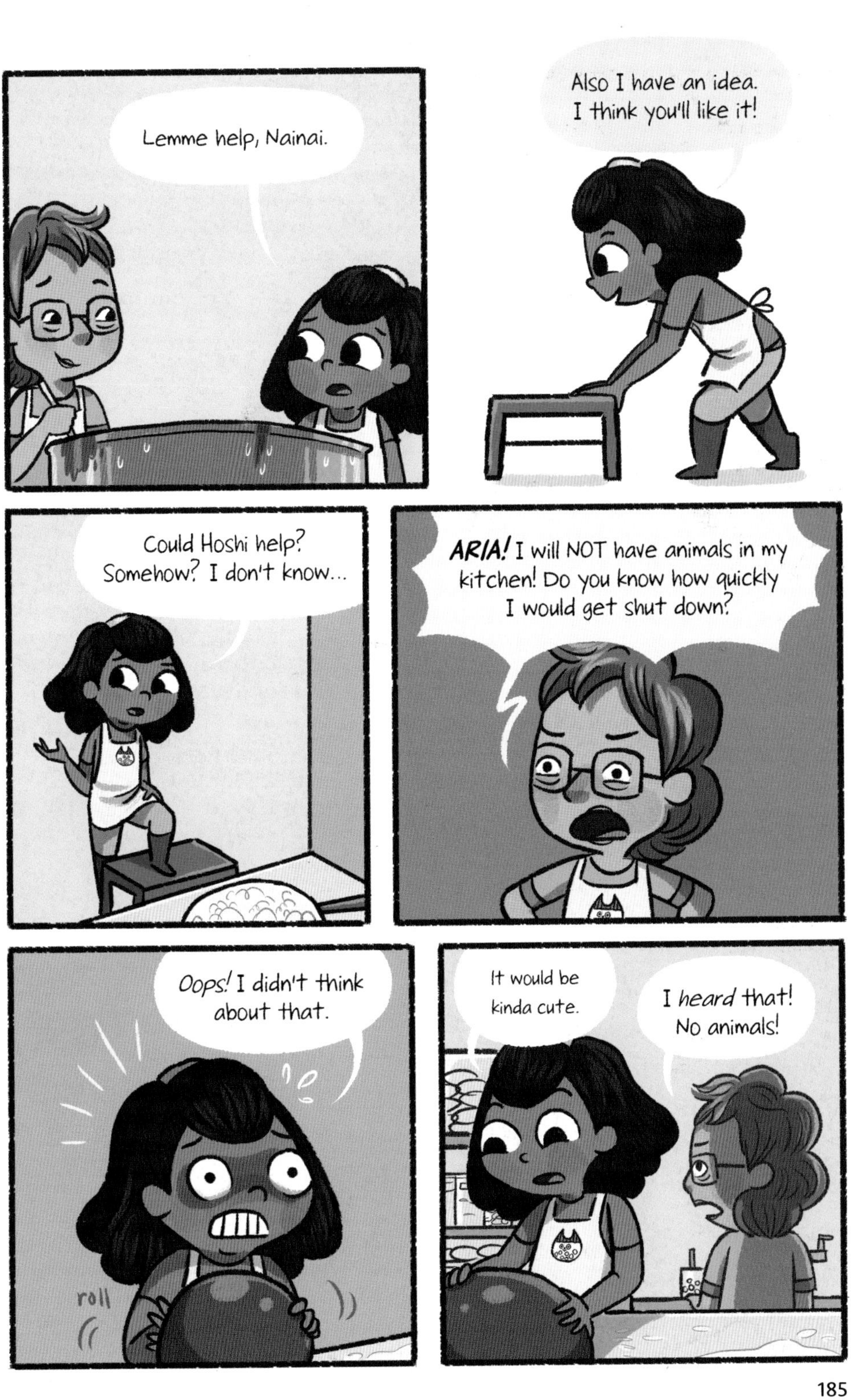
Lemme help, Nainai.
Also I have an idea. I think you'll like it!
Could Hoshi help? Somehow? I don't know...
ARIA! I will NOT have animals in my kitchen! Do you know how quickly I would get shut down?
Oops! I didn't think about that.
roll
It would be kinda cute.
I heard that! No animals!

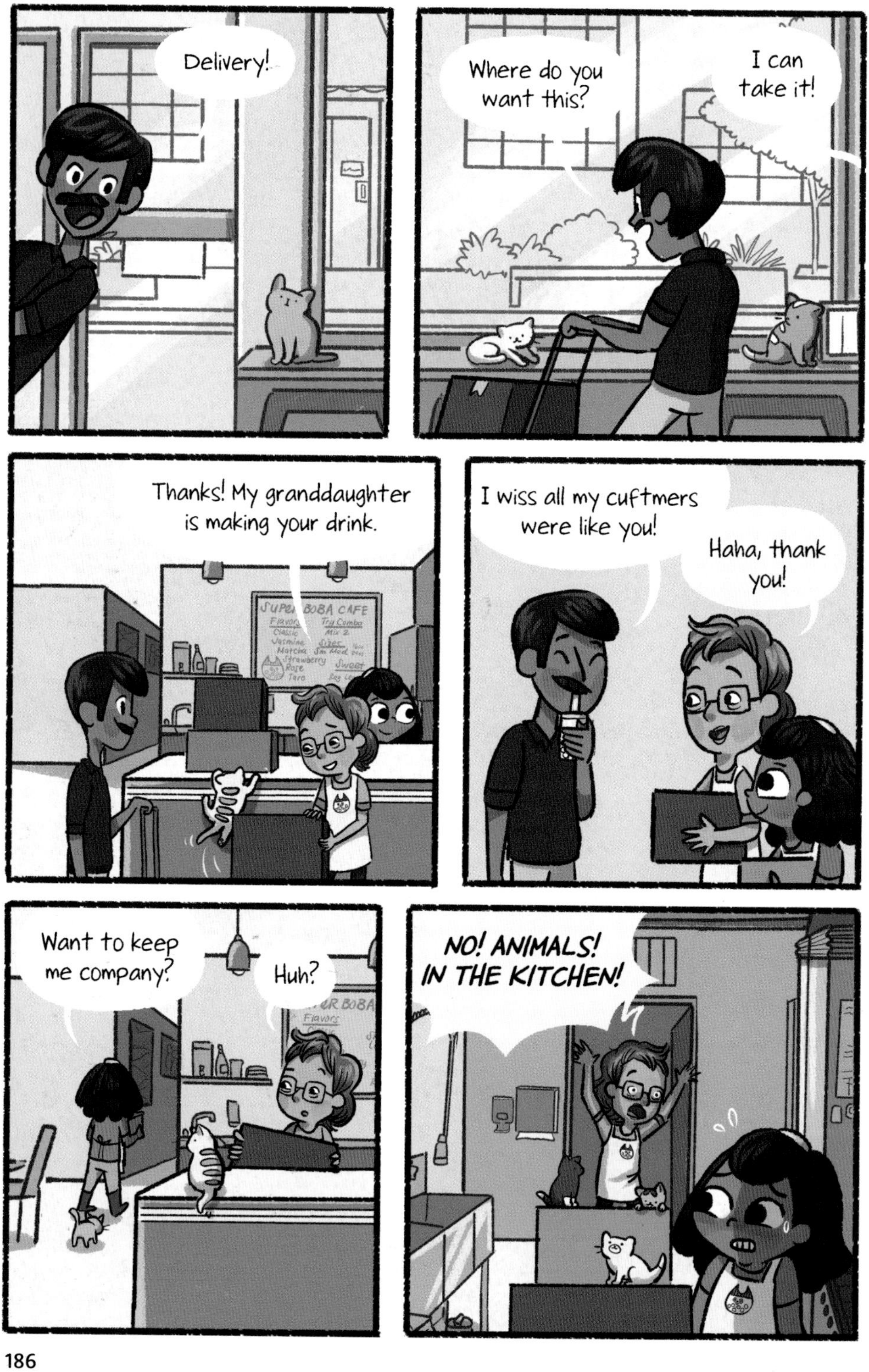
Delivery!
Where do you want this?
I can take it!
Thanks! My granddaughter is making your drink.
I wiss all my cuftmers were like you!
Haha, thank you!
Want to keep me company?
Huh?
NO! ANIMALS! IN THE KITCHEN!

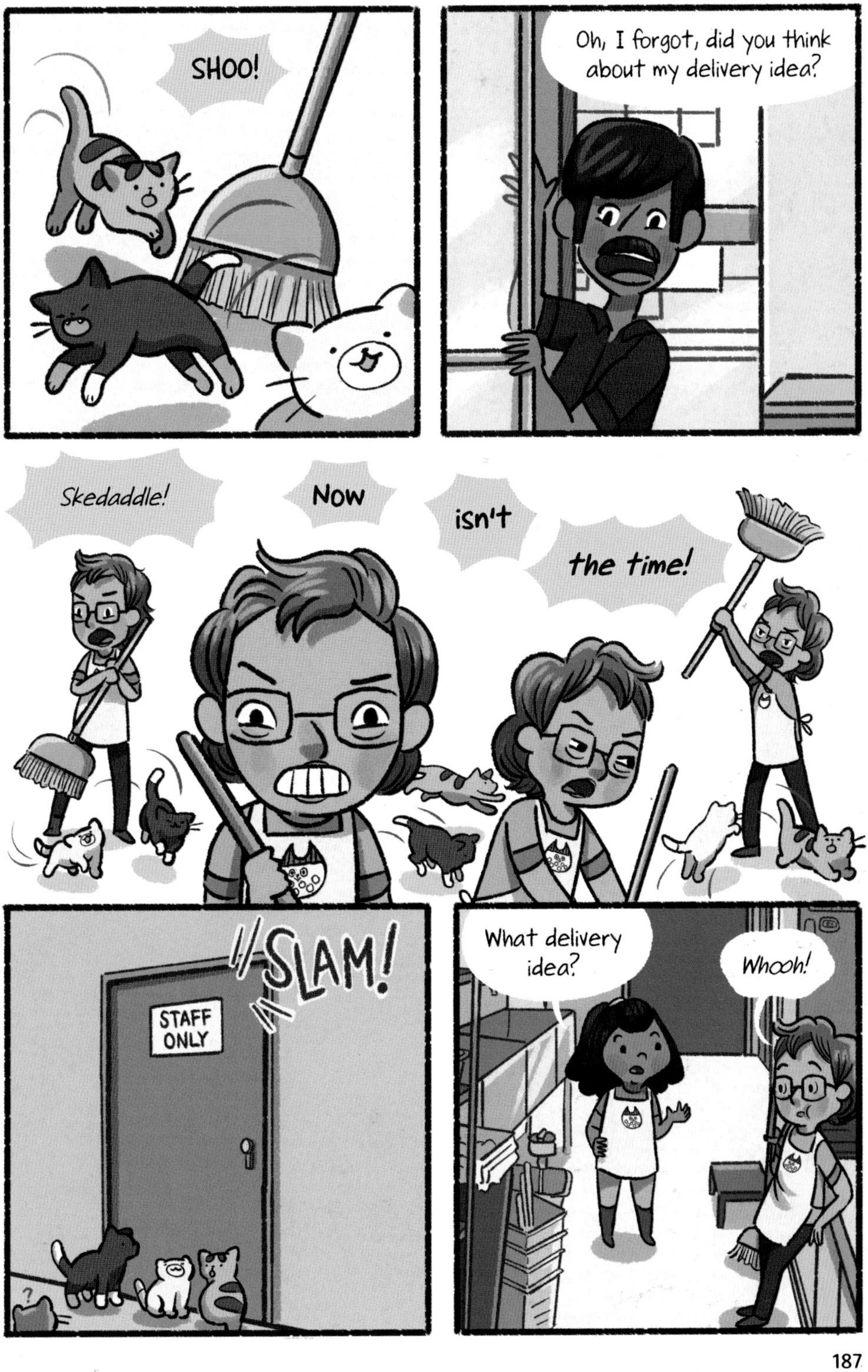
SHOO!
Oh, I forgot, did you think about my delivery idea?
Skedaddle!
Now
isn't
the time!
SLAM!
STAFF ONLY
?
What delivery idea?
Whooh!

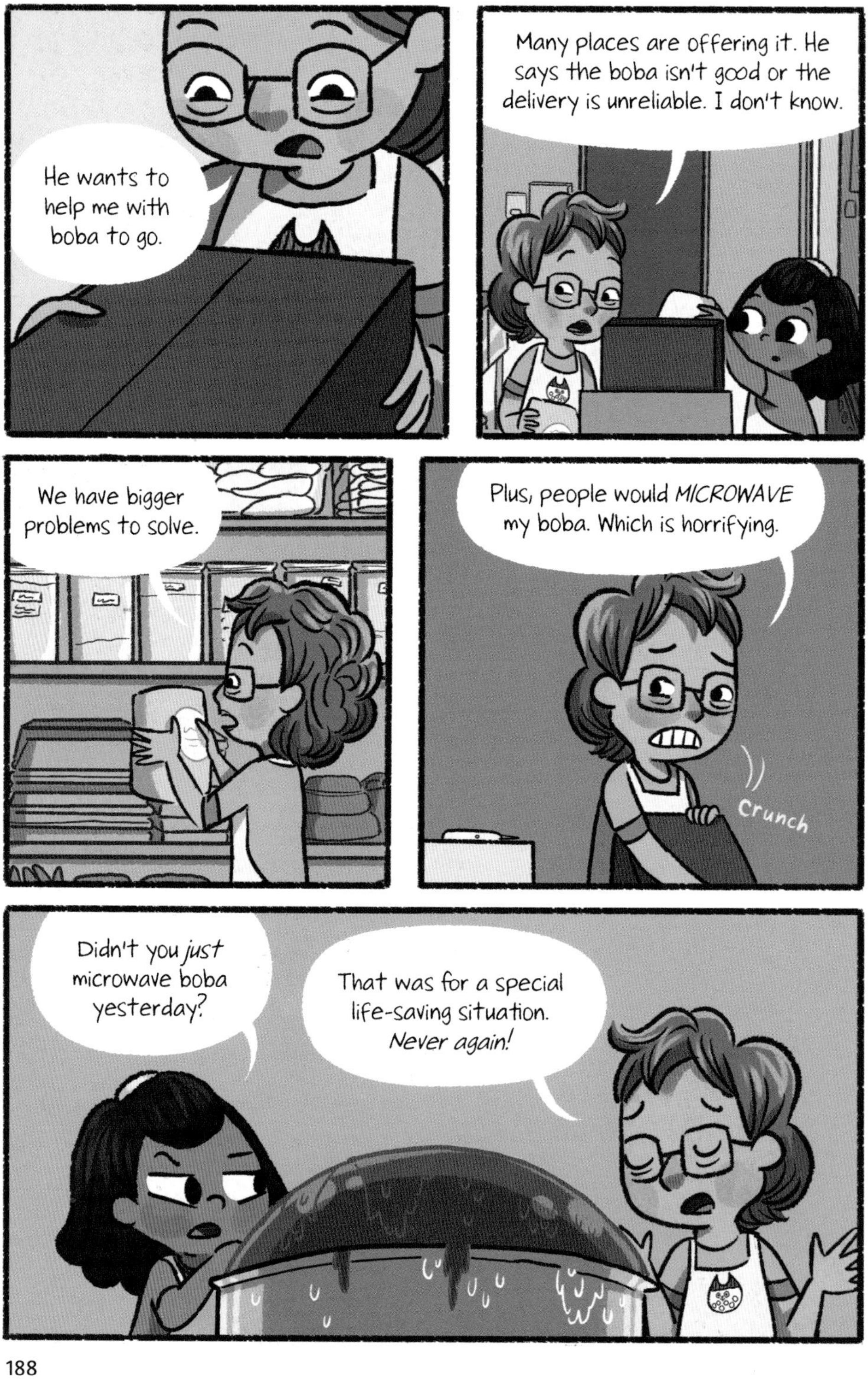
He wants to help me with boba to go.
Many places are offering it. He says the boba isn't good or the delivery is unreliable. I don't know.
We have bigger problems to solve.
Plus, people would *MICROWAVE* my boba. Which is horrifying.
Crunch
Didn't you *just* microwave boba yesterday?
That was for a special life-saving situation. *Never again!*

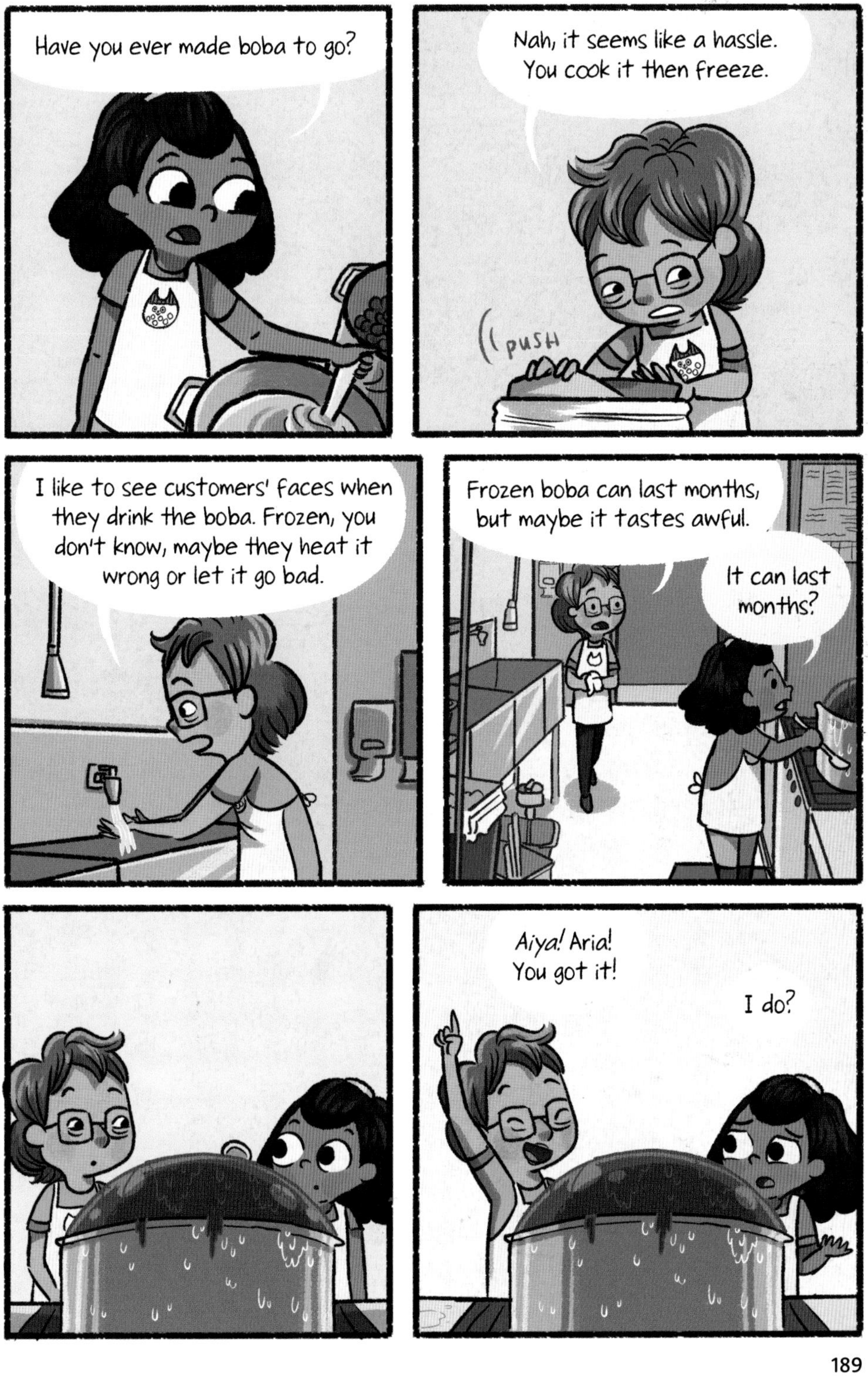
Have you ever made boba to go?
Nah, it seems like a hassle. You cook it then freeze.
PUSH
I like to see customers' faces when they drink the boba. Frozen, you don't know, maybe they heat it wrong or let it go bad.
Frozen boba can last months, but maybe it tastes awful.
It can last months?
Aiya! Aria! You got it!
I do?

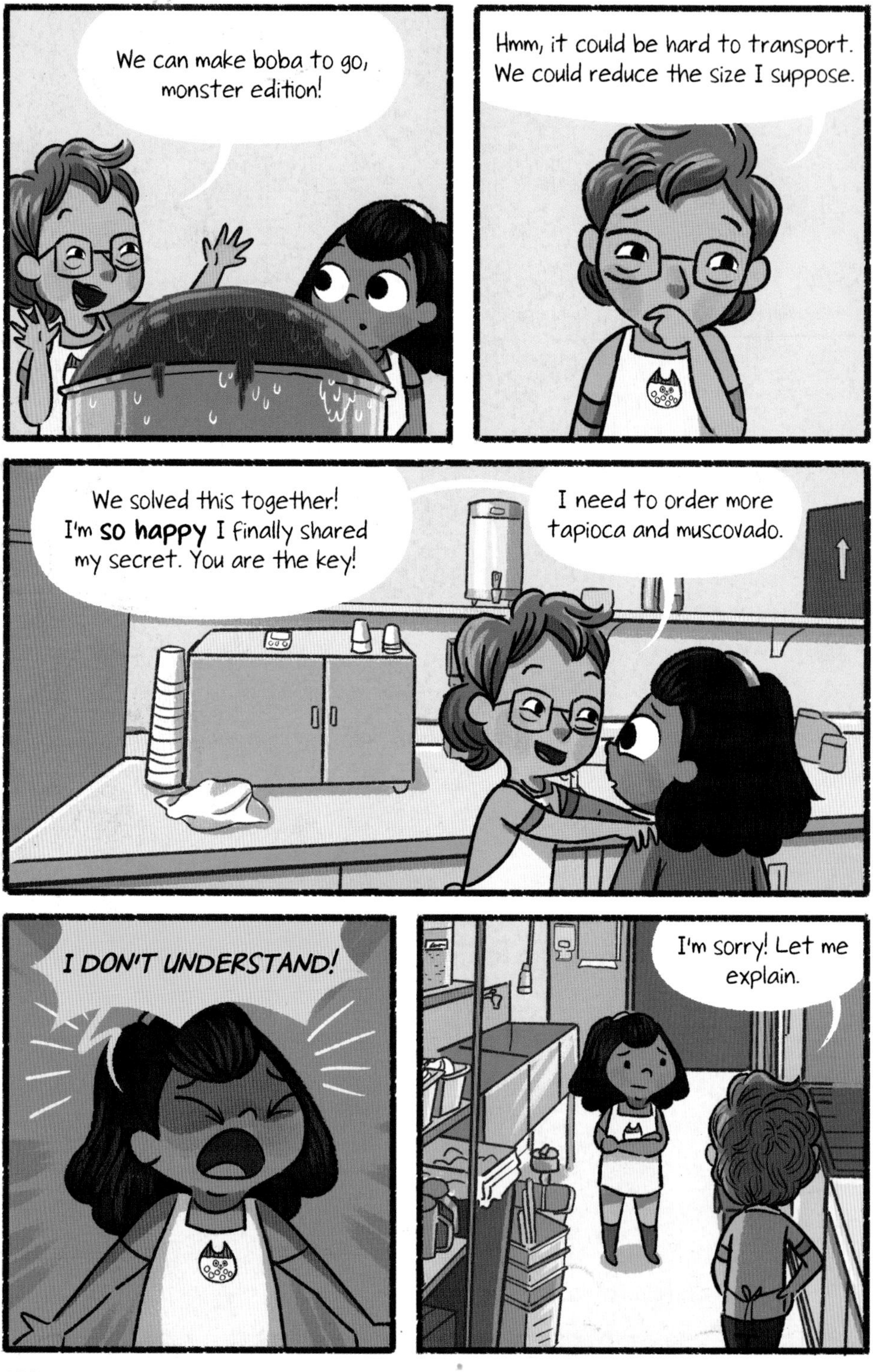
We can make boba to go, monster edition!
Hmm, it could be hard to transport. We could reduce the size I suppose.
We solved this together! I'm **so happy** I finally shared my secret. You are the key!
I need to order more tapioca and muscovado.
I DON'T UNDERSTAND!
I'm sorry! Let me explain.

I will freeze the super boba to go. Slightly smaller for transport.

We drop them down.

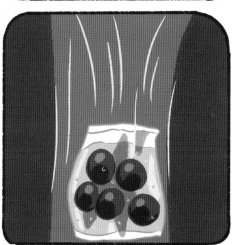

The first time, you will need to explain the new boba to it.

Push them to the monster and...

Drat! I forgot we need heat!

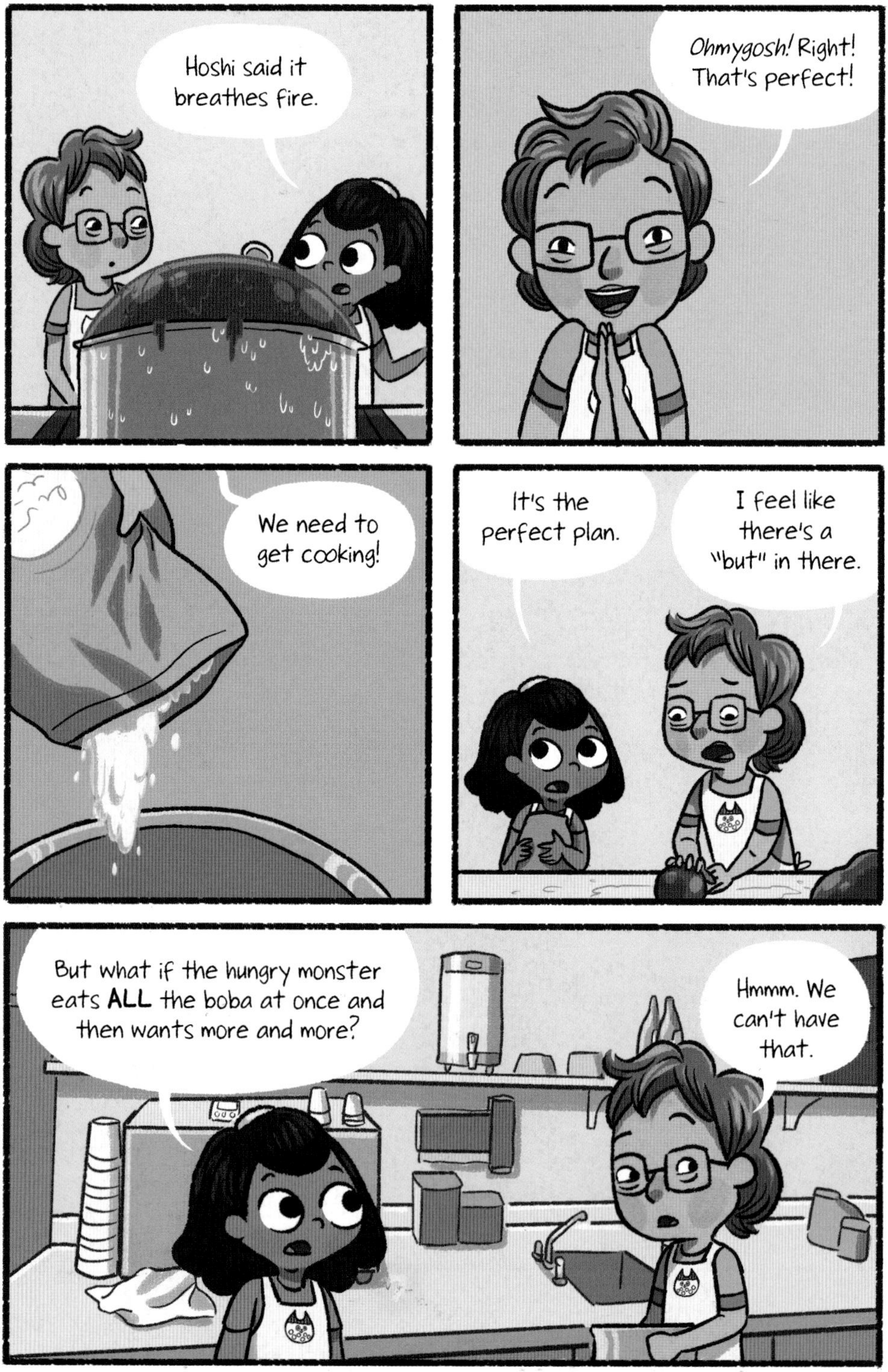
Hoshi said it breathes fire.
Ohmygosh! Right! That's perfect!
We need to get cooking!
It's the perfect plan.
I feel like there's a "but" in there.
But what if the hungry monster eats **ALL** the boba at once and then wants more and more?
Hmmm. We can't have that.

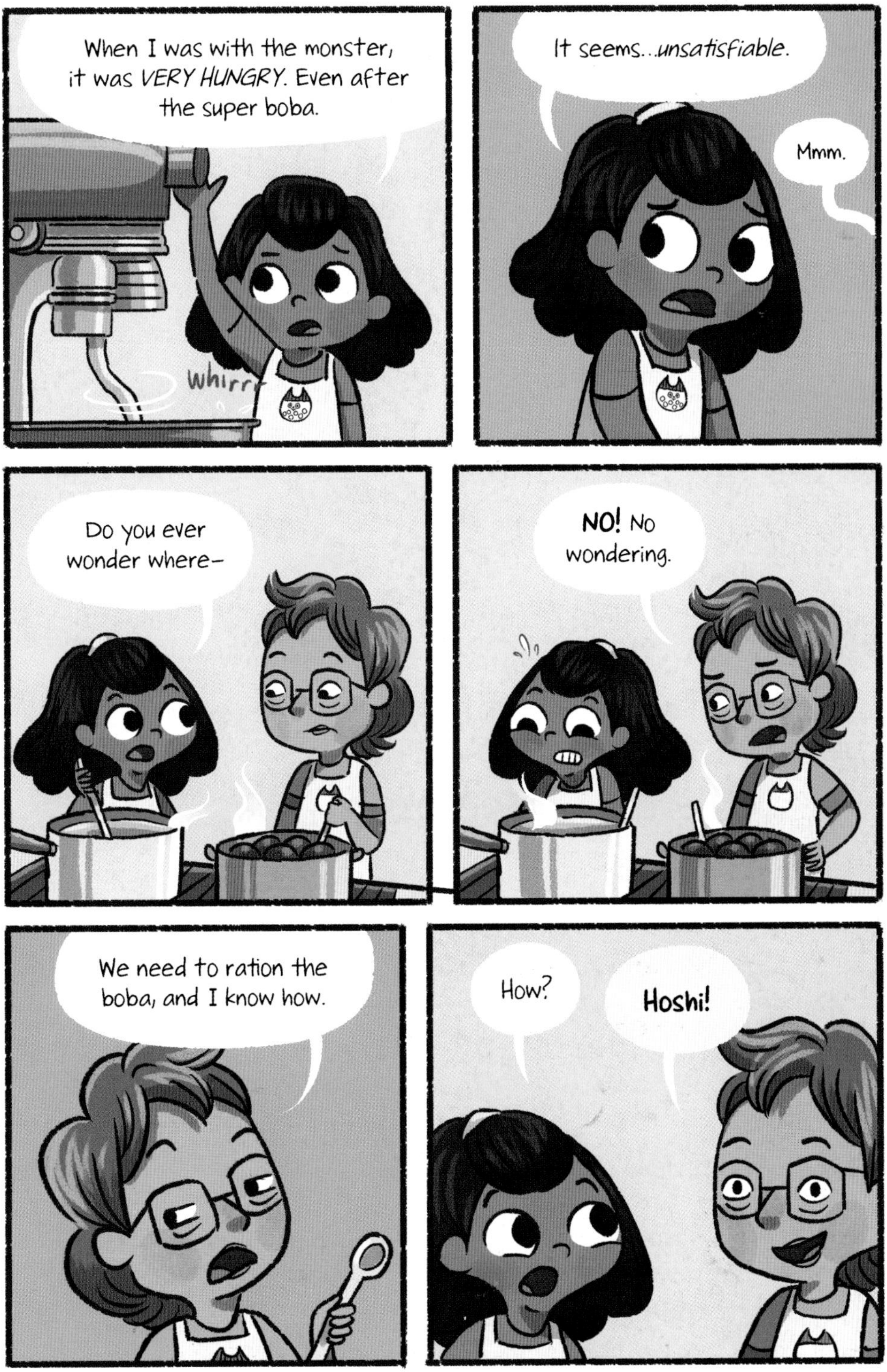
When I was with the monster, it was *VERY HUNGRY*. Even after the super boba.
whirr
It seems...*unsatisfiable*.
Mmm.
Do you ever wonder where-
NO! No wondering.
We need to ration the boba, and I know how.
How?
Hoshi!

You will show the monster how to cook it once but won't deliver the rest.

Hoshi will dig a passage.

A place to store the frozen boba.

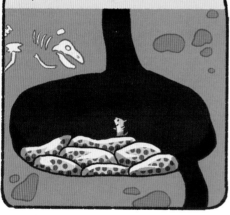

The prairie dogs will deliver on a schedule to the monster.

It's perfect!

Thank you!

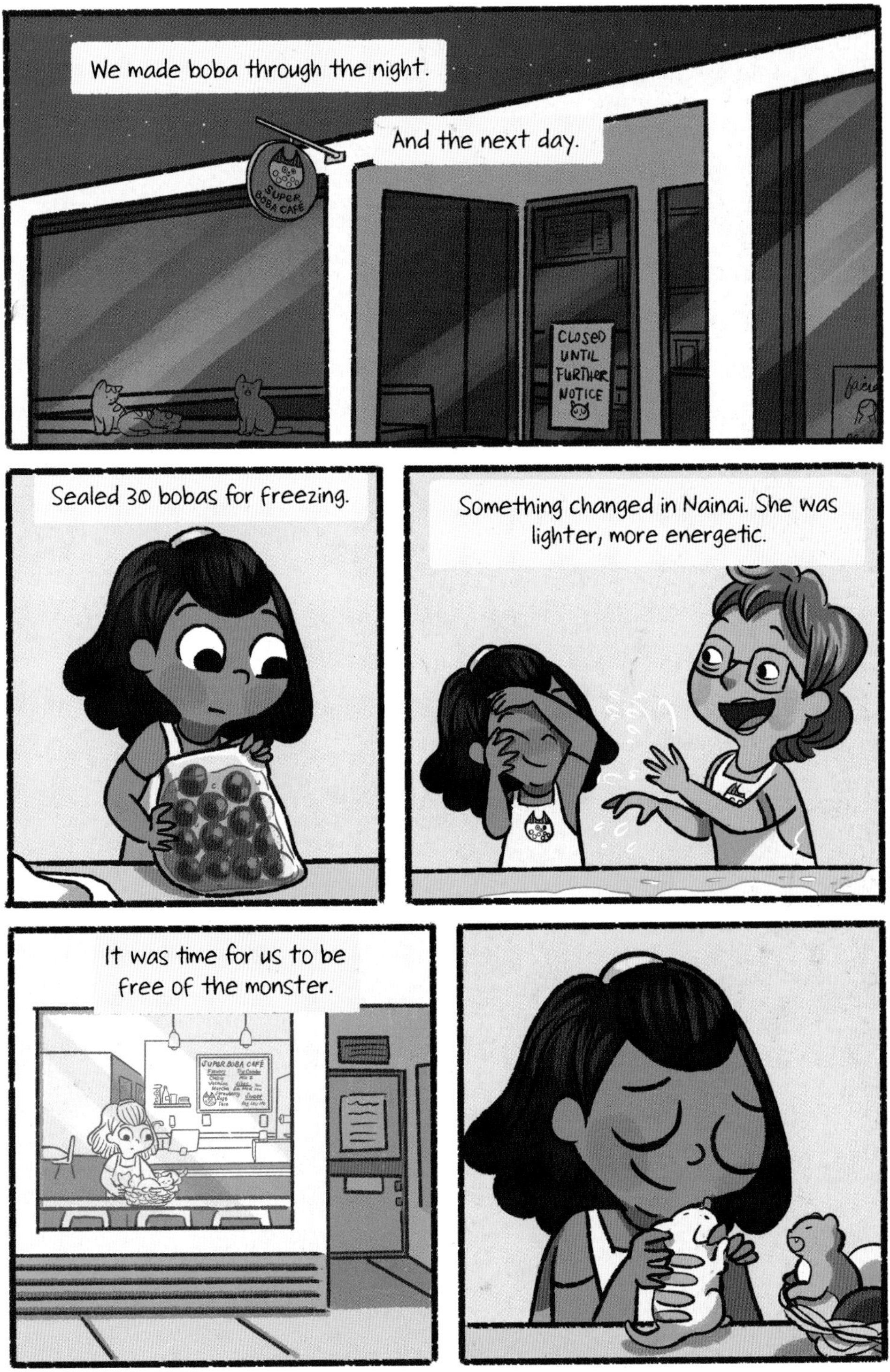
We made boba through the night.
And the next day.
SUPER BOBA CAFÉ
CLOSED UNTIL FURTHER NOTICE
Sealed 30 bobas for freezing.
Something changed in Nainai. She was lighter, more energetic.
It was time for us to be free of the monster.
SUPER BOBA CAFÉ

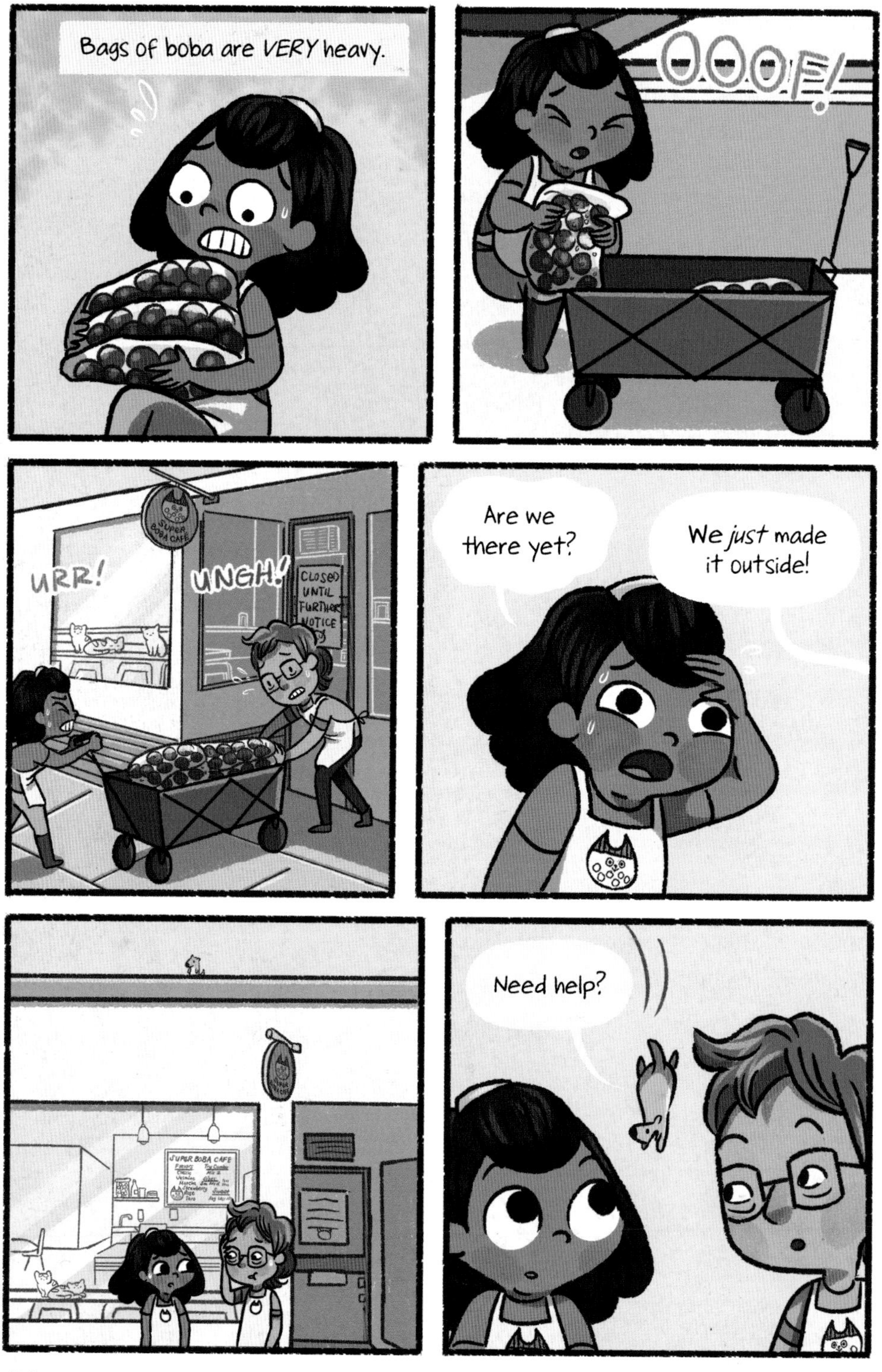
Bags of boba are VERY heavy.
OOOF!
SUPER BOBA CAFE
URR!
UNGH!
CLOSED UNTIL FURTHER NOTICE
Are we there yet?
We just made it outside!
SUPER BOBA CAFE
Need help?

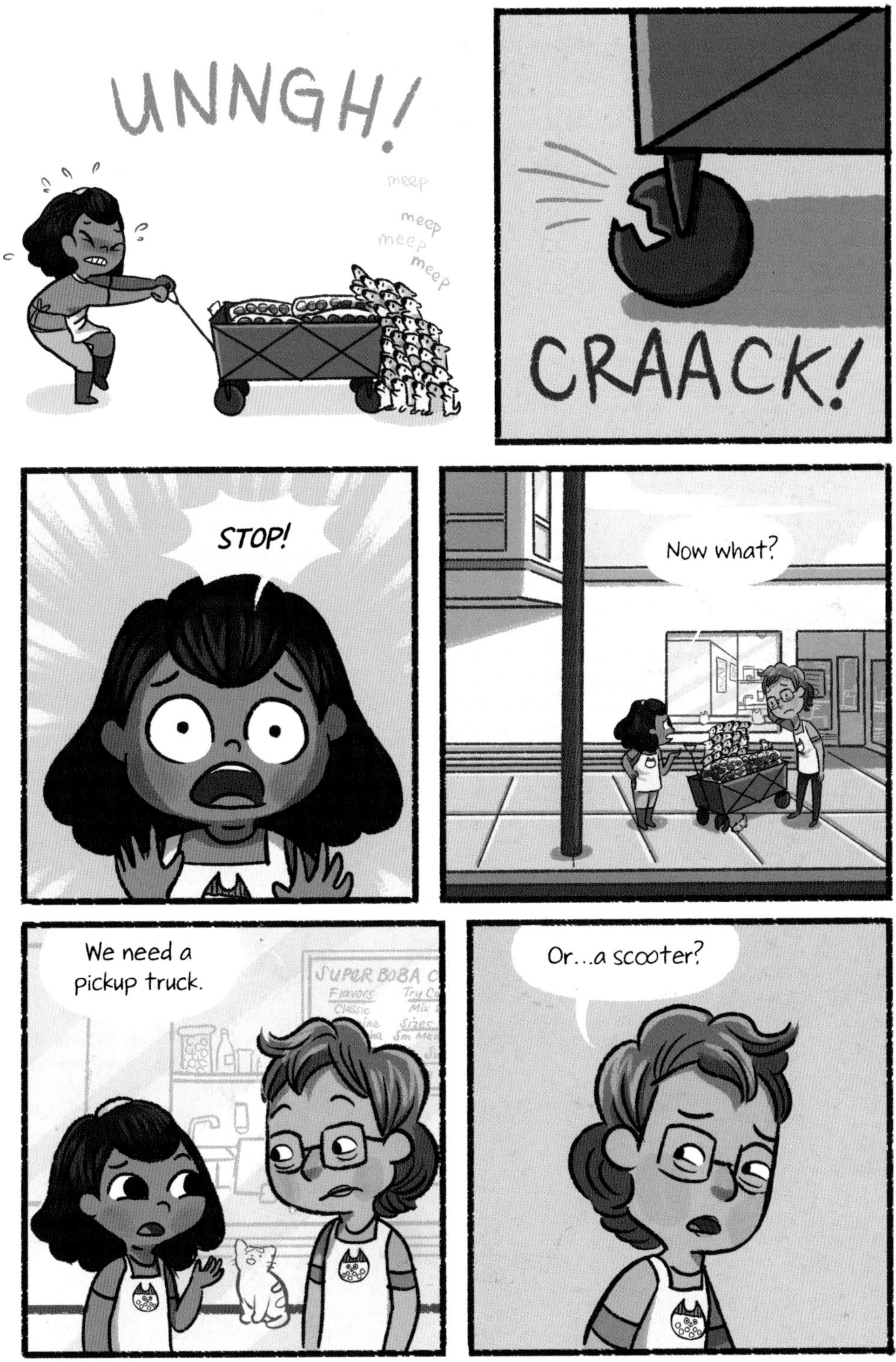
UNNGH!
meep
meep
meep
meep
CRAACK!
STOP!
Now what?
We need a pickup truck.
SUPER BOBA
Flavors
Classic
Sizes
Or...a scooter?

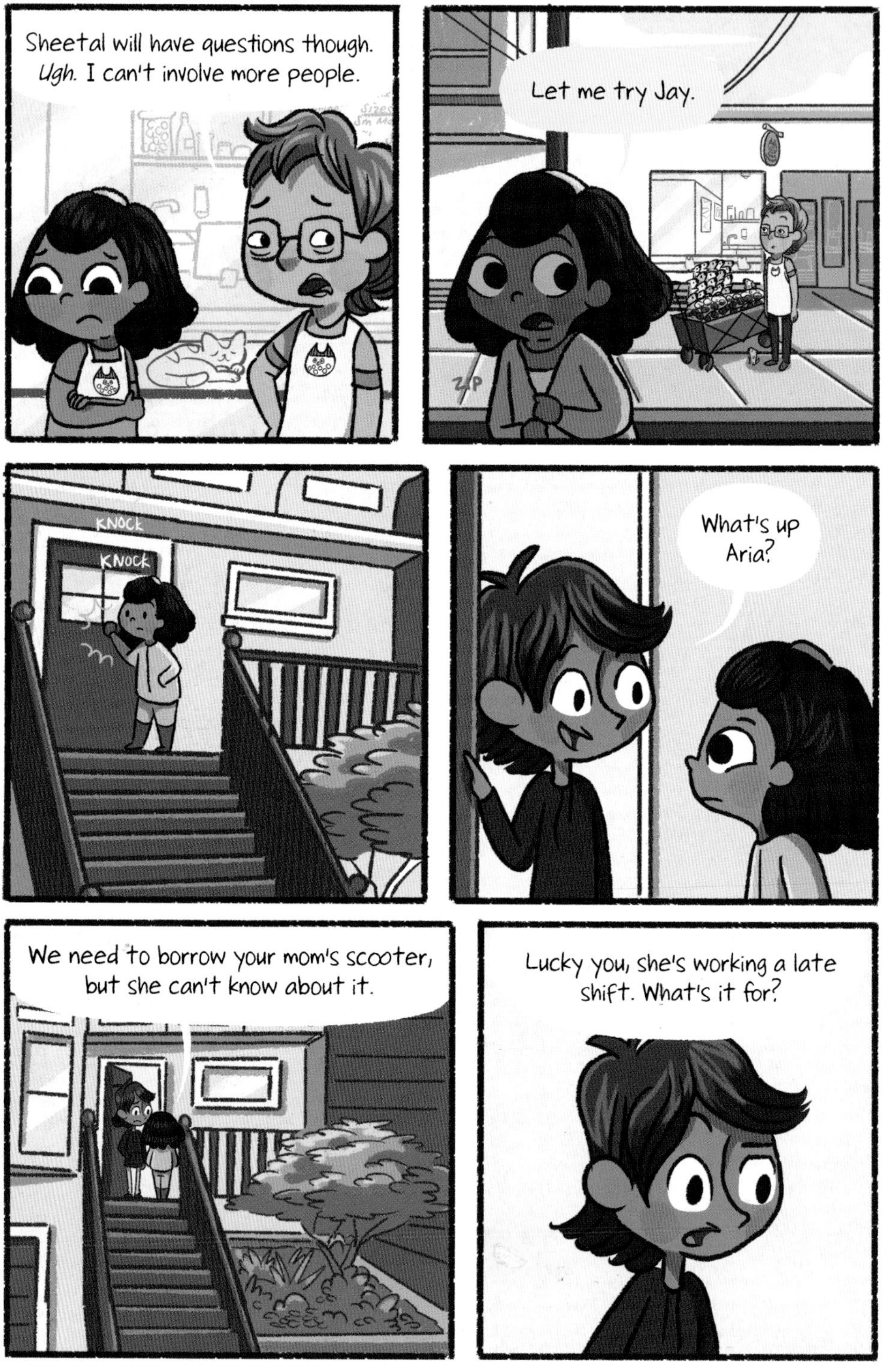
Sheetal will have questions though. *Ugh.* I can't involve more people.
Let me try Jay.
ZIP
KNOCK
KNOCK
What's up Aria?
We need to borrow your mom's scooter, but she can't know about it.
Lucky you, she's working a late shift. What's it for?

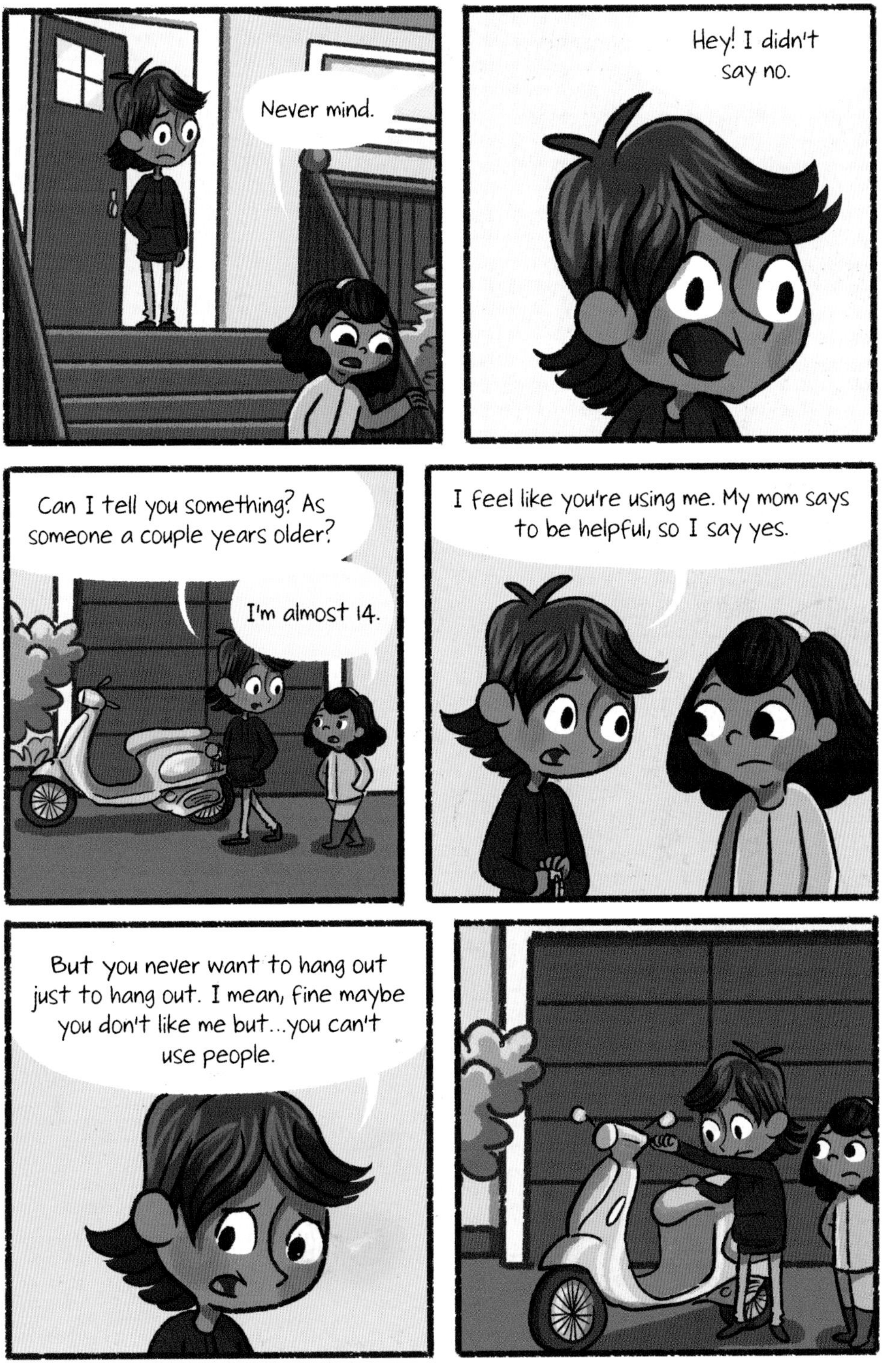
Never mind.
Hey! I didn't say no.
Can I tell you something? As someone a couple years older?
I'm almost 14.
I feel like you're using me. My mom says to be helpful, so I say yes.
But you never want to hang out just to hang out. I mean, fine maybe you don't like me but...you can't use people.

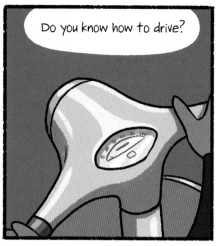

Do you know how to drive?

Right, you're 13. I can take you.

Almost 14! And you're only 16!

And I can drive a scooter a couple blocks. Unless you want to wait for my mom.

C'mon!

Thanks, Jay.

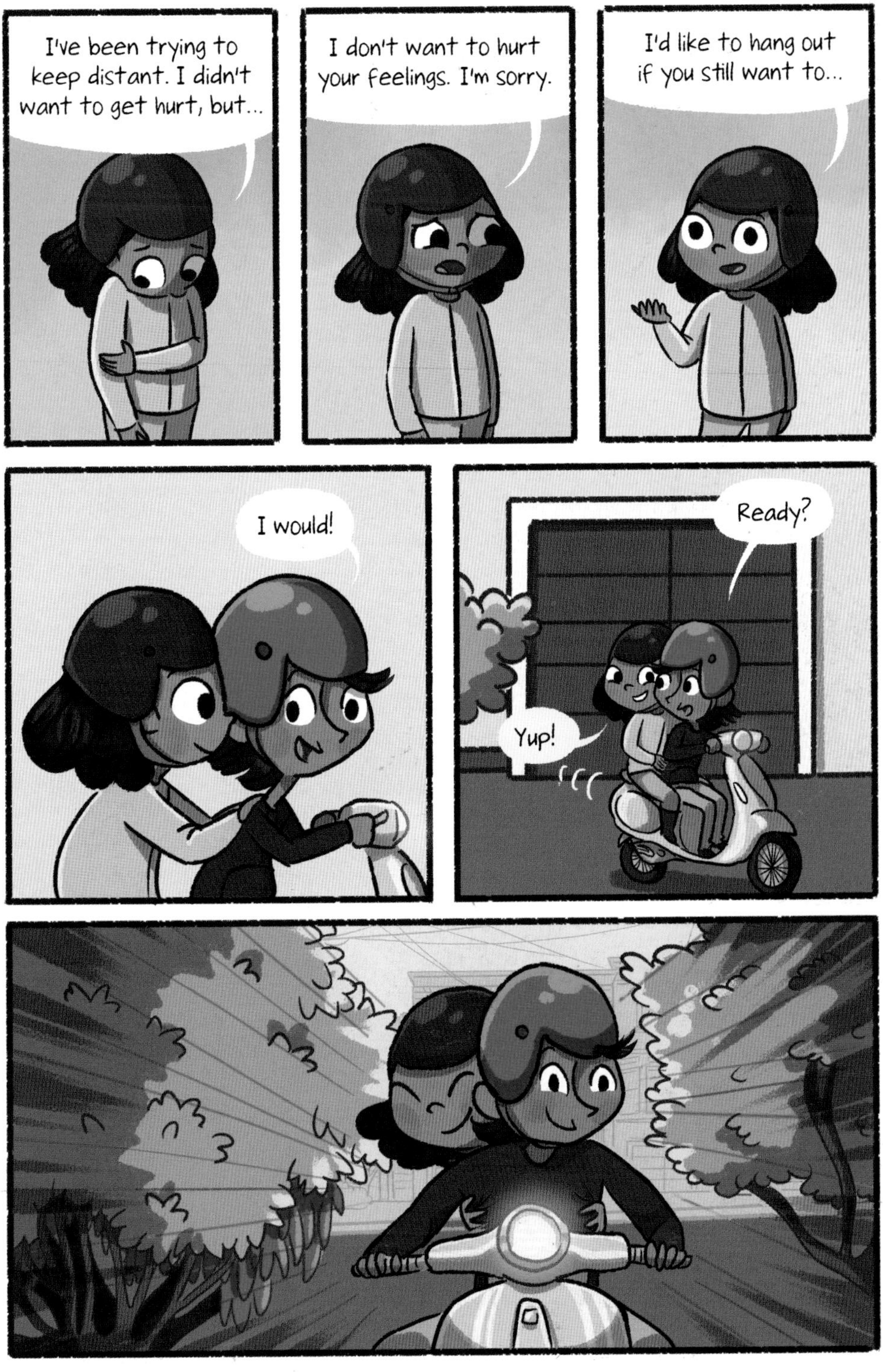
I've been trying to keep distant. I didn't want to get hurt, but...
I don't want to hurt your feelings. I'm sorry.
I'd like to hang out if you still want to...
I would!
Ready?
Yup!

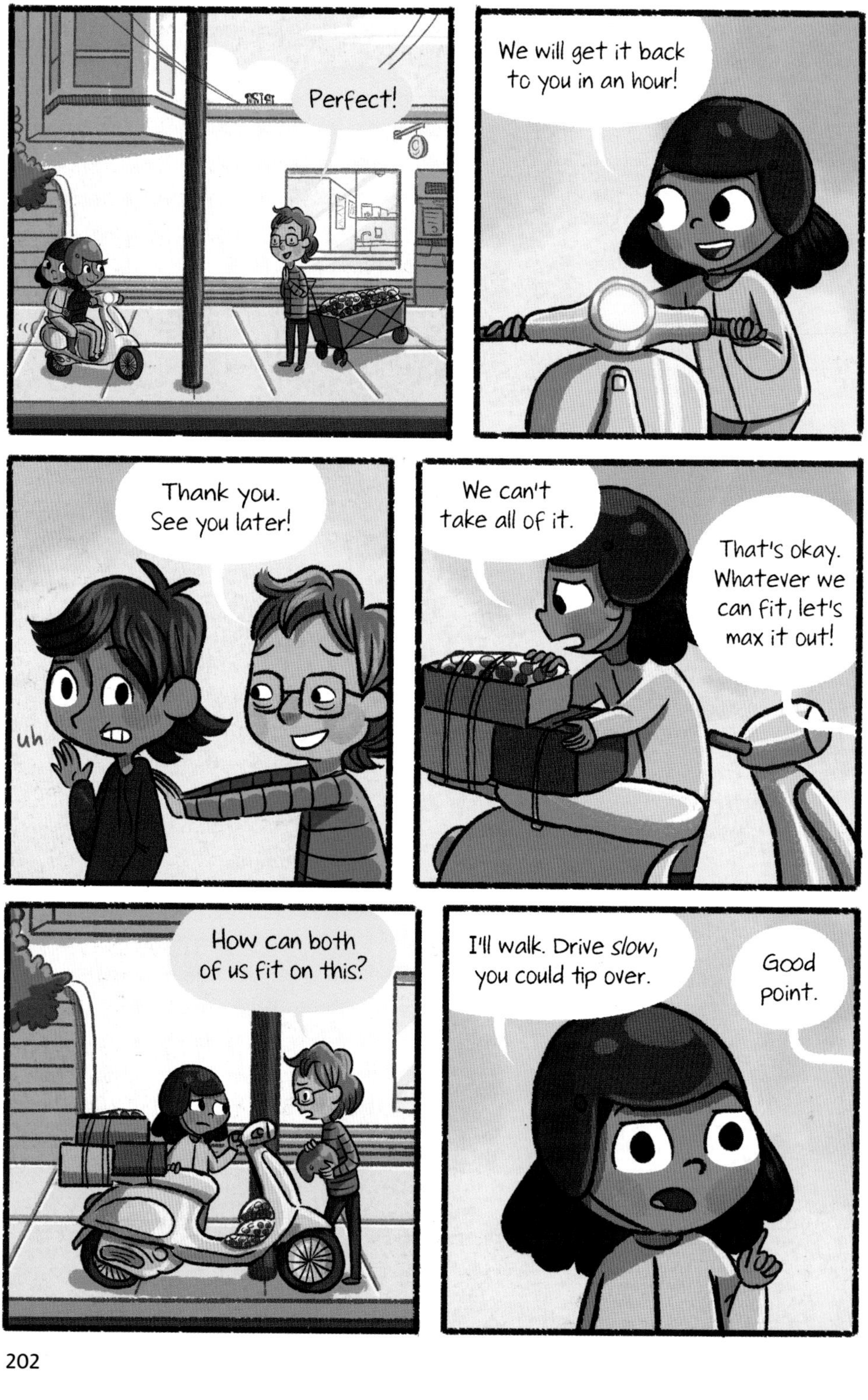
Perfect!
We will get it back to you in an hour!
Thank you. See you later!
uh
We can't take all of it.
That's okay. Whatever we can fit, let's max it out!
How can both of us fit on this?
I'll walk. Drive *slow*, you could tip over.
Good point.

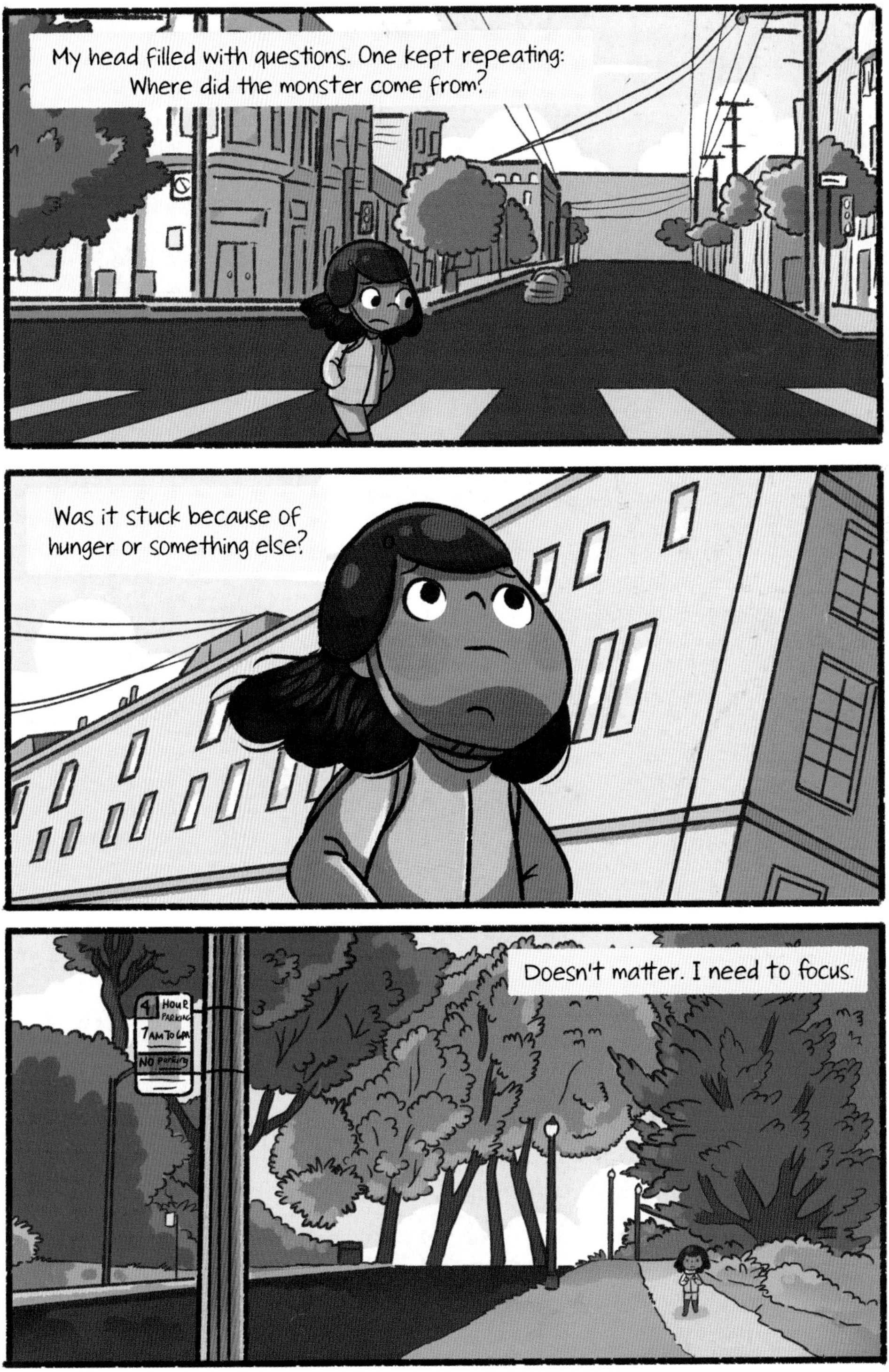
My head filled with questions. One kept repeating: Where did the monster come from?
Was it stuck because of hunger or something else?
Doesn't matter. I need to focus.

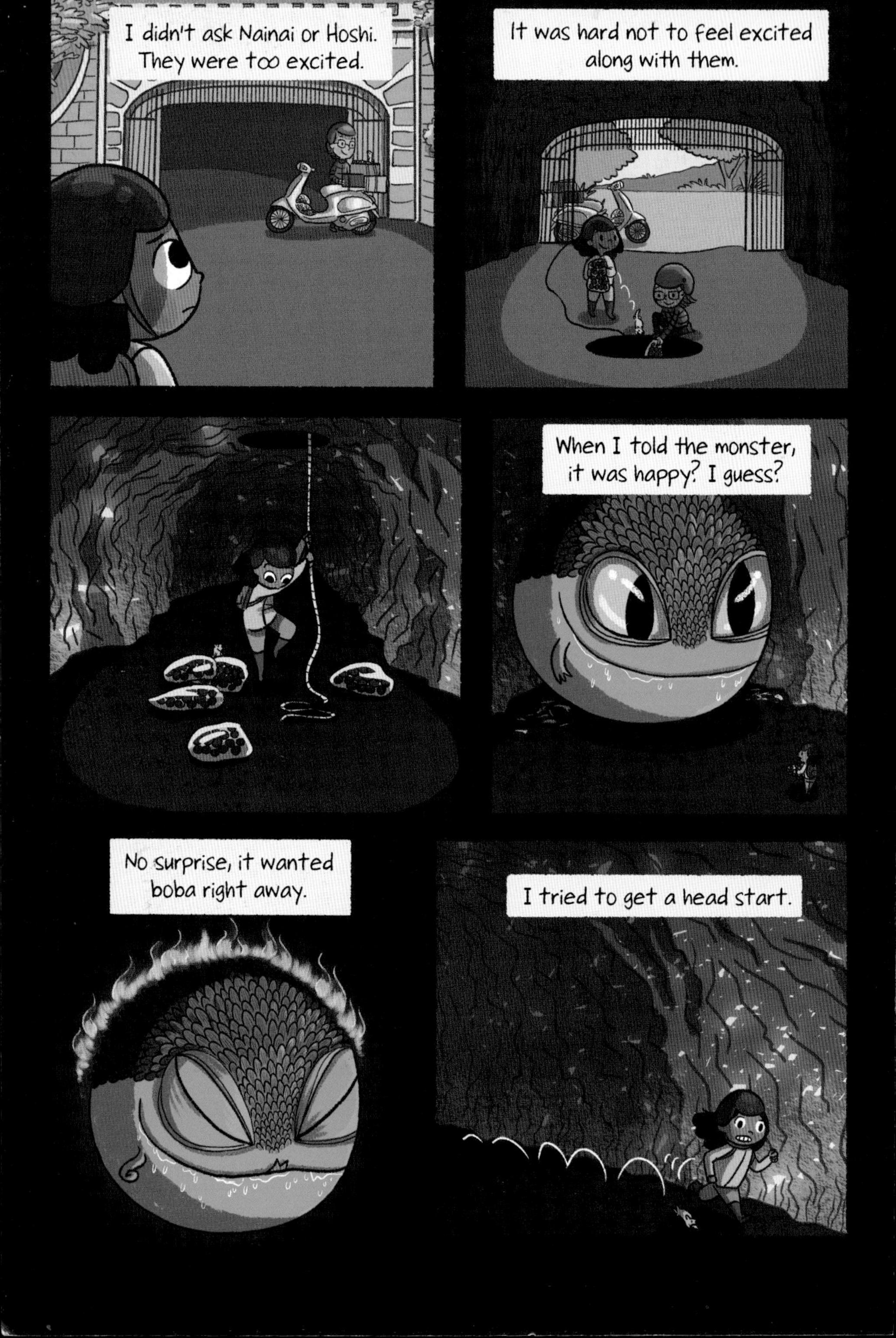
I didn't ask Nainai or Hoshi. They were too excited.
It was hard not to feel excited along with them.
When I told the monster, it was happy? I guess?
No surprise, it wanted boba right away.
I tried to get a head start.

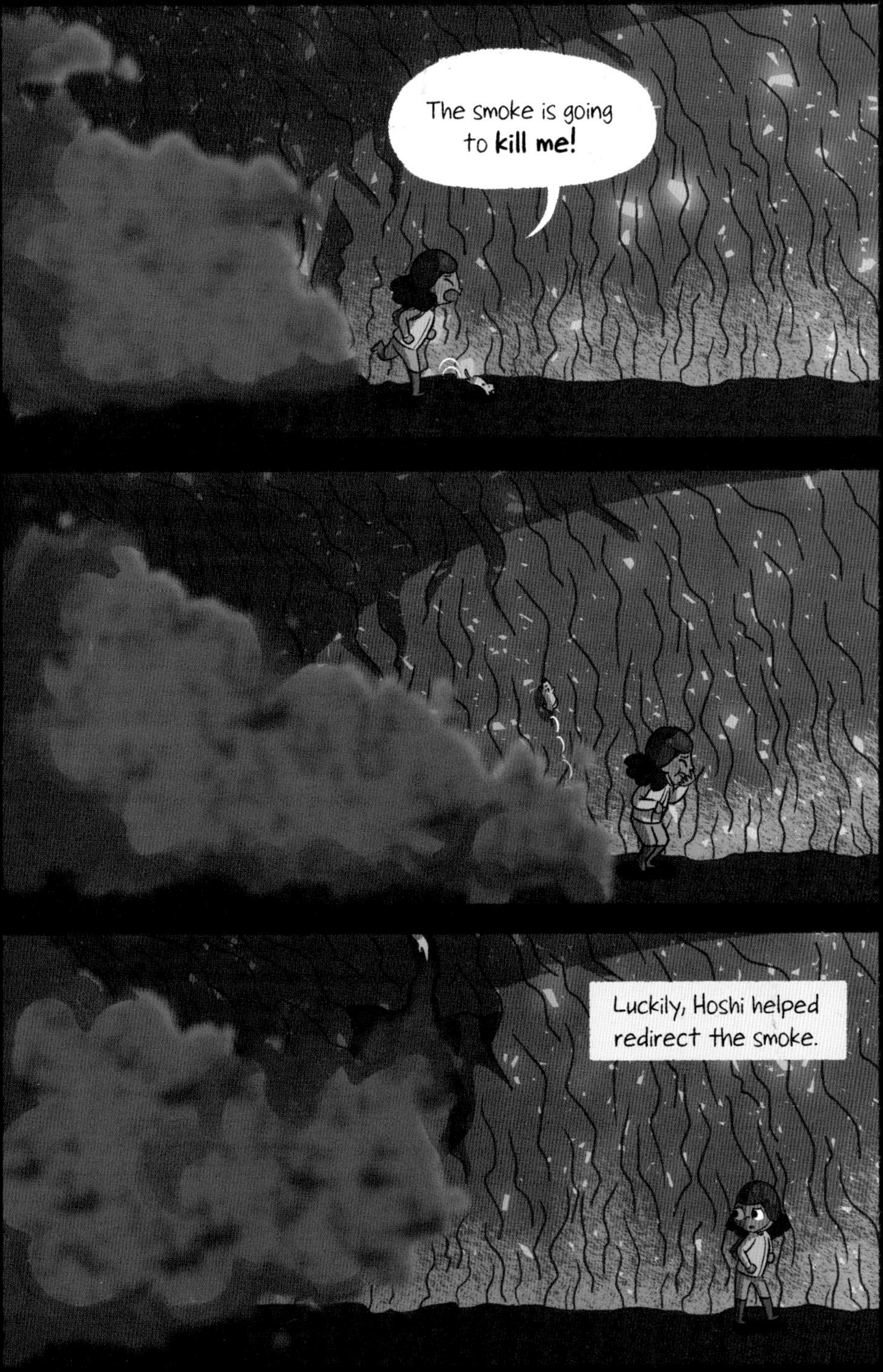
The smoke is going to **kill me!**
Luckily, Hoshi helped redirect the smoke.

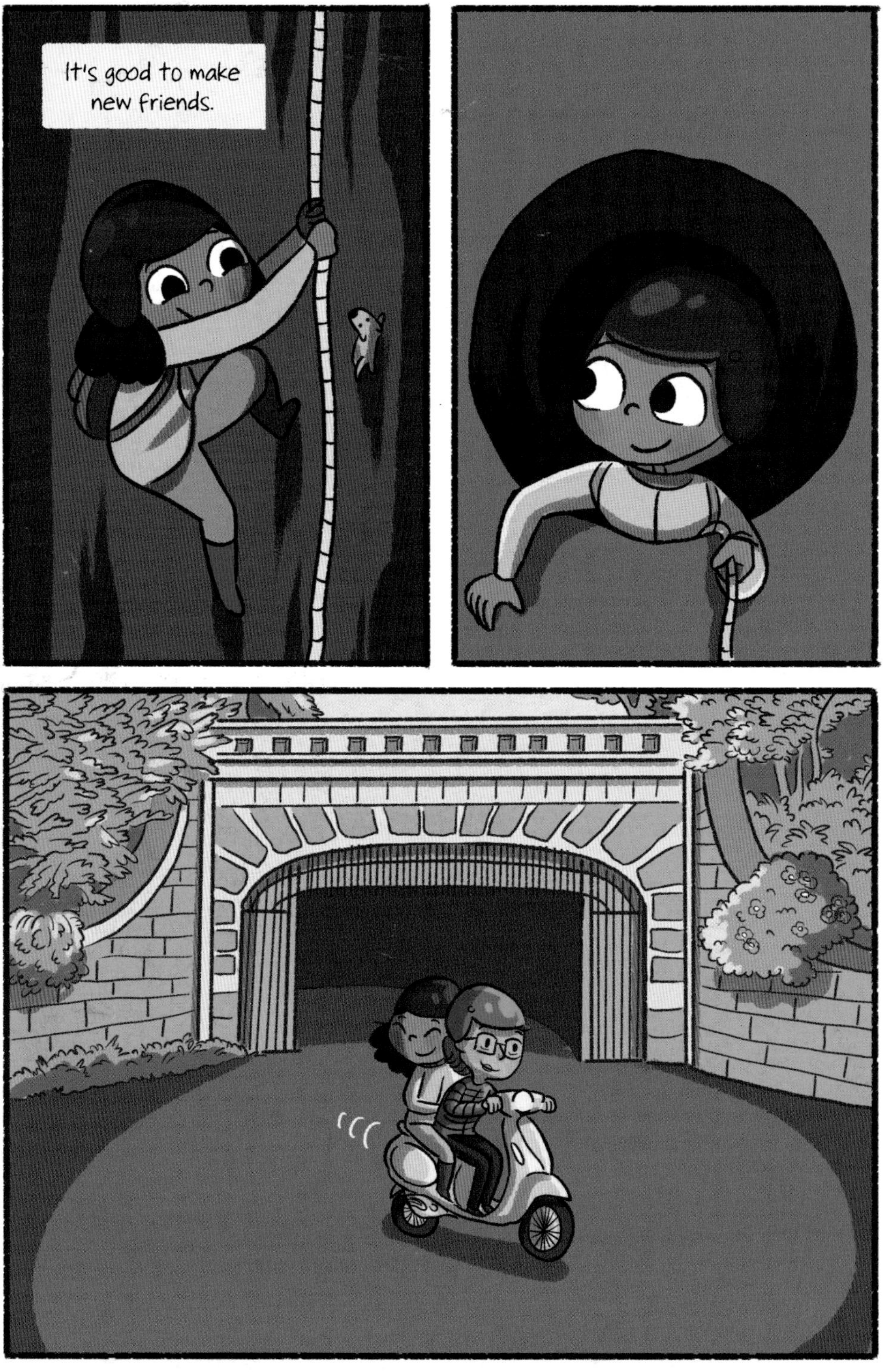
It's good to make new friends.

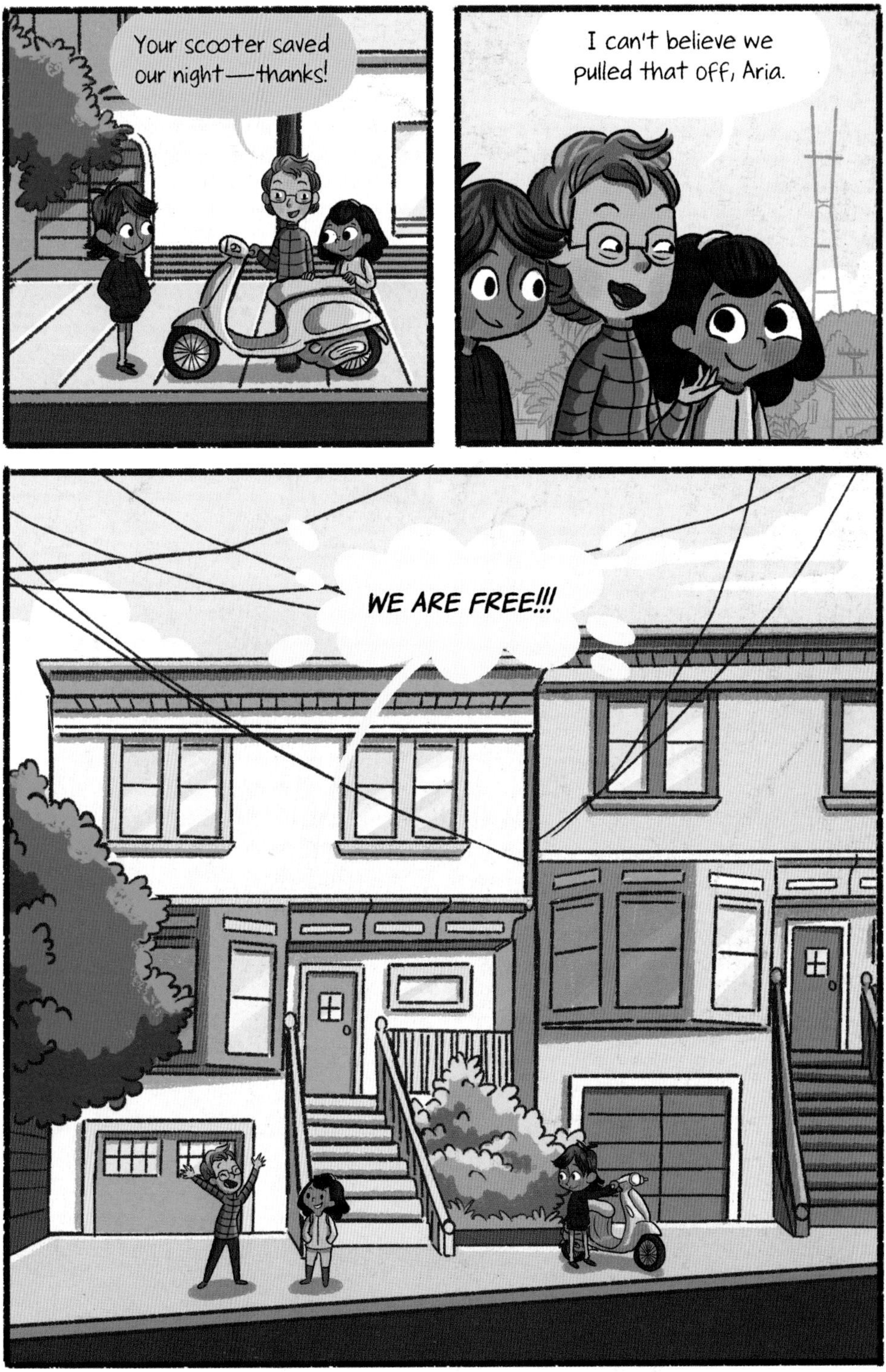
Your scooter saved our night—thanks!
I can't believe we pulled that off, Aria.
WE ARE FREE!!!

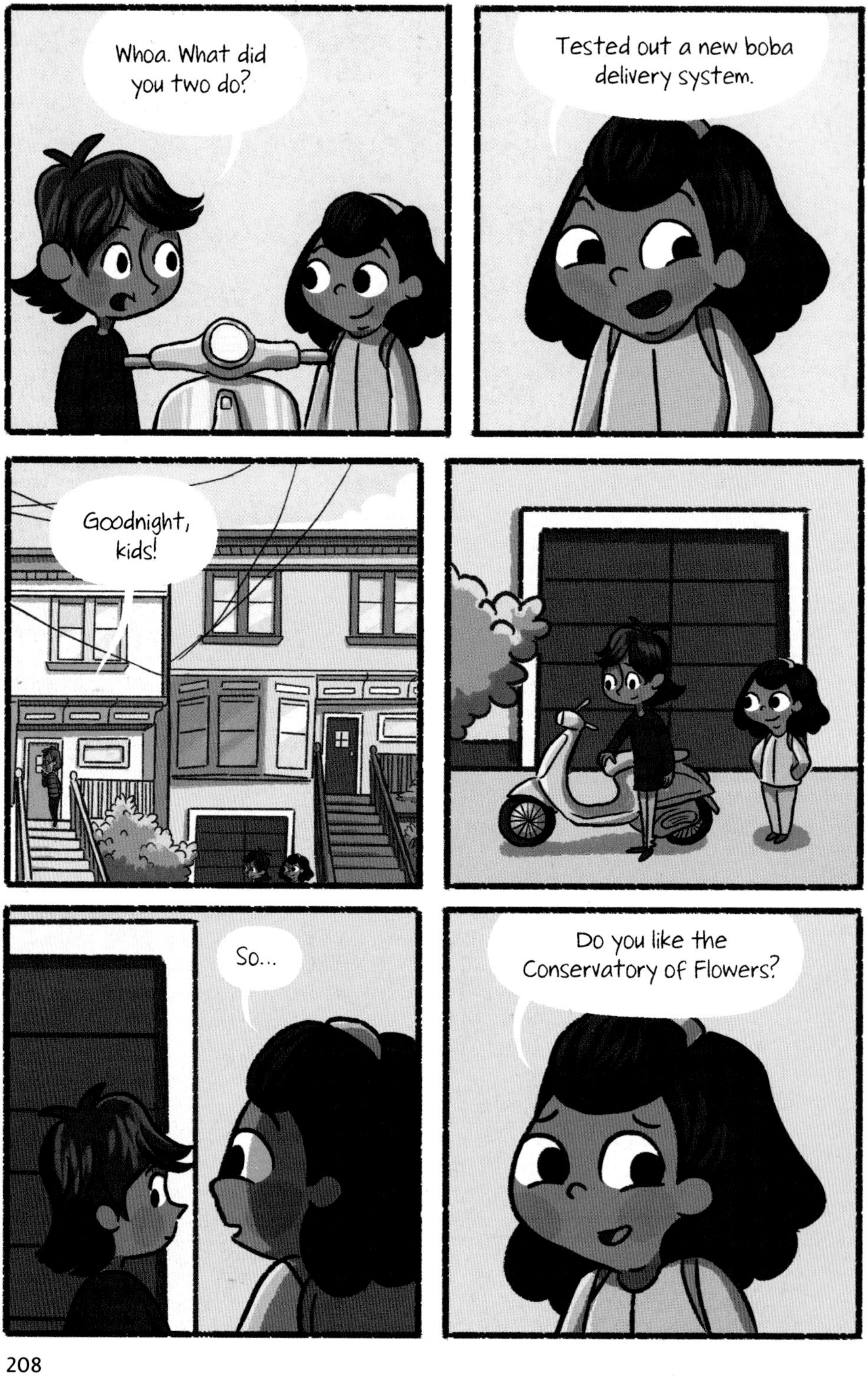
Whoa. What did you two do?
Tested out a new boba delivery system.
Goodnight, kids!
So...
Do you like the Conservatory of Flowers?

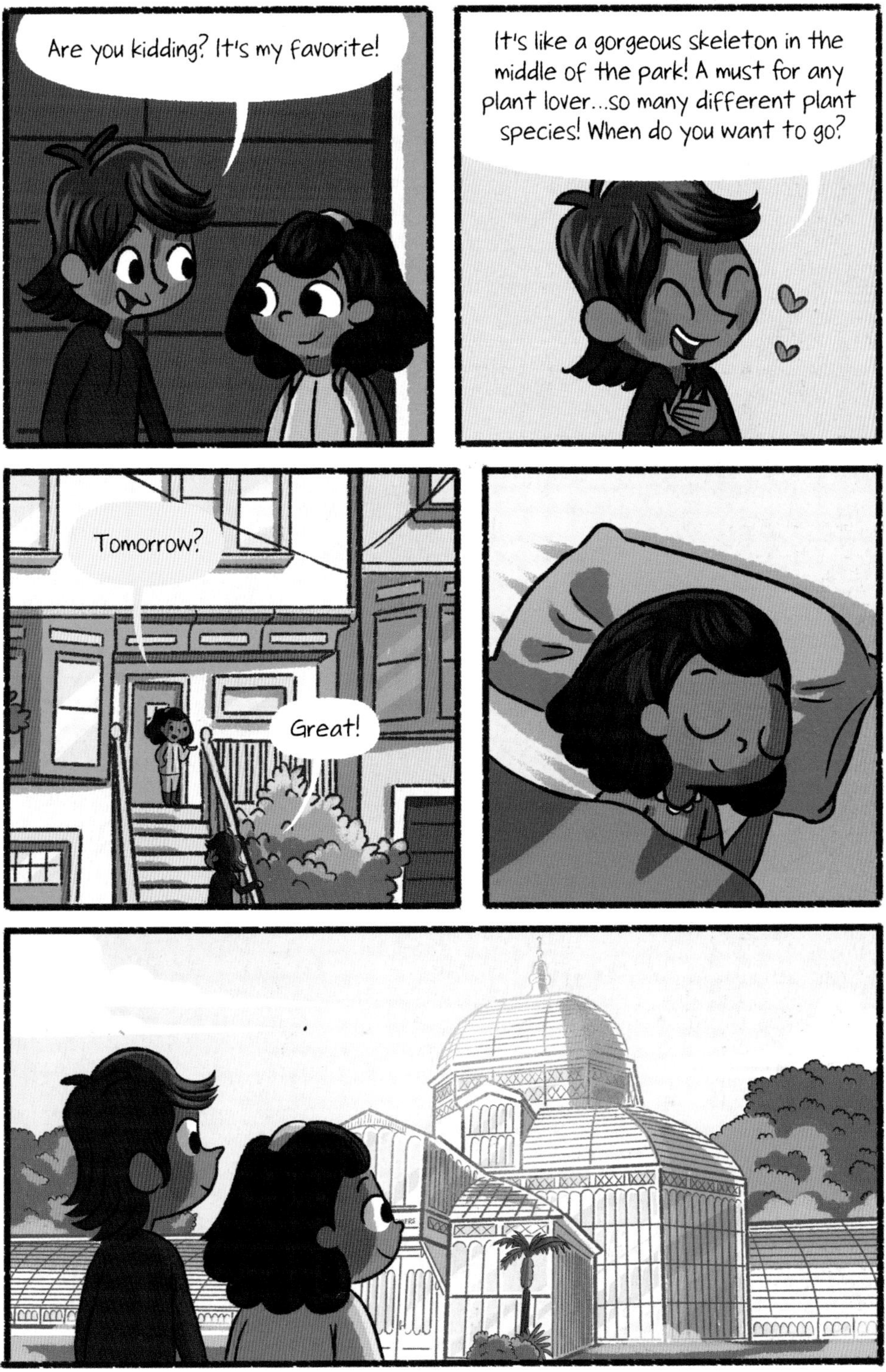
Are you kidding? It's my favorite!
It's like a gorgeous skeleton in the middle of the park! A must for any plant lover...so many different plant species! When do you want to go?
Tomorrow?
Great!

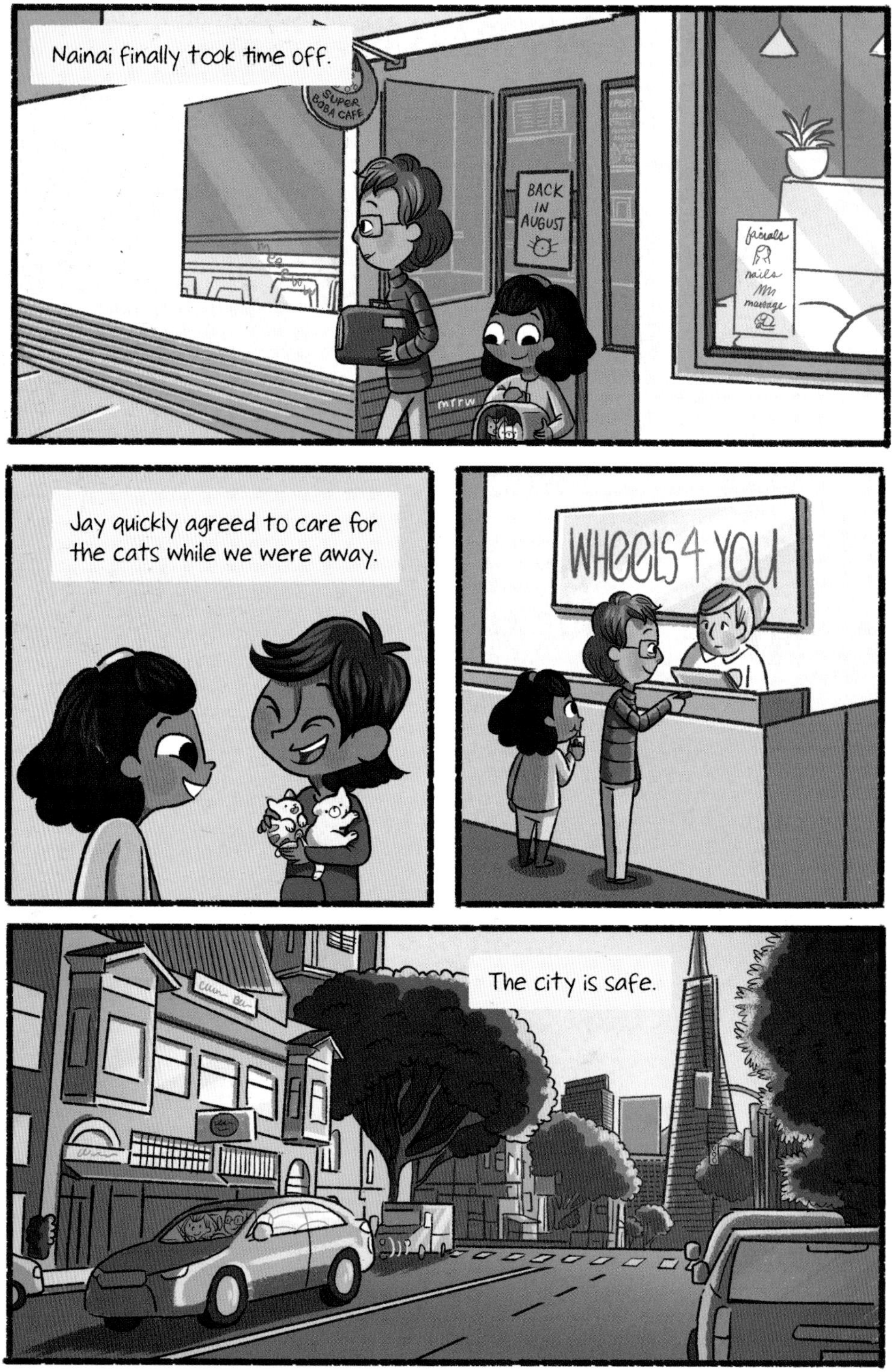
Nainai finally took time off.
SUPER BOBA CAFE
BACK IN AUGUST
facials
nails
massage
mrrw
Jay quickly agreed to care for the cats while we were away.
WHEELS 4 YOU
The city is safe.

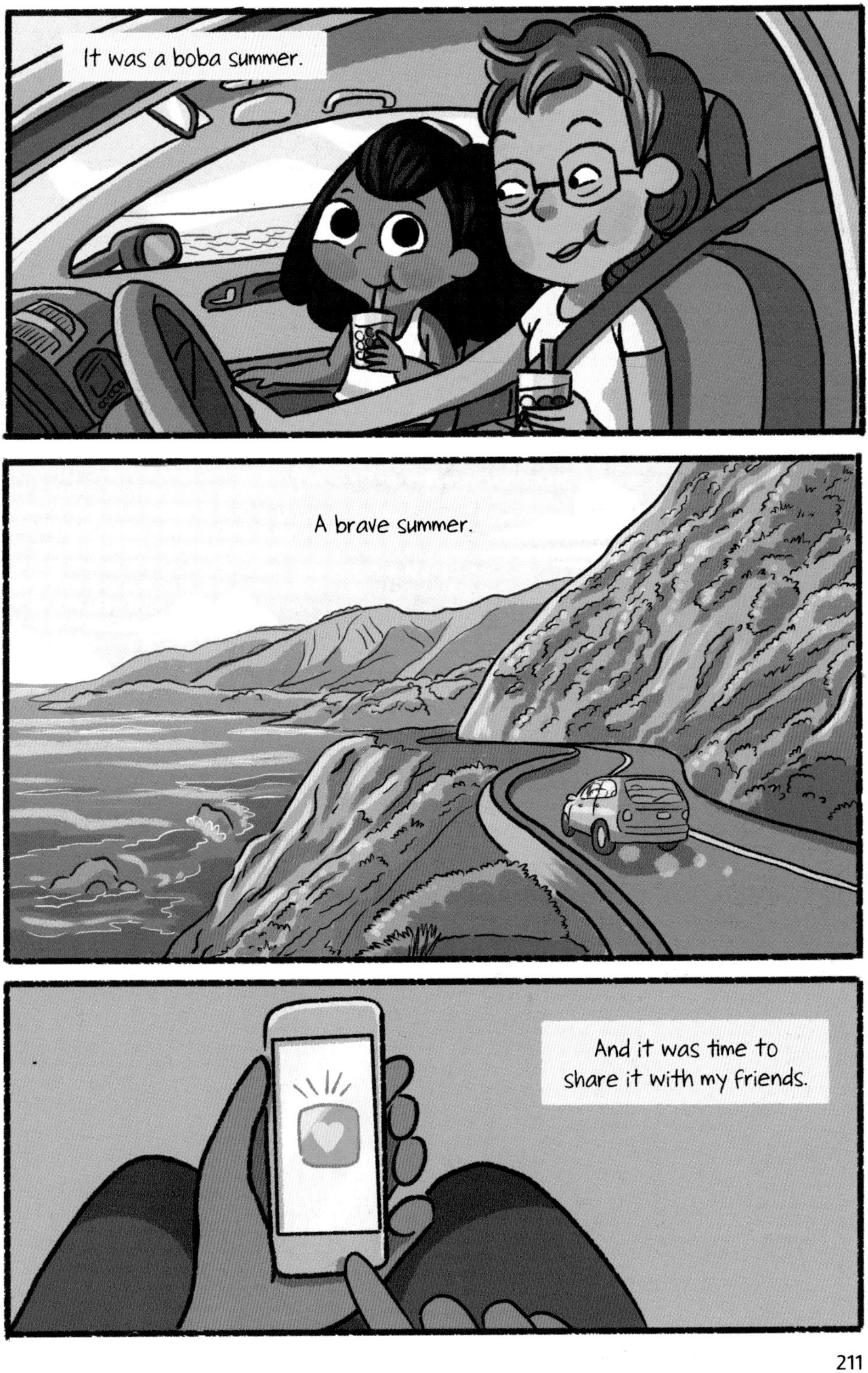
It was a boba summer.
A brave summer.
And it was time to share it with my friends.

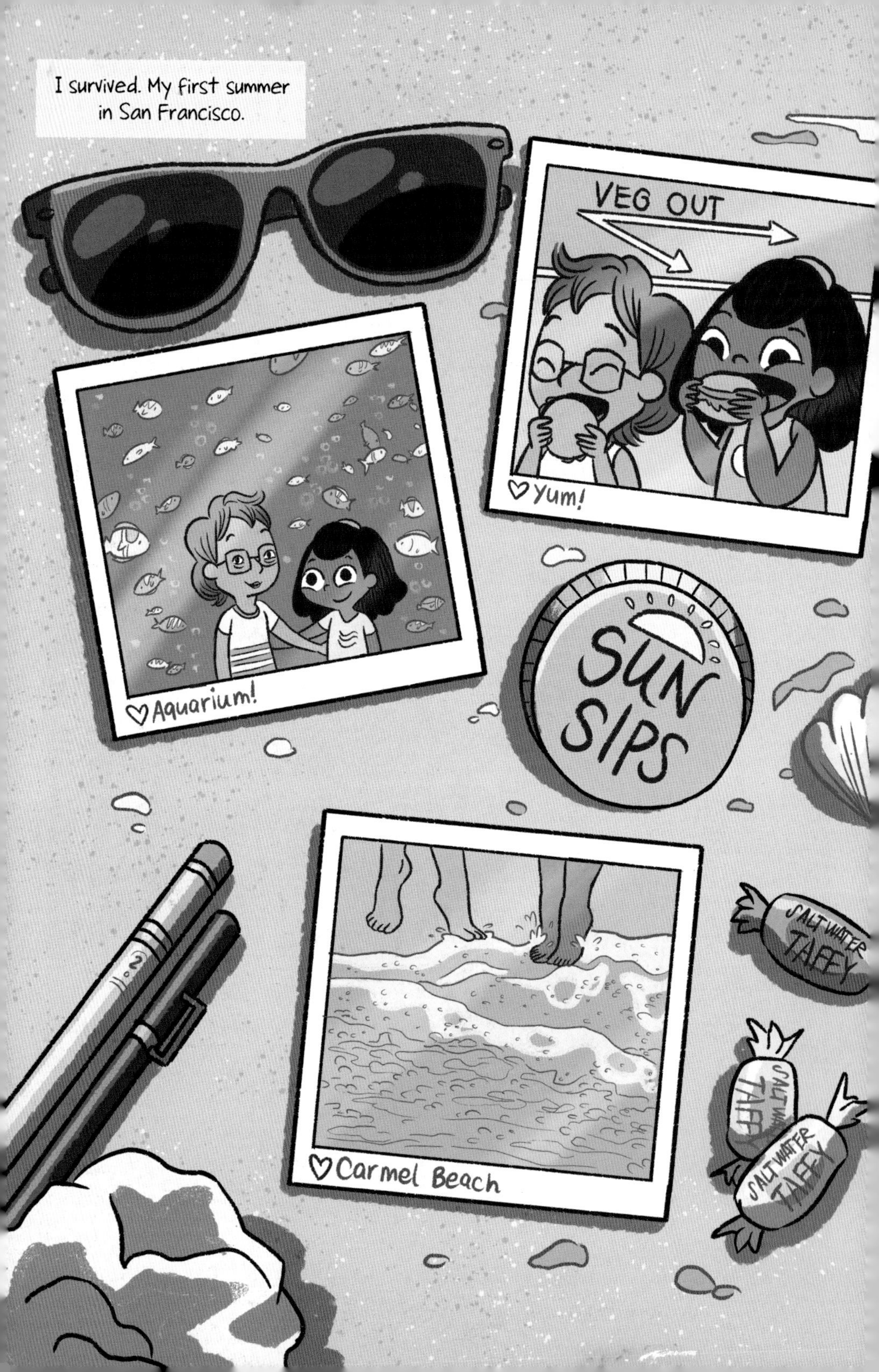
I survived. My first summer in San Francisco.
VEG OUT
♡Yum!
♡Aquarium!
SUN SIPS
♡Carmel Beach
SALT WATER TAFFY
SALT WATER TAFFY
SALT WATER TAFFY

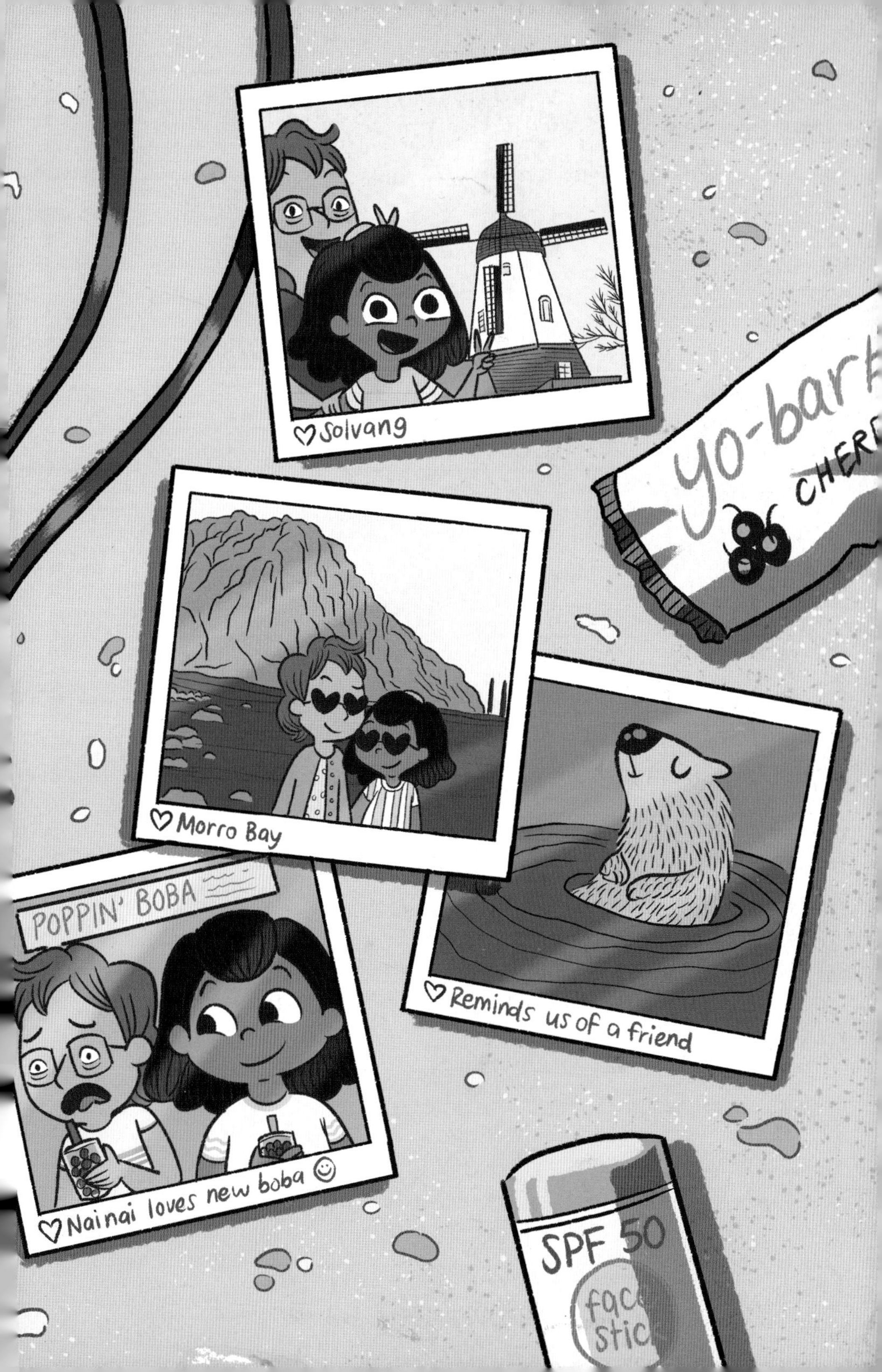
♡Solvang
yo-bar
CHER
♡Morro Bay
POPPIN' BOBA
♡Reminds us of a friend
♡Nainai loves new boba ☺
SPF 50
fac
stic

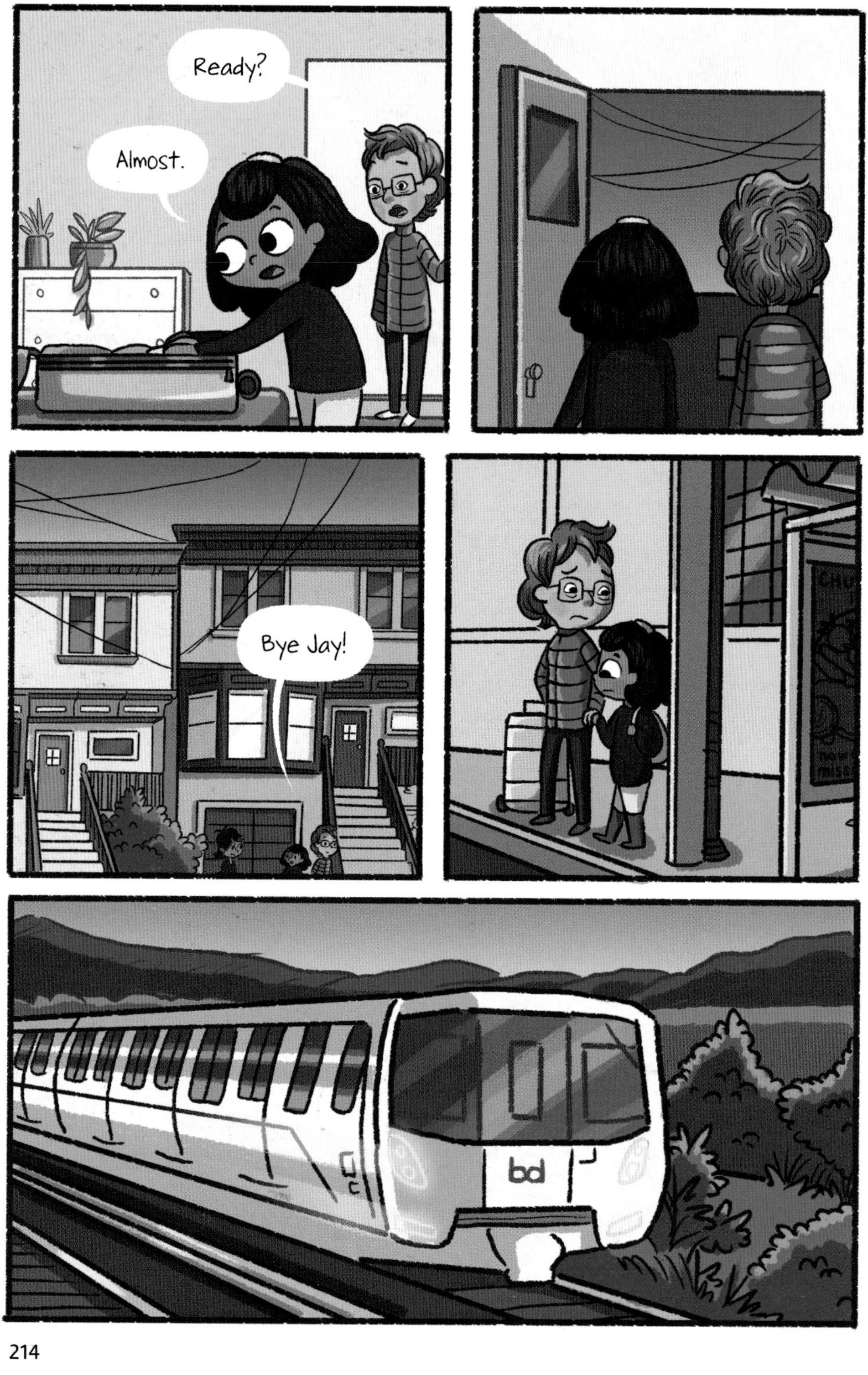
Ready?
Almost.
Bye Jay!

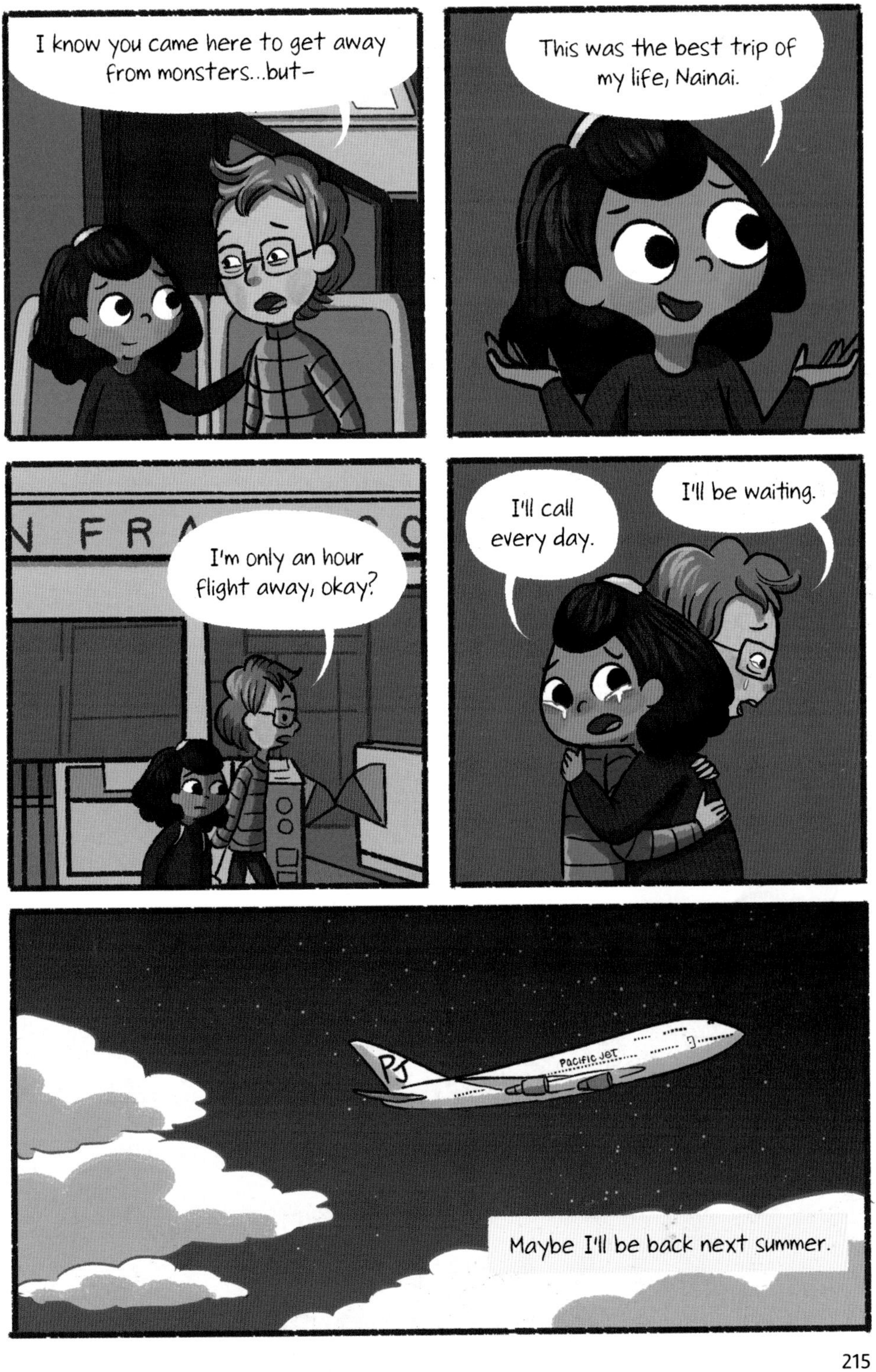
I know you came here to get away from monsters...but-
This was the best trip of my life, Nainai.
N FRA
I'm only an hour flight away, okay?
I'll call every day.
I'll be waiting.
PJ
PACIFIC JET
Maybe I'll be back next summer.

Or sooner...

Thank You

Thank you Sarah Davidson, colorist extrordinaire! Every page of this book is bursting with life because of your beautiful work.

To my dearest Pomodoros, Dashka Slater and Marcus Ewert, you are my daily dose of sanity in this overwhelming creative life. Dashka, your feedback and honesty is a balm. Marcus, you are such a beacon of light. You made the lonely journey of inking a graphic novel bearable. I am forever grateful for our friendship.

Thank you Maggie Lehrman, my gifted editor. Your vision for *Super Boba Café* made me believe in the depth of Aria and Nainai's story.

Thank you to Binglin Hsu for your kitten inks, they're purrfect.

Thank you to the entire team at Abrams: Andy Miller, Marie Oishi, Elisa Gonzalez, Kim Lauber, Hallie Patterson, Emily Daluga, Rachael Marks, and Andrew Smith for all your work bringing this book to life.

To Nickole Caimol and Teresa Huang, my closest friends in art and story, I am grateful that we can reflect and nurture each other's light.

To my agent, Jodi Reamer, you help me reach for the stars. Thank you for your steadfast support and encouragement.

To my friends who helped me stay coherent while making another graphic novel during a pandemic, Lyla Warren, Faheema Chaudhury, Corey Peterschmidt, Praveena Gadiraju, Maneesh Yadav, Sheetal Jain, Jonathan Hill, Aron Nels Steinke, Jessixa Bagley, K-Fai Steele, Evan Hamilton, Sunila Rao, Susie Ghahremani, Suzanne Kaufman, Matt Silady, Eric Rosswood—thank you.

My family, who lift me up in the many years it takes to make a graphic novel, I couldn't push through without you. Nick, I'm still pleased that you laughed multiple times when you first read *Super Boba Café*. Leela, thank you for always asking to see my work and your loving praise. I am better because of you two.

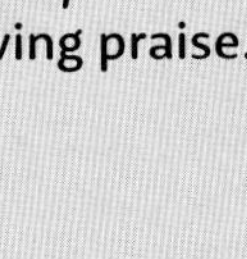

Refined character turnarounds

Early character designs

Aria

Nainai

Jorts

Harvey Milk

Pearl

Squish

Kitty Key
Many of the names came
from folks on Twitter—
thank you!

Mewlong

Noodle

Boba Gump

Mewni

Process

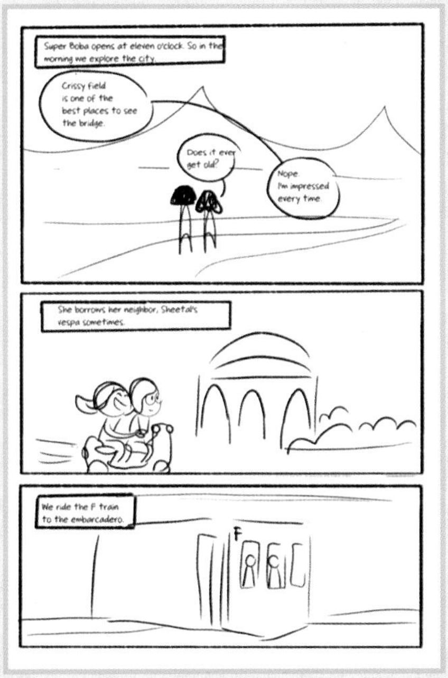
Super Boba opens at eleven o'clock. So in the morning we explore the city.
Crissy field is one of the best places to see the bridge.
Does it ever get old?
Nope. I'm impressed every time.
She borrows her neighbor, Sheetal's vespa sometimes.
We ride the F train to the embarcadero.
F

Thumbnail

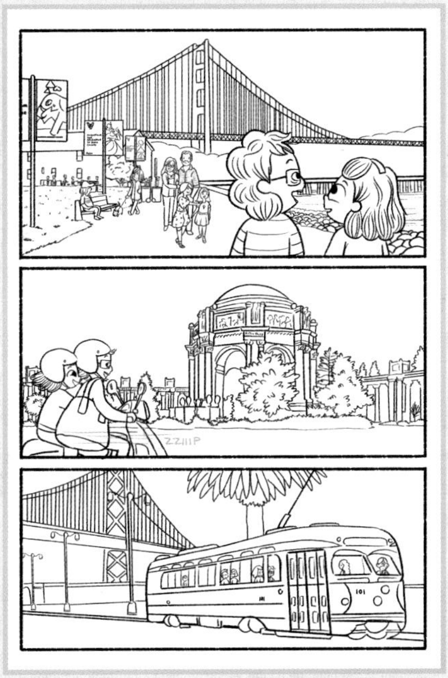

Inks

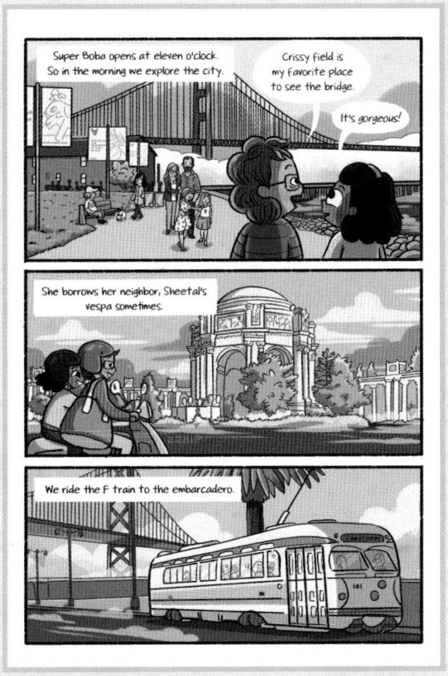
Super Boba opens at eleven o'clock. So in the morning we explore the city.
Crissy field is my favorite place to see the bridge.
It's gorgeous!
She borrows her neighbor, Sheetal's vespa sometimes.
We ride the F train to the embarcadero.

Color

To Mom/Grammy Giordano,
for your sweet and silly relationship with
Leela that inspired these characters

Library of Congress Control Number for the hardcover edition 2023932718

Hardcover ISBN 978-1-4197-5956-7
Paperback ISBN 978-1-4197-5957-4

Text and illustrations © 2023 Nidhi Chanani
Colors by Sarah Davidson
Book design by Andrea Miller

Printed and bound in China
10 9 8 7 6 5 4 3 2 1

ABRAMS The Art of Books
195 Broadway, New York, NY 10007
abramsbooks.com